Acclaim for *Skin of Sunset*

"*Skin of Sunset* is a complex, funny and intelligent exploration of our frailties – perhaps above all our ability to endlessly and helplessly repeat our most damaging mistakes."
    -- A.L. Kennedy, author of *Day, Paradise* and *So I Am Glad*

"David Johansson's novel and his characters' insights remind me of Bukowski with a bank account, Baudelaire with a sense of humor. The undeniable truth of Mr. Johansson's testimony made me laugh out loud, and shed a few tears. For that, I am indebted to him."
    -- Jay Atkinson, author of *City in Amber* and *Legends of Winter Hill*

"Pick of the Month." Recommended.
    -- Bookviews.com

"*Skin of Sunset* is intense yet meditative, and ever-verbally playful. Johansson moves deftly from one character's worldview to the next, capturing by turns the manic, quiet, and depressive sides of a love triangle that is dysfunctional even by American standards."
    -- Dr. Robert Von Achen, Oxford University

SKIN OF SUNSET

SKIN OF SUNSET

A NOVEL

For Nancy,
After sunset,
come the stars —
David Johansson '09

David Johansson

Squire Press

SQUIRE PRESS
411 Fourth Avenue
Melbourne Beach, FL 32951, U.S.A.
skinofsunset.com

Copyright © David Johansson, 2009
All rights reserved

Cover art by Nancy Baur Dillen
Author photograph by Xochitl Ross
Design by Jonathan Gullery

Publisher's Note: This is a work of fiction. Names, characters, places, and incidents either are the product of the author's imagination or are used fictitiously, and any resemblance to actual persons, living or dead, business establishments, events, or locales is entirely coincidental.

LIBRARY OF CONGRESS DATA
Johansson, David
Skin of sunset / David Johansson.
p. cm.
ISBN 978-0-615-18950-5
1. Youth and middle age—Fiction. I. Title
PS3610.J64 2008
070'.59—dc22   2008901861

Printed in the United States of America

First Edition

Apart from the cover art and brief excerpts which may be used for review purposes, no part of this publication may be reproduced in any form without the written permission of the publisher.

This novel is for

Harry Crews

whose apprentice I was

Part I

1

Discovery Motions

HELMUT was annoyed with the universe. Alone, he sat at the hotel bar, his face greenly illuminated by the recessed, aquamarine lighting, his nostrils assaulted by the odor of stale peanuts and flowery disinfectant. Classic rock floated from invisible speakers and the career alcoholics sat hunched over their drinks. Over the bar a TV flickered soundlessly, displaying an emerald baseball field. Helmut ran his finger around the inside of his collar and sighed. The submarine atmosphere of the place might've turned a cheerleader to suicide. Was it this awful on purpose? Or was this the best you could hope for in Kansas? Certainly the bar made you want to get drunk.

He looked at the clock.

Well, she'd made a fool of him.

Tipping up his glass, he let the ice cubes knock against his teeth. With his shiny bald head, his protruding brown eyes, his sallow face, his prominent nose and receding chin, he had the look of an enraged canine. Why, he'd even dressed up. He had on his taupe nail-head suit, with a blue silk tie with gold stripes – his favorite.

Casually lifting his index finger, he called for another Grey Goose and tonic. The prospect of another law conference had been rendered bearable only by his expectation of the frolic with the senator's wife, in the senator's bed, under the senator's well-documented eye, staring at him from the nightstand.

Now that was ruined.

He crushed an ice cube and ground it to cold bits across his tongue. So this was the verdict. Expect frustration and you wouldn't be disappointed. Anticipate a hot woman and you got a mouthful of icy slush. As an attorney, he accepted injustice, except in his own affairs, where he expected the universe to throw itself on his mercy.

He'd met her at a previous conference and they'd made a party of it, although his law partner, Barton Squire, had declined his invitations to strip clubs and dive bars and, most annoyingly, to dinner with the senator's wife and her sister, a refusal Helmut now credited with his sitting alone in a hotel bar in Index, Kansas.

"What a water boy," he said softly. Barton had refused to come because he'd been unable to get a call through to his wife, Jordan, to whom he was obscenely devoted.

Overhead, on the bar's TV, a baseball player tugged at his crotch while Helmut poked his drink with a swizzle stick. The bartender, wearing a black vest with a bow tie, polished a brandy snifter and stared blandly at the screen.

Conferences – what frauds. Helmut squirmed on his bar stool and the sciatic nerve in his right buttock lit up like a live wire. His eyes watered. Justice wasn't blind. She had it in for him. His body was a traitor, the world a kangaroo court.

Shifting his weight and grunting, he blinked when the scales of Justice tipped his way, because who should appear but the woman herself – not the senator's wife, but that blazing supernova, that star of his youth – that Jordan Kelly.

Standing in the doorway, she cast her eyes around the bar. Her hair was the color of the ripe wheat rippling the Kansas fields, falling in loose waves over her shoulders. A spray of freckles dusted the bridge of her upturned nose and prominent cheekbones, and her pulse throbbed delicately at the hollow of her throat. Biting her lip, she squinted over the crowd. She had on a hammered silver medallion necklace, a cotton gauze embroidered top, and a denim skirt. On her feet she wore silver macramé flats.

Inwardly, Helmut checked his blood-alcohol content. The needle swung to glowing, halfway to drunk. He swallowed and belched into his fist, then shook his head and sucked his teeth, checking for debris. His tongue dislodged a juicy tidbit which he wrapped in a napkin.

Squaring his shoulders, he drew a deep breath and put on his game-face, preparing himself to brave the force of nature which was Jordan.

The bartender approached her, but she shook her head and said something Helmut didn't catch.

He felt a grin deforming his face and quickly twisted it off. The nerve in his right buttock increased its voltage, hurting so much he ground his teeth.

Wait for it, he thought. *Don't look.* He feigned interest in a player scuffing the dust beside home-plate.

"Helmut!" Jordan's voice curved upward, a gold thread of sound reeling him toward her.

He raised his nose, scenting the air. *Wait.* She called his name again, more urgently. Stretching his arms over his head, clearly satisfied with his own company, he turned on his bar stool and yawned, summoning the vast reserve of his coolness. Of course he'd *meant* to be sitting all alone, joining the locals to watch the game – even as he brainstormed brilliant legal strategies on cocktail napkins.

Jordan waved her hand and charged toward him, her hair flying out behind her as she knocked into chairs and spilled people's drinks.

"It's me!" she called breathlessly, crashing up to the bar. She had luminous milky skin and a wide smooth forehead, with aqua-blue eyes and plump russet lips. "Where's Barton?"

Helmut stood up and pulled out a bar stool. Up close, under

the flickering glow of the television, he could see that something was wrong with her. She was drunk or she'd been crying. Her breath smelled of apples cut with something minty, and her body had gone slightly rank with sweat.

"Grey Goose and tonic for the lady," Helmut called to the bartender, "same for me – double." The bartender wiped a glass and nodded.

Jordan kissed Helmut on the cheek, and as her lips brushed his face he got another hot whiff of her – jasmine shampoo and a slightly funky *Eau de Jordan*. He closed his eyes. Even her stink smelled good. He shook his head. His partner Barton Squire was a lucky man, though too much of a fool to appreciate it.

"Jordan," Helmut said, as though he'd been expecting her. "You're just in time. I was getting too much blood in my alcohol stream."

Her eyes gazed over his shoulder, staring past him into the middle distance.

"I suppose you're looking for your boyfriend," Helmut said.

A frown creased her wide forehead. "Husband, Helmut. *Husband.*"

Helmut cupped his hand to his ear. "What's that? Well, if that's your story. Say . . . wait, Jordie. I seem to be remembering something."

The drinks arrived. Helmut put his hand on Jordan's fingers, finding her skin surprisingly cold. Her bones felt brittle and thin. *She's aged,* he thought.

"I'm sorry," he said, not knowing why. Something had put her over the top, but what? "I read part of my paper today," he said, " 'The Charismatic Close.' Probably publish that bad daddy in the *Yale Law Review*."

Her mouth twitched and she widened her earnest, candid eyes. "Give me a second," she said quickly as her breath caught in her throat. Helmut leaned back, angling his face toward the TV, enjoying the weight of stares, even from such yokels as inhabited the bar.

What could she be doing in Index, Kansas? he wondered. He doubted it was to hear the legal team of Knight and Squire read "The Charismatic Close."

Could Barton have died? He'd seen him at lunch, but still . . . perhaps he'd dropped a blow drier into the bathtub, been stabbed by pitchfork-wielding locals . . . who knew? In the heartland, anything could happen.

Helmut's veins tingled, precluding any guilt he might've felt for wishing his partner into the Kansas earth. Best friends died, didn't they? There was nothing could you do. Grieving widows had to be comforted.

"So Jordan," he said, "what brings you to this God-haunted hinterland?"

Without warning she wailed his name and threw her arms around his neck, wobbling him on his bar stool. Helmut's mouth opened and closed. To his great surprise, he found himself speechless. He had a heart, of course, yet as with all his organs, he preferred that it should remain anonymous.

Because for all his aloof reserve and snotty posturing – the secret of his success with women – the sudden heat of her flesh unnerved him. Her hair engulfed his bald head with unspeakable softness, and he felt drunker than he had in years. Braced against the soft crush of her chest, he patted her back while she wept onto his neck, heaving rhythmically. He brought his drink to his mouth through the blond canopy of her hair, and as the liquid ran down his throat, her hot tears wet his shoulder.

"Careful," he said, feeling the legs of his stool lift off the floor, "Jordan, honey. You're going to knock me over."

She leaned back to stare into his face, as if surprised to find him there. Her skin was mottled, her cheeks streaked. She wiped her eyes with the back of her hand.

"Sorry." She blew her nose into a napkin, honking loudly. Helmut blinked. "I'm a train wreck," she said.

Ordinarily, he would have objected, because the Jordan he knew was bright-eyed and healthy, radiant with animal vitality, with the looks of a cheerleader, an all-American-girl-next-door. She had a face that could sell toothpaste. Shampoo. Toxic waste. Anything. Hugged by Jordan, squeezed by her strong arms, he felt like candy melting in the sun. *Loved.*

Casting a keep-your-distance look at the bartender, he confiscated a handful of cocktail napkins. "Okay," he said. "Don't throw a mood." He dipped a napkin into his drink and wiped her face, while she sat motionless, her expression blank. Her submissiveness excited him. Adjusting his buttocks on the bar stool, he reawakened his sciatic nerve, sending a bolt of lightning down his right leg.

"Are you hurt?" Her voice was clotted and her lower lip protruded, glistening wetly under a neon Budweiser light.

Helmut moaned under his breath. God, he liked a look of woe. The moist red eyes, the heaving breast. The vulnerability. Was anything sexier than a woman whose eyes had been sanded by grief? The delicious pain in her face fogged his vision.

Tenderly, she placed a slender hand on his forearm and he went lightheaded, aroused by her tapering pink fingers, the pearl ovals of her nails, the cool caress of her fingertips.

Taking a deep breath, he commanded his crotch to stand down, to become reasonable and prudent. He was reacting like an animal, for God's sake. Then, too, wetness and redness were sexual stimuli for all primates. Yet here in Kansas, of all places, he'd be damned if he'd share his family tree with a monkey.

Why this woman should unman him, trounce him with her royal flush, he couldn't say. Not even the author of "The Charismatic Close" could beat her hand.

And people said *he* was manipulative.

Jordan sniffled and shivered and hugged her hands in her armpits. "Where's Barton?" she asked again.

Helmut glanced at his watch.

"Went to a strip club with some Rastafarians."

"What?"

"Well, at least they *defend* Rastafarians. Whatever. Let's wet our tonsils in my room."

Her eyelids were heavy, her eyes shiny. Sighing, she said, "Oh, Helmut. I'm in a bad way."

He stood and took her arm. "C'mon . . . we'll look for wonder-boy."

Why did he want her so badly? It wasn't for beauty and it wasn't for money. He had money, and money could buy beauty. No, what he wanted was *to be noticed and appreciated* – not only by her, but also by others – mysterious strangers, envious colleagues, anonymous bartenders, homeless bums, wealthy clients, sworn enemies. *Helmut wanted to be seen.* He *had* to be seen. Attention, for him, was like air. Without it, he'd suffocate.

For as he expanded into middle age, Helmut had found himself approaching sexual invisibility, a romantic vanishing point, that place where pretty girls no longer smiled at him. This was death to Helmut, who had to be observed, whether positively or negatively. Like an electron in the quantum universe, he lacked a position unless under scrutiny.

And Jordan drew scrutiny. She always had, what with her hair. Fluffy and blond might be out of fashion, but it still made you look. Feeling the furtive eyes of the locals, Helmut felt famous. Lit by Jordan's golden glow, he shone like Apollo. Everyone in the bar was staring.

Jordan lifted her glass and sucked at her drink, finishing it in a single draught. Helmut snapped his fingers and another drink appeared. He might be rude, but he settled his tabs with hefty tips, so he had the right.

Jordan's pale throat worked as she emptied another glass, then her lower lip pushed forward. "Muh-muh-my uncle," she sputtered. "My uncle Anton." Her mouth was trembling. "When I was a kid I used to visit him here – near Independence."

Helmut scowled, processing the information. So Barton was

still alive, damn him, although presumably he wasn't in the room they shared, or why would she have checked the bar?

"Your uncle," he repeated. He didn't even know his own uncle's name, much less if he was still alive, so this kind of grief was beyond him. "Well, we all die," he thought of saying, but no, that was the sort of statement Barton prevented him from making to juries because it lacked "sensitivity." Helmut knew this because he'd attended their firm's Sensitivity Training Seminar, for which he'd earned a handsome certificate.

But wasn't this another fat thumb on the scales of Justice, tipping them against him? The unfairness of the universe! Helmut had spent his life learning *not* to be sensitive. Wasn't that called manhood? Why else endure the horrors of growing up with other boys, if not to join them as steel-hearted men? Helmut was a bull and proud of it.

Exciting as her tears might be, this grief business put him off. What did people say? "I hear old uncle so-and-so set down his knife and fork." Or "I'm sure he was proud to have been an uncle." Was that even an achievement? Probably. He might've even gotten a certificate. People often took credit for their own biology. Look at the way parents expected to be congratulated for reproduction. Too much! thought Helmut. To hear people crow over their newborns, you'd think they'd cracked cold fusion or cured cancer.

"I'm so sorry for your loss," he said, as he touched Jordan's shoulder.

Her eyes peered out of her reddened face and she hugged him again, brushing his naked head with her hair. Her arms squeezed him with surprising strength, pressing the breath from his chest. Helmut squeezed back, unnerved, while under his hands her pulse thumped invitingly.

Good God, she felt good. It was criminal.

She was so warm. So alive. So Jordan.

He'd had so many women, but none like the one in his arms.

He released her and they leaned away from each other and

stared into their empty glasses, allowing the rawness of the moment time to scab. "Turn 'em over and they're all sisters," was one of his favorite sayings, yet this one bewitched him, enticing him with her *aura*, a word he despised.

Yet there it was. Her presence burned through his skin, branding him down to the calcium of his bones. The scent of her yellow tresses – yes, *tresses!* – her skin's odor of sandalwood, combined with her armpit's aroma, burned off the alcohol in his blood and cast him into a hellish funk. Where Jordan was concerned, he couldn't win the case against his icy heart, couldn't prevail in his argument that he ought to see through her. He wanted to snarl. For Helmut hated losing, even to himself.

"I got the call from my aunt," she said, her voice quavering, "right after I dropped you two at the airport."

Ah, Jordie! Helmut thought. The familiar venom flooded his loins, rising up to his eyeballs. An unpleasantly clear voice in his head prophesied doom.

"I've been driving all night," she said. She shook out her hair as if to shake out grief, then put her hands on her lower back and straightened her spine. She wrinkled her nose. "I stink, Helmut. I'm sorry."

"I love your stink," he said, surprising himself. He didn't use syrupy baby talk. Someone else had spoken, some romantic fool, some idiot like her husband.

And yet . . . he recognized that voice. His younger self, Helmut Knight, the college man, *the one with hair*, the one she'd coaxed into the light as no one had before or since. And it wasn't so much that he'd loved – *did love* – her, but that he loved who he was when they were together, a more substantial man, weirdly, than he could ever be when he was alone.

"My uncle showed me Times Square," she said, "when it was all muggers and dirty movies. When I was eleven he took me to a Broadway show. He showed me Chinatown and the Empire State Building. We looked at the skyline and . . ." Her voice dissolved.

Helmut massaged her shoulder and his hand crept under the warm curtain of her hair and onto the back of her neck. Thank God the senator's wife hadn't shown!

"Are you here alone?" she asked, shrugging lightly.

"Who took you to a dirty movie?" Helmut wasn't playing. His capacity for self-absorption was so profound that he often lost the ability to believe in the reality of other people, much less remember what they were talking about.

"No one took me to a dirty movie," she said.

Helmut didn't say anything.

"I need to find Barton," she explained, and smiled gamely, "you know, your law partner, your best friend – my husband?" She shrugged again and Helmut removed his hand.

"Oh. *Him*. I told you. Gone to a strip club with some dudes from Miami." Helmut's mouth supplied the words, although he had no knowledge of his partner's whereabouts. In this he was innocent. "Probably be out all night," his mouth added helpfully. He raised his chin toward the bartender. "On my tab," he said, then, to Jordan, finding her drunk enough now that she could be led, "Trust me, honey, and I'll get you through this. I took a course in sensitivity. Now," he clapped his hands, "let's visit that mini-bar and wait for what's-his-name."

The bartender sighed as the two of them walked out, arm in arm. Polishing a glass till it squeaked, he reached up and loosened his bow tie, wondering if tears and alcohol weren't secretly the same substance.

Or perhaps, and this struck him so that he shook his head, the two liquids simply gave rise to one another.

2

Consultation

"DO us proud, Grandpa!"

The door closed on Helmut's back and I began typing on this machine, a decrepit laptop abandoned by the firm's last intern, some of whose hair remains stuck between the keys. In any case, I'm not really his grandfather. It's a kernel of endearment hidden inside a husk of sarcasm. This is Helmut's style, an effective tool, since one always wants to please him, to merit his non-sarcastic praise – who can say why? It's his gift. Why, even this curmudgeon, your narrator, begs a pat on the head.

Anyhow, my physician suggested "journaling" to keep my mind "limber," whatever that means. Presumably it's the opposite of rigid, which I gather is to be avoided, though "rigidity" in mental function has always seemed to me to be the benchmark of sanity. In any case, while I laughed in my doctor's smug young face, I've taken his advice.

Now, beginning with The Kansas Incident, I don't claim to have been present at every event depicted here, although they were all related to me by one, or in some cases, even all of the principals. So while I've invented mood and dialogue, the fact pattern remains accurate. This is how it really happened. Of course, the chronology is muddled. And it can't be helped, I'm afraid. I am an old man.

To wit, you find me in the beginning stages of Alzheimer's

disease. My doctor informs me that, with the latest pharmaceuticals, I may expect another year of lucidity. And while a gentleman doesn't discuss his afflictions, I feel compelled to make a full disclosure regarding my condition, lest you consign me to the dustbin of narrators deemed "unreliable."

Indeed, despite being of sound mind and body, the more I grasp at the airy present, the more I'm thrown onto the hard ground of the past. Sprawled on its dust, I find no helping hand, certainly not from the buffoons who nurse me here in this dreadful place, this "home."

This is why I elect to spend my last days telling the story of Barton Squire.

I wish to testify.

For Barton Squire was a hero – my hero. He made a blood sacrifice, serving his passion courageously and faithfully, and though in the end his faith wavered – still he served his master – his life, his love: Jordan Kelly.

I've never seen the like of it, and given the brief span left me, I never will. In short, I envy him. Consequently, I've become his audience, chronicler of a love which, to my sentimental bachelor's mind, blazes bright enough to merit "divinity" as its inspiration.

Barton Squire made me believe in fate. And as I sit here typing, one of his wife's paintings – of two naked figures wading hand in hand into the sea at crimson sunset – hangs above my desk. A deeply private man, Barton remained opaque to all but the painting's creator, with the possible exception of his lifelong friend and business partner, the infamous Helmut Knight.

I offer his case, then, not to a jury, but to you, my silent companion – my hanging judge. It is, *ergo*, an appeal.

For as the tangled proteins of my brain unmoor me from the calendar, I begin to see the counting of days and hours as humanity's greatest fiction, a tale of birth and death I no longer accept on linear terms.

The world is turning, unseen, and my mind has become a flat stone skipped across a pond, where the water is time.

This story is the sound of that skipping.

Bear with me.

– Alexander Colin, Attorney at Law (ret.)
Green Glade Assisted Living Community
Sebring, Florida
July 3, 2008

3

ANYTHING YOU SAY

LIKE a Mayan priest with a stone dagger, he carved out a man's heart on the conference table. Exhausted, Helmut slumped back in his chair, surveying the altar, which dripped with blood.

"I see where you're going with that," Barton hastily assured the pasty-faced young lawyer whose heart had been removed. Smiling, Barton winced at the young man's cheaply cut blue suit, the fraying cuffs of his shirtsleeves, his plastic watchband. "But Helmut's got a point." The young man's eyes brimmed with tears and Barton sank his voice into its most melodious, jury-charming tone. Thumbing pages, he said, "But I wouldn't go with that particular statute." He raised his eyebrows and flipped a page, "Or that precedent." Glancing up, he grinned encouragingly, even as the young man's face beaded with sweat and he assumed a suicidal expression – perhaps as he considered the jaw-dropping balance of his student loans.

Helmut had stunned the senior partners, including yours truly, Alexander Colin, when he'd slid the new lawyer's brief across the conference table, announcing he couldn't read anything so riddled with "*dipshit freshman errors.*"

No one touched the brief and it lingered forlornly until Barton reached out and rescued it. In the meantime, Helmut leaned back in his chair, inspected his fingernails, and offhandedly called attention to the young lawyer's suspiciously thick-browed, "frighteningly simian forehead," an *ad hominem* attack which evoked dry chuckles from senior partners Gart and Lanus, while your narrator squirmed in his chair.

"In any case," Barton continued, distributing his eye contact around the table, "this one's distinguishable on the facts, so Helmut and I will rewrite it. All right? Next item."

Barton had salvaged another ego, although Helmut was right: the brief *was* freshman work, especially as its author had employed "clearly" as if it were a legal term, an unforgivable offense.

With juries, too, Barton often interceded, rising from his seat in court to interrupt Helmut's theatrics, as when he'd directed a five-year-old amputee to *"show 'em your stump, kiddo!"*

Barton had cleared his throat with a volume just short of comedy. "Of course, I can see how we might seem too aggressive," he said, caressing the jury with his velvet voice and silencing Helmut with a dark look, "but we are defending not only our client but also the very body of laws this case represents. For in some sense, we are all maimed, crippled," he paused for dramatic effect. *"And wounded in spirit."*

These were set speeches. Yet Barton delivered them with such gusto that when he summed up his case he believed his own argument and, more important, so did the jury.

Meanwhile his partner would snort and stare glumly out the window. Helmut couldn't help it. Barton's sermons soured his guts. Seated at the plaintiff's table, he'd focus on the hum of the air conditioning, shuddering whenever Barton's voice broke through the wall of his mighty reason.

Yet if sentimentality won the day, what could you do? Helmut let Barton jerk the tears and trusted his own style, which was more direct. (You want a dunce's attention? Hammer a gavel onto his knuckles.)

Back in the conference room, left alone under the fluorescent lights, Barton caught his partner's sleeve. Helmut glanced up, beetle-browed, dark-eyed – annoyed.

"Yes?" His voice rose upward.

Barton's tone was pleasant. Smiling with his eyes, he said, "I'd like a word, if you don't mind."

Helmut bowed deeply from the waist, staring smugly up at his partner, who towered over him, although Barton set his feet apart to mitigate his height.

Helmut wouldn't have believed it, but Barton frequently downplayed his height *and* his good looks. Because with his chiseled features and lanky body, Barton turned heads, both male and female. In early middle age, he was trim and muscled, having kept his rangy bones in shape. He looked like he had twenty years ago, at twenty-three. His shaggy blond hair, which he wore short over his ears and long on top, had remained full and thick, with reddish streaks. His forehead was wide and strong, his nose big, though well-formed. He thought his pores disappointingly large. His lips were full yet masculine, and they never glistened. He was a man who kept his tongue at bay. A pale stubble covered his lantern jaw and prominent chin. His eyes were cornflower blue. He was *almost* movie-star handsome, but his eyes weren't arranged symmetrically in his face. One was noticeably higher than the other and this gave his features a hastily assembled look, so that if one supposed there was a God, Barton Squire was one of those men blessed with the finest materials, but whose face looked like a rush job.

Glancing around, he lowered his voice to indicate *gravitas*. "Listen, Helmut . . . you've got to stop being so nasty. You feel me? Leave your hemorrhoids at home. I know you don't mean it, but sometimes you hurt people. You getting this? Because now I've got to go make sure that guy hasn't hung himself in the bathroom."

Helmut narrowed his deep eyes, flaring his nostrils. His body trembled and Barton wouldn't have been surprised to see black smoke rise from his head. Nobody could fume like Helmut.

"Think of your blood pressure," Barton said, clapping his friend on the arm.

Helmut glared at the hand and Barton withdrew it. Barton might be the taller of the two men, yet somehow Helmut managed to stare down his hawk-like nose. His eyes smoldered, then slowly cooled. He may have even smiled. After all, Barton was only a harmless, if meddlesome, fool.

Opening his mouth, Helmut spoke in his own polished tones, the camouflage of the professional. "Sure, Barton. I hear you. No worries, partner."

"It's a problem, Helmut. Understand? It's an issue."

"With these plebs? Please."

"The stares you give people. It's bad, Counselor."

Helmut glowered, feeling found out. But since no one likes to be unpopular at the office, he socked Barton in the arm, affecting a brogue.

"We'll 'ave none of that, eh laddie? Nay wonder yer talking shite, young Squire! Let yer Knight buy ye a pint. Ye cannay refuse. Off to the pub now, eh?"

Barton shook his head. His hair had grown unkempt behind his ears and Helmut observed that Barton looked like he'd just stepped out of a fashion magazine, his hair wind-tousled, his complexion rosy. Sighing, Helmut silently despised his partner's casual good looks, disliking himself, in the meantime, for even caring.

"It's not unmanly to show a little compassion," Barton said, reaching out to squeeze his partner's shoulder. Helmut stood motionless, tolerating the contact. "That's all I'm asking."

"You're a prick too," Helmut said, shrugging off the enormous hand like some giant fleshy spider. "You just hide it."

An ugly moment ensued. Screw this ageing candy ass, Helmut thought, *and* his fancy wife. He'd had it with both of them, except that he couldn't stop thinking about the fancy wife. What of it! She wasn't made of ice-cream. Her breasts were as hard as biceps and she was too skinny, but there it was – he burned for her until he thought the fire would incinerate him.

He understood *longing*.

If any fault obtained, it lay in taking so long to identify Barton as a dangerous buffoon, a sticking point in the long haul he meant to steer toward Jordan. No doubt about it. He'd have to eliminate this obstacle, with professional help, if need be.

"Earth to Helmut – I'm talking to you."

"I'm thinking. Do you mind?"

He might take out an insurance policy on Barton's life, but it wouldn't do to tamper with the firm's finances, not after he'd tapped into the escrow account to cover a scary margin call from his broker.

Barton snapped his fingers in front of his partner's face.

"Okay, okay!" Helmut said. Don't get your panties in a wad. What're *you*, the moral authority?"

"I'm not, I – "

Helmut closed his eyes and shook his enormous head. "I will comply with your demands," he said evenly, opening his eyes. "I'll make nice, okay? Now let's get back on billable time. I'm not here to hold hands."

Barton grinned, displaying his well-flossed, highly polished teeth. "There's the Hell Mutt we all know and love. He's off his leash!"

Helmut's forehead relaxed. They made a good team – he had to admit it. Ever since they'd won their first case in moot court at the University of San Francisco School of Law, even dour judges had applauded this earnest pair. Superb researchers, they simply out-studied their opponents. And Barton's jocular, all-American-boy routine mitigated Helmut's edgy wit, for Helmut's booming baritone too often included the subtext: "if only you weren't a mental-defective, you'd see that what I'm saying is both obvious *and* true. So you're not only an idiot, you're also an *obstinate* idiot."

Consequently, outside his office, both underlings and colleagues tended to see things Helmut's way. They were afraid not to. His technique was simple, with most of his questions hung along the rhetorical line of "So were you lying *then* or are you lying *now?*"

In court, once he got a witness flustered, he'd close in for the *coup de grace*, and lest he seem too predatory, he cracked jokes all the way to the kill. For like many merciless advocates, Helmut was a talented comedian. Winking and shuffling, elbowing them as if they were fellow geniuses, he'd offer the jury his witty company, presenting his conclusions like so much ripe fruit, but only to the elect – those lucky enough to be his audience.

Outside the conference room, secretaries and clerks and other lawyers threaded their way past them and Helmut began digging through his briefcase, thumbing manila folders, oblivious to members of the firm he deemed "worker bees." An object of loathing among the secretaries, he secretly cherished his role as sarcastic commentator since it meant he'd been noticed and – better still – talked about.

This was something Helmut could admit: Barton might have the looks, but he – Hell Mutt – had all the charisma.

And the *cojones*.

And the teeth.

"I didn't mean to offend you," Barton said. "I just wanted to let you know . . . as a friend."

Helmut remained silent. What was this need for full disclosure? Barton was always confessing, always owning up. Helmut considered it fortunate they didn't practice criminal law or they'd be doing lethal injections right there in the office.

Barton touched him lightly on the shoulder. Helmut glared. *Again*, with the touching?

"So the issue's resolved?"

Groaning, Helmut rifled his briefcase in search of a legal pad which had meanly gotten itself lost. Alarmed, he'd remembered an outstanding debt regarding his foreign exchange account.

"Well?" Barton asked.

Helmut snapped shut his briefcase, nostrils flaring. "All right, already!" He turned up his hawk-like eyes. "I'll play well with others, if it makes Dad happy." He allowed himself to leer. "That about cover my sensitivity training, Counselor?"

"See? That's just what I'm saying."

"Oh, for crying out loud!"

"All right then," Barton said, as though they'd resolved something.

Helmut accepted his partner's extended hand and, smirking, found Barton's grip disgustingly strong and warm and dry. Barton thumped his partner on the bicep, while Helmut thought of ways to poison him.

Even before The Kansas Incident, the way Helmut saw life, he had no choice but to destroy Barton. Because for reasons he couldn't name, Helmut needed to feel superior to Barton. And he *was* superior. He wrote more incisive briefs, published better articles, and he made more money, but in the end, Barton irked him beyond saying because at a fundamental level Barton enjoyed life more than Helmut. For this, Helmut could never forgive him.

Yet he also admitted that murder was too extreme, a schoolboy's unproductive fantasy.

He'd have to get Barton fired.

It was only equitable. If Barton got Jordan, he couldn't also be a partner.

Helmut meant to put his thumb on the scales of Justice.

Because why would Justice be blindfolded, if not to let him right a wrong?

4

The Heat of Passion

"SO this stuff is mellow, right?" Barton asked. "It won't freak me out?"

"Trust me, Big Bart." Bill frowned good-naturedly and compressed his bushy eyebrows into single, furry line across his forehead. He had a heroic nose and a black beard, and with his barrel-chested body and thunderous voice he reminded Barton of a Roman soldier. It was easy to imagine him on horseback wearing a bronze breastplate and a helmet with a crest on top.

"It's White Widow," said Bill, his brown eyes aglitter, "the taste is red wine and citrus with a hint of chocolate in the body, then the finish is pine and mint." Bill couldn't stop smiling. He was very enthusiastic. "You'll *love* it!"

Holding it by the stem, Barton held the bud under a lamp so as to better admire it. With its red and purple hairs, the bud looked more like an insect than a plant. White crystals of resin sparkled on its manicured leaves.

"I haven't gotten stoned since the earth cooled," Barton said. He grinned at Bill. They'd been buddies since law school and their friendship was of that rare, timeless variety, the kind of camaraderie where years apart passed like hours. Their twenty-year dialogue never stopped – it only took breaths. Now they were two floors above Helmut and Jordan, sitting at a table inside Bill's room at the hotel.

"Careful," Bill warned, "this stuff expands."

Puckering his lips, Barton inhaled and the ember of the joint crackled and filled his lungs. He allowed his eyes to bulge theatrically. Sputtering, he held his hit and handed the joint to Bill.

Bill sat on the edge of the bed. "One of my clients paid me with this stuff."

"Is that wise?" Barton asked. "You think it's reasonable and prudent?"

Bill's laugh was deep and merry. An inside joke from law school, they'd found the concept of "the reasonable and prudent person" as absurd as it was hilarious.

"Doubtlessly not," Bill said.

Hiding his reluctance, smiling, Barton accepted the joint and filled his lungs with the resin-heavy, pine-smelling smoke.

"Got it from a guy I defended on a DUI," Bill said, holding his hit before releasing a stale-smelling cloud.

The two lawyers sat in stoned silence. Layers of smoke hung in the air, gently wavering, while Barton glanced up at the ceiling, at the unblinking red eye of the smoke detector. His skin itched.

"It wasn't in a car though."

"Not in a car," Barton said mechanically, as though he were taking a deposition.

Bill raised his substantial eyebrows. "Nope." He stared admiringly at the ribbon of smoke streaming off the joint.

"A mule!" he hollered. He slapped his knee. "I defended a drunken man riding a mule down Duval Street! Turns out the mule was drunk too, though he wasn't charged."

"You're fine and brilliant man," Barton said, and he pushed himself to his feet, eyeing the hideous floral print on the bedspread with something like alarm, adding, "I've always said so."

"Stay," said Bill, holding out the extinguished joint, "I don't want to be high all by my lonesome."

"Can't," Barton said, shrugging, "got to read my paper tomorrow."

"Forget those yahoos," Bill said, "conferences are for losers."

"Then what are *we* doing here?"

"Ah. Resting our cases."

Barton looked at his friend. Bill was a generous man and his charm was a potent guilt-reliever. Barton could see why his clients liked him.

"Brother, I can't," he said. "I'm officially a one-hit wonder and – " Barton's eyes widened and he frantically patted his back pocket, reassured himself that his wallet was still there, breathed a sigh of relief, then checked it again. "See what I mean?"

Bill pushed his heavy, bear-like body to its shambling feet. "I hate to break it to you, pal o' mine – but no one cares – these conferences, they're all about playing hooky and . . . *fringe benefits.*" He held out the roach. "I mean, who doesn't love a junket?"

Seeing the roach was unlit, Barton didn't take it. He was thinking about his presentation. He was proud of "The Charismatic Close" and hoped to publish it, even though Helmut's name would appear first, as ever, given that K came before S. He'd wanted to ask Helmut if he'd consider alternating the order, but he wasn't up to the shower of mockery such a request would earn. In the end, and in the spirit of what he thought of as Buddha-nature, he let it go.

Seeing Barton frown, Bill frowned too, snapping Barton out of his mood. Ever Mr. Good Cheer, Bill grinned so widely that his eyes vanished into fleshy slits under his tremendous brow. His whole face smiled. He set his meaty hands on Barton's shoulders and shook him. "You're a master of jurisprudence!" he bellowed into Barton's face, then dashed to the window and swung it open on the black Kansas sky: *"Barton Squire is the greatest legal mind of his generation!"*

"Put it on the street, brother."

Bill shrugged and fell backward on the bed with his feet still touching the floor. "See you at rooster time." He closed his eyes and exhaled. "Think of me when you trip out."

"You coming to my song and dance?"

Bill had his eyes closed, drowsing in bliss. "I wouldn't miss it, Counselor."

"Your honor," said Barton, crossing the room and bowing, "I bid thee good night and heartfelt thanks." Hearing Bill snore theatrically, he gently pulled the door until it latched with a soft click.

Outside, blazing tubes of fluorescent light traveled the hall ceiling. Barton squinted and protectively held up his hand, feeling his skull begin to throb while his ears started humming. Unsteady on his feet, he ran his fingertips along the wall, gagging from the reek of disinfectant rising from the carpet. His nose wrinkled. Given their human traffic, one didn't want to consider the hygiene of hotels too deeply, particularly when stoned. All those dead skin cells. Pounds of them in every mattress, hair follicles blowing from every vent – a regular shower of strangers' DNA.

Barton grunted softly, expelling such thoughts, and shivered from his toes up to his skull. Outside Florida, he chilled easily, a sorrowful admission for a born-and-bred Yankee, and a distinct indicator he'd crossed forty.

In front of the elevator, he pressed the button and waited. Bill wasn't lying. This was some fine marijuana. This was hallucinogenic. The elevator announced itself with a soft ring of its bell and its doors parted in what seemed like a friendly way. Barton suppressed an urge to thank it.

Stepping inside, he pictured the deathly dark shaft looming under his feet. Smacking his dry tongue against the roof of his mouth, he illuminated number 7, hoping Helmut would be unconscious when he arrived.

He wasn't up to facing his partner just now, because he seemed to be getting higher every minute, every second. *Le Buzz Magnifique!* Translucent floaters danced in the aqueous humor of his eyes, teasing little twists like fishing line which kept spinning out of sight.

In the stucco on the wall he perceived an old man's bearded face, surmounted by a wizard's cap.

Unlocking the door to his room, he discovered his best friend on top of his wife, the two of them sprawled across a flowered bedspread identical to the one in Bill's room. Barton blinked and shivered – hallucinating, or so he thought.

Helmut's bald dome covered Jordan's face but not her golden hair, which surrounded Helmut's gleaming skull like a nimbus around the head of a saint. Barton's wife struggled to sit up and Helmut tried to hide, burying his naked cranium in the riot of her tawny curls.

Barton's pulse throbbed in his temples and his gorge rose and he swallowed against the sour taste in his mouth. *I'm tripping*, he thought, *I must be* . . .

Gulping air, he ground his fists into his eyes. His tongue felt like a dehydrated lizard, slowly desiccating in the desert of his mouth.

A giant penis with a flesh-colored head and wheat-colored pubic hair lay on the bed, its gargantuan shaft concealed by the hideous bedspread.

"God, that's good pot," Barton croaked.

Two muffled voices whispered frantically. Barton shook his head. A recreational drug connoisseur during his law school years, he'd once fought down a cat-sized albino dinosaur gobbling up his sneakers outside the library, so he wasn't about to let some pot-inspired penis get the best of him now – not after he'd passed the bar and become an officer of the court. He raised his hand to object.

"I'll castrate your ass," he declared.

"Hi, sweetheart!" called a disturbingly familiar voice.

So the giant penis had a pet name for him, did it? Well! The monstrous organ struggled and thrashed under its honey-colored ruff, twisting itself up in the bedspread. Barton frowned and clenched his jaw. For a penis, the thing sure had a girly voice. Vaguely, he recognized it, but those musical tones belonged at home in sultry Florida, not here in bone-chilling Kansas.

The penis grew arms and struggled with itself, writhing under the bedspread. It was beginning to masturbate. Ugh! Barton's eyes darted around the room, searching for something sharp, suitable for circumcision. Hallucinations were one thing, but *obscene* hallucinations were another. He wouldn't stand for it. No, sir. He lived by a code, one which didn't include oversized, self-gratifying sex organs.

"One second, honey!"

What nerve. Unsatisfied with pleasuring itself, the penis was coming on to him. And in his own room. This he could not abide. At the height of his indignation, the penis underwent parthenogenesis and suddenly his wife turned up her face. Meanwhile the penis slithered off the bed and disappeared, dragging the flowered spread behind it like a snake with a half-shed skin.

Barton squinted in disbelief, in horror. His jaw unclenched. He felt the air on his dry tongue. His senses were wide open, his nerves roaring.

"Jordan?"

"Barton?"

Husband and wife exchanged names again, as if they were unmasking each other at a masquerade. The air conditioner thrummed and rattled.

"I just got stoned," Barton said helplessly.

"You look stoned," his wife said. The instant lingered. Their mouths opened and closed and they blinked at each other, unable to breathe properly. Together they waited for time to pass, to fan its cooling wings over the hot wound of the moment.

They stood shifting their weight from one foot to the other, daring to make eye contact, only to break it off and re-establish it. It was hard to know what to do, where to look. Their bodies seemed unnatural extensions of themselves.

Thankfully the air conditioner kicked into higher gear, mitigating the terrible silence. Jordan had on a white brassiere and blue panties with lace trim. Her macramé flats were still on her feet.

Covertly, she ran a slender hand through her tangled, bed-head hair and, feeling the cool air raise goose bumps on her nearly naked body, she seated herself on the edge of the mattress, trying to make herself small.

"So do you," he said.

"So do I what?" she asked.

"Look stoned." Or drunk, he thought, momentarily distracted by his horror of her using alcohol.

"I've been crying."

"Oh."

Both hoped this conversation might establish something, might make sense of the encounter, but it didn't. Another painful moment ensued.

"So how do you like Kansas?" Barton asked idiotically.

Jordan widened her raw-looking eyes as though confronted by a lunatic. Of course, in his present condition, he *was* a lunatic.

"It's very flat," she said, then – inspired, "like Florida!"

Her husband waited. Geography was an interesting topic, but he let it pass. Perhaps if they kept very quiet, the awkwardness of the moment would mutate, evolve – become bearable.

But no, the awful moment expanded until it filled the room, the town, the state, the galaxy. Husband and wife were overwhelmed. Time left them skinned, their guts exposed to the air.

And where had that giant penis got to anyhow?

"Why're *you* crying?" Jordan asked, bending forward. Her hand touched his knee.

"Crying. What? I'm not."

"Yes, you are."

"No, I'm not. I'm just high."

Her lips were trembling. "Oh," she said.

Her husband looked at the ceiling, at the mocking red eye of another smoke detector. He rolled his neck, trying to ease a cramp. Shivering and sweating, he couldn't tell if he was hot or cold.

"Why're *you* crying?" he asked.

"My uncle passed away and . . . oh!" Gasping, she clutched her heaving chest and hiccupped with incredible force. She shuddered down the length of her body and, swallowing painfully, slowly regained herself. She drew her feet onto the bed and clasped her slim, rose-brown ankles with her hands. She yanked loose the mattress pad and dabbed at the corner of her eyes, blinking rapidly. "He lived in Independence – near here, so I decided to drive to the funeral. I thought you might want to come with me. Oh. I loved him, Barton." She sniffled loudly. "Oh, honey, I did!" Her face convulsed and she began to weep – great tearing sobs which lacerated her husband's heart – no matter that he'd caught her *en flagrante delicto*. She *was* his heart.

And so he felt he knew what it would be to be drawn and quartered. The sound of his wife in pain was more than he could bear.

"*I am so sorry*," he said, because there was never anything else to say to grief. He held open his arms and his wife sprang into them, knocking him backward so he had to retreat a step to keep from falling. The heft of her body felt sweetly familiar, as solid as home and hearth. Nuzzling her soft hair with his nose, he caught the tangy scent of her, the close smell of a long road trip taken in the middle of the night.

"Ollie, Ollie-in-come-free!" a voice called. The bald crown of a head peeked out from under the bed and Helmut's bulging brown eyes peered up, the rest of his face hidden by the floral spread. "Can I come out now?" The toe of Barton's foot tingled, ready to punt his partner's head out the window.

"Not a reasonable and prudent action," Helmut warned. "As your attorney, I suggest you refrain from violence."

Barton laughed humorlessly. "Prepare for death or great bodily injury, Counselor. You've reached the penalty phase."

"Barton," his wife said. She rested her hands on his shoulders. "Barton, let him come out."

Fists clenched, Barton growled, then pulled back his head to stare into his wife's eyes, unwilling to believe she was begging for mercy for Helmut. He could forgive *her*, but his partner? No mitigating circumstances. No pardon.

Jordan set her hands on her hips and flipped her hair over her shoulder with an awkward jerk of her neck. It was an unconscious gesture, Barton believed, a nervous tic, but it won her point. Perhaps long ago, as a child, she'd learned its persuasive value and then forgotten it, leaving this fossil in the adult. He sometimes wondered how well he knew her, though they'd shared a bed for twenty years.

"It's all a misunderstanding," she said. Her cheeks were flushed. Barton thought about her high blood pressure and pressed his finger to her lips to stop her from talking, then using both hands he gripped her upper arms and held her at arm's length. Her sapphire eyes blinked helplessly out of her flushed face. She shrugged and mouthed *sorry!* He groaned and let go of her. She was a piece of work, he admitted, but he loved her completely.

And what, pray tell, can a man do about that?

Scowling, he recalled the errant penis. Drawing a long breath, he remembered why he'd stopped getting high or drunk. Those kinds of days started out so well and ended so badly.

"Brilliant," he said in the British fashion. "We'll be a long time dead, but you guys are really seizing the day, eh?"

Helmut wriggled out from under the bed and gained his feet.

"Toasty under there," he said, pulling at his collar. He extended his short neck and rolled the great ball of his head. He had on a white dress shirt and red boxer shorts.

Nobody spoke.

Standing there before his law partner and his wife, Helmut glanced in the mirror over the dresser, gathered his pants from a heap on the floor and stepped into them as if he were alone. Zipping up, he adjusted his scrotum and turned to his friends as if they were adoring intimates who wouldn't mind watching him dress.

Raising his eyebrows and smiling, his dark eyes gleamed out of his head. "Anyone care for a highball?" he asked brightly.

Barton panted, inhaling the follicle-laden, stale air. He took a step forward.

Helmut raised his hands. "Easy there, young Squire. Jordan just got here. I was fixing her a drink. Comforting her. Her uncle passed on – so let's show some respect."

Barton stuttered and smacked his fist into his palm.

"And here she is," said Helmut, seizing her hand and kissing it. Jordan snatched it back. "Our one and only Jordan Kelly. Or are you signing yourself 'Squire' these days? One of those hyphen jobs? I'm drawing a blank." Helmut tapped his temple with his finger and his eyes protruded from the egg-shaped dome of his skull, glittering and – Barton was sure of it – *twinkling*. "Now we'll have our nightcaps!" Helmut announced. Light on his feet, he made for the mini-bar as though it might escape.

"So what *were* you two doing?" Barton asked, keeping his voice level. His heart thumped inside his chest like a wounded animal, although at least he'd gotten his lungs under control. Helmut stood with his back to him, trying to keep his hand steady while he poured a drink. Normally a cool customer, he wasn't in the best of shape himself.

Barton sighed. Neither wife nor partner met his gaze. When he turned toward the window their eyes had a private conversation behind his back, a visual conspiracy, an alibi-maker. Jordan quickly pulled on her clothes.

Barton shook his head, feeling betrayed. Hell, he *was* betrayed. He felt the blood of a fool pump in his veins. He didn't feel noble and wronged, but self-righteous, wounded and vain. Why should he expect others to adhere to his morals? By what *right* did he expect justice? Because he was legally wed? No. The law held more fiction than literature. "Christ," he said, although he wasn't a Christian, "preserve me now and at the hour of my death." Waiting for them to explain themselves, his temples throbbed, his guts burbled, his teeth hurt. Worst of all, he was still high. Bill was a good guy, but Jesus . . . he was a bad influence.

At the window, Helmut fixed a triple vodka gimlet and slyly positioned himself behind the TV, ready, if need be, to drop his drink and hurl it at his partner.

"I'm prepared to offer you both the benefit of the doubt," Barton said, unpleasantly aware he'd slipped into his lawyer voice. Weak in the knees, he sat on the bed, but that left the two of them towering over him. He stood up and they backed away. He saw with pleasure that they were mildly afraid of him. "So please don't blow it."

Helmut and Jordan hung their heads. They shuffled their feet. They looked away. Obviously no lawyer had coached them on how to appear before a jury. At least not in the capacity of defendants. Barton attempted to ignore their self-prosecuting body language. Still, they wouldn't look at him. Helmut slurped his drink, making obscene sucking sounds with an undersize drink straw. Barton wondered if he was doing it on purpose and decided he probably was.

"I've known Jordan for twenty years," Helmut said abruptly, thrusting out his chin and preening. Jordan and Barton looked at him in surprise. Helmut cleared his throat and set his drink on the television, suddenly emboldened, safe behind the TV. "So don't take this out of context, Barton. Her uncle's death has traumatized her. And I was offering solace – that's *all*. You can see we're both fully dressed." Hearing his own authority and lofty tone, Helmut became indignant. He brought his hawk-like gaze to bear out of his nostrils. "That's two decades." Staring into space, he suddenly stopped, hearing how drunk he sounded.

From the way his tongue slid off his teeth, slurring the "s" in "decades," Barton judged his partner's blood-alcohol to be well within the "diminished capacity" range, but that was no defense.

Barton moaned. Physically, he was strong enough to lift Helmut off his feet and hurl him through the window. Both men were aware of this, and as they made eye contact this knowledge hung between them, a double death sentence.

Then Barton blinked and Helmut smiled. There would be no violence.

For Barton believed that if you didn't forgive people you'd become a slave to your own mind, where you'd be force-fed revenge fantasies. More to the point, he aspired to be a Buddhist, while acknowledging that aspiration and Buddhism were incompatible concepts. Still, attachment and aversion were delusional. All life, though it might appear separate, was a single phenomenon, if you could stand to admit it. To Barton, this was pretty obvious.

So why this lust for the crack of bone, this hunger for the smell of his enemy's blood?

"What *were* you doing?" he asked, striving for *satori*, for the inner peace required not to throw his partner out the window or to want a drink like the one in his rival's pudgy hand.

"I've explained it to you," Helmut said, as though speaking to a slow learner, "I was *comforting* her."

"Right," said Barton. "Absolutely." He turned to go but Jordan caught his arm and squeezed it. She dug her nails into the skin and left a row of red crescents.

"We were kissing. I admit that." Her voice was high, desperate, her eyes imploring and cobalt, the color she somehow saved up for desperate moments. "I'm sorry, honey. I fell off the wagon and we came up here to look for you and I was upset about my uncle and . . . Honey, I'm sorry."

Helmut sipped his drink and studied Barton over the rim of his glass. Barton scrutinized his partner's eyes for any hint of a twinkle.

Helmut held himself in check, drawing the curtain down on even the suggestion of a twinkle, although he could feel his eyes tempting him, itching with desire.

"The two of you," Barton said, returning halfway to his senses as Bill's marijuana began to wear off, "you're in your forties and you act like teenagers and . . . you know what?" Barton clapped his hands. "Fuck it," he said happily.

Helmut raised his eyes and Barton saw his partner's bald head exploding on the pavement beyond the dark window. "It's a good thing I'm a Buddhist," he said. "You guys do what you want. I'm going to the bar."

His wife made an awful noise in her throat and Barton opened the door and strode into the hallway where he bit his knuckle. He fought down the urge to howl. A sensitive man, he nevertheless subscribed to the notion that grown men didn't cry, much less howl. How else could you tell they were men? He and Helmut agreed on this point.

Striding down the length of the reeking carpet under the blazing lights, he recognized his wife's footfall behind him, a sound he adored – ordinarily. He fought down a thickening of the throat, a hot heaving behind his eyes. The elevator arrived with a self-satisfied *ping!* and Jordan roughly grabbed his hand and spun him around. She kissed him on the mouth and eyes, his cheeks, even his hands. She sank to her knees and kissed his knuckles.

"Barton, please. *Please!* I was out of my head." Her voice was breaking. "I was drunk. I *am* drunk. I love you. I do. What do you want me to say?"

Goodbye, thought Barton, terrifying himself.

The elevator door opened, lurching and clanking with mechanical authority. Inside it was empty.

"You forgive me?" she asked. She was still on her knees. Her eyes were wide.

Barton inflated his lungs. "You're my wife," he said. He helped her off the carpet and together they stepped into the elevator.

"And you're my husband," she said, reaching for him. The doors closed.

"It's already history," he said. "Forget it."

She turned up her face and pressed her hand to the rough stubble on his chin.

"You really promise to forgive me?"

He nodded and held her close, while the elevator floor dropped from beneath their feet.

5

Habitual Offender

IN summiting a mountain of mental anguish, one is faced with two routes: the aesthetic and the *an*aesthetic. You've got your Beethoven or your heroin, your Shakespeare or your vodka, your Picasso or your cheesecake. Either climb may conquer the peak of your shining pain, but neither flag flaps long in those chilly winds. By expedition's end, you're either liberally educated or badly hung over. Perhaps both. Glory is noticeably absent.

The only hope lies in flight, in retreating to that land you inhabited before you climbed pain's blue mountain. To discover those virgin foothills you've got to isolate the muscle of your memory and flex it backward, training it to return you to those fertile lowlands, where the seeds of anguish lay as yet unsown. Straining hard, you remember who you were, the one without the deformed heart, the maimed soul, the crippled disposition. The one who wasn't so nasty. In Barton's case, to the T. B. J. – *Time Before Jordan.*

How else to survive the treachery of adult life, that tainted jury of your peers?

Your questionable honor . . .

He remembered his life in the T. B. J., which began in his freshman year at the University of Florida when he'd nailed his thumb to the wall.

* * *

"Goooooood Gawd A'Mighty!" Helmut said, glancing up from his dorm room desk and affecting a southern drawl, "What da hay-ell you doin'?!?"

Barton swallowed against the knot in his throat, a grim look on his face. A hot bead of sweat rolled down his back.

"I just nailed my thumb to the wall," he said. He chewed his lip and hung there against the drywall, bleeding. Twin red streaks dribbled down the white paint. "It hurts," he said.

Helmut scowled and pushed his chair away from his desk. He narrowed his eyes.

Barton explained: "The most beautiful girl in the world walked by and – ouch! Do you mind? Can I get a little help here?"

Reluctantly, his roommate stood up. This introduction didn't bode well for the future. Helmut disliked accidents and the people who had them. They were losers, weren't they? It seemed obvious, although like so many obvious things only *he* could see it. He sighed. Genius walked hand in hand with loneliness. This was a hard truth, but even at eighteen he was man enough to accept it.

Later, the most beautiful girl in the world would ask, "So you didn't help him?"

"Put yourself in my place, Jordie. Here I'd just met the guy and he crucifies himself. Is that normal? I thought he might be like one of those Filipinos. The ones who bloody themselves till the Easter bunny comes."

A few days earlier Helmut had been sent by the housing office to replace Barton's first roommate, Alejandro Sanchez, who'd died of AIDS. A disco-dancing, man-loving Miami Cuban, Alejandro was a long way from the long-locked, heavy metal Barton, who was fresh from New York and wild-eyed with lust for every coed on campus.

And yet it was Alejandro who gave virginal Barton his first good counsel on women – as in remember she's got a heart like you, an approach which thunderstruck Barton, who simply couldn't see beyond the screen of healthy female flesh. In a flash he had what their literature professor called *an epiphany*. Women were mind-blowing in the flesh alone, but if you loved the soul inside?

Certain doom.

You soldiered on, in any event. First living and then dying with HIV, Alejandro had taught Barton something about courage.

Remembering the funeral as he stared at Alejandro's mattress, stripped bare on the other side of the dorm, Barton jumped when a key scratched inside the lock and the door opened, admitting a bright rectangle of sun. A wiry young man stepped into it and set his hands on his hips, screwing up his face. He had a small, wiry frame and tidy muscles. Blinking and waiting for his eyes to adjust, he surveyed the room with the air of Napoleon inspecting his domain in exile. Raising his nose, he wrinkled his nostrils and sniffed the air, seeming none too pleased with it.

Barton cleared his throat.

Helmut perked up his eyebrows and regarded his new roommate, squinting as he took in Barton's athletic body, his earnest good looks, his blue eyes and lantern jaw. He seemed not to see the red pimples dotting Barton's chin, although for Barton every pustule was an eruption of mortal embarrassment.

Barton tossed back his long hair and nodded cheerfully. Smiling, he stood up and held out his hand.

Helmut polished his lenses on his shirttail and replaced them on his long nose. "So," he asked, "you gay?"

"Excuse me?"

"Just asking. I don't want you to blow me or anything."

"Gee thanks," Barton said.

Helmut shrugged. "Just making sure I've got the right room. No offense."

"Why would I be offended?"

"Hey," said Helmut, "I'm sorry about your lover, but – "

"*He wasn't my lover,*" Barton said too loudly. He lowered his voice. "He was my friend." He clenched his fists at his sides. He didn't care for his new roommate's voice, a baritone ripe with self-assurance, a voice which ought to have come from a much larger man. The voice had the sound of the country club in it, a slick ring born of the in-ground pool enjoyed in childhood, of summer sailing and scuba lessons.

Compressing his lips, Barton took in Helmut's surf shop clothes, his O'Neill baggies, his Ray Ban sunglasses, his Sperry topsiders. He might have walked off a tropical beach, the insouciant, slovenly millionaire, his long brown hair professionally tousled.

Helmut produced a slip of paper verifying his room assignment. While Barton read it Helmut gazed over his shoulder. "Are you married to that spot by the window?" He raised his chin toward the sunbeams shining through the slats of the blinds. "Because I need to sleep there."

Barton looked up and handed back the paper. "Sure. I can move my bed."

Helmut sucked his teeth. "All right then. *So*. What about you?"

"What about me." Barton made it a statement.

"You gay?"

"What?"

"Just asking, dude – not that I care."

"I just told you – no – *dude*." Barton scowled. A young man given to enthusiastic gesturing with his hands, he'd sometimes been mistaken for a homosexual, especially since he'd moved to the south, an error which scandalized him.

Helmut chuckled and clucked his tongue. "Only inquiring, dude. I sleep naked and I can't have Captain Butt Pirate sailing up my stern, eh?" He socked Barton in the arm in a spirit of athletic, heterosexual horseplay. Barton didn't return the contact. He wasn't that kind of guy. High fives and the like struck him as ridiculous.

"Just so you know," Barton said, "Alejandro was my best friend, okay?" He allowed himself to loom over his new roommate. He wanted his size to register with this little emperor. "Just so you know," he repeated.

"Oooohh!" Helmut turned his head and addressed an imaginary

confidante, wagging a limp wrist and raising his voice an octave. "*He's so butch. I love it!*"

Barton glowered. But no, he wouldn't start off this way. He blinked and drew a deep breath. "Let's be friends, okay?" He extended his hand again.

Helmut eyed it until Barton let it drop. *Let's be friends?* Helmut thought. He narrowed his dark eyes. "You're not some kind of Christian, are you?"

"Ummm . . . no . . . I'm a Buddhist if you're interested."

"Not particularly, but . . . Jesus Christ," Helmut said, "I thought college was for *rational* people."

"Listen. Maybe you should ask for a single."

"Dude, I tried. No dice. Anyway, there's some talent around here." He bugged out his eyes and caressed imaginary breasts. "I've seen it."

So Helmut had seen her too. That shiny girl with the sun-flecked hair.

The one who'd strolled past their window and who'd so distracted Barton he would later nail his thumb to the wall in the midst of hanging a Van Gogh print.

Helmut crossed the room and frowned at the bloody mess pinning his roommate to the drywall. He turned up his lip, baring his greenish teeth, then his nostrils twitched, disclosing black hairs which, out of some strange vanity, he refused to trim.

Barton writhed. "I'm stuck," he said. Twin red blood trails trickled downward, lurid against the wall's dingy white.

"I hope you realize we're liable for the damage you're doing to that wall," Helmut said. "I have a deposit to think about."

Barton wriggled and beads of sweat rolled down his face. His cheeks were blazing. "I can't get myself loose."

"You aren't some kind of masochist, are you?"

"Just go get somebody, will you? Come *on!*" Barton's thumb abruptly came free. The blood had loosened the drywall and crumbled it into a paste of gooey pink plaster. The pink paste blocked up the hole in the fleshy part of his thumb quite nicely. The blood streaks dried on the wall.

Outside, Jordan strode past their window again, a bombshell of cleavage and teeth. Atop her slender neck, her hair bounced and glinted in the Florida sun, as gold as Spanish doubloons.

Behind the glass, the two roommates stared out at her while Barton cradled his mangled thumb.

Observing their gaping mouths, she rolled her eyes and hurried on, averting her gaze from the astonished circles of their eyes. "Oh my," she thought. "*Great.* More high school."

Ever since her freshman year men had looked at her as if she were an entrée, as if she were more food than human, as if they'd like to stick a fork in her. Shaking her head, she walked toward her dorm. In college she'd hoped to be considered human, but pretty girls knew better than to expect any sympathy.

Inside, Helmut guffawed and rubbed his hands together. "Daddio," he said, slapping his knee, "*that* is some *serious* talent!"

Barton sucked his thumb, tasting salty blood. "Tell me about it. I may never give a thumbs-up."

"Or hitch a ride," Helmut smiled crookedly. For all his country club bravado, he was a lonely freshman too. He needed friends. Who didn't? "I'm sorry about your roommate," he said suddenly. "AIDS sucks, man. I hate condoms."

A strange moment ensued as, simultaneously, they realized that in the dark they'd be masturbating in each other's presence. They'd be sharing a single room, after all. They were college freshmen. They were eighteen and surrounded by half-dressed girls – a sea of tanned midriffs and silky thighs and the wondrous odor of Coppertone.

They couldn't help it.

6

DIMINISHED CAPACITY

AFTER he'd caught her with Helmut, Barton sat at the bar with his wife in the hotel lounge in Index, Kansas, studying the fractal patterns of melting ice in his glass, thinking of order and chaos. On the whole he preferred order. Jordan spun around on her bar stool, her yellow hair flying. Husband and wife were decidedly off the wagon and on top of something else.

It was happy hour. The bartender, who had the sleeves of his shirt rolled up to reveal tattoos as blue as bruises, set down a fresh round. He'd seen it all before. These professional types in their designer clothes didn't hold their liquor any better than the locals who reeled around the dance floor in overalls and cowboy boots.

Barton set a crisp fifty on the bar, neatly creased along its length. The bartender picked it up, raised his eyebrows, met his customer's heavy-lidded stare and acknowledged Barton's keep-the-change wave.

Happy hour, the bartender thought, depositing his tip in the jar beside the register. What a name. More like, *I wish* I was happy hour.

Holding his drink up to the neon glow of a beer light, Barton rattled the ice cubes in his glass. Given alcohol's contribution to criminal behavior, the stuff ought to have been scheduled alongside cocaine and heroin, but here it was, running in rivers from sea to shining sea. He drank to the perversity of it, smacking his lips over its solvency, the evaporative feel of it on his tongue, its odor a cross between bug killer and paint thinner. And this was the good stuff. He smiled mirthlessly. The trip from top shelf to rock bottom was like gravity – it started slowly and ended quickly.

Jordan spun around on her bar stool and swung her face up from under the blond tent of her hair as if performing a dance move. Having sobered up, she was now a little drunk again. Soon, her husband realized, it would be more than a little. It would be a lot, a ticket to La La Land, and then . . . God help them. Anything could happen, as it had so often in the past.

"See this in the big picture," she said in a hard voice, quite unlike her own, the aggressive edge of the alcohol creeping in, "See it in *el foto grande,* Barton. I won't let you throw your whole life away. Uh-uh, no way." She poked her finger between his ribs. "*You got that?*"

"Sure thing," he said, snatching her hand and kissing it.

Jordan said, "Well!" with a sudden explosion of breath, her azure stare undercut by a sudden attack of hiccups.

She raised a slender hand to her mouth. "Are you – *hicket!* – pat – *hicket!* – pa-tronizing me?"

"Certainly not," her husband said. Her eyes flashed but her temper subsided as she fought her hiccups. Feeling the alcohol work, Barton entertained such profundities as *time is weird.*

Hearing a familiar song on the bar's sound system, his memories of young love surfaced like the bubbles in his drink. Glory days and salad hours, but so what? The moment, *the now,* was all that mattered, and there wasn't enough *right now* left to spend it wallowing in *back then.*

"Satisfaction," he said. He drank and looked at his drink. It seemed made of disinfectant. "I'd die for it."

Jordan's white teeth crunched an ice cube. "*Hicket!*" she said, swallowing. "Now, oh yeah, Mr. Astronaut. I remember why we don't drink."

Barton shrugged. She was right about the booze, more than she knew. Alcohol put a spit-shine on bad behavior, including his most recent diversion, which was violent fantasy. For since he'd decided to rid the earth of Helmut, he'd felt giddy with freedom, like a man paroled.

Sweet revenge. Fresh as mountain air and worth any price, including prison. Oh, there'd be some dark days on the cell block, but they'd be lit by the flame of recollection, that look on Helmut's face when Barton would stand before him and Helmut would blanche, realizing he was about to take his final breath in this world.

Barton grinned.

"Hicket!"

Certainly worse villains walked the earth, but Helmut was *his* villain, and the more he thought of killing him the clearer it became that this was his moment, that this was his, dare he think it?

Destiny.

Of course it would also be his vanishing point, that place where he began his exile from society, and, most agonizing of all, from his wife, the matchless Jordan Kelly.

"Hicket!"

Yet didn't every hero pay his price? Hadn't he written term papers to that effect? Well, this was the real thing. Glory never came at a discount.

To rid the earth of Helmut. To win. To conquer. Victory! Barton bared his teeth and sucked at his drink, savoring his fate, chewing it like a cherry.

"Hey," said his wife, holding her chin to her chest and speaking quickly so as to seize a brief respite from her hiccups, "you should see how you look." She spat out the last words in a breathless whisper.

Her husband raised his eyebrows and leaned over on his bar stool.

"I feel like a god," he said.

"Well. You look like a fiend." She tossed back her drink and slammed her glass on the bar. The bartender shot her a warning glance and she mouthed "sorry" and shrugged.

Barton didn't notice, sunk in sodden reverie. Revenge on Helmut wasn't a new idea, nor was his attempt to dismiss it. Ever since college he'd tried to argue himself out of a whole catalog of violent fantasies, including an experiment with the old living-well-is-the-best formula.

The glitch in his brain wasn't so much Helmut as the disturbing *concept* of Helmut. Helmut trod the recesses of Barton's skull in dirty boots, invading his dreams, his memories, even his sex life, staining the shiny paths of his psyche with muddy footprints.

"Maybe we should – *hicket!* – get back onna' wagon," Jordan said, wiping her lips with the back of her hand and waving her empty glass at the bartender. "Maybe iss time for a lil' vegan detox." Her tiny fist socked Barton in his bicep. "Whaddaya say? Time to get out the ol' juicer again? Start livin' on smoothies?"

He turned his face to her. Her eyes, like twin blue marbles, wobbled inside their sockets.

"Dang," he drawled, "you're smarter than Einstein. How 'bout we start in the morning? Now, even."

Jordan slapped herself across the face. "Oh!" she yelped, startled, and raised a hand to her burning cheek. "Be good, Sassy Box."

"Well?"

Holding her breath, she waited. Barton wondered who they were talking about. Her eyes darted back and forth, expectant.

"You got it," she bellowed. "Another round to celebrate."

"You're welcome," her husband said, clutching the bar to keep from toppling over.

In another, more sober part of his mind, he wondered: did he envy Helmut's sexual freedom? He couldn't say. Irked by his own loyalty, Barton couldn't cheat on his wife any more than he could stop breathing. Infidelity wasn't in him, whereas Helmut felt compelled to seduce every divorcee who entered the office. "Doing Discovery Motions," he called it, winking and cackling, elbowing the law clerks in the ribs as he pointed out "the talent." Barton remained in awe of the man's audacity, his cheek, his chutzpah. Half the secretaries in the office had done a stint on their knees under Helmut's desk, although it wasn't like he harassed them – on the contrary, to Barton's dismay they went willingly – with a gauzy film over their eyes, a side effect of his partner's dark charisma.

Certainly it wasn't his looks which had the ladies shucking their brassieres and approaching on bended knee. The man was entirely unnoticeable, until he turned his bird-of-prey stare on you and shrunk you to the size of a mouse. Scrutinized by Helmut Knight, you felt insanely vulnerable, naked before his unblinking gaze, pierced by his brown eyes.

Paunchy and bald, with chronic halitosis (a fishy yet beefy smell, like ripe salami) Helmut's ability to make his case with intimidatingly beautiful women baffled Barton to distraction. Helmut had the knack for easy teasing and confident flirtation which Barton lacked. This shyness had led Jordan to propose *to him* while Helmut had proposed to *his* wife (a freckled, shy, stoop-shouldered woman) soon after she'd entered the office on the wrongful death case of her three-year-old son, after Helmut had learned that the success of his upcoming bankruptcy hearing depended on his being married.

Thus, his nuptials. Debts dismissed, assets hidden under his wife's name, Helmut hadn't even broken stride in his parade of conquests at the office. His wife remained at home, where she languished in a haze of Valium and soap operas.

And if he had to juggle some of his assets in other currencies at his bank overseas . . . well, she simply had to understand that a traveling man picked up a nail now and again. Having tossed her an amber pill bottle of Amoxicillin after his last trip, he'd whacked Barton between his shoulder blades and said, "You should've seen the look on her face!" His hearty laugh echoed through the halls of the office and tears of mirth streamed from his eyes. He wiped them away with his sleeve, then stepped back and socked Barton in the arm, hard. "What *am I like?*" he demanded, and his salami-smelling breath steamed his partner's face.

Jordan lowered her head to the bar and slurped from her new drink, making extravagant kissing sounds. The bartender shot Barton another warning look and Barton raised his eyebrows and turned up his palms in a gesture indicating good-natured helplessness.

He had to steer a careful course around alcohol, but its effects on the electronics of his brain weren't magnetic, unlike Jordan's, whose cerebral cortex came completely unwired.

Still, she'd get herself sober. She always did. AA. Psychiatry. Acupuncture. Therapy dog. Whatever the cure, it would last about a year.

"So this is all talk, eh?" she asked, turning up her pink face. Her cheeks were flushed, her eyes glassy. She sucked an ice cube into her mouth, then spat it back into her glass with a ringing sound. "You aren't a murderer, are you, Barton?"

"Course not," said her husband, thinking *not yet anyway*.

The nights were the worst. In the dark, he couldn't blot his partner's face from his mind. Helmut's round head bulbed out of his rotund body and his eyes bulged like fat brown marbles pounded into the egg-shaped dome of his skull. Hell Mutt indeed. He bore a passing resemblance to a cross between a Chihuahua and Benjamin Franklin. Still, the man had taste, Barton had to admit it. Helmut was a connoisseur of twentieth-century painting. He spoke French. He knew the pleasures of wine and opera, and he could ferret out the coolest jazz joint in any city. Helmut acted as if he were handsome – movie-star handsome, and that's how he got treated – while Barton, who with his lantern jaw and cornflower-blue eyes and high cheekbones actually *was* handsome, acted as if he were funny looking, and that's how he got treated.

Yet together, Helmut and Barton could work a jury like two fast-talking carnival hustlers shaking down an audience of country bumpkins. Barton hamming it up with his movie-star chin, his sky-blue eyes, his pecan hair and white linen suits. While

Helmut shambled around with his soiled shirttails flying, his hand continuously hitching up his trousers due to his complete lack of an ass, his pot belly as round as a bowling ball, his eyes as shiny and protuberant as those of the Chihuahua he somehow resembled.

Together they hypnotized juries with phrases like, "the totality of the circumstances," and "the reasonable and prudent person." They shouted and performed – while juries wept and defendants paid. With their charismatic close, judges shook their heads and cracked their gavels, while Helmut and Barton slapped each other on the back. They were the *wunderkinds* of the firm, the *enfants terrible* of the bar. The awards piled up. And so did the money. Their small bankruptcy and divorce firm grew into such a success that they were gobbled up by Freeman Enterprises, which retained the name of Kelly, Knight and Squire, though as far as actual ownership, the name was all Helmut and Barton had left. Jordan had long since abandoned the law so she could paint.

Thus Knight and Squire reverted from owners to employees. Helmut buddied up to the parent corporation and the senior partners at Colin, Lanus and Gart, including yours truly, your narrator Alexander Colin. Back in the twentieth century, we founded one of the biggest law firms in central Florida, with offices in Orlando and the smaller community of Melbourne, the working class city which supported the more affluent seaside town of Melbourne Beach, which was home to our trio.

In fact, without Helmut's influence, Barton might not have gone to law school at all. Confronting his college graduation, he'd said, "I'm not even sure I *want* to be a lawyer."

Helmut sneered. "You're an English major. What else can you do?"

"I could go to grad school. I could teach."

"Pah!" said Helmut. "No money, no respect. You want to be a wage-slave? Get a basement office? Work for the state?"

"Our profs enjoy the ivory tower."

"And look where they went to school – Harvard, Yale, Brown,

Princeton. And the best job they could get was at UF, in *Gainesville*, for God's sake. The hinterlands."

Barton didn't say anything.

"Trust me. You get a Ph. D. in English and you'll end up at East Blowfish Community College. Is that what you want?"

Barton didn't answer. His plan, to teach at Berkeley, had been ludicrous. He was smart and he had his act together, but he wasn't up to batting in that league and it shamed him. Helmut knew it and now he knew it too, although as usual Helmut had beaten him to the punch line.

"Well?" Helmut demanded.

Barton sighed and put his pen back to paper. "I guess I'm going to be a lawyer."

Jordan too, as it turned out. The three seniors worked on law school applications: safety, possibility, and dream. Their safety was their *alma mater*, UF; at possibility stood the University of San Francisco – and for dreams, Jordan chose Berkeley; Helmut, Harvard; and Barton, Stanford. If the trio broke up, fate would own it, but if they attended the same law school they'd be set as roommates. Neither Barton nor Jordan talked about what would happen if geography separated them. They were too young to sustain a long distance relationship and so, early on, they faced the great dilemma of the modern American couple – whose career was more important?

But since none of their dreams offered admission, the issue never came up.

"Now I know why Hemingway thought Fitzgerald was pathetic," Jordan said, leaning onto the bar and staring into her drink, her head sunk between her shoulder blades.

Barton blinked, startled, then looked at his wife. She lifted her straw and sucked off a drop of clear liquid.

"He was impressed by the country club set even after he'd grown up," she said, "when he should've known better. Hemingway warned him." She burbled her glass with her straw. "He was right."

"Are we talking about literature now?"

She arched her eyebrows. "Why? Am I going too fast?" She widened her eyes, lightly mocking, playful.

"No, I just missed a transition."

"Well, keep up, Counselor. Barkeep! Bring this man a drink." She laughed and pounded the bar with her fist. "A *real* one and none a' yer crap!"

"Jordan."

"Well?" Her voice curved upward and she worked her features into a scowl. "He's givin' me lip." She put her face in Barton's. "You think I need that? I mean – *really!*"

"Easy, honey."

"It's ironic, innit?" she said vehemently. "Gatsby gets killed goin' into that world, which is fake anyway. But old Scott couldn't convince himself with his own novel." Her eyes welled up and her lower lip pushed out. "Oh, poor old Scott!"

Drunk as she was, she'd revealed herself, and her husband too. Something about Helmut Knight radiated money, power, privilege. He belonged to Gatsby's crowd – the yacht club set, The Beautiful People. Noses aloft, snubbing the world. And for a lower middle class kid like Barton Squire, a child of the meat-and-potatoes district of upstate New York, to be asked to join this crowd – this was thrilling, like being blessed by royalty. Helmut Knighted.

Barton shuddered. Didn't he remember how Scott's novel ended? How shallow was he? Would he forsake his past to join the elect, the upper crust?

He hoped not.

Feeling woozy, a hot whispery voice breathed in his ear, and what this familiar said was beautiful, musical, *divine*.

Murder, it intoned, and Barton salivated. He dreamt of staving in his partner's skull, *with a hammer*. He dreamt of blood . . . of its sticky redness, like crimson syrup. Of death under his hands. Barton, the executioner. Barton, the taker of life.

A sudden crash. On the floor, stretched out along the dingy

blue carpet, his wife waved her hand from beside her overturned bar stool. "I'm all right," she announced loudly. "Nothing to see here." She chuckled but neither the bartender nor her husband shared her merriment. Their faces were long, their eyes sullen.

"Ouf!" she huffed, pushing herself onto her elbows as she glanced around, "I seem to have gotten the rough end of the pineapple down here."

Barton slid off his bar stool and worked his hands under his wife's hot armpits. Her body seemed to be constructed of several unconnected sections and he had trouble getting her to her feet because she wouldn't let go of her glass. Barton slipped and went down beside her, hurting his knee.

"I beg your pardon," a smooth voice intoned. "Are you two having a moment?"

Barton swiveled his head and Helmut's shiny face appeared above him, as round as a balloon and grinning down at him with faintly lime-colored teeth.

"I'm happy to see all is forgiven," he bellowed, clapping his hands. "But now you're overdoing it." He frowned at them sprawled there on the floor, then shook his head and laughed cheerfully. "You alkies," he said, taking hold of Barton's arm, "what would you do without me?"

"Get your mitts off me!" Barton said. He shook off his partner's hand.

"My mitts?"

"Piss off, will you?" Barton's knee throbbed and his face burned. Two bearded locals in denim overalls eyed him over the tops of their beers.

"Hi, Helmut!" Jordan saluted him, raising her glass. "Get a round and come down here. Iss innaresting."

"I would, but Barton's holding a grudge – though since I ran into Bill I don't know why. Your husband's an unreliable witness."

"Hicket!"

7

Death or Great Bodily Injury

BARTON grabbed the front of Helmut's shirt and slammed him into the wall beside the dried blood streaks. A year had passed since he'd nailed his thumb and Jordan had painted the blood streaks into a mural depicting a crucified Venus, complete with dripping stigmata. Below the goddess's eye, Barton grimaced and smelled his roommate's sour breath. Under his hand, Helmut's heart skittered. Barton hoisted him off the floor and Helmut turned his face away.

The delicacy of Helmut's body surprised him. He'd expected such a big personality to weigh more.

"So you *did* do it!" He lifted Helmut's body so that his feet dangled like a hanged man's. Helmut kicked and the toe of his right shoe caught Barton in the shin. Grunting, Barton closed his eyes, seeing blood in his eyelids. If he didn't reign himself in, he'd really hurt this guy, and he didn't want to do that.

Helmut's face turned an ugly red. His bulging eyes went black, shining with hatred.

"Why do you have to *own* everything?" he asked. "Peace, pot and microdot, my ass," Helmut's voice was strained. "If you were *really* a hippie you'd share her." Flecks of warm spit flew into Barton's eyes.

Barton got in close enough for a kiss. His voice hissed hotly in Helmut's ear, a whisper: "I should break your pencil, little man."

"Do it, you loser."

Feeling the sweat peel down his back, Barton allowed Helmut's feet to touch the floor.

"Ha!" barked Helmut, "what a candy ass."

Barton let go of his roommate's shirt, clenched his fingers into a rock-like fist, and punched a hole in the drywall beside Helmut's head.

Helmut looked at the hole.

"You going to pay for that?"

Barton's blue eyes were like patches torn from the Florida sky, so full of promise when he'd started college . . . and now? He couldn't say, but falling in love made people crazy, as far as he could tell. Perhaps life was better spent as a sane, single person. It bore consideration.

Helmut chuckled, shook the drywall dust from his hair and strode across the room. He set his hand on his powerful guitar amp, twice the wattage of Barton's. Preening, he opened his mouth, but then, thinking better of it, snuffed through his nose.

"No encore?" asked Barton, rubbing the knuckles of his hand and addressing an imaginary audience, "Ladies and gentlemen! The mighty Helmut Knight has gone mute. Had the shit scared out of him, you might say."

Helmut clapped his hands. The applause echoed off the walls of their dorm. "Great show, Bart! Awesome. Has it been fun? Did it get you off? That's what this is all about, isn't it? Getting you off? That's pretty much your whole life, right?"

"Helmut, I'd shut up if I were you."

"It's all about Barton. A Barton-centric universe. The dominant paradigm."

Barton turned and tackled Helmut and pinned him to the floor and straddled his chest. He supported his weight on his knees.

"You're a selfish prick," Helmut gasped, "but you're *so* selfish you can't see it. But you do know you're hiding behind bourgeois morality. Semantics! Boyfriend, girlfriend. It's bullshit."

Barton let his full weight rest on Helmut's chest.

"I don't want your romantic picnics," Helmut wheezed, his face going red. "All your baby talk and stupid jokes. I have this little thing with her, and that's all. I don't want more and neither does she. Why can't you grow up, *mein ubermensch*? I'm not a fucking threat to you!"

Barton took his weight back onto his knees.

"You want to be like the rest of this sick society?" Helmut demanded. "Nobody says we have to play by their rules."

Barton climbed off his roommate. He might've farted on him but he didn't. Whenever possible, he strove not to inflict humiliation. He wasn't sure of any absolute values, but not being a deliberate asshole seemed to be a winner. It was a proposition you could build your life around: *not being an asshole.*

Still, Helmut tested him.

And more, for as he massaged his smarting knuckles he realized that Helmut had struck the truth. Jealousy was a learned behavior – learned as in, *not really him.* He *should* share Jordan, he thought, but he couldn't. He wasn't that generous. So his best friend, he had to admit it – got left empty-handed.

So this is college, he thought. *L'Éducation sentimentale.* It was too much. They ought to be climbing mountains or fording rivers – hiking the wilderness you didn't have time for *angst.*

After all, who took Nietzsche on a fishing trip?

Helmut got a broom and a dust pan from the closet and swept up the fine white dust and loose chunks of drywall.

"Barton, listen." Helmut didn't look at him, sweeping up debris. "We were . . . in a blackout." Helmut upended the dust pan into the wastebasket beside Barton's desk. "Think of how young we are. In twenty years . . . man, we'll be old and it won't matter. We're young, brother. For Christ's sake. You want to nail me up like some plaster Jesus?"

"*You're* the idealist, Helmut. It won't work. What a bunch of babies we are. A whole generation of arrested development! 'It's not my fault I have no morals. I'm an incest survivor. My parents were alcoholics. I have a club foot. My dog has the mange. There's a cyst on my ass. My uncle was a handicapped Eskimo. My cat is a libertarian and my goldfish has joined Hamas. I'm a child of war. If I'm a cheater, it's not my fault. I'm a victim of prejudice and I should be compensated. My lawyer says so.' "

"Jesus, what are you on?"

Barton sat on his bed and held his head in his hands, feeling his skull might detonate.

It had all begun with a giant pimple. The Hiatus, that awful spell where Jordan had declared her need of "space," had wreaked havoc on Barton's skin. "Growing a second nose," Helmut called it, as Barton smeared on Clearasil, Blemish Buster, salicylic acid, cortisone, toothpaste . . .

Preparing for sleep, Helmut had studied his friend from across the room. Barton lay on his narrow bed, propped on pillows stacked against the wall, reading. Both were in white-face – their cheeks and foreheads and noses smeared with a reeking mix of sulphur and benzoyl peroxide.

Leaning up on one elbow in his bed, Helmut's dark eyes gleamed out of his white mask.

"There's something I need to tell you before you hear it from somebody else," he said. His voice was strange. No condescension – he sounded sincere. Barton shivered and closed his copy of *The Sound and the Fury,* adjusting the pillows behind him, sitting up straight, attentive.

"You're a Butt Pirate and you're in love with me. Am I right?"

"Quit being an asshole."

Comic repartee of every description suggested itself, but Barton refrained. Helmut's earnest demeanor, so out of character, unnerved him.

"So spill it, brother."

"Jordan and I . . . well, we sort of got it on over Christmas break."

Barton blinked out of his white face. "What do you mean by 'sort of' and what do you mean by '*got it on?*'"

"Which should I answer first?"

"Got it on."

"Oh. Well. You *know*. Conjugate the verb."

"Jesus Christ, Helmut."

"It only happened a couple of times, and you were on The Hiatus. Remember?"

Barton blinked and the nickel dropped. His head popped with light.

"A COUPLE OF TIMES?" Wearing only his cotton underwear, he leapt from his bed. He hadn't sprouted chest hair yet and his body was growing out of adolescence into manhood. He was nineteen. "She told me it was only once!" He started across the room and Helmut hid under his sheets. Towering over the lump in the bed, fists clenched and his heart thundering, it occurred to Barton, as it would so often later in life, that he might have to kill Helmut, even if he *did* share his prescription acne medicine.

Barton yanked back the sheet and exposed his roommate. Helmut lay in his bed with his protuberant brown eyes gleaming out of his white face. Barton huffed and puffed. He smacked his fist into his palm. "You," he said, "you Judas!"

"This is really awkward," Helmut said, "what if somebody walked in and saw you assaulting me?" Barton glowered. Helmut reminded him of a scrappy little dog, cowering before it bit you. "Don't get your bowels in an uproar, Bart. You know it makes you break out. Think of your second nose!"

Barton leaned in close. From Helmut's perspective, a ghostly face hove into view. "You understand I could snap your neck like a chicken bone?"

Embarrassingly, this was true, although they often forgot it. Helmut's self-confidence, his razor wit, his ease with pretty girls, all contrived to make one forget his diminutive body, his short stature, his dog-like face.

Barton unclenched his fists and straightened his spine. Years of karate lessons, along with his father's advice, had taught him self-control. "You ever get in a fight and hurt somebody," his father had said, himself a barrel-chested, ham-handed man, "the judge'll take one look at you and say, 'this big sonofabitch is just a bully.' And then, son, you're looking at a state institution."

"Institution?"

"Prison, son."

And so Barton, who'd never struck another human being in his life, maintained his perfect record, his no-hitter.

"Do not, I repeat, *do not* go near her – you got that?"

"We have mid-terms."

"Keep away from us," Barton said, breathing his hot breath into Helmut's face, "until I say otherwise."

"Barton."

"What?"

"We have mid-terms."

Barton shook his head, knowing there was no help for him. He honored the trio's unspoken code: no matter their personal problems, nothing interfered with school. Study was their religion. An asteroid might be careening toward the earth or an appendix might be bursting, but none of them ever missed a due date. Lifelong teacher's pets, the habit of slacking just wasn't in them, nor would it ever be, even *en extremis*.

Barton returned to his bed, clicked off his lamp and turned to the wall.

"Dude," Helmut said. He reached up from his bed and switched off his light, plunging the room into darkness. "Dude," Helmut repeated.

"What is it?"

"Dude, I'm . . . I'm sorry."

Barton lay with his eyes adjusting to the dark. He'd never heard

Helmut apologize – for anything, including farting loudly at dinner at their English professor's house, but this – this was something new. Helmut's voice. It was naked. My God, thought Barton, *Helmut is human!* Could it be true? *Herr Übermensch* a mere mortal? Barton's eyes widened. So Mr. Country Club wasn't perfect.

It was almost disappointing. Blinking at the patterns emerging on the ceiling, Barton understood *camaraderie*. A letting go of hubris, that life-haunting word, the one he'd learned in Greek Tragedy. Of course, camaraderie also meant learning to forgive, and then it became clear – forgiveness was a form of courage.

There might not be any frontiers to conquer, but by God, he could be brave. He could take up the words of Lao Tse: *the truly strong nature is yielding and gentle . . .*

"It's done. Let it die."

"You got it, champ. It's dead and buried."

Barton froze. Was that a hint of sarcasm creeping into "champ"? From the Greek, *sarkasmos*, "to tear the flesh from the bones like a dog." He swallowed, feeling the teachings of Lao Tse recede. Already, his new-found camaraderie began to crumble, undermined by Helmut's familiar smugness.

It didn't matter. Helmut had revealed himself. He was naked and small. Vulnerable. Just like everyone else. What a world. Barton drifted off to sleep contemplating the nature of *epiphany*, his English professor's favorite word.

He supposed there'd be more to come.

8

Evidence

"WHAT'S this?" he said.

Wearing flip flops, cut-off denim shorts and an un-tucked T-shirt with LED ZEPPELIN embossed on the front, Barton held up a square of gold foil, torn across the top. His hand shook embarrassingly. He'd thought the case against Helmut was closed last semester, but here he'd uncovered fresh evidence implicating his One True Love.

Jordan's face drained of color. Muttering, she turned away and began pacing the room, tucking her hair behind her ears. She had on a white cotton "peasant" dress seemingly made of wrinkles, with a wide lacy collar which lay atop her prominent shoulder bones, tanned to rose-brown. Around her neck she wore a necklace of blue beads imported from Africa. She'd strung them herself. Her feet were bare – pink and healthy between the toes, the soles grimy. Her toenails were painted turquoise.

"So how do you plead?" he asked.

The gold square of foil glinted in the Florida sun slanting through the window. In his other hand he held her broom. He'd been helping her clean her filthy dorm and he suddenly realized how he must look. Jordan bugged out her eyes, fluttering her lips and making a sound like a horse, a kind of whinny which was her way of easing tension.

"This is bad information," he said. His hand was shaking. "This is evidence."

Jordan blinked rapidly and glanced out the window. This wasn't the happy day she'd anticipated when she'd climbed out of bed, smiling at the birds chirping on her balcony, but here it was, alongside the best laid plans. Outside, the green fronds of the palm trees waved in the breeze, carefree against the molten blue sky. For a moment, she was lost, watching the leaves dance.

"Condom wrapper," she confessed in a rush of breath.

"Correct! My brand, too . . . except I didn't open it."

She didn't know where to look. It was shaping up to be a bad morning indeed.

"You must've left it here."

"You let Helmut use one of my condoms?"

"Oh!" She shook out her hair impatiently. She was, we must recall, only nineteen. "Would you rather it was unsafe? For the millionth time, Barton, WE WERE ON THE HIATUS!"

The Hiatus. That desolate stretch when Jordan had "to get her head together," whatever that meant. For Barton those months remained a wasteland, a terrifying sample of how his life would feel if she weren't in it. She was his *anima*, his spirit scrubbed clean of all the grit of the world.

He'd even written a poem about it. Love as a boat wrecked on the shoals even as – *too late!* – the sailors sighted the glow of the lighthouse. Well, he never said it was good. But love didn't *have* to be tragic, did it? In an essay for Greek Tragedy, he'd redefined the word.

Tragedy: when what could be, won't be.

But no, he'd fight it. Together, they'd build a new boat, one to navigate the future's treacherous currents, a vessel to steer them clear of the rocks which middle age would heave under their keel.

A captain and his mate!

And walking the plank, a cutlass at his back: the traitor Helmut, blindfolded.

Jordan peered out from under the blond curtain of her hair. Parted in the middle, with bangs, its long layers hung past her shoulders. She kept her mouth shut because she'd just finished reading a book on the Mafia where she'd been struck by one of their aphorisms – *silence makes no mistakes.*

Good advice in matters romantic, she thought, adopting her own personal *omerta.*

"Why did it have to be him?" Barton asked, and cringed. He was whining, never an attractive quality – even if you *were* in the right. He pressed his hand to his mouth and sought the calm light of Buddha-nature. He tossed the condom wrapper into the wastebasket next to Jordan's desk.

"He mesmerized me," she said. "You know his eyes." Seeing Barton's stricken face, she realized she should've stuck with her code of silence. Still, she blundered on. "Forget it was him," she said. "It could've been anybody." Another mistake. She was batting a thousand. Barton's mouth fell open. "I'm telling you – *it didn't mean anything!*"

"It meant something to *him.* Me too."

"What're you talking about?"

"He'll hold this over me for the rest of my life!"

"Oh my God. This isn't a big deal unless you make it one."

Still holding her broom, he looked over her head out the window at the trunks of the palm trees bending in the wind. "Helmut Knight is a lie. He's a fiction. He's his own creation. And that's his problem. And ours. He needs us to exist. We're his audience."

"It's all a lie," she said. "How else could we go on? Death and rot. Without lies, there couldn't be any love." She crossed the room to her bookcase and ran her finger along the spines of Hemingway and Fitzgerald. "*You're* the fantasy-maker, Barton. You've made me into a character in your *own* story, and you get mad when I don't behave according to plot."

They were both breathing hard. They'd reached a juncture in

their lives, a fork in the romantic road. Barton considered letting her go, thinking she might be happier with Helmut.

Why not? She and his roommate shared the same emotional *genus*. She and Helmut had hard shells. Compared to them, Barton was a cephalopod. Resilient but soft.

Meanwhile Jordan wondered if she could marry Barton, knowing he could read the invisible sign around her neck. *Love, keep out*, it said. *Love, go home!* All her life she'd feared confinement, and what was love if not a tie that bound? She sensed this fear of love lurking inside her, patiently waiting to thrust its filthy snout into the light.

"Helmut's pure evil, Jordan. I'm telling you."

"You make him sound like Hitler."

"He's *worse* than Hitler. He'd fuck a snake if somebody held its head."

Jordan looked at him. "What have you been reading?" she asked. "My word."

"Hitler didn't think of himself as evil," Barton said. "He was criminally insane. Whereas Helmut *knows* he's evil, and he goes *on* being evil. And it's not the girls that thrill him. It's screwing over their boyfriends. He loves it."

Remembering how she'd made Helmut's toes curl and how he'd hooted with glee, she disagreed, although now she had sense enough to follow her Mafia advice. She squinted. "Then why are you friends with him?"

Barton shrugged and sat on her bed. The springs squeaked and the sound conjured an unpleasant image.

"Excellent question." He shook his long hair, feeling it warm and soft on his neck. "I'm under his spell, too, I guess. I mean, he's like a drug high – you hate it, but you love it."

"Go with that."

Barton looked at her oddly, knowing she was taking Psychology. Tall and slender as a flower, she slid her rear end onto her desk and sat there, crossing one thigh over the other and dangling her bare foot. Barton focused on her turquoise toenails.

"Around Helmut I feel famous," he said, feeling the thrill of confession, "or like I'm going to be famous. He makes you feel powerful, you know? . . . *in control* . . . like you've got the world by the short hairs and you aren't ever letting go. Know what I'm saying? Helmut knows which wine to order, how to steer a sailboat, how to play a lick in B flat. He's got the inside track on *la dolce vita*. All of life's little extras."

Including my girlfriend, he thought with horror, hearing himself rattle on.

"Well, he certainly *acts* as if he's famous."

"He's got flash," Barton admitted. "That's our Helmut. Enter a crowd, and he automatically aims his big honker skyward."

Jordan smiled and studied her young lover, wondering what he had to be jealous about – Barton with his wide, smooth forehead and shaggy blond hair, his strong Scandinavian nose, his straight white teeth and full lips. He had a square jaw which she enjoyed sketching, making a head-of-a-coin profile so unlike Helmut's, whose chin receded and whose mousy brown hair was already thinning. Their bodies, too, couldn't have been more different. Helmut was compact and dense, with a pugnacious build, whereas Barton was long-limbed and surprisingly graceful for a man his size.

No wonder Helmut had it in for him, she thought.

In bed, too, there were contrasts. Barton was a gentle grizzly bear – Helmut a quick cunning fox. And in matters of the heart? Helmut was a question. Barton was an answer.

"Oh, Bee!" she said. She launched herself from the desk and flung her arms around him and knocked him backward onto her bed, pressing her warm mouth to his lips, impaling him with her young tongue. "You know it's got to be you," she whispered into his ear. She peppered his face with kisses and whispered obscene endearments.

For Barton, the weight of her body was bliss. If this was death he would accept it. "I wish I could trust you," he said, "but I guess I'll have to take what I can get." He looked into her blue eyes, a shade darker than his own. "Can I do that, Jordan? Can I trust you?"

"I wish you'd look at what you've got instead of what you *haven't* got," she said, reminding him annoyingly of Helmut. "All this will pass." She extracted herself from his arms and sat on the edge of the bed. Her stare was lost in the middle distance. "Our youth will end soon." Shivering, she hugged herself. "God, think of it. We're going to get old. We're going to die. In a weird way, it's kind of thrilling."

"And one day the sun will run out of hydrogen," Barton said. "Doomsday will dawn. Now can I trust you or not?"

She turned to him, rolling her eyes. "You can trust me," she said doggedly. She held up three fingers. "Scout's honor."

Barton made a noise in his throat to indicate he was less than convinced. He disliked having to extract things from her.

"I wish you were a little more willing," he said.

"Oh, I'm willing," she got on all fours on the bed, "want me to prove it, Master?"

"Don't call me that."

"You used to like it, Master." She batted her big eyes. Those eyes! They changed like the tides – sometimes like the ocean after a storm – an aquamarine sunlit glow, a blue-green transparency, full of depth, yet reflective too. Her eyes were portals to undersea kingdoms – shimmering crystal vaults, palaces of diamonds and ice.

"Oh, Barton Squire," she sang in her lilting, musical voice, "won't you come out to play?" She turned her head and grinned, glancing from the corner of her eye, mischievous and playful, the cat that ate the canary.

Yielding, he fell on her, because Helmut wasn't the only one who mesmerized people. Jordan cast spells too. Not like Helmut's, but just as powerful in their way. So did Barton. He admitted this.

The three of them weren't like other people. They were leaders, motivators – or manipulators, depending on your point of view.

"Take off your clothes," he said.

Her lips drew back and she bared her teeth, strong and white and sharp.

"Is that a command?"

The question echoed in his skull. He hadn't meant to sound so bossy, but there it was, and oh, what a moment!

Is that a command? Arching her honey-pale eyebrows, the tip of her tongue slid between her parted lips.

"You best believe it, baby."

Rolling onto her back with feline grace, she drew up her knees and slipped off her panties, folding them neatly at the foot of the bed, then she stood and stepped out of her dress and hung it in the closet.

Naked, she crossed the room. Barton could only stare.

On the bed she lay down and stretched, putting her arms over her head and moaning contentedly, stretching her back and striking a pose which for Barton constituted irrefutable proof of God's existence, a perverse, sadistic God, to be sure, but God nevertheless. His pupils dilated and fastened on her lovely concave abdomen, her flaxen mound of Venus.

Lazily, catching the sunbeams slicing through the blinds, she turned onto her stomach while his gaze traveled from her delicate shoulder blades toward the blond down dusting the small of her back, where a spray of tiny hairs caught the light before disappearing into the twin eddies of her sacral dimples. The globes of her buttocks were as firm and round as two big biceps, her cleft the tawny heart of mystery, her lover's fleshy shrine.

"Oh, womanly woman," he whispered.

She craned her neck and looked at him over the smooth curve of her shoulder. She puckered her lips. Barton swooned. Yes, that's right. There's no other word for it. He *swooned*. Stripping off his shorts and T-shirt and kicking off his flip flops, he leapt into bed and folded her naked body into his arms. Given glorious free reign, the palms of his hands and his fingertips traveled the length of her, exploring her smooth skin, so soft it felt other worldly.

Transported beyond joy, he thought, *I am fucking doomed.*

He understood he'd found his One True Love, his blood's companion. Perhaps their meeting had occurred when he was still too young, but there it was. Nothing he could do would change it. You accepted Fate or you died resisting it. God or Buddha or the Great Whatever scheduled all your significant moments whether you found the timing convenient or not. Your calendar was not your own.

His cheek brushed the honey-butter skin of her breast. She smelled of Coppertone and youth.

He rested his head on her rib cage and listened to the steady drumming of her heart while her fingers stroked his hair. Barton sighed and closed his eyes. An arrow had pierced his chest, and was now stuck fast by its barb. This was something the ancients understood – something he'd learned in Greek Tragedy – Cupid was a god to be feared.

Shifting her weight, she put her lips to his ear. "What freaks me out," she said, feeling him squirm under her hot breath, "is that if we stick with Helmut we're going to be ungodly rich." She slid down his body and kissed his left nipple while he struggled up onto one elbow, turning on his side to look at her. The mention of his roommate's name had tainted the moment.

"I thought you didn't care about money."

"Everyone cares about money."

"Really? What happened to your mission? What happened to world literacy?"

"Books cost money."

"I thought you had money."

"My parents have money. Not me." She pressed a fingertip to his lips. "That's one thing they teach you in New England. Before you inherit the fortune you're supposed to have made your own. My grandfather used to say, 'Hunger is the best inspiration.' "

"And you agree?"

"Absolutely. You've seen the rich kids here. 'Spoiled' is not a metaphor."

"You're *my* inspiration," Barton said, snuggling his nose into the hollow of her neck, taking in her most personal odor, the one like freshly baked bread. Without really trying, he realized, they'd repaired their hearts without missing a beat, a pattern they'd repeat all their lives. He ran his fingers through her hair and held up the gold silk to the light before letting it fall softly across his face, as, together, they lolled in the Florida afternoon.

"I can't tell if this is heaven or hell," he said.

She looked at him, her eyes darkening to cobalt. "And what about later, when I'm all sags and wrinkles? Will you know then?"

"Won't matter."

His hand went tingly under her weight and he struggled to reposition his arm. She adjusted herself to fit his body and settled back into him.

"You're a real romantic," she said, sighing. "You know how dangerous that is?"

"I've heard."

Together, they found a rhythm and began breathing hard.

Meanwhile in the wastebasket beside Jordan's desk, a square of gold foil glinted in the sun, forgiven if not forgotten.

9

Pro Bono
(For the Good)

INSIDE his corner office at Kelly, Knight and Squire, Helmut sat at his vast mahogany desk. Polished to a glassy sheen, its surface reflected him with perfect fidelity as he pressed a measuring tape to the great dome of his skull. Marking the tape with his finger, he removed it and held it at arm's length, tilting back his head and reading. His reflection's mouth fell open, as did his. Impossible! His hairline had receded another two inches.

His reflection blinked at him and he mouthed an obscenity. The axis of baldness was on a blitzkrieg across his scalp, wiping out any resistance as it deposed the last tuft on his crown. A few doomed prisoners sprouted over his ears, but they were so cowardly he'd put them to the razor himself, the fuzzy little traitors.

Running his hand over his head, he found the skin on his skull appallingly smooth and tight and slick. *My head feels like a big dick,* he thought. His cheeks burned. He didn't care if people *thought* he was a prick, but he'd rather not resemble one. With only two inches to go until his receding hairline met his bald spot, the reign of his hair would soon be over, his youth forever wiped off the map.

Digging into his desk drawer and exchanging the measuring tape for a woman's compact, he eyed his naked pate in the circular mirror, turning his face from one side to the other. Using his fingertips, he gently brushed the few remaining wisps over the top of his head.

Dear God, no!

To strangers he would no longer be "that guy," but "that *bald* guy."

Of course, he could get a transplant, but there was only one problem.

He was afraid of surgery.

Perhaps he could sue for peace. Collaborate even. Submit to the comb-over. But no. Never. He had *some* honor. He'd rather go down with his hairy boots on. If he was going to be bald, then he'd be bald and proud. He wouldn't sweep himself under a rug, even if he did look like a prick. He'd take his own advice, for which his clients paid good money; that is – if you've been deformed by another's negligence, wear your injury with pride.

Show 'em your stump, kiddo!

Aside from your settlement, it was all you had.

Turning his face in the mirror and tugging at the incipient turkey wattle under his chin, he grimaced and bared his teeth. He'd inadvertently purchased a compact with a magnifying mirror and every pore in his nose gaped like puncture wound. And those teeth. They were unspeakable, but his terror of dentists exceeded even his fear of surgeons.

Perhaps this ugliness was a trick of the light. Sighing, he worked his feet and rolled his chair to the window to examine his cranium in natural light, hoping the sun might prove more charitable. But no . . . the word *ghastly* came to mind. He despaired. It had been years since he'd picked up a comb without fear, lest he dislodge a golden follicle, or – catastrophe! – a great shank of the irreplaceable mop itself, cruelly ripped away by the comb's pointed fangs. Inevitably, he thought of Samson.

Well, man was built for suffering.

He pressed his thumb and index finger into his eyes and resisted the urge to pray. Faith was too easy. And dangerous. If salvation existed, so did damnation. Scaly red demons dancing in the flames of hell, tapping their hooves and claws. Who needed it? Or the other? White-winged angels with golden halos astride cottony clouds, fording rivers of milk and honey . . .

He'd take a pass, thank you, as heaven served on the same board as hell, creating a conflict of interest. Both belonged to the Middle Ages. And the last thing he needed was the Bible haunting him. Jesus could just stay out of his head, thank you very much. His Father, too.

And the devil? Was hair restoration within *his* powers?

Helmut sucked his teeth, considering. But no, he wouldn't sell his soul for the pleasure of seeing a barber, nor would he pray for follicles. He wasn't that weak. And he refused to be that needy.

Scrunching up his nose in the mirror, he caught sight of two large brown eyes peering wetly out of a kind face. This was not actually in the mirror but behind him, though it took a terrifying instant to figure this out. Startled, he whirled around.

"Christ," he said, "I thought you were the devil!"

A small woman crouched beside a mop bucket and a cleaning cart. Smiling shyly, she met her employer's eye, revealing her own neglected teeth.

Helmut snapped shut the compact. "Well," he demanded. "What do you think? Am I beautiful? Answer honestly. No pressure just because I'm your boss."

"*Señor Helmut es muy guapo.* Berry handsome!"

"Brilliant. Not here a year and you're a black belt in bullshit. You'll go far, Graciela."

"Sorry, Mistair Knight. I no interrup' you."

"Trust me, Graciela. You've done me a favor. Here. Want a compact?" He held out the little mirror with its make-up and powder puff. "Take it. I said take it. I won't be needing it anymore."

Helmut had crossed a line. He was through squandering potentially billable hours observing his body and he saw real danger in becoming self-conscious. Because if you *were* an actual egghead, you had to forget your Humpty-Dumpty looks and unleash the industrial grade charisma. He had this in plenty, he told himself. In court he *was* beautiful. His razor-sharp wit could reduce a jury to peals of laughter, even as he carved up a hostile witness like a Christmas goose.

Graciela grinned broadly with her unfortunate teeth and her face was lit by what Helmut could only describe as joy. She seemed to be seeing God Himself and for a wild moment Helmut thought she was looking at him until he realized her stare had gone deep focus. Frowning, he turned his leather chair toward the window.

Outside, under the shade of an Australian pine, a squat, brown-skinned man wearing a sombrero leaned on a shovel and waved. Helmut smiled, thinking himself the recipient of this greeting until Graciela said, "Oh! Ees my – 'ow do you say in English? My Oooosbaaahnn!" She pronounced this with satisfaction and waved her hand at the dark-eyed man in the sombrero. Helmut observed her experience real love – not a facsimile – but the original. She might be standing next to his chair, but in spirit she'd gone through the glass.

"We 'ave two shillren," she said. Helmut started. He'd been about to shut the blinds, but even he understood that this might be considered rude.

Barton stuck his head inside the door. "Graciela's mother is moving in with them," he announced, as though this might mean something. Helmut waited, drumming his fingers on the desk. Barton blinked. Helmut raised his eyebrows and cocked his head to the side, opening his hands in a gesture of dubious welcome. Barton comprehended. "We need to show her how to get tax credit for an elderly relative. I told her that as long as she came in on her day off to clean your office you'd help her out."

Helmut blinked. Barton was too much. Really, the man had problems.

"Does she want her committed?"

"I'm sorry?"

"Placed in a home. When my father started crapping himself and babbling we stashed him in Kissimmee, next to some swamp land."

Barton sighed. "How's that worked out?"

"Great. Haven't heard a peep from him."

"I don't think so."

"It costs me three grand a month, Counselor. And you think my worthless brother or sister chip in? No. They leave it to me to be the good son."

Barton didn't point out that Helmut's inheritance from his mother paid for his father's care, because Helmut wouldn't have grasped the argument. Legally, he'd inherited the money and it was his. Case closed. Barton set a folder on his desk and Helmut picked it up.

"Aren't we about maxed out on the *pro bono* here?" he asked. "I thought this was Jordan's baby. Cause this," he shoved the file across his desk, "ain't billable."

"She'll do it, Helmut, but she's got the flu today, so I thought you might run interference. I'd see to it but," he looked at his watch, "I'm due in court."

"The flu," Helmut repeated. "That Latin for hangover?"

"Fine. I'll take care of it myself."

"No, you won't." Helmut snatched up the file and thumbed through the pages. "*Señor* Helmut is always happy to help the Miranda family."

Graciela hadn't been following the conversation, but her eyes darted up at the sound of her name.

Eager to please, she smiled and nodded, hoping this was the appropriate response. Indeed, in the sort of Dickensian coincidence which occurs so plausibly in life and so seldom in fiction, the Miranda family had literally washed up on the shore of Jordan's life. Jogging along the beach through the mist of a winter morning, she'd discovered a small red boat stuck in the sand. Hammered together from scraps of lumber, the make-shift craft had huge blocks of

Styrofoam lashed to its sides. Painted in crude white letters along the stern, she'd read its name: *Felicidad*.

She was touched. Such optimism. *Felicidad*, or *Happiness*. Happiness they'd pursued all the way from Havana, Cuba, hoping to find it on this beach on the Atlantic coast of Florida. And who could blame them? The Mirandas didn't want their children growing up in the cult of Fidel and had they been able to foresee history they might've waited, but who knew Castro's reign could end? Outliving so many U.S. presidents he'd seemed an immortal sort of troll, so off they'd gone, into the unforgiving seas.

Raising her hand to her heart in surprise, Jordan quickly discovered that the boat was occupied. Inside, she found the Miranda family, shivering, starving and dehydrated. They stared at her with baleful eyes, speechless with misery. Jordan gasped and bit her knuckle.

"*Buenos días*," Graciela croaked, extending her puckered hand and smiling wanly.

At home Jordan fed the family hot chicken soup and her homemade multi-grain bread, recalling enough of her high school Spanish to establish that they were seeking asylum. Now, for Cubans, ordinarily this wouldn't have been a problem, but Antonio had already been deported when he'd tried to prepare the way for his family, stowing away on a cruise ship from whose deck he'd jumped into the oily waters of Port Canaveral. Fished out and sent back to Havana, he'd tried again with his family aboard the *Felicidad*, rendering her unsinkable with the Styrofoam blocks.

Unfortunately, he was already "in the system," and the only way out of that labyrinth was to find a lawyer.

"I don't represent wetbacks," Helmut had informed her. "Not unless they're *rich* wetbacks."

"I'm not asking," Jordan said. "I'm doing it myself."

"What? *L'artiste* is going to set aside her holy grail and deign to practice with the Philistines?"

"I'm still a member of the Florida Bar," she reminded him. "I'm still an officer of the court. Law school was three years of my life I won't get back, Helmut. Don't begrudge me the chance to recoup a little of that investment."

"So what're you charging?"

"Ha ha. It's *pro bono*, Counselor."

"Not at my firm, it ain't."

"My name's still on the sign."

"So it is – got to do something about that, eh?"

"Helmut, come *on*. All I need is a secretary and an office. I won't be long."

"Get wonder-boy to do it."

"He's helping, but he's already buried under the research you've assigned him. He's hardly got time for his own cases."

"Great. Now we have two lawyers off the clock. What the hell. Legal aid is downtown!"

"Thanks, Helmut," Jordan called cheerfully, declaring victory. Helmut rolled his eyes and waved her off. Really, she thought, he wasn't as bad as Barton made him out to be. He just took some handling.

And he was right about the case's difficulty. The judge wanted to deport Antonio, while letting his family remain. Fortunately Jordan's research skills hadn't been dulled by her sabbatical, so her well-documented brief, along with her impassioned argument on the sanctity of the family, allowed Antonio to stay with his wife and children. Their case was also helped by the white dresses she'd bought for mother and daughter and the suits she'd provided for father and son, creating the picture in court of the new all-American family, whose cinnamon faces and chocolate eyes shone postcard perfect from their table, the Cuban equivalent of Mom, Dad, Buddy and Sis, except that their names were Antonio, Graciela, Esperanza and little Esteban – *el gordito de la alegria* – their little fat boy of happiness. Their citizenship hinged on employment, which Jordan promptly guaranteed, finding Graciela work as a maid at Kelly, Knight and Squire. She found Antonio a job as a groundskeeper, working for all the suburbanites who couldn't bear to push their own lawnmowers, what with global warming and it being Florida.

So Antonio came to be standing outside Helmut's window, sweating and leaning on his shovel, waving his muscled brown arm and grinning. Graciela waved back over Helmut's bald head, beaming with *felicidad*. Her employer followed her gaze to the suntanned man with the high cheekbones, who, when he removed his sombrero to wipe his brow, revealed an obscene amount of lustrous black hair. Helmut snorted. Antonio's hair was so black it was almost blue. In the sun it shimmered.

Helmut wished he would put his hat back on and, as if reading his thoughts, Antonio obliged.

Graciela continued smiling at her husband with her bad teeth, but then, seeing Helmut watching her, quickly covered her mouth with her hand.

"*Señor* Helmut, d'joo know what *macho* mean?"

"Ummm. Tough guy?"

"No. Antonio. He gentle. Not hurt fly. But macho. Berry macho."

"Hmmm?" Helmut was writing on a yellow legal tablet.

"Macho man support hees wife and shillren." She tapped her head with her index finger. "Strong in hees mind." She patted her heart with her hand. "Strong in hees soul." Overcome with happiness, she blew her husband a kiss. "Hi, macho man!" she called.

"Graciela, do you mind?"

"Oh – sorry!" She rolled up her cleaning cart beside Helmut's desk, pulled on yellow plastic gloves, got down on her hands and knees and scrubbed at a stain beside Helmut's shoe. Seated at his desk, he went on writing, allowing her to work around his feet.

Finished with the stain, she backed out from under his desk on all fours while her employer admired her pert rear end and athletic legs. Feeling his gaze, she stood up and peeled off her yellow gloves.

"*Señor* Helmut, can I ask you sometheeng?"

Helmut abandoned his memo, part of a bankruptcy filing for

another lawyer. "Sure, Graciela . . . I only charge three Benjamin's an hour, but what the hell . . . I'm at your disposal."

"Are you happy, *Señor* Helmut?"

He shrugged and said, "Ehhh!" as if he'd had better days. Graciela emptied his trash into the bin on her cleaning cart and inserted a fresh liner into his wastebasket.

"I only ask because Antonio and I . . . we are so grateful. Ms. Jordan is so good to us and . . . you too." Her eyes suddenly filled and reddened. "And you work so late, with no family at home . . . If you like, you come to dinner at our house."

She smiled shyly with her mouth closed and her moist brown eyes glanced at the carpet. Helmut compressed his lips and found his throat constricted, feeling a strange heat press from behind his eyes. She'd caught him by surprise. He knew he was cold but . . .

He smelled the olive oil she brushed into her hair.

"*Muchas gracias,*" he said, speaking the Spanish without sarcasm. He drew a breath. "So do you like it here? In the States, I mean. Is it what you thought it would be?"

Helmut waited, genuinely curious. Certainly she knew what *his* life was like, since she'd had to dispose of the panties abandoned by various female clients, or, in one case, her employer's boxers, when Helmut had occupied the role of client.

How did she stand it? he wondered. How did anyone stand it – *it* being the job, the life, the universe? What were their lives even like? Helmut shuddered. He supposed he didn't really want to know. It was too horrible – the interior world of a fellow human. What a dump! And the smell. Really – what were people but cleaned up baboons?

He chuckled. No wonder he liked the look of a freshly spanked ass. Those red cheeks!

Still, it wasn't like his life had been free of pain. Once when he was eleven years old, his older sister and two of her friends had tied him to his bed with his own reversible Cub Scout belt. Exciting at first, the game turned ugly when they stripped off his clothes and hooted loudly at his boyish erection. Wild with glee, they took turns flicking the thing with their middle fingers.

Crimson-faced, young Helmut howled so loudly his little brother came to his rescue while the girls fled shrieking into the woods behind the house.

For the rest of his life, every woman would pay for that indignity.

With interest . . .

"Oh, yes. Ees wunnerful. Esteban and Esperanza bring home prizes from school. And I tell dem – deese is land of opportunity. You can be any-ting. We so happy!"

A shadow crossed Helmut's face, but Graciela wasn't playing The Grateful Immigrant. She and her family had spent seven nights on a homemade boat with a mile of water below them as the Atlantic heaved and bucked, sending waves crashing over the sides like an enormous beast licking its chops. The little family clung together, a fleshy knot of fear atop the merciless deep as the *Felicidad* drifted further north, beset by prowling sharks in the daytime and howling winds in the dark, so that now, with her *familia* safe on dry land, Graciela offered up thanks for every breath she and her loved ones took into their lungs.

Her prayers had been answered.

"That's nice," said Helmut, who hardly ever said things like "that's nice."

"*Gracias, Señor* Helmut." She turned and pushed her cleaning cart out of the office and wheeled it squeaking down the hall and – what was that music? She was humming! Helmut's face reddened as it had when he was eleven years old and humiliated beyond saying. Why, he made more money in an afternoon than she and her beaner husband made in a week . . . in ten weeks. So why were they so happy? *How* could they be so happy? What right did they have?

"Third world expectations," he muttered. He picked up the folder Barton had left on his desk and set to work getting Graciela the tax credit for taking care of her mother.

Glancing up, he noticed the compact on his desk. What nerve. That ingrate. Furrowing his brow, he growled and said, "What *in the hell* am I doing?"

He tossed her folder into the fresh liner in the wastebasket.

10

Assumption of the Risk

FOLLOWING The Kansas Incident, the weather in Florida was autumnal, with the air as clear as a well-made lens, rife with that invigorating coolness New Englanders describe as *crisp*, as if the world had been brought into focus overnight. Overhead, the sun blazed out of an immaculate blue dome, dazzling the suburban lawns with cinematic intensity. Blades of grass shimmered gold and green. A light breeze gusted off the Atlantic.

Parked in his driveway, Barton started his Toyota pickup truck. Flakes of rust pocked the body, corroded by ocean salt. Still, he refused to buy a new vehicle. This one started and ran. What else did you need? Cars, Barton thought, were motorized wheelchairs with poisonous exhausts. Worse even – lined up in traffic, they reminded him of metallic lice, pests which fed on and fouled their host, the uncomplaining earth.

Sitting with his hands on the wheel, with the truck vibrating under his thighs, he smiled at his wife as she approached her door. He leaned over and opened it for her and she squeezed in beside him, warmly pressing her thigh against his and balancing a cup of coffee in her hands.

Barton said, "Top of the morning, hottie."

Jordan groaned. Her husband kissed her bare shoulder and wisely shut up. The woman needed quiet in order face the day.

Without a gentle approach to full consciousness, a smooth ramp from bed to morning, she'd become a real crab. If that happened, he'd burn up his whole morning rehabilitating her mood, soothing the sourpuss, returning her to her natural good humor. Because he wouldn't, or couldn't, let her be.

Still, blazing a trail for her to greet the day was never a chore. No matter his wife's emotional valence, her presence energized him like the best drug God ever conceived. Her tousled hair smelled of apple-scented conditioner and her breath was like freshly picked mint. From her lap, white wisps of steam rose off her coffee cup.

"Careful," he said, shifting into reverse.

Jordan brought the cup to her mouth and puckered her lips. Barton waited, watching her. A lover of heat, she held the cup with both hands. She sipped noisily, slurping at a layer of foam.

"I need to pile up some more Z's," she moaned. The tip of her tongue licked off her milk mustache, and with her face still puffy with sleep, she looked vulnerable and girlish. Turning to her husband, she blinked and yawned, widening her eyes. "Hi, honey."

Her plan this morning was to accompany Barton to the law office before taking his truck to Meehan's, an art supply store where a blank canvas awaited. Picturing her *tabla rasa,* she rolled down her window, savoring the air as it ran coolly up her nose. The prospect of freshly stretched canvas filled her with a sense of the miraculous, of the wonder of possibility. All that pristine space! Perfect because it contained no errors. Only potential.

"We've got to pick up your partner," she said suddenly, scrunching shut her eyes.

"What?" Barton's high spirits evaporated as quickly as the steam drifting off her coffee. This had been the one morning when his first thought hadn't been of murdering Helmut, a reprieve he attributed to a renewed commitment to Zen meditation. But now black clouds gathered in his brain, blocking out the light of *satori.*

"I'm sorry," she said. "He asked me to ask you, but I've been afraid to."

Taking slow, measured breaths, her husband backed out of the driveway, careful of the two golden coconut palms they'd planted on either side of the entrance. Their house stood several blocks from the beach on the barrier island, a narrow sandbar between the Atlantic Ocean and the Indian River Lagoon.

"You know how he is," she added.

"Yes I *do* know how he is," Barton said. "Unfortunately. How'd he get hold of you?"

"Email."

"That – " Barton stopped. He refused to begin his day with a curse.

"I'm not hiding anything," she said quickly. "And I'm through drinking. *Consumatum est.* Anyway, I'll tell you my password and then you can read his emails. Delete them if you want. It's up to you."

"I don't *want* to know your password," Barton said more vehemently than he intended. He hesitated. "I mean, we can trust each other, right?"

Looking at him over the rim of the cup, her eyes peered at him through a tiny cloud.

"Of course," she said.

"Okay then." He put the truck in drive and started off slowly so that she wouldn't get burned by her coffee. "For better or for worse, eh?"

"Sure thing," she said.

Together they drove through the affluent enclave of Melbourne Beach, navigating the palm-lined streets. In front of Helmut's house, with its winding cobblestone drive and orange Spanish tile roof, its date palms and ornamental shrubs, its golf-course green grass, they pulled to a stop and waited, listening to the engine tick. Antonio Miranda, Graciela's husband, emerged from around the corner and set down his weed-eater. He wiped his brow with his forearm and, noticing the Squires, grinned at them with his whole face, revealing two missing teeth.

Behind him, Helmut's stucco walls rose serenely from the

manicured grounds. The driveway continued behind the house to the special garage he'd built to house his Ferrari. Barton called it the Folly, since the machine preferred to spend most of its time in expensive repair shops rather than on the highway. The Folly! Barton thought. The most impractical car imaginable, like a rare breed of dog with a permanent skin condition. Hard to drive, no AC, no stereo. Of course, the engine throbbed with phallic authority and godlike potency. When it ran, that is.

"Hi, Antonio!" Jordan bellowed out the window, waving her hand as enthusiastically as if he'd been passing on a parade float. Barton tapped the horn and gave a little wave of his finger from the top of the steering wheel.

The front door opened and Helmut sauntered down the walkway swinging his calfskin briefcase. For a man with a belly, he moved with surprising agility. Like a predatory ape, thought Barton, frowning.

Helmut piled inside and bumped Jordan so that she sloshed her coffee onto Barton's crotch. Wincing, he clenched his teeth and kept his mouth shut. He kept an extra suit at the office for just such occasions. Helmut slammed his door too hard and Barton, who was sensitive to sound, jerked upright, feeling his skull begin to throb.

"Who's dressing you now?" Barton asked, shaking his head. Helmut laughed boomingly. For all his hedonic expertise, his knowledge of The Good Life, he was peculiar about his clothes. Apart from the one good suit he'd worn to meet the senator's wife in Kansas, he refused to invest in them because of his hatred of mirrors. Only at his Barton's insistence would he dress properly for court. Other days, he looked like a bum outfitted with a suit from the Salvation Army.

"What's got your knickers in a twist?" Helmut asked, noting Barton's frown and winking. "Trouble with the wife again?"

Jordan turned her face toward her husband and wrinkled her nose. Helmut's breath smelled as if he'd wolfed a garlic and salami hoagie and washed it down with cat piss.

"Buddhas of past, present and future," Barton intoned, feeling a strange pain constrict his chest, "get me through this day." He rolled down his window and took them onto the highway and into morning traffic.

Ascending the causeway over the blue stretch of the river, the sun shone from the east, scattering its gold light across the frothy chop on the water. Elevated so that sailboats could navigate the Intracoastal waterway without a drawbridge, the top of the causeway afforded a view of both the approaching mainland and the receding barrier island, comprised of a long crescent of sand giving onto the Atlantic beach. Descending the western side, they rejoined the main body of America, the world of Helmut and Barton's work, the land of plaintiffs and defendants.

Helmut drew a noisy breath through his congested nose, enjoying the pressure of Jordan's thigh. Freshly showered, the cleanliness of her body came through her clothes. An odor like the incense they used to burn in college rose from her hair and he took it deep into his lungs. Her nearness opened his nasal passages.

"So what's wrong with the Folly?" Barton asked.

"I couldn't say," said Helmut. "You'd have to ask my grease monkey."

Barton's hands tightened on the wheel, leaching the blood from his fingers and turning his knuckles a sickly green. His wife and his partner had to have their fancy cars, yet his rusty black pickup was the only one that ran dependably. Jordan's own car, a teal Mercedes coupe, had developed a mysterious ticking sound, which meant it had joined the Folly on a pricey vacation at the garage. Barton didn't mind playing chauffeur, but the car issue was another example of how Helmut and Jordan waved off common sense as if it were a bothersome insect.

Feeling another twinge in his chest, Barton wondered if he would ever understand them.

Turning off the causeway onto U.S. 1, he headed up the highway, which was as wide as a runway. Four lanes of traffic careened along each side of the grassy median. The Department of Transportation had recently added two lanes and it had taken all the legal muscle of the firm to save the century-old live oak growing at the edge of their parking lot. It was a stately tree, with its majestic green canopy and its impossibly thick brown trunk, but it made for a dangerous obstacle as he slowed to make the turn into the office.

Traffic shot past an orange-and-white hazard marker alongside the massive trunk, and no wonder the Department of Transportation had wanted to cut it down. Even with the newly added lane, Barton had to turn sharply, jerking the wheel and swerving to avoid getting clipped from behind, while at the same time making sure that he didn't hit the tree or their sign.

Kelly, Knight and Squire
Attorneys at Law

This particular morning, however, the rearview mirror was clear.

"Slow down," said Jordan, "this coffee's like radioactive."

"That isn't news to me," said Barton, whose crotch was still steaming. He bore down on the accelerator.

"Barton, slow down!"

"Know what the Lakota said before battle?"

"Rah-rah-ree, kick him in the knee, rah-rah-rass, kick him in other knee!" Helmut grinned.

Barton laughed mirthlessly. "No, they said, *today is a good day to die.*"

"I thought that was from *Star Trek*," Jordan said.

"They got it from the Indians," Barton said. "The point is that your accounts ought to be square so you'll be ready."

Helmut yawned. "Is this going anywhere?" he asked. "You know how I am with too much blood in my alcohol stream."

"Oh, we're going somewhere," Barton said.

Beside him, Jordan stiffened in her seat. She heard a catch in her husband's voice and she didn't like it. It was scary.

"Barton, come *on*," she said. "You've made your point."

He floored the gas and the white lines of the highway shot underneath them.

"Hey!" said Helmut, bracing his shoes against the dash, "you trying to kill us?"

"That's the idea," said Barton. Turning, he aimed the truck at the brown trunk of the oak tree.

"Honey, stop it." Jordan dropped her coffee and put her hands against the dash. The oak tree filled the windshield.

Inside the law firm, on the second story of the building, Graciela emptied a wastebasket in what was once my office and peered out the window.

Wasn't that Mr. Squire's truck? She blinked and rubbed her eyes. And why was it going so fast? And why was it aimed at the big tree?

She clutched the gold crucifix Ms. Jordan had given her and whispered a prayer, appealing to the Virgin Mother to protect the three lawyers.

Outside, the Florida sun shone down like a white-hot ember which had popped out of hell, while Barton hit the brakes and squealed his tires, raking two black lines of burned rubber across the asphalt as he did a power slide into the parking lot.

Helmut stumbled out of the truck, gasping and holding his belly, while Jordan glared at her husband across the seat.

"What?" Barton said. The pain in his chest had lifted. "You weren't in any danger. I was just having some fun."

"*Fun? Is that what that was?*" Jordan was breathing hard. "Barton, I'm – "

"Go ahead," he said, despising himself for the tone in his voice, "scream some heavy lines."

"I'm disappointed in you," she said at last, very quietly. "You and your one man show . . . your little theatre of kamikaze."

He climbed out of the truck and stood under the lacy shade of the oak tree. Shafts of yellow sun glimmered through the leaves.

His wife slid behind the wheel.

"You don't understand," he said.

11

DEADLOCK

"YOU'RE obsessed," she said, "why can't you just let it go?"

That night in their king-sized bed, caressed by their cool sheets, his wife widened her eyes, cupping her husband's face with her warm hands. *The Yale Law Review* had published "The Charismatic Close," which was cause for celebration, but when Barton took it out of the mailbox and saw Helmut's name in print above his own he'd gotten a whiff of the past, transporting him back to The Kansas Incident.

"Let. It. Go." Her breath had the odor of pears whose skins have started to mottle.

Barton worked his face free of her hands and turned onto his side, bunching the top sheet between his legs. A strand of her hair caught the stubble of his beard and hung across his eye like a golden thread.

"A Buddhist would let it go," she said, her voice going throaty as she encircled him with her arms. She nuzzled her nose into the nape of his neck.

Her husband held his body rigid, his eyes wide open, staring at nothing. They were a couple in a Mexican standoff, tempers locked and cocked. Sensing the danger, both realized this was point-blank conversation, that zone where any mistake, any offense, might prove lethal to their marriage. Love trembled as if facing a firing squad. Loyalty wore a blindfold.

Barton stared through the translucent yellow hair. "I'm an aspiring Buddhist," he said. "I never said I'd achieved *satori*."

"So, you're working your way up, like belts in karate?"

She didn't say this sarcastically. She was curious.

Her husband considered the nature of Zen. "Yes and no," he said, which seemed an appropriately Zen-like answer. His wife's hot breath tickled his neck. Her hand squeezed his upper arm and she peppered his back with kisses.

"So why don't you enlighten me?" She licked his spine with the flat of her tongue, making him shiver and raising gooseflesh.

"If I let it go, Jordan. If I let it go . . . I should commit hari-kari. Or something. Otherwise, I have no honor."

She nibbled his ear, then stuck her slippery tongue into it. Barton writhed and her tongue withdrew, leaving a cold spot. Her hand dropped to his groin and joggled him heartily. Barton felt the marrow of his bones flicker as the blood rushed from his head. She was winning her point, he realized.

Could she be right? Should he let it go? His memory felt alarmingly fluid and looking back he saw shimmering, mirage-like images.

Sometimes he recalled The Kansas Incident one way, sometimes another.

If only he hadn't gotten high . . .

Yet during nakedly honest moments, he remembered it all with horrifying clarity. Bloody-eyed and impossibly stoned on Bill's hybridized marijuana, he'd stumbled back to his room long past midnight, surprising his wife *en flagrante delicto*. Helmut sat on the bed and her blond head bobbed over his lap.

Barton blinked. Had it really been like that? He'd assumed he was hallucinating. But Helmut had grinned at him. He'd actually grinned, baring his awful yellow teeth.

Barton realized he might not have been hallucinating.

Now, he remembered: Helmut's jaw fell open as he coughed and groaned, his eyes rolling back until they were white and he came with a shudder.

There'd been a scene. Perhaps there'd been screaming. Certainly there had been tears. The threat of violence had loomed. Helmut decamped hastily. Barton felt like a fool and a coward.

Then it was over.

And yet, following The Kansas Incident, the partners made amends. They had to. They were making too much money to become adversarial. So they got on with life, no longer friends but professionals. Colleagues and co-workers. Their careers advanced and life regained its balance. But then Helmut hit a hot streak, publishing three articles in the *Harvard Law Review*. He got the well-heeled clients and the corner office, then later the business trips and the posh suites in Manhattan.

Helmut accepted these accolades as smilingly as if they were his birthright, while Barton tried not to envy him. Helmut put in the hours and did his homework, Barton often reminded himself. He worked like a machine. And he was a good advocate, which Barton never denied. But after they sold the firm to my partners and me, we advanced Helmut into our own ranks, allowing him to abandon personal injury and join the club – that of tax shelters for the wealthy, home of The Really Big Money.

Barton got the leftovers and two choices: he could follow his colleague around like a freshman law clerk, or he could keep his own cases, the sort of working-class folk whose children had wrongfully smeared their guts under the wheels of one of Helmut's Hummer-driving clients.

With his name still emblazoned on the sign outside, even as his status diminished inside, Barton felt horribly old, as opposed to indisputably middle-aged. But that was chronology in America. Middle-aged *was* old. And for Barton, who was nostalgically inclined, the passing of youth grieved him daily. Sitting at his desk, staring at the backs of his hands, he wondered: *whose old paws are these?*

They didn't belong to anybody *he* remembered.

And there were other things. His first gray pubic hair, which, oddly enough, recalled puberty, because hadn't he just *gotten* pubic hair? And the way a pretty young intern might offer him a forced but kind smile – the fossil of flirtation, he understood grimly. Soon that too would vanish and he'd become a tottering geezer, standing on his lawn gazing at his sprinklers, another wizened Floridian, another hapless cuckold.

It wasn't too late. He could still contribute to the world. But how? Sometimes he thought he might journey to the slums of Africa, find a family and rescue them from poverty. He could raise five-hundred thousand cash inside a week, and in a third world country that could save a family from extinction.

Of course, it wasn't that simple.

But what if it was?

He understood himself to be at a crossroads.

He'd never had children, yet he had the power to save a family. To kill death itself. And here he was obsessing about himself, his wife, and a blow job.

Not exactly the stuff of tragedy. More like theatre of the absurd. More pathetic still if what you wanted was epic. On the verge of howling, of baying at the sky and beating his chest, he could hardly believe he'd given up on his happily-ever-after. But when youth passed, so did opportunity.

Yet possibilities remained. He could still mark his grave with glory. Life could still *mean* something.

Why not?

I am not old, he often reminded himself, although if he kept at it long enough, he figured, pretty soon he'd have to amend it to *I wish I was not old*.

Meanwhile a sea of suffering humanity called from the television, from the newscasts in Africa, silent pleas issuing from refugee tents, all those dark desperate faces and black imploring eyes.

But Jordan. Sweet Jordan. Buddhas of past, present and future!

How could he abandon her? Jordan dressed up for court in a smart blue suit. Jordan in a slanting beam of sun. Jordan strumming her guitar, about to sing. Jordan with her cat-that-ate-the-canary smile.

After he'd scared them with the truck that morning, he'd nearly done in his partner that afternoon. Hanging one of Jordan's new paintings in his office, a crimson abstract shot through with streaks of silver, the upholstery hammer had been in his hand.

Finished with the picture, he'd stood outside Helmut's office under the fluorescent lights, his fingers pumping the hammer's rubber grip. His eardrums whistled. The air conditioning hummed and voices drifted through the walls. Shining sparks danced on his retinas. He felt . . . there was no other word, *divine,* because he knew now, at last, what he was going to do.

Barton looked at the hammer. He'd considered employing the silver machete Antonio used to hack off dead palm fronds, but he was afraid of bungling the crime. The blade might be dull and he didn't know how to sharpen it.

He'd ruled out firearms too, because he felt murder ought to be a hands-on affair. In this he adhered to his belief that you ought not to eat anything you wouldn't be willing to kill. Consequently, he ate fish and birds because he believed he could kill them, but a cow or a pig or a lamb?

Never.

But Helmut?

Easy.

Now his prey sat before him, his door open, his back turned as he yammered on the phone. His head glinted under the light like a giant egg, and as he shifted his buttocks on the chair, squeaking the leather, Barton knew that Helmut knew that he was behind him and that Helmut was happy to keep him waiting.

His heart thumping, Barton knew he wasn't going to do it. Or was he? If he did, it would be an accident. He was hanging a picture and Helmut's head got in the way.

Ker-splat!

Giddy with desperation, he nearly laughed out loud and quickly bit his knuckle. The Kansas Incident. That was the sticking-place. That was the heavy weather.

Since that dark night at the hotel, he hadn't got back on the wagon.

Hadn't bowed down to Buddha-nature.

Hadn't meditated on the divine *Om*.

Hadn't exercised.

Hadn't been free of searing heartburn.

Barton's arm swung in a terrific arc and the hammer connected with Helmut's bald dome, traveling through skin and skull and brains till it came out the other side, shattering his jawbone and spattering all that Helmut had been into a sticky red pile on the floor.

Barton tossed the hammer into the wastebasket and sucked in the stale office air. A blazing white flash burst in his skull.

This was glory.

During the sentencing phase of his trial he imagined his lawyer asking, "You think he's in hell now?"

"I hope so, but I think he's probably just dead."

"You understand it's better if you express remorse?"

"I *do* feel remorse. I wish I'd paralyzed him. He didn't suffer enough."

His lawyer sighed and shuffled his papers.

"We're not pursuing an insanity defense," the lawyer reminded him.

Barton laughed humorlessly.

"You'd have to be crazy *not* to want to kill Helmut," he said. "I just did what a lot of people only dream of doing."

"And that makes all the difference," his lawyer advised. Barton bit his lip, remembering the soapy smell of his wife's hair, her smooth and sturdy shoulders, her honey-butter skin, her breath as fresh as citrus.

Back in the real world of the office, Helmut snapped shut his phone and spun around in his chair. "So spit it out, Big Bart."

That he would steal Jordan's pet name for him was too much. The man had to go, Barton thought. He really did.

Helmut chuckled warmly. "Seriously, Big Bart. What's up with the hammer? Learning a trade? It never hurts to have a second career – just in case."

Barton counted his breaths and fought down his anger, feeling unworthy of Buddhas past, present and future. He sought detachment, the ego-absence of Zen . . . even as he felt his brain bubble like cheese under a broiler.

Helmut smirked. Barton's fingers tightened on the hammer grip. He couldn't get past that smirk, that country-club-kid superiority. Helmut *deserved* the death penalty. Why, hadn't he confessed to Barton that if he had a woman in her own bed, his favorite thing, his absolute top-shelf experience, was to fix his eyes on the bedside family picture so that he could stare into her husband's eyes? For Helmut adored the cuckold more than the conquest.

Observing Helmut's bony Adam's apple work up and down as he took a swig from his office flask, Barton thought, *the sickening thing is that I was ever friends with this creep.*

"Don't look at *me* like that," said Helmut, replacing his flask in his desk drawer. "It was *her* idea, man."

"The truly strong nature is yielding and gentle," Barton told himself, reciting the ancient teachings of Lao Tse. *The truly strong nature is yielding and gentle.*

A vein jumped in his neck. Apparently *satori* wouldn't be his today, or ever, at least not while Helmut drew breath. Yet Barton accepted that he was also at fault. In his younger days he'd found Helmut's conduct attractively outrageous, even bold, but now this shamed him. Wincing, he faced the knowledge he'd concealed from himself. He was an accessory after the fact. Helmut was a pervert, a satyr, a centaur, and through silence Barton had aided and abetted his crimes. Gripping the hammer, his hand felt as though it were holding a gavel.

Guilty as charged, he thought, the both of us!

But what of a pardon? Could he purge himself of the fruit of the poisonous tree? Become the man he was before he fell under Helmut's spell? He wanted to swing a hammer through his whole life. The drive to work. The greed of clients. The pompous judges. The corrupt insurance adjusters.

Seeing Barton walk down the street with his pretty wife, passers-by would've called him a success, but they were unreliable witnesses. From where he sat, Barton identified an upper middle-class lawyer, age forty-three, with an unfaithful wife and no children, and such years as were left him looked like more of the same, a long desolate plain with an open grave at the horizon. The expression *over the hill* accrued literal meaning. Perched on life's peak, he wondered: was this where dreams ended? In tawdry compromise?

He had come to a reckoning.

For what had his life amounted to? He would leave no heirs, no legacy, no art. So far his contribution to American culture consisted of three articles in *The Yale Law Review*, two of them co-authored with Helmut.

Gazing into the future he saw himself living under a bridge, toothless and unshaven and gray, sucking at a bottle of red wine with a screw-on cap, because his life as it was cancelled the life he'd foreseen, that happily-ever-after with his one and only, his Jordan, his Juliet – and wasn't a man entitled to give something back after that kind of disappointment?

Groaning, he begged his mind to shut its eye on these revenge-on-Helmut fantasies and leave him in peace.

And so he returned to his king-sized bed, where he lay awake beside his wife. Behind his long and slender body, snuggled close, Jordan began dragging air through her nose and drooling down his naked back. Her husband kept very still, not wanting to wake her. Listening to her steady if nasal breathing eased his throbbing heart. He wanted her to rest. He wanted her to stay healthy. He wanted her to find serenity. He wanted her to be in love with him. He wanted her to be happily married.

"Sweet dreams," he whispered, as much to himself as to her.

12

ADDENDUM

BORN in 1965, our trio belonged to a generation never labeled – one caught between Baby Boomers and Generation X. Too young to be hippies, too old to be hip-hop, they came of age in the now seemingly innocent 1980's, without war, without terror, without children and without religion. Then somehow they found themselves stranded in the new millennium, successful by society's standards, yet nagged by an unsettling feeling that something essential had been mislaid, forgotten – a part of life left out in the rain, yet despite all their years of education, they couldn't name it.

Back in college, when ageing was something that happened to other people, they'd begun to become aware of their place in history.

"There's something I've been meaning to mention, young Squire." Sitting at his dorm room desk, Helmut thumbed his *Viking Portable Nietzsche,* then turned on a Smith Corona portable typewriter. The machine hummed importantly. "You should cut your hair."

"*What?*" Barton shook out the long blond curls he'd sported since high school. "I'm a hippie," he said. "I *can't* cut my hair."

"These are the eighties, you goof. The sixties are long gone." Helmut began typing. Each key was like a tiny gunshot – *rat ta tat! ta ta tac!*

"Not for me they aren't. But what's the difference? You get left out of the summer of love?"

"Oh, please. Spare me the peace and paisley. But if you're really going sport that rock star mop, you need to own it. Get yourself some black silk pants embroidered with dragons, Elizabethan shirts with frilly collars – something. Cause you're not wearing your hair, man, it's wearing you."

Barton ran his fingers through his lustrous mane, as soft as a girl's. "You don't like it?"

Helmut's typewriter idled as though powered by gasoline. "Don't ask. You need to go GQ, Squire. Time to grow up. And don't even think about a ponytail. You'd look like a construction worker."

"Jordan likes it long."

"Oh, Jesus." Helmut tapped a pen against his teeth. "End of conversation. You look ridiculous – just thought you'd want to know." He turned back to his typewriter.

Barton wasn't an *ubermensch*, Helmut thought. He was an Everyman. Sentimental. And the way he obsessed over his girlfriend!

"She's hot," Helmut had told him. "I'll give you that – but turn 'em over and they're all sisters."

Across the room Barton felt his hair hang warmly against his back, but Helmut was right. He was a retro ass. The hippie era had fossilized. They might ape the bygone counterculture (Jordan with her long straight hair, parted in the middle, complete with embroidered head band and ceramic love beads) but they'd arrived too late, even on campus. The legendary rock and roll acts had either died or broken up, and Haight Ashbury was only a street corner.

Tomorrow, he'd ask Jordan to shear off his locks.

Helmut wouldn't have believed it. All evidence to the contrary, he claimed Barton ignored his advice. Helmut thought it was the story of their lives.

Hey, Barton, cut your hair.

Hey, Barton, apply to law school.

Hey, Barton, let's sell the firm.

Hey, Barton, don't marry Jordan.

Even in middle age, Helmut would never understand his college roommate. Barton had acquired wealth and a modicum of power, but also a crazy-ass wife. She cruised through life with her lights off. There was no help for it, Helmut figured, because some people just *wanted* to be losers. How else to explain the choices they made?

Marriage, kids, commitment: what a heaping feast of bullshit! Why not report directly to the penitentiary? Helmut didn't get it. And he never would.

Rolling his head to ease the tension in his neck, he closed his *Portable Nietzsche* and began writing a paper on Jean Paul Sartre and the search for "the privileged moment."

And so it went. The moments added up into years, and the years piled up into decades. Roommates Knight and Squire became attorneys Knight and Squire – and with the addition of the Kelly name and the prestige of Jordan's family, the trio soared into the corporate world, players at last. Then greed overtook them and they sold their firm to Colin, Lanus and Gart, itself a subsidiary of that global behemoth, Freeman Enterprises.

Yet in the dorm room where Helmut typed on his Smith Corona portable, the year was still 1985. The Age of Computers peeked over the horizon, slashing the sky like dawn on the Atlantic and bearing information on blades of light. Soon every American would have more passwords than a secret agent.

Into that storm of information, with its electric arcs creasing the sky and the coming millennium, marched Jordan, Barton and Helmut, heads held high as they journeyed west toward San Francisco, into the promised land of the American future, where happiness would be pursued through the still new world of a thing called the Internet.

Anything could happen.

Part II

Green Glade

"MAKE us good, Mr. Colin."

The door banged shut and Barton's feet padded down the hall, strangely quiet for a big man. Strange too that he should echo Helmut when I told him I was writing their story, but it must've cost Barton a lot to lay The Kansas Incident to rest. Then again, he may have been humoring an old codger, feigning interest in my literary aspirations. It's hard to say. Barton's a faithful visitor, calling odd Wednesdays, when he leaves books he believes I'll find instructive. Just now I'm staring at the smiling gold Buddha on the cover of Alan Watts's *The Way of Zen*. A magnificent book: I hadn't the heart to tell him I'd already read it.

In any case, bear with me, dear reader. For as Alzheimer's disease conspires to loosen my grip on the present in order to hurl me into the past, I struggle forward into the future, fighting the mighty headwind of memory.

And yet, perhaps the flashbacks in my story render me new-millennial, reflecting the physicists' latest conception of time, one prismatic and relative as opposed to one monochromatic and linear, one more reflective of Einstein than Newton. Indeed, I seek but cannot find a unified field. I am full of dark energy.

But this is no time for apology. In truth, I am alone. I have no one to edit me. The isolation is profound. As a lifelong bachelor I've always been a solitary creature, but never a lonely one. Still, I refuse to convey my living, or should I say dying, conditions. I am an inmate in Death's clearinghouse, yet I won't allow its odious sights and smells to invade these pages, for this manuscript has become the one durable product of my fast-crumbling mind.

As I brief my characters' lives, then, I implore you to quash your impatience, as forays into the past will soon cease entirely, with flashbacks giving way to action and, I hope, catharsis.

Finally, I refer to the principals as "characters" only as a figure of speech. Of course they were real human beings, and, in any case, we're all "characters" in the lives of others, aren't we? Typecast, we play the parts they assign us, cast in dramas where we alternately star or scrounge work as extras.

Those readers desirous of a more linear view may consult the relevant dates in *Florida Today* newspaper or the Orlando Superior Court record of DeVaughn *et al* v. Glib and Stone Pharmaceuticals.

– Alexander Colin, Attorney at Law (ret.)
Green Glade Assisted Living Community
Sebring, Florida
August 14, 2008

1

Next of Kin

"I HAVE an emergency!" cried the portly old woman, her sad gray eyes gone wide in a permanent state of alarm. Stuffed into an aluminum wheelchair, she had on a pink housecoat and matching slippers, with a face corrugated by wrinkles under a silver helmet of hair, one of the many faces parked in wheelchairs and lining the hallway of Apple Blossom Park, a nursing home in Palatka, Florida.

"I have an emergency!" Her toothless mouth chewed the words. "I said . . . *I have an emergency!*"

No one even glanced at her. Catheterized, sedated, and forgotten, the other residents looked like they'd weathered too many emergencies of their own to bother with hers.

Flinching, Jordan hurried past her through a tunnel of cavernous, sunken faces, feeling their rheumy stares catch at her flesh. Her face burned and she kept her eyes pinned to the grimy floor, pumping her thighs as she fled down the hall.

Coward, she thought, look up. *Smile. Be nice!*

She couldn't do it. She was ashamed of her own vitality, her still-blooming body, her ability to escape this geriatric prison. A piercing scream was hastily muffled by a slamming door.

"I have an emergency!"

A nurse with platinum hair and black roots, who was so obese her massive chest threatened to pop the buttons from her uniform, trundled past the woman in the pink housecoat, ignoring her emergency. Jordan flattened herself against the wall so the nurse could pass. The nurse pushed a wheelchair occupied by an old man listing dangerously over the armrest. His face was corpse-green and although she'd been trained as an attorney and not as a physician, Jordan diagnosed his ailment. He was dead, in her amateur opinion, but who knew? She hadn't majored in biology and what disturbingly came to her mind was an expression of Helmut's: "One foot on a banana peel, the other in a coffin."

It might've been the motto of Apple Blossom Park.

At the end of the hall she reached her destination and, pausing with her hand on the cool doorknob, she gritted her teeth and stepped inside.

The room was dark and she fought off a panic attack. From behind a half-drawn curtain a low moaning escaped from the client beside the far wall, but Jordan couldn't go to her any more than she could the woman with the emergency. She was sorry, but there it was. The woman moaned and Jordan understood she was hearing a ghost, or someone who'd soon become a ghost.

Blinking in the dim, beige-colored light filtering through the filthy window, she turned to the room's other occupant.

Barbara Kelly, age eighty-nine, threw off a blanket and sat up in her bed – no more than a cot, really, just a threadbare mattress and a wire frame, without even a box spring.

"I knew you'd throw a punch for me, Sassy Box. Ha! Sweet Baby Jordan. None of these mental cases believed me. But I knew. Ha ha! Oh yes, I did!" She cocked her head toward the hallway. "You hear that, you gasbags? Ha ha!"

Her eyes were as vividly blue as her granddaughter's, like swatches slashed from a tropical ocean. She had on a wrinkled polyester dress of sea-foam green and a navy beret. She'd applied lipstick to her thin and colorless lips, but her unsteady hand had left a crimson smear across her chin. Jordan took a tissue from the nightstand and dabbed it with spittle and cleaned her up. Blinking rapidly, Jordan tried to force her own mouth into something resembling a smile.

Her grandmother scowled and said, "Get that pout off your mug, sweetie, you ain't makin' up a stiff quite yet."

Quitting with the tissue, Jordan tossed it into a wastebasket overflowing with blood-spotted cotton balls. "I'm here for you, Grandma." Her voice quavered in the dim light, while her grandmother's roommate softly moaned.

"Oh Lord," her grandmother said, wagging her head, "I ain't made of glass. Honey, I've *been* ready. Now get one of those quacks in here and sign my papers!"

Jordan took hold of her grandmother's hand, which felt like a small dry paw. Its grip was tenacious. Swinging her arm around her hip, she helped her off the flimsy bed. Her grandmother's body was appallingly light.

Together they walked down the hall, braving the lane of cadaver-like faces and gaping astonished mouths and the woman with the emergency. At the front of the building Jordan swung open the door on a Florida afternoon, with its dazzling light and sultry, orange-blossom air. Overhead, a spray of clouds, like heavenly ocean foam, roamed across the expanse of blue.

"I've won," the old lady croaked, shaking her cane at the sky, "you thought you had me fixed for a dirt nap, but you were wrong!" Her voice was raspy but strong. Turning, she wobbled on her feet and banged her cane on the door of Apple Blossom Park, where two aides in white uniforms stood watching her through the glass, their mouths working over large candy bars. "And *you*. You fat buggers. Go pound salt up your asses!"

"Grandma?" Jordan said, sheepishly ducking her head and glancing toward her red rental car glinting in the sun. "Shall we go?"

"Don't rush me, Sassy Box. I got things to say and people that owe me. They stole my clothes." She dusted off her dress and straightened her neck, flapping wattles of skin and looking, Jordan thought, like a parched old turkey. "But that's a battle best fought another day, Honey Bunny."

Shading her eyes, her grandmother observed her reflection in the building's mirrored windows. Shrugging, she said, "Not bad for an old broad."

Jordan's face was pained. The old lady reached up and pinched her granddaughter's cheek with fingers as strong as pliers, leaving a red mark and forcing a tear from her granddaughter's eye. "I only meant that the staff should pound salt," she said in a milder, more grandmotherly tone. "I feel bad for the lunatics still trapped in there." Jordan rubbed her smarting cheek.

Inside the car, the old lady primly allowed her granddaughter to reach across her lap to fasten her seatbelt.

Her steely eyes softened. "Thanks, Pussycat. You're my true blue." The old lady batted her eyes in a theatrical way and chuckled and coughed, then leaned her head against the window and promptly fell asleep, snoring lightly.

On the highway Jordan set the air conditioning so that it wasn't too cold and adjusted the vents so that they didn't blow directly on her grandmother. Navigating traffic, her eyes darted between the sleeping old woman and the passing cars. Cries of *it's an emergency, it's an emergency* echoed in her head.

God! Was that what life had in store? Gasping, she hit the gas and passed a tractor-trailer loaded with oranges. She imagined the truck crashing and all the oranges spilling onto the highway.

I'm not afraid of dying, her grandmother had written her, care of the law school in California, *but I don't want to do it here. They take you out through the back door. In a bag. Black plastic, with a zipper. I've seen it. Rescue me, Jordan. Hurry.*

– Grandma K.

Listening to her grandmother snore, it occurred to Jordan, then twenty-three, that it would be less than a tragedy if she didn't have children. Reproduction offered no guarantees. Liabilities, yes – assurances no. The corners of her mouth turned up. It was a rare day when you actually learned something about yourself.

Now, when a soon-to-be-child-bearing friend asked, "Aren't you afraid you'll be lonely when you get old?" she'd reply, "Sure, but I'll just be lonely, whereas you'll be lonely *and* abandoned."

It might sound bitter, but her grandmother was her evidence. Her own parents, and all her aunts and uncles, had been too busy with their own lives to care for their aged mother, much less move her into their homes, even on a rotating basis. How could they manage? It simply wasn't feasible. The old lady's presence would be too inconvenient. She smelled like an old person and she made inappropriate remarks. She wasn't good company. What could they do? They were helpless.

Her granddaughter was not. She might be in the middle of a semester in her first year of law school, but for her the blood bond of kin outweighed any legal obligation.

She had led her grandmother out the *front* door of Apple Blossom Park, by God.

The old woman woke up and clutched her heart, her eyes wild. Her hands shook.

"Never sell the land!" she thundered. Her faded blue eyes darted back and forth, "Never never never!" Just as suddenly she fell back asleep.

Never sell the land had been the Kelly's mantra, and had been for ten generations. Jordan could trace her lineage all the way to the wooden deck of the *T'Bonte Koe*, the ship which had sailed from Holland and brought her people into what was then the port of New Amsterdam. Her family had lived on Whitehall Street, in what is now New York's financial district, although in those days it was as much farm as city.

Losing eight of his eleven children to malaria, her oldest traceable ancestor, Jacob Bokee (pronounced like "bouquet") abandoned the fetid confines of colonial New Amsterdam and moved his family upstate to Dutchess County. And from those rocky hills and blue lakes and pine forests, the family contributed officers to both the Revolutionary and Civil Wars.

With Jordan still in pigtails, the farm had been sold to a couple of executives who'd made a fortune in syndicated television. Along with mineral rights, the new owners acquired title to the ancestral bones buried under the granite markers behind the postcard red barn, which, like the farmhouse, with its oak banister which Jordan had slid down as a child, would be bulldozed to make way for a new house, complete with solarium.

Well, she thought, *my country 'tis of thee*. What had she learned in law school? The first draft of the Declaration of Independence read: *life, liberty and . . . property*. The pursuit of happiness had been a lofty revision.

Yet that same spirit had led to her previous visit to Apple Blossom Park, when her grandmother had patted her shoulder and said, "You were always a good girl, Jordan. Helping me with barn chores. So quit worrying. I'm fine here." She'd tapped her cane on the wall. "Course . . . any place works for dyin'."

"But I'm *not* a good girl, Grandma." *Or I wouldn't leave you here.* An anonymous, colorless room, the light above the cot had burned out and there wasn't even a radio. On the wall beside the door, her grandmother had taped up pictures of New England foliage, resplendent with fall colors. Proud of her Yankee stock, she was the sort of woman who made the best of things.

"We were always poor, living on the farm. But now that we've…" the old lady closed her eyes against the memory, "*sold the land* – you're not poor. But don't let that stop you from *being* somebody." She squeezed her granddaughter's hand and peered into her eyes. "Now go on, honey. Go back to law school and make something of yourself."

"Those sound like two different things, Grandma."

"Honey, sometimes you've got to do the wrong thing so you can find the right thing. In the end, don't think it to death. Trust your gut, Sassy Box."

But then Jordan had got the letter, and made a beeline for the Dean's office where she filled out a request for a leave of absence.

The Dean, who was also Jordan's criminal law professor, leaned back in her creaking wooden chair and smiled professionally, keeping her lips pressed tightly together. She held Jordan's leave form in her hand and looked at it over the tops of her reading glasses.

"Reason for withdrawal," she read aloud. " 'Need to liberate my grandmother.' " The Dean removed her glasses and set them on the desk beside a miniature silver gavel. "I'm sorry, Ms. Kelly, but I don't understand. Is she seeking asylum?"

"No, she's *in* an asylum." Jordan leaned forward with her hands on her lap. "That's the problem. She needs to be rescued."

"Ah. I see." The Dean sighed heavily and clucked her tongue. "We went through something similar in my family." Her tone became professional. "But Ms. Kelly – *Jordan* – most students who take a leave of absence never return."

"Oh, I'm coming back. I love the debates in your class. When I've got my own practice – "

"Ms. Kelly," the Dean said, holding up her hand as though she might be taking an oath of office, "that's another issue – your whole class – I've fostered the wrong atmosphere, I'm afraid. We talk a lot of theory in there, but it's academic. It's not the judicial system."

Jordan furrowed her brow.

"I seemed to have created a misconception," the Dean said, thawed by Jordan's earnestness. Perched on the edge of her chair, Jordan tilted up her chin, her ears bright pink, her eyebrows raised expectantly. "You think I represent the profession. But I don't. I'm not a lawyer."

Jordan blinked and smiled politely. She had no idea what the Dean was talking about, but she remained eager to please. Let us remember she was only twenty-three. With her large clear eyes and sunny disposition, it was no wonder every teacher since kindergarten had loved having her in class. She was a natural pet.

"I'm not a lawyer," the Dean repeated, pressing her fingertips together and staring into the tent of her hands. "I'm a *law professor.*"

Jordan experienced what her favorite English professor in college had called "an epiphany."

"Oh no," she said, sinking back in her chair as the blood rose to her cheeks. The woman in front of her, so dynamic in class, so full of authority and femininity, had revealed herself, an unworthy idol. She didn't practice. Like Jordan's literature teachers at the University of Florida, she didn't make the material – she taught it – an academic. What horror. Technically, this woman might be an officer of the court, but she lived in an ivory tower. Jordan fought back the hot flush boiling behind her eyes. This woman had duped her.

And now it was clear. Jordan understood.

She should never have applied to law school in the first place.

Barton and Helmut had talked her into it because that's what English majors did: they went to law school. What else could they do? Write? *Haikus Wanted.* You hardly ever saw that in the newspaper. Teach? Fill freshmen heads with enough literature to ruin their cubicle futures? She didn't think so. So she went to law school, a path trod by so many of her generation. In her bones she'd *felt* it was a mistake, but now she *knew* it. Ah! So life was going to be like that, eh? A world of second guesses.

Already, she sensed that the law firm of Knight and Squire would include her in name only. She might be a partner, but in their predictably testosterone-centric way, Barton and Helmut would consider themselves her superiors, yet she'd be damned if she'd spend her life knocking on the door of the boys' clubhouse. Jordan Kelly would not be a glorified secretary, not for them – not for anybody.

The Dean ground her eyes with her thumb and index finger. For an academic, she seemed hugely fatigued. "Any second thoughts?" she asked, the tip of her pen poised over Jordan's form.

"No, ma'am."

The Dean scrawled on the line and handed the form to Jordan, wishing her luck.

So Jordan rescued her grandmother, although she could do nothing for the woman with the emergency, whose voice she'd hear in her dreams. Years later, after she'd passed the bar, she did penance working for legal aid, defending the elderly against predatory landlords.

"Beautiful," Helmut had told her, "you take a lucrative profession and discover its only poverty niche." He drew a deep breath and coughed. "Even Barton's not *that* stupid."

Leaving Florida behind, Jordan and her grandmother took a small apartment set on a hill overlooking the blue of San Francisco Bay. To the west stretched the green of Golden Gate Park. The old lady enjoyed the views. Jordan returned to the University of San Francisco School of Law and in the dry California air her grandmother promptly recovered her health, and then just as promptly, she passed away.

After the funeral, Jordan attended class in a wide-eyed daze, finding her only relief in what her grandmother had taught her. For Barbara Kelly had introduced her to the siren odor of paint and the seductive texture of naked canvas. When Jordan wasn't studying Evidence or Torts, her grandmother instructed her in point-line drawing and color theory. Together, they consumed hours before their twin easels, even as Jordan kept up her grades in law school. It was a weird and exciting time.

Gazing at Alcatraz, its white stone fortress jutting from the cobalt bay, Jordan thought she knew how the convicts must've felt on the nights they could hear the jazz bands playing on the waterfront, when a saxophone's brassy solo drifted over the bay to torture the prisoner in solitary.

She dreamt of escape, too, of early parole from her self-imposed life sentence. She couldn't deny it any longer. She didn't want to be a lawyer. Yet she wasn't a quitter. If she had to forego sleep in order to mimic her heroes, Pollock and Chagall and Klimt, while also writing outlines for Constitutional Law and Contracts, then case closed.

Outside, on her porch one morning, invigorated by the stiff Pacific wind and the cumulus clouds stirring in the blue, she threw her arms over her head and hollered, "Grandma, please. Please let me paint." The sky remained silent. Jordan lowered her arms. The gesture was juvenile but so what? It felt good. It felt fine. She inhaled the cool air through her nostrils, smelling the pine trees from Golden Gate Park, sucking their green odor deep into her lungs. Purpose filled her like a drug.

In need of a tube of cadmium yellow, she strode into the Haight, her beloved hippie neighborhood, passing head shops and vegetarian restaurants, liquor stores and clothing boutiques, smelling the peculiar odor of the street, a mix of steam and tar, spices and grease. She had on hemp sandals and denim bell bottoms and an embroidered cotton blouse decorated with sequins. Around her neck she wore an orange scallop shell strung on a length of fishing line. A riot of loose curls spilled down her back and her skin glowed with animal vitality, burnished the color of honey by the California sun. She fit right in.

A bell jingled as she pushed open a door and entered Sir Charles, her favorite art supply store.

Running her fingertips along the soft bristles of the brushes, she gazed at the wooden easels, the tubes of paint (arranged in a rainbow) the stacked assortment of frames. She imagined heaven might look like this. Shivering, she silently thanked her grandmother for showing her the way. A wave of bliss stole through her. Under the lusty eye of the clerk, she felt the thrill of San Francisco's power. In this city you became who you were. Care to sport a full beard with a taffeta evening gown? Have at it.

Life here was recognized as something too brief to waste being the wrong person.

Examining the stretched canvases, she found them beautiful – they were blanks, little acres of possibility.

Her belly clenched. Would she become one of those arty parasites on family money, the sort who paid off gallery owners? Bribed columnists? Wrote her own reviews?

With talent, came doubt, because she didn't *have* to practice law, not with her inheritance from her grandmother. In a portfolio which she kept like a guilty secret, she had assets in cash, bonds and stock totaling $863,721.06. She also had a safety deposit box filled to its sparkling brim with one-ounce, 24 karat Canadian maple leaves. "Not a fortune anymore," her grandmother had said ruefully, sighing, when she'd shown her the will, "but I will say," and she grinned broadly, "it *does* beat a poke in the eye with a sharp stick."

Even so, their ancestral home was gone and nothing could get it back. They had *sold the land*. The farm was too valuable to keep, what with the taxes. Jordan saw it in other families too: once the matriarch died and the land was sold, the whole family collapsed. Nuclear elements might remain, but full-scale reunions for Thanksgiving and Christmas were as long gone as the wooden wagon wheels and Civil War uniforms she'd played with as a child, leftovers from what her grandmother called "the olden days."

But who painted anymore? Was she supposed to sail to the south seas, strip off her shirt and daub canvases with mangoes? It was too absurd. Yet wasn't accepting your own foolish nature – even loving it – the whole point of life?

But what if she proved inept? Query: should you follow your heart's desire, even if you weren't any good at it? Or should you pursue the brass ring in front of you? She could charm a jury, that much was certain. They thought she was "feisty" and "plucky." And they trusted her.

It didn't matter. Even before she'd passed the bar, before she left San Francisco to return to Florida, Jordan had cast her lot with the artists of the world, that motley band of painters and actors and writers and singers, the ones who forged pleasure out of pain, alchemists all. When she permitted herself to feel this truth, the glorious rightness of it, she hugged her arms across her chest and felt her grandmother's heart throb inside her. So what if the road bruised her feet? So what if it hurt? Making art left you bloody, but so did all birth.

Stopping at the cash register and digging for change in a lint-filled pocket, she paid for the tube of cadmium yellow, hearing a familiar voice whisper in her ear.

2

OFFICER OF THE COURT

THE campus of the University of San Francisco School of Law abutted Golden Gate Park, where Barton and Jordan strolled down a hill with the tendons in their ankles working hard against the grade. Passing under towering pines and redwoods, the ground leveled off and they strode onto the wide green lawn before the park's Victorian greenhouse, a fairy-tale castle with ornate white spires and high arched windows. The air in California had a different smell than in Florida – fresher, somehow, heady with pine resin and the rich loam of the soil. Clouds of cool mist and swirls of fog rolled inland off the Pacific.

Jordan turned her head to look at her boyfriend as their footsteps pattered softly along the ground, thinking that the term *boyfriend* had grown more than stale. It had begun to wear on her nerves. It made her feel old, which seemed an unfair emotion.

"Can we talk?" she asked, tilting her head. She had on a bright yellow blouse and a denim skirt, dangling silver earrings set with jade, and a necklace strung with tiny olive seashells. Her toenails, painted a lighter shade of jade to match her earrings, peeked out from her hemp sandals.

Inhaling the strawberry scent of her through her clothes, Barton felt his guts loosen. In his experience the phrase, *we need to talk*, never heralded good news. Had she met someone? Was she leaving him?

Did she have cancer? That was it! His girl with her pink hands and slender ankles and her laugh like a waterfall – she was dying!

"Please don't look at me like that," she said.

"Sorry." Barton shook his head as if to shake out worry. He'd cut his hair since college, though a few shaggy blond curls still peaked out from behind his well-formed, rather small ears. He had on black converse sneakers, jeans with holes worn through at the knee, and a black sleeveless T-shirt with Bob Marley's face embossed on it. "You're freaking me out," he said.

"Relax, Barton – you're the tensest person I know. You're like a drawn bow."

"I'm a natural wire. It's true."

"Listen. In the greater scheme of things, this is nothing."

"Uh-oh."

"What?"

"It sounds bad."

"I'm trying to sort a few things out," she said.

"Is it sexual?" he asked, lowering his voice. "You want some strange?"

She stopped on the path and stared at him, fixing him with her blue eyes and frowning mightily. "Are you insane?"

"It's that guy in Constitutional Law, isn't it? The Swedish God, the swimmer with the body – "

"Barton, what in God's name are you talking about?"

"I don't know." They started walking again, passing a bed of purple crocuses bordered with daffodils. The red pagoda of the Japanese tea house rose in the distance before the pointy tops of a blue spruce. A jogger in a shiny track suit huffed past, trailing a pungent reek.

"Our sex life is fine."

"Only fine?"

"Terrific then." She rolled her eyes. "My word, Barton."

Inwardly, he kicked himself. He knew better. They made a point of not bragging to one another about their outstanding sex life.

This was something she had also come to understand. To be a success at anything you had to keep secrets, and aside from her infidelities with Helmut, her deepest secret was her heartfelt conviction, somehow sexual in nature, since it was entertained alone and with her own eyes averted, that she was destined to become . . . *a great artist.*

And yet she knew better than to name such knowledge. Putting words on it would curse it, so she treasured the wonder inside, sheltering it like a solitary candle.

She accepted that she might be suffering from delusions of grandeur, but the only way to find out would be to work her herself raw. "I'm not afraid of failing," she said, "it's eating your own liver that's hard."

Barton felt a great weight come off his shoulders. His chest expanded. "Well, any fool can be a lawyer," he said. "Learn to spot the issues, take a bar review course and you're in business. But art — that takes talent."

"I hope not," she said. "Because no one's ever said I had any. Anyhow, I'll still take the bar . . . but . . . the life of an artist . . . I mean . . . it sounds so pretentious, doesn't it? It's not what people think. It's a grind beyond belief. Full-on obsessive compulsive. I want to warn you, honey." She stopped talking. "Is that the kind of wife you want?"

Barton's head rang like the gong in the Japanese tea house. "The kind of *life* I want?"

"*Wife,*" she said in a small voice, very unlike her own. She scuffed the toe of her sandal on the edge of the path, taking great interest in a clod of dirt.

"*Wife?*" Barton stood alongside a bed of red tulips bordered by yellow roses. Somehow, he'd stopped understanding English. Over the crown of Jordan's head, a prehistoric-looking fern sprouted from the earth. Its leaves were emerald, tapering to delicate tips. A shiver zippered up Barton's spine.

Jordan blushed. She couldn't look at him.

He set his hands on her warm shoulders. "Jordan. Are you proposing to me?"

Ducking out from under his hands, she got down on one knee and spread out her arms. She might've been doing a Vaudeville act, except she was serious. She turned up her oval face and widened her eyes. Flecked with silver, her corneas reflected the low clouds scudding overhead. Barton fell into them, lost in the sky.

"Barton Squire, will you marry me?"

His mouth fell open.

"Don't leave a girl on her knees, honey." She glanced down the path. "It's unbecoming."

"My God. Yes, Jordan!"

He took her hand and helped her to her feet and she said, "Well, *that's* settled," and together they continued arm in arm toward the red pagoda of the tea house.

"I am as high," he said, sucking in the cool piney air as they walked through the empty seats surrounding the band shell, "as the proverbial kite."

"Well, come back to earth, Big Bart, cause there's more."

"Oh?"

"I won't be joining Knight and Squire."

Overhead the clouds broke apart and a shaft of sun lit Jordan's hair, which gleamed like something polished. Barton had a wild urge to wrap its flaxen strands around his head.

"Absolutely," he heard himself say. He wondered what he was talking about.

A frown creased her face but she shook it off. She had a moment of fear for his future clients, but given the bombshells she was dropping she supposed he could be forgiven for drifting off. His head was in the clouds, quite literally. So was hers.

"Wow," said Barton. He blinked at her. Words failed him. The sun shone warmly on his face, illuminating the interior of his skull. He seemed to be in the midst of a religious experience.

She held his gaze. Ever so slightly cross-eyed, her ocean-colored orbs confounded him, so that he felt as dizzy as if he'd got into a staring contest with a Siamese cat.

"And you say you still want to take the bar exam?"

"After three years in Kafka-land? Hell yeah. I put in my hours – same as you and Helmut."

"But you don't want to practice?"

"I'll still do legal aid, not-for-profits, environmental stuff. Greenpeace, if they need me."

"Wow."

"I'll do some tax shelters, too. This woman's got to eat."

Barton didn't say anything.

"You're not upset?"

"No. I'm still taking it in."

"It's absurd. I realize that. And old-fashioned, too, huh? I mean, it's like announcing I've devoted my life to scrimshaw. Juggling. Mime . . . I don't know. *'I'm a painter'* sounds asinine when you say it out loud."

"No, it doesn't."

"No?" She arched her tawny eyebrows. "Your parents will think I mean *house* painter."

Gazing at his future wife – *his wife!* – Barton's spine ached. What a face. He loved that face. He'd have stood by her if she'd declared a plan to crochet a ladder to the moon.

"Kick ass and take names," he said. "To hell with the world. It's our one and only life, hon. Blink and you'll miss it."

The ragged edge of a cloud obscured the sun and a fine, stinging mist began falling out of a sky the color of pewter. The air took on a chill it never had in Florida, as if the Pacific had more authority than the Atlantic.

"One last detail," she said. "Though I hesitate to mention it."

Barton clenched his teeth, awaiting some godawful confession regarding Helmut and their college days. He'd hoped to be spared this, but no . . . full disclosure loomed like the angry-looking storm clouds now massing in the west.

"I won't make much of the folding stuff. Not until I get into a decent gallery."

"Not a problem," he said. "It'll still be Kelly, Knight and Squire – then you can work when you want."

"Better clear that with Helmut."

Barton turned his head and pretended to spit, suggesting Helmut's opinions were moot.

"I can't leach off my family," she said, "and I'll pay off my own student loans and buy my own art supplies, but – "

He pressed the tips of his fingers to her soft lips. "Say no more, lover. I've got your back. Always will." They kissed in the rain. "Let's celebrate," he said. "Let's score some champagne!"

The rain increased with a rushing sound and soaked their clothes.

Jordan said, "That's just it, honey. I've got to go home and paint. The muse is on me."

"I get it, baby."

"Go ahead," she said. "Tie one on for me at The Bullfrog. Call Helmut."

"Our best man, I suppose."

She raised the back of her hand to her forehead in mock horror. "God help us."

Barton snuffed through his nose. "Imagine him in a tuxedo!"

"You sure you won't be mad if I go paint?"

"Never! All else passes, or some such."

"You sure? We just got engaged."

He cupped her face in his hands and peered into her eyes. "Jordan, I swear I get it. You're marrying me but you married Art first, right?"

She nodded. The rain was darkening her hair from gold to wheat and pasting her curls to her face. "I did," she said.

"Course you know he'll beat you up."

"Beat me up? Art's going to kick my ass, black my eyes, break my nose – you name it."

"But you love him anyway."

"Art can be violent," she said. "But I need a beating. Hell, I *want* one!"

"Then get in a few licks yourself. Fight dirty!"

She jumped forward and pressed her warm laughing mouth to his and then she was off, her hair dripping against her back as she bounded along the path, working her way up the hill beyond the beds of tulips and daffodils.

Barton felt as if he had no body. If the soul exists, he thought, trembling through his bones, *I'm feeling mine right now.* The background hum of the universe, he thought. Creation's echo. He had to stop himself from bursting into song.

Halfway up the hill, in a stand of dripping pine trees, his love halted and turned around. She waved at him in the rain. Barton stood grinning, getting drenched, watching her.

She'd painted the happiest man alive.

3

Disorderly Conduct

"In high school I was an exchange student in Sweden, in tenth grade?" In her youth Jordan had a vocal tic, born of not wanting to brag, of ending her sentences with an upward curve in her voice, as if she were asking a question or checking the details of her own story. "And in Sweden they let you touch the artifacts in museums, like spear points and axes? But the coolest thing was this wagon wheel from the Middle Ages, from around 1200. The spokes and the wheel were wired down to a display, but you could run your fingers over the wood. It was all gray and smooth? I mean, I touched the Middle Ages! With my fingers running along those wooden spokes I could feel what the carpenter felt. His work. So it was a human connection. Across history? It was wild."

Helmut cleared the phlegm from his throat and seemed to stare at her through his hairy nostrils. She'd been explaining the chief example in her term paper.

"I give up," she said, exasperated. Her ears flushed bright pink. "God's right in front of you." She was shouting. "Just open your goddamn eyes!"

"Good heavens," Helmut said, feigning offense, "reign in thy tongue, woman."

"What the hell. You're a hostile reader. You're not even trying."

"Please. This is some Freudian thing I don't even want to get near. But answer me one question – why do you need a Daddy who lives in the sky?" He slid her paper across the desk as if it might dirty his fingers. He spoke as though to a wayward child. "And take it out of that plastic cover. You're not in high school."

"I'm following instructions," she lied, mortified by the cover and worse, by the artwork which adorned it, a garish sunset she'd painstakingly drawn with colored pencils, "but the conscious mind arises from an *un*conscious intelligence and – when did you say Barton would be back?"

Helmut cocked his head to the side, then yawned and stretched his skinny arms over his head. He had on pleated khaki pants and a white Oxford shirt, unbuttoned to show off the tuft of hair between his small chest muscles. "They go out for margaritas after class. I hear they really tie one on. Orgies. Ritual sacrifice. It's a scene, man."

"I guess he'll be late then?"

Helmut nodded. His mousy brown hair, parted in a chalky line running down the center of his head, fell in long wispy strands to his shoulders. At twenty-two, his locks were already thinning. "*Real* late," he said, leering, raising his nose and sniffing the air. He smiled slyly.

"Uh-oh," she said, and stared at the flecks of lint on the carpet. Then both of them started panting because they knew what they wanted to do. His dark stare held some mysterious power over her, an animal magnetism she couldn't understand.

"Get on that bed," he said. His eyes glinted and then they were on Barton's bed, tugging at each other's clothes and grunting. Helmut produced a condom in a gold foil wrapper. He tore it open with his teeth and tossed the wrapper off the side of the bed. Unseen, gravity locked it inside the bed's metal frame.

Their tryst was over in the time it takes to smoke a cigarette.

Helmut sat up in bed with Barton's thick down comforter bunched up in his lap, producing a small white stain which his roommate would later stare at in bewilderment. "So was that a mother lode?" Helmut asked, preening.

Naked, Jordan stood and felt his insolent eyes rove over her body. Quickly, she slipped on her panties and, picking up the pile of her jeans, she hopped from one foot to the other and crammed herself into the worn, tight-fitting fabric. She faced him topless. "Not even a nugget," she said. Helmut stared at her breasts, which looked alert, with inquisitive pink nipples.

"I'm sorry," he said from the bed, glancing into her eyes. "Did you say something?"

Jordan retrieved her bra and picked up a T-shirt with GREENPEACE embossed on the front. She turned her away to dress, feeling Helmut's eyes poke her in the rear.

"I'm sure I don't need to tell you to shut up about this," she said, keeping her back turned. Helmut's gaze rose to the delicate flutes of her shoulder bones.

"I understand," he said, leaning forward on his elbows and reaching out to pinch her firm right buttock between his thumb and index finger, "Psyche speaks!"

Jordan yipped like a puppy. The pain woke up her conscience. *Agenbite of inwit.* Why did she act the way she did? Why did anybody? Perhaps she'd simply been created without good character.

It had all begun so innocently, as guilty acts so often do. She'd written a paper for her Comparative Religion class on the existence of God and she wanted Barton to proof it (this in the days when college students still labored over typewriters) except she'd forgotten he'd be at his evening seminar on Romantic Poetry.

At the dorm she found Helmut working on a paper for the same class. His was titled, "Corpse of the Almighty."

And then things had come to this unlikely pass . . .

That's what Helmut had meant when he asked if their sex was a "mother lode." He'd horned in on the private language she shared with Barton, a metaphor they'd adapted from Nabokov and which had gotten mixed up with a history Barton had read on the gold rush in California. In this case, "dust" described an acute perception, a flash in the space between moments – say the sudden silence which might puncture the excited babble of a party, when everyone stopped talking and stared at each other, mouths agape – that instant, Barton claimed half-seriously, when an angel flew past.

A "nugget" lasted longer – when the universe held so still you could take a bite out of space-time, when the watcher and the watched became one. Last came the "mother lode," a succession of nuggets which became a vein in memory, the future's treasure.

Dust. Nugget. Mother lode. Gold stars pasted on to the black pages of age and death.

Only one problem: though you might search the hills for ore, you couldn't mine the gold, any more than you could stare directly at the sun. Treasure-moments just had to happen.

Now, as Jordan slipped on her sandals, Helmut had staked his claim on this private code, though he thought the metaphor painfully obvious. It was the sort of sentimental cliché his roommate adored.

Naked, he climbed out of bed and slapped himself happily on the buttocks. "Well, it was a nugget for me, baby. Hell, a mother lode!"

Jordan shook out her hair impatiently. His comment didn't amuse her, as it alluded to her paper's thesis: that sense perception constituted proof of God's existence. The experience *was* the message. You stood in the sun loving life and you knew you'd *remember* standing in the sun loving life. What else did you expect? The archangel Michael in golden clouds of glory proclaiming, *There is a God*. No. God wouldn't be gaudy.

Her paper would later receive an A, although one of the professor's comments would stun her. In green ink, he wrote, "You're arguing in terms which don't support a logical argument. In my opinion, faith is non-rational, and cannot be 'proven.'"

What struck her was not the criticism but the professor's self-conscious remark: that "in my opinion," a disclaimer designed to spare her tender sensibilities but which left her feeling patronized. Furious, she decided that if people couldn't see the Deity in a dandelion, such was their loss. She was sorry she couldn't explain it better, but she wasn't the missionary type.

Helmut zipped up his fly and chuckled. Jordan scowled as he pulled on his shirt, tearing out a few long hairs which fluttered to the carpet.

"That was awesome, dude." He dug his feet into his sneakers, straightened up and saluted her.

Jordan sighed.

Glancing in the mirror over Barton's bed, Helmut ran his fingers through his hair, tilting his head first one way and then the other. Satisfied, he clucked his tongue and shrugged. One thing about Helmut, you couldn't call him vain. He looked how he looked, he figured, and the world was lucky to have him, however he appeared.

"Tell Barton I left him half the pizza," he said, shouldering a blue canvas backpack stuffed with books, "– as instructed." He lingered. "Or you could eat it yourself, I guess."

Jordan set her hands on her hips and met his hawk-faced stare, his bold brown eyes. Having got what he wanted, she was history. She suppressed a scream. What could you do with a man like this? He had no conscience, or if he did it was toothless. For him, guilt was a whining child, begging to be slapped.

"Goodbye, Helmut. I don't need to tell you – "

He held up his hand in a "stop" signal. "Don't insult me, Jordie."

Hearing his footsteps fade, she sat on the edge of the bed and held her head in her hands. Her tears weren't for herself or even her boyfriend, but for God Himself, who didn't exist. Helmut had broken up their relationship. Because he was right. Her paper was sophomoric. God was dead and she had proved it. God hadn't seen her sin. Never had, never would. Might as well admit it. Humanity's sweet dream, and hers, was over.

Sliding along the bed to the desk, she grabbed her paper and tore it length-wise into strips, letting them flutter into the wastebasket.

Watching them fall, she wondered if she would go to hell for cheating on her One True Love. Without God, there was no hell, right? But there might be a Devil. In fact, she felt one beginning to stir inside her. The Kandinskys and Van Goghs papering the walls spun in a poisonous whirl of color. She pressed her palm to her forehead, unsurprised to find herself burning, her skull filled with a hell of her own making.

Biting her lip, she thought, come *on*. Get hold of yourself. Men! They had to shoulder *some* of the blame. They glorified sex to inflate their own egos, because with all their jealousy they thought more about their own honor, if you could call it that, than the women they said they loved.

Barton and Helmut wanted to mark her like territory, fence her with *no trespassing* signs. They wanted to own her, as if she were a hot property.

So what did that make her? Part of the farm? A cow? A sow? The south forty?

On Barton's desk she found the end of a joint in an ashtray and lit it with the lighter she discovered in the top drawer. She focused on nothing but the moment, thinking, *I am sitting cross-legged on the bed. I am lighting a roach. I am smoking a roach. I am inhaling. I am getting high. I am a cheating bitch. I am a fucking whore.*

She blew a smoke ring which grew larger as it drifted through the motionless air. Bending forward she puckered her lips and sucked it back into her mouth, then she stubbed out the joint and stood up and walked to the bathroom and turned on the shower and put her hand in the stream.

Waiting for the water to heat, she stripped off her sandals, jeans, panties and T-shirt, and hung them on a towel rack. The tile was cold against her bare feet and raised gooseflesh on her thighs. Testing the water with her instep, she found it hot and stepped into the shower. The spray felt like a rain of dull needles. Thin clouds enveloped her body and she wished she could disappear, rise upward like the steam and vanish into the air, like vapor, be anywhere but where she was, standing over a dirty drain with its foamy suds making a tiny whirlpool, with Helmut's come dripping warmly down her leg.

Along with her self-restraint, the condom had burst.

Why, oh why, had she cheated? She and Barton had founded a Civilization of Two. They'd created their own language and culture. The Civilization filled him utterly, yet on some days she choked on it, finding their world claustrophobic. On those days he'd follow her around wanting to know what was wrong and how to fix it.

"Getting away from me would be a start."

The look on his face!

"Please don't make me into an idol," she said gently. "It's oppressive. I've just got to be *me* for a while, all right?"

Barton cut his eyes away from her.

"Come *on*, Big Bart, quit acting so *wounded*."

Ah, that voice. It wasn't hers. It belonged to some demon bawling from inside her rotten heart. Barton conjured it somehow, with his innocence, his privilege, his lack-of-suffering. Nothing really bad had ever happened to him. In the face of the heavy load of emotional scar tissue *she* carried, he hauled about a feather's worth.

The shower reddened her skin. I'm like Eve, she thought. I've eaten the apple and the apple is Helmut. She could still taste the salt of him on her tongue. And what a bitter, garden-killing flavor it was. Pah! She spat into the drain and scrubbed his come off her thigh with an evil-smelling washcloth.

Turning off the shower, she stepped out of the stall and toweled off her long-limbed body.

She had no excuses, not even lust. For earlier – *that day* – Barton had reduced her to a quivering heap. Mr. Homework had actually read up on cunnilingus and had startled her with his new-found skills, his patience, his natural aptitude. What *was* he doing down there? When his face finally surfaced, rising between her thighs and grinning stupidly, she'd lost count.

"Dust?" he asked, wiping his mouth with the back of his hand.

"Nugget," she said, panting. "Jesus. Mother lode."

Later, returning to his dorm so that he could read her paper, she found Helmut instead and . . . God!

His bold dark gaze depraved her, excited her, lured her, promising secret sexual knowledge, whiffs of the exotic and the foreign, opening the gate on a private garden, a forbidden tree. He *was* her apple – bitterly sweet. Her teeth pierced his skin and her tongue caressed his flesh. Her throat worked and she gulped his bitter seed. Oh, the pleasures of vandalism. Who could resist wrecking paradise? He had a power over her she couldn't name, and because she couldn't name it, its intensity grew until she believed that through surrender she might discover the cause of his magnetism, the source of his pull, the energy of his composition.

Why, he didn't even care that he was getting sloppy seconds.

Barton's key scratched in the lock. Naked and guilty, she glanced up, hearing him call her name through the bathroom door. Her whole body blushed.

He'd never suspect her, but she'd scrubbed herself raw anyway, with such holy water as she could find.

4

LARCENY

AFTER Barton and Helmut read "The Charismatic Close" at the law conference in Kansas, Barton and his wife renewed their attack on Mount Sobriety, eyeing its summit with a mixture of hope and despair. They'd made their base camp in San Francisco, as far back as law school, when pounding hangovers had ceased to be a source of low-brow amusement. Prior to enlisting in AA, they'd maintained the balance in their lives by becoming alcohol accountants. They audited themselves, crediting every ounce, debiting every excess. They followed a protocol. No drinking on an empty stomach. No getting drunk two days in a row. Above all, no shots.

Like a time bomb, the system ticked until they entered "the program." Both liked AA, although as a Buddhist, Barton felt hypocritical when the praying and hand-holding started, since in Buddhism *you* were your own higher power, without ego – not exactly an easy concept to convey at a meeting of tattered, tortured souls.

In any case, they hadn't signed on as lifelong members and, growing weary of rock-bottom stories, the ravaged faces and endless histories of woe, they'd slowly let the "hello-my-name-is" business slip from their lives.

Meanwhile Helmut never broke stride. He drank more than he

ever had – Crystal and Dom Perignon – sucked down at 35,000 feet in the company jet, in constant celebration of his success as he soared over all the potential defendants below.

Then one day, when Helmut was warmly lit and Barton precariously sober, Helmut called his partner into his office. He had the corner now, with its floor-to-ceiling windows, its view of the wide green lawn, the leafy canopy of the live oak towering over their sign, and the white-capped, blue river beyond.

Barton, looking sharp and upright in his navy suit and the white shirt he'd ironed that morning, stood before Helmut's mahogany desk, which Graciela had polished to a mirror-like sheen. In its surface, Barton was startled by how glum his face looked. He tried smiling, but the effect was ghastly. Staying sober without the hand-holding wasn't easy, even for a Buddhist. About that he had no denial.

Helmut cleared his throat and ran his finger around the inside of his collar. He had on a wrinkled gray business suit with a soiled white shirt and a silver tie with a diamond clip. The gem was worth more than Graciela made in a year.

"We've been friends a long time, Big Bart, so this isn't easy."

Barton shifted his weight from one foot to the other, scratching his Achilles tendon with the toe of his shoe. He hadn't been invited to sit down on Helmut's sleek new Danish couch, handcrafted from the wood of endangered trees. Instead he stood before his old roommate like a freshman law clerk. In his hand he held a coffee cup with "I'm from New York – What's Your Excuse?" emblazoned on the side.

"I'm glad you think we're still friends, Helmut. I suppose it's very adult of us – considering."

"Indeed."

Barton sipped his coffee and scalded his upper lip, burning off a small flap of skin. What sort of pompous fool, he wondered, actually used the word "indeed" in conversation?

Helmut smiled tightly. He was a man who seldom looked

uncomfortable. He was in control of himself and his circumstances, and yet now . . . perspiration beaded his upper lip.

The hair on the back of Barton's neck stood up and his skin itched under his shirt. Had Helmut's color begun to rise? Impossible. Too much gin before breakfast, Barton thought, but no – there was something else.

He had the disturbing sensation that his entire life had been leading up to this moment, some crowning humiliation. His forehead went hot, but maybe it was only the coffee boiling in his stomach. He set down his cup on the desk and Helmut eyed it disapprovingly. Barton picked it up.

"Don't look that way, Barton. You did this to yourself. Taking all those long-shot cases with their doe-eyed plaintiffs. What – "

"Long shot?"

"The gimp. The paralytic."

"That driver was negligent. Open and shut." Barton sipped his coffee, which remained superheated.

"Who says otherwise?" Helmut said mildly. "That's not the issue." Without waiting for a rebuttal he began leafing through a folder. Barton stared at his partner's head, glinting under the recessed lighting. His hand tightened on the cup's handle and he saw himself swinging it onto the center of that unsuspecting dome until his partner was no more than a pile of blood and brains.

In legal terms, his crime was "inchoate." That is, uncommitted. Still, and this shamed him, just *the thought* of murdering Helmut raised his spirits.

"Joint and several liability," Barton explained. "*Ergo,* we add the deep-pocket defendant. Change the venue, name the Department of Transportation for negligence, and we're golden."

Helmut busied himself inspecting a settlement offer. "Am I to infer your client has no insurance?"

Barton scalded his tongue. He wanted desperately to spit and then soothe his burnt mouth with an ice cube.

Helmut looked up and frowned. "What's that? Speak up, Counselor."

"No insurance," Barton said quietly. "That's why we want the Department."

Helmut clapped his hands. "Okay. But you weren't thinking of taking the jet to Vermont, were you?"

"That's where the deep pocket lives."

"For one thing I've reserved it for my trip to Napa, and for another – " He slid a paper across his desk and his voice took on the courtroom edge he used to flay hostile witnesses. "Read 'em and weep, Counselor. You can't sue city hall in Vermont."

Stunned, his partner read the statute. A state agency could be sued, but not without the defendant's consent, an unlikely proposition.

"That is one dipshit freshman error!" Helmut roared. "Kee-rist!"

"My mistake," Barton admitted, sweating, "I apologize. But if I show up they'll settle. They can't *not* settle when they see the pictures. God, Helmut, he's just a kid. His face is mangled. He can't walk."

"And if they don't? Even if you win against those yokels in . . . where was it? Vermont? Land of sap suckers and tree huggers? The appellate court will reverse."

"The kid doesn't even have a decent wheelchair. He's fifteen years old. A lifetime of care. He's still a virgin – and with a busted spine he always will be. You're telling me that's not pain and suffering?"

"So blow him. Get him a whore! I don't care. Jesus, Barton, this is a major law firm. It's not Kelly, Knight and Squire anymore. I don't care what it says on the sign. Now read my lips: *Pro bono – consumatum est.* We're not running a charity, understand? We're here to make money."

"Gee, and I always thought this was a soup kitchen."

"On your bike, Barton. Take the day off. Take the week off."

"There's more to lawyering than the bottom line," Barton said, and cringed, hearing himself. "There's room for compassion." Even in his own ears, his voice sounded self-righteous, yet he believed in *pro bono* work, in defending the poor, the downtrodden. He'd sworn as much when he passed the bar and became an officer of the court.

Helmut didn't say anything and fixed his partner with his unblinking stare, full now, of undisguised hatred. His eyes were like pincers. Barton shook his head and Helmut smirked, seeing his stare draw blood. This was his talent. First he shrank people, then he bled them. And in the legal world, when Goliath appeared, David settled.

Relenting, Helmut rolled a pen between his fingers. The pen was made out of gold and his signature was engraved along its length. "I wasn't going to say anything . . . but we both know it isn't working out, don't we?"

"What're you – breaking up with me?"

"This isn't funny, Big Bart."

"Fuck off, Helmut."

Helmut pretended he hadn't heard anything. "You're not fitting into Colin, Lanus and Gart," he said, "and they are the owners of Kelly, Knight and Squire, in case you've forgotten."

"Helmut, don't do it. You and I were the ones who dreamt up this place."

"Unfortunately it's not ours anymore. Or don't you recall signing a contract to that effect?"

"It's ours in spirit."

Helmut opened his mouth to laugh, then closed it and sighed, shaking his head. "True enough, but that doesn't change the law. Or the ownership. Consult an attorney if you like."

"I have obligations, Helmut. My parents can't get by on social security. I subsidize their prescriptions. They need me. I have a mortgage." Embarrassed, he shut his mouth. He was babbling.

Helmut played with his gold pen, touching it to his colorless lips. He appeared to be resting his case. Reflected on the desk, Barton's face looked as if he'd just received a life sentence.

"I helped *found* this firm, remember?"

"Then you shouldn't have agreed to sell it, my friend. Or didn't you notarize your signature?"

Barton closed his eyes and rested in the reddish dark behind his eyelids. He couldn't believe this was happening, although he understood that a sense of injustice was not a legal defense.

When he opened his eyes, he found himself shaking. He set his coffee cup on the shiny desk, while his partner, his *former* partner, frowned at the ring it would leave.

"Helmut, so help me, if you fire me I'll – "

Helmut's eyes flashed and he shoved his gold pen back into its holder. "You'll what?"

"I'll wipe that goddamn smirk off your face!"

Helmut laughed boomingly and leaned back in his chair, squeaking the leather. "Relax, Counselor." He gestured toward his couch. "Now sit your ass down." Barton sat on the couch while Helmut laced his fingers together over his paunch. "Nobody's firing anybody," he said. "Jesus, you're so dramatic. I mean, I ask you here out of loyalty – *out of friendship* – in order to save your ass, and this – "

"So you're not firing me?"

Helmut cupped his hand to his ear and turned his head. "Christ, is there an echo in here or is it just me?" He straightened the lapels of his rumpled suit. He appeared to have worn it for several days, with the shirt going yellow around the collar. Look, it seemed to say, I'm so slick I can *afford* to be a slob. "The Big Three came to see me this morning, and they want you gone. You're a bleeding heart, they say." Removing his gold pen from the holder again, he absentmindedly tapped his bottom teeth with it. "You've become a liability, I'm told."

Barton cleared his throat. "Colin too?"

"Oh, he put in a word for you – not that Lanus and Gart were persuaded."

"Why's that?"

"You didn't hear?"

"Evidently not."

Helmut rotated his index finger around his right ear, indicating insanity. "Good old Alexander Colin's got the brain rot. Alzheimer's. Early diagnosis, asymptomatic. Anyhow, who's going to take him seriously? *Non compos mentis,* eh?"

"That's terrible," Barton said, feeling his own troubles shrink by comparison. "We just had him over for dinner and he never said a word. Jordan loves the guy. He always wants to see her new paintings. She thinks he's lonely."

Helmut shrugged. "He's about to get lonelier. Lanus and Gart want him gone, too." He met his friend's eye. "The both of you."

"But he's a genius."

"Irrelevant. How can you try a case when your lead counsel's got one foot on a banana peel and the other in a coffin?"

Like a good Buddhist, Barton put aside his own troubles and pictured his boss – his friend, Alexander Colin – bathed in the gold light of compassion. Poor Alex! Thrown out on his ear after a lifetime of service.

Helmut banged his desk with the flat of his hand and said, "Jesus, *are you crying?*"

Barton blinked. "My name's not Jesus, and no, I – "

Helmut pursed his lips and eyed the ceiling. He held up his hands in supplication. "Please tell me, oh Lord, what have I done to deserve this?" He leveled his gaze at Barton. "*I'm* the one who took the bullet for you, Big Bart – not Alexander-the-Great-Colin. I'm telling you. He's out of the loop. For good."

"So here we are."

Helmut nodded. "Indeed," he said.

That it had come to this! Once Barton had imagined a brilliant future at a Manhattan law firm, dreaming that after they sold their partnership they'd launch themselves into The Show – The Big Time in The Big Apple.

But then Jordan quit all but her *pro bono* practice, donating hope to the hopeless, and somehow they'd all become middle-aged. Jordan had her painting, but Barton was stranded on a professional plateau awaiting the transformative event which never came. Whereas Helmut would march his shining bald head into the office every morning acting as if he *had* made The Big Time. Watching him strut before the secretaries, Barton's hands tingled. He wanted to smash something.

Say . . . a skull?

The law delayed him. Buddhism delayed him. Worse, his violent fantasies filled him with shame. Either he ought to rise above them, or he ought to act, ought to kill.

But that was illegal. Anyway, was it Helmut's fault if Barton found life disappointing? Little Barton, the smartest boy in class, the teacher's pet. Great things had been expected of him, but what had he become?

Heart surgeon? Distinguished author? Concert violinist?

A lawyer. Professional parasite. But what could he do? At his age he was stuck. Best put a torch to the dreams of youth. Burn them down and good riddance.

Because there was more.

He knew that in the top drawer of his desk, Helmut kept a bottle of specialty stain remover. Add this to the in-need-of-legal-counsel-aspiring-model, on her knees or in a prone position and . . . one gets the idea. Barton could've had one too, but even if he hadn't been smitten with his wife, he didn't operate that way. A man of principle, he wouldn't stoop to adultery. He'd never be like Helmut. A man had to rise above his instincts. Otherwise, face it. People were primates. Shit-flingers. Baboons.

Helmut cleared his throat and spat into his wastebasket. "So . . . you know you can't remain a partner, right?"

Barton swallowed, feeling his throat knot up. "Sure, Helmut, I saw it in my crystal ball last night."

"You think this is funny? You're lucky you've even got a job. Gart's after your ass, I'm telling you. And he's not the only one."

"That include you?"

Helmut's eyes widened. He wasn't an easy man to surprise, but this had startled him.

"Did you miss my summation? I'm the one saving your job, dipstick. If it wasn't for me you'd be writing an application at the public defender's office."

Barton raised his coffee cup to his lips and drained it, feeling fine, black grit lodge in his teeth.

Helmut said, "Do your job, that's all I'm asking."

"I'm aware of my duties."

"I'm sure you are. But you don't . . . umm, what can I say? *Perform* them."

Barton frowned and shifted his weight from one buttock to the other. "You've lost me."

"Turklovsky."

"Oh. That."

"Yeah. *That.*"

Helmut had him. The last time Barton fell off the wagon he was too hung over to get out of bed and missed a bankruptcy hearing. Worse, it was a deep pocket case Helmut had thrown him, a rare favor. Afterwards, outside the conference room where the senior partners held court, Barton overheard the words "malpractice," and "disbarment."

"So anyway," Helmut said, "we've decided that you're going to work as my assistant, do the leg work on the big cases. That all right with you?"

"*We've* decided?"

"Okay. *I've* decided. That better? Lanus and Gart have brought me on board as a senior partner."

The two former colleagues regarded each other over Helmut's desk. Neither man blinked.

Once second they'd been college roommates writing term papers, and the next, Helmut was his boss. The things that happened when you didn't pay attention! Father Time marched right on by.

The only up side to the passing years was that while Helmut had grown a cannon-ball-sized gut, Barton had stayed thin, though his cropped blond hair was going gray at his temples.

And, of course, it was Barton who'd captured the heart of Jordan Kelly. He touched the gold ring on his finger.

Helmut's mouth slowly turned up at the corners. "Want me to break the bad news to the wife?"

Keeping his voice level, Barton said, "Nice of you to ask, but I'll handle it. And since we're on the subject of full disclosure, let me advise you of something."

"Proceed," said Helmut, without interest.

Barton waited. His new boss picked up a file and started thumbing pages.

Barton said, "I'm considering a murder – specifically, it would be yours, you cocksucker."

Helmut's eyes darted up from the file. He was smiling, trying not to laugh. "*Cocksucker?*" he asked. He raised his eyebrows. His voice had a lilt in it. His eyes twinkled.

Barton blushed and, feeling his face go hot, blushed more deeply. For all his size, his hours in the gym and his powerful arms, he wasn't a fighter. He might fool other men, but Helmut had known him too long. Before his former roommate's unblinking stare, Barton felt found out – naked and unmanned.

He covered himself with a joke. "Great meeting," he said, rising, "send me the minutes."

"Don't forget your cup!" Helmut called cheerfully.

Barton turned and snatched it off the desk, noting it had not left a ring.

Outside in the hall, he closed the door so that it latched precisely with a singled well-tumbled click.

Threaten the man's life and he mocked you! Barton felt like howling, but instead he stood there holding his empty cup, while a row of secretaries glanced up from their computers. He couldn't look at them.

From behind his door, Helmut yammered into the phone in his confident baritone while Barton slunk down the hall. Out of pity, the secretaries furiously shuffled their papers and averted their eyes. They liked him, because aside from Mr. Colin, he was the only lawyer who ever gave Christmas presents – magnums of Crystal champagne. He was also the only lawyer who let the staff call him by his first name, a lapse in discipline not appreciated by the senior partners, and now . . . Helmut.

Knight, thought Barton, takes Squire.

Checkmate.

Objection!

Overruled!

Inside his airless, windowless office, hideously aglow with fluorescent lighting, he squatted down and dug into his filing cabinet, looking for the Turlovsky folder. He couldn't find it. And he knew he'd never find it. Since he'd been drinking at the time he might've stored it anywhere – in his truck, in Jordan's studio, at the bottom of the river. His knees hurt and, finding nothing but a gray layer of dust, he was about to stand up when something caught his eye.

Swooning, he remembered what it felt like to be twenty-three years old. In his hand he held a flashcard from law school. He blinked at it, astonished he'd managed to preserve it when so many other things had been lost, swept away by the broom of blackouts past.

Giddy with nostalgia, he ran his finger down the edge of the card, now as yellow as parchment. A study aid, he and Helmut had used it for their Criminal Law exam. On one side, written in black capital letters, stood a single word:

LARCENY

He didn't need to turn it over. He knew the definition by heart.

Larceny: the trespassory taking and carrying away of the personal property of another with the intent permanently to deprive the owner thereof.

Checking his answer, he fanned his face with the card and thought, *What shit I've stuffed in my brain!* He should've chosen a different profession. He should've learned a trade – unclogged septic systems, practiced mortuary science – anything but law. Lawyers were leeches. Feeders on misery.

Then too, Graciela probably didn't relish scrubbing the men's room urinals, but what choice did she have? Barton had nothing *but* choices. And this was the best he could manage? Sick with self-loathing, he tossed the card into his wastebasket. His hands trembled.

Back in his office, Helmut would've already forgotten him. Helmut didn't dwell, didn't obsess . . . not like Barton.

The man has no heart, Barton thought. Helmut's emotional vocabulary didn't contain passion – it was too time-consuming – not to mention expensive, although he enjoyed observing it in others.

"Larceny," Barton said softly. He sat down at his desk, constructed of particle board with a faux wood finish. He pressed his fingers into his eyes. "Larceny," he whispered, removing his fingers. *Trespass.* His eyes widened. He sat up straight. "Helmut stole my life," he said.

A laugh, a sob, caught in his throat. He touched his wedding ring. "Helmut stole my wife."

5

HEIRS OF THE BODY

LIKE millions of stoic, lonely men, Helmut stood in front of his stove after work, frying his dinner in a pan. He'd put himself on a diet, one that featured plenty of protein and fat. He hadn't lost any weight, but he liked the program. It required iron discipline, but he was up to it – in this case a pound of bacon.

Using a wooden spoon, he turned over the pink and white strips of flesh bubbling in a layer of grease. Sighing, he felt as if the meaty smell were coating his frayed nerves. For contrary to what Barton imagined, he *did* have an emotional life.

The life of the worker. Stirring his bacon, he recalled that once he'd believed he'd been born for something more, something historical, something great. Now, at forty-three, the possibility of that fate seemed decidedly slim.

Instead he'd die poor and obscure, exiting the way he'd come, the debit of death marked off against the credit of birth. Rolled up in such gloomy thoughts – Barton was his only friend, after all – his mind wandered and the coil on the stove glowed orange and the grease crackled and spat. A droplet shot from the pan and burned his hand.

Sucking his skin, he released his finger and squinted at the red dot on his pinkie. Absurd that a wound so small could hurt so much.

Standing there in his white cotton underwear, his paunch hanging over the elastic waistband, he allowed himself a pleasant memory, a balm for his burn. In the era of his thinness, he'd been able to look down over a flat stomach and see his penis, instead of the view he currently enjoyed: the hairy hillock of his gut, that curved and hirsute horizon beyond which . . .

His hand fell and groped and yes – there it was – his flimsy member hung faithfully in place, somewhat the worse for wear and tear, but still in working order.

Giving it a ferocious yank, he ran his other hand across his slippery cranium, remembering that the era of his thinness had also been the era of his hair. And what a mop he'd sported. Rock star locks. How many adoring fans had run their fingers through it! He thumped his gut and shuddered. Glory days were like dead animals: odorless till you disturbed the bones, but then, *pah!* – what a reek.

Outside, the neighbor's dog barked. His fingers tightened on the wooden spoon, going green at the knuckles. The dog howled as though it were being skinned, but the staff at animal control had said that when dogs barked they were simply communicating.

"Well, this one must be writing a novel," Helmut had replied, "*War and Peace,* I should think."

The dog barked in a higher key and the skin at Helmut's temples tightened with stress.

Heading outside to investigate, he stood on tip-toe to peer over his fence. There was nothing wrong with the dog, a large yellow mutt. The dog was bored and lonely. Helmut sympathized. He spoke to it soothingly, as though hypnotizing a jury. The dog cocked its head and stared at him with its shiny eyes. Helmut went back inside and no sooner had he entered the kitchen than the dog called out to him with earnest little yips of canine longing, begging the man with the nice voice to return.

Helmut was sorry, but he'd closed the argument. He'd have to sue the dog's owner, although he believed there weren't any bad dogs, only bad people. Even so, filing a lawsuit would confirm his worst fear: that he, the legendary Helmut Knight, had shed his cool and become an old fart.

Scratching a sudden itch in his crotch as the bacon browned at the edges, he felt something wet on his face and wiped it off. Appalled, he licked the tear from his fingers, tasting his body's salt. He had to get hold of himself, he realized, and soon. Time was getting the best of him. Hell, it *had* had got the best of him.

And that army of age – what a lethal arsenal it had – stealth tumors, covert blockages, insurgent nodules. Who knew what malignant missiles *already* creased the sky?

He reached for the eggs in a cardboard carton on the counter. Expertly cracking one on the edge of the pan, he dumped it into the grease where it hissed and whitened.

He laughed hollowly. Eggs weren't the only things going broke that day.

He was, too.

Watching the eggs thicken, he recalled how he'd demoted Barton, restoring the Squire to his place, serving the Knight. After their little scene, Barton had made a ridiculous show of not slamming the door, presumably to prove what a great Buddhist he was.

Meanwhile the Knight, feeling he'd won a key battle in their life-long rivalry, tilted at windmills best left alone.

Foregoing the stock market earlier in the day, he'd logged onto his foreign exchange account and, shorting the dollar against the euro, promptly lost forty-two thousand. Trading currency with a leverage of 100 to 1, you could do some heavy financial lifting, but you could also do some heavy losing, too.

Assuming a new position, he shorted the dollar against the yen, costing him another seventeen thousand.

Pressing his face to the blue glow of his computer, he moaned, "*Oh, no!*" while the numbers plunged, bleeding his account too quickly for him to square the deal and staunch the hemorrhage. He'd never seen numbers turn so quickly. And in the wrong direction. His fingers frantically tapped the keys. Too late! His position was changing so rapidly he couldn't escape it. The weight was chained to his ankles and it pulled him down, into the abyss, those murky depths reserved for losers.

Hitting the featureless gray bottom, he couldn't cover his position.

His loss for the day? Fifty-nine thousand. Even for a player, that was a stinger. He'd have been all right, too, if the Fed chairman hadn't unexpectedly opened his mouth in Zurich, but what could you do? You put down your money and you took your chances. Still, it wasn't gambling; it was speculation. A big difference. The former required luck, the latter brains.

There was only one problem: it wasn't his money. Half of it belonged to Barton, although it wasn't like the Squire needed to know how the Knight did his jousting. Helmut protected Barton, or so he told himself. In fact, when Barton had overheard Lanus and Gart talking about "malpractice" and "disbarment," they referred to the Knight and not the Squire, because in the course of his currency speculation Helmut hadn't set an automatic sell, so that when the Japanese Prime Minister painted a gloomy picture of his economy, he might just as well have tied lead weights around Helmut's ankles and thrown him overboard.

For in the space of an afternoon, when storm clouds hung like bruises outside the picture window of his office, Helmut had lost close to half a million dollars – funds he'd been holding in escrow for an elderly client, a former professional wrestler, of all things.

Of course, he intended to replace the money, which was what he'd been doing when he lost the other fifty-nine thousand, half of it Barton's.

Ah, technology! Amazing what you could do with the right set of codes and a computer. At best he'd be disbarred; at worst, without restitution, he'd spend a decade in a federal prison brushing up on his ping-pong skills.

Using his worn wooden spoon, he turned over the bacon strips, then turned off the stove and moved the pan to an unlit burner. The refrigerator popped and whirred, while Helmut stood there in his underwear, blinking at his dinner.

He was alone. His mousy, anonymous wife had long since left him, though he hadn't really thought about her, not really, not until her attorney served him at the office. Papers signed, he immediately forgot what she looked like, that is, until now, when his life had taken a distinct turn for the worse.

He required a back rub and a blow job, but his spouse had broken her vows. Now, it wasn't his nature to feel sorry for himself, but still . . . The Bachelor Life. Not for the candy-assed. The solitude was hard, especially when the financial waters turned into a whirlpool.

In time like these, he thought, snapping off a piece of bacon and grinding it between his molars, a man needs a family.

But shit-stained diapers and baby squalling and urine-stink and sagging breasts and good God just the images tickled his gorge! Of course, he'd probably lose his appetite and bowling-ball gut amid all that excrement. What did Barton say? Always something to be thankful for. But sometimes it was hard to see.

He munched another strip of bacon, giving his thoughts over to family, to dreams of blood and kin.

The same woman every night? With the same name? How medieval. Vaguely incestuous too, after a time. He wiped his mouth with the back of his hand.

But what if junior got a paper route? Or became a child actor? He could earn money and kick some to Dad and . . .

Advancing into middle age, Helmut was filled with fear. And suddenly everything became clear: not having children had been a fatal mistake. Pursuing wealth and fame, he'd raced beyond the breeders on his way to *success,* only to find that, like tortoises, the family men were slowly crawling past him, approaching a different kind of success, one which gleamed like a pot of gold at the end of the rainbow.

Whereas *he* was dashing toward an unvisited grave. Because who was going to peruse a back issue of *The Yale Law Review* into which he'd poured his very soul?

Nobody.

Now, if he'd made it to the appellate bench they'd have been reading his opinions for years, but as it was he'd be a footnote, a "wannabe," for God's sake.

The grit of the bacon caught at the back of his throat. Alone, without heirs, he might choke to death.

Was that the answer? Was that why humans bred? To have someone to come to your rescue? To be important to somebody?

I am your father.

He couldn't imagine uttering those words . . . and yet, what a fool he'd been not to pass on his brilliant DNA.

Swallowing, he guessed he wasn't the sort to bring home any bacon, except for himself. He was too much of a pig. Still, he wasn't the sort of pig to be left out of anything, so if nothing cropped up before he turned sixty he might pop off to the third world – Romania or Bolivia – somewhere they envied good plumbing and American greenbacks. In knightly fashion he'd tour the lobbies of the upscale hotels, select the most desperate young candidate (doubtlessly with brat in tow), import her to the USA, and sire an heir of his body before his flesh expired.

Now *that*, he thought, chewing, a sly smile turning up the corners of his mouth – *is an action that will lie!*

"Just me and the wife and kids here," he imagined bragging, hooking his thumbs into the elastic of his underwear and cocking his head toward his imaginary brood.

Strutting around the kitchen, he thrust out his chest, feeling paternal. Suddenly, he felt mightily important. So that's why the masses reproduced so prodigiously. He was right. The breeders waded through all that poop and snot in order to feel like big shots. *Of course. I am somebody's father.* What a kick from the balls!

A cold fear cramped his gut. How did the progenitors stand *that* part? His tongue cleared his mouth of grit and he tossed his spoon into the sink where it clattered against the drain.

No children, he decided. Ever. Tomorrow he'd make an appointment to get a vasectomy.

For in the blackest recesses of his mind, a devil cackled and rubbed its hands together, licking red, carnivorous lips, stamping its hooves.

Helmut knew something. He had no personal experience of evil, but he knew it existed. Evil was more real than God and Helmut knew *it* had it in for him.

If he ever had a child, he realized in a secret place inside himself, somebody would rape it. And kill it. As sure as he drew breath, he knew that would be just his luck. And then what would happen to his family, his well-rounded life?

"Jesus," he said.

He stood very still in front of his stove. Next to the bacon in the frying pan, his eggs hardened into a white and yellow disc.

As far as becoming chickens, they never had a chance.

Part III

Green Glade

WHILE Helmut stared at his eggs, Jordan said, "Give us our happily-ever-after, Alex."

Her sweet face hung above me, brushing my cheeks with her hair, kissing me full on the mouth and surprising me with a flicker of tongue, all nimble and wet. Ah! Today was my birthday and she wasn't shamed by an old geezer's unspoken wish, so she gave me back my manhood, if only for that hot liquid moment when her lips touched mine.

Hearing her footsteps echo along the hall and down the stairs, taking them two at a time in her sing-song, merry gallop, I wept with gratitude.

Oh, beloved reader, I have an emergency!

How I long to howl it from my window. I've been transferred to a new ward and my room has become a cell, one of those on death row. Fresh from an examination performed by a physician young enough to be my grandson (if I had an heir) I've been informed that the mode of my execution will not be Alzheimer's disease but pancreatic cancer.

"Staged" at IV, this means I have less time to complete my story and, alas, no granddaughter to come to my rescue. On the up side, I'll be spared the long death-march toward dementia, that land of purple-faced ghosts who drool and shuffle. The lethal nature of my latest malady is even cause for gratitude, for when I expire I won't be wearing diapers, and I'll still know my name. I may go naked, but at least I'll be able to say goodbye.

"Alexander Colin, Attorney at Law – regretfully no longer at your service."

I won't be considered young when I die, but I've never cared for the concept of "youth" in any case. Whoever began the tradition of counting birthdays must've truly despised humanity. Dragging these fragile, high-maintenance carcasses to and fro, performing all the business of the world which we imagine is so important (the greatest fiction of all) one might think we had enough to worry about without stamping ourselves with an expiration date.

Yet year by year we add up the numbers like a tree counting its own rings, branches trembling, awaiting the lumberjack and the saw.

Time is a trickster, my silent companion. One sunlit morning you're on a playground, hollering and running bases in a kickball game, then by noon your grim-faced spouse is offering you a divorce, so that by dinner only one question remains: burial or cremation?

Time is kinder to children. In youth, an hour is fat with duration. Life stretches out like a vast plain, all blue sky and endless horizon, then youth grows into middle age and you realize that what you took to be a wide-open space was only a city block and – *horrors* – you've crossed it.

I object – but the point is moot, dear reader. Enough. Let us kill death standing side by side, my invisible comrade. Let us proceed with our story, waving goodbye to the past even as we open our arms to the future.

(Regarding my own case, my withering life outside the world of Barton, Jordan and Helmut, I have nothing further to add at this time.)

– Alexander Colin, Attorney at Law (ret.)
Green Glade Assisted Living Community
Sebring, Florida
September 1, 2008

1

Trust Fund

BARTON had lost his lunch. Now he kneeled before the toilet, his face lowered into the bowl above the water. Feeling his knees press against the hard tile, he reached up and pulled the lever. A gushing roar sucked away his half-digested toast and a whoosh of air rushed past his face.

"You all right in there?" Jordan called. Her voice was muffled by the bathroom door but he could tell she was worried.

He let his forehead rest against the cool rim of the toilet bowl, feeling the skin on his back dance with pinpricks.

"I feel," he croaked, swallowing against a hot wave of nausea, "like I've got to park another custard."

"What did you say?"

Barton dry-heaved with tremendous gusto.

Retching and tripping, he thought, spitting sour bile into the bowl. With such distractions, who had *time* to be depressed?

Finished, he hoped, he avoided his eyes in the mirror, brushed his teeth and gargled and splashed his face with cold water, wondering how anyone who hadn't experimented with LSD could survive an anti-depressant. For nausea was only one arrow in a whole quiver of side effects. Others included visual disturbances, tinnitus, flatulence, sweating and dry mouth. And those were the mild ones.

So far, he was hanging in there.

Making a mental note to clean the bathroom before Jordan saw what a mess he'd made, he slowly gained his feet. Well, at least there was something to be thankful for. In his current condition, neither Jordan nor Helmut could bum rides to the law firm. Nausea was a license of sorts – a license not to drive.

His particular brand of anti-depressant was called Fokus, the latest in a new generation of serotonin uptake inhibitors. The stuff even looked like LSD, especially for those 20th century psychonauts old enough to remember purple microdot, although these new and improved pills were diamond-shaped and crimson. He'd begun taking them at Jordan's insistence, after she'd pointed out that his obsessive thoughts and homicidal fantasies were seriously threatening their marriage. Those were her words.

Seriously threatening our marriage.

Shocked at such talk, and frightened by it too, he admitted the sanity of her suggestion and so, head hung low, he relented and saw a bland man in glasses, who, after a ten minute exam mumbled "depressive something paranoia something psychotic ideation something." The doctor produced a prescription pad and installed Barton "on the Fokus regimen," which sounded to him like a corporate catch-phrase, which it was.

Emerging from the bathroom and leaning against the door, the patient smiled bravely. Good and bad, his moods had come unstuck from his person, so that now he carried them around outside himself like a set of ugly luggage. Just now he pictured a garment bag of despair slung across his back.

"So," he asked, tightening the drawstring on his white cotton pants, "how do I look?" He had on black sleeveless T-shirt with a smear of chicken soup dried into the shape of Florida over his left nipple. He squared his shoulders impressively.

"You look," his wife said, clucking her tongue and wagging her head, "like a mental patient."

"Well, I *am* a mental patient."

Furrowing her brow, she picked up a blister pack of diamond-shaped red pills and read the warning printed on the back. "It says these may cause suicidal behavior." She looked up, her eyes wide. As a couple, embarrassment and denial were luxuries they couldn't afford. They still loved each other, after all, and they still wanted their happily-ever-after. "Do you feel suicidal?" she asked.

A fresh wave of nausea rolled in and broke warmly on the shore of his stomach. Sweat appeared on his forehead. Gritting his teeth and remembering all the bad trips he'd survived in college, he swallowed heroically.

There. He'd beaten it. Hooray! Uh-oh. What's this? His eyes bulged. Changing its tactics, the drug moved further south, rumbling his bowels with volcanic force. He clenched his buttocks to forestall any leaks, thinking he ought to get out of white pants at the first opportunity.

Jordan raised her voice. "I said, DO YOU FEEL SUICIDAL?"
"ONLY WHEN I TAKE THE PILLS."

His wife shrugged and silently mouthed, "Sorry." She'd given herself the day off to nurse her ailing husband, so that all she had on was her white terrycloth bathrobe. She pressed her cool palm to his forehead.

"You're burning up, hon."

As she leaned forward her robe fell open and revealed her buttery skin and pink nipples. Her husband smiled wanly. Sick as he was, he understood that only a very lucky man got pampered by the likes of Jordan Kelly Squire.

He reached up and cupped a warm breast. It filled his palm and he enjoyed its hefty plumpness, the smooth feel of her flesh. "I'm not deaf," he said, "just depressed and obsessed."

"Okay, Mr. Squire," she said, gently disengaging herself, "no copping feels from the nurse."

Barton closed his eyes and opened them, steadying himself with a hand on the towel rack. From his mouth to his anus, he felt like a long, unhealthy worm, an image which writhed in his mind with horrifying clarity.

Feeling his scalp tingle, he shivered from his heels to his hair. "In sickness and in health," he said, attempting good humor. He raised his eyebrows and grinned good-naturedly, feeling sorry for his wife, who had better things to do than nurse a lunatic with a sour stomach and loose bowels.

"Bee? You all right?"

"Ouf." Using his fist, he struck himself in the belly and burped. "Sorry, honey. I feel like a dog's dinner."

"Well . . . you took care of me in Mexico. I'm returning the favor."

Accepting her hand, he allowed himself to be led from the bathroom. He and Helmut had a court date that morning, but he was in no position to dress, much less appear at the plaintiff's table. Jordan had already notified Helmut, who Barton had correctly guessed would accuse him of malingering, given his recent demotion at the firm. What Barton didn't know, however, was that Helmut would secretly welcome his absence, as it would allow him to spend most of the day on the foreign exchange attempting to replenish the firm's escrow account.

Barton pressed his hand to his head, unable to tell whether it was his palm or his head that felt hot. He was suddenly drenched. Sighing, he stripped off his sweat-soaked clothes and tossed them into the hamper.

"Better break out *The Tibetan Book of the Dead*," he said, only half-jokingly. "Feels like I'm about to lay down my knife and fork."

Never one to appreciate gallows humor, his wife pinched his rear end and said, "Quit it," then took his elbow and escorted him to their bed.

Moving as gingerly as an old man, he felt as though his bones and joints had been replaced by balsa wood and Elmer's glue. Blinking, he realized that if he survived, this is what his body would feel like in old age, that is to say, *fragile*. And yet, catching sight of himself in the mirror above their bed, he was relieved to see that, naked, he was still a man in his prime. At forty-three, he still had his flat, muscled belly and hard shoulders, the fruit of endless dull hours at the gym.

"Whoa! I'm listing to starboard, honey." His left side had gone numb and he couldn't feel the floor.

"Coming about?" Her hand reached down and gripped his sudden, unexpected erection. She'd misunderstood, but what the hell, he figured. He might be insane but he wasn't crazy.

Leaning together, they regarded the thing in the mirror. As hard as a pump handle, its head resembled a plum.

"Oh my," said Barton. Sometimes, as now, its sheer bulk was embarrassing. Next to his wife's delicate body, his blood-hardened appendage made him feel like a gorilla.

She shook him enthusiastically. "I could hammer nails with it," she said brightly. She gave him a good squeeze and grinned.

Barton rolled his eyes. His penis had a private life, a personal philosophy and sacred beliefs. Curious, it always wanted to poke out its head, to get some air. It was very interested in females. Its owner disapproved of this interest, unless it was directed at his wife.

Consequently, Barton and his penis had had a very stormy relationship over the years, although he never let it forget who was boss. Not once did he let it foul up his marriage. He loved his wife too much.

Jordan released him and gently set her hand on his shoulder. "Get to bed, Big Bart."

Her husband turned away and smartly flicked his penis with his middle finger. Wincing, he hoped it might deflate and leave them in peace. But no, it got even angrier, throbbing with a pulse all its own.

You fiend! he thought.

"What did you say?"

"Huh?"

"Bee, what's wrong?"

He shook his head, blinking.

"You're talking to yourself. And your face. Your expression changed. Really fast." She sounded worried.

Forgotten, his penis shrugged and hung limp. All its energy had shot to Barton's forehead, souring his mood, taking him somewhere dark, someplace violent.

He heard himself blurting, "I'm going to kill that bastard. I'm going to tear off his head and puke down his lungs!"

His wife looked aghast. "Who?"

"He's a rat with a gold tooth. *He's the devil!*"

"Barton, what's wrong?"

"What?"

"You're shouting." His wife's face grew pale.

Barton knew she knew he meant Helmut, but seeing the frightened look on her face and catching sight of himself in the mirror, he thought better of speaking the hated name. Jordan held open the covers and he caught the odor of raw sewage.

"I'm smelling things," he said. He sniffed the air. "An outhouse . . . and now – " he sniffed, "waffles cooking."

"It's the side effects," she said, her sharp features pinched with worry.

"Well, if it's working why do I still want to kill him? Why can't I stop thinking about him? I feel like Macbeth. Bloody hands and ghosts and witches – I've got the whole show in my head."

"It takes a few weeks. That's what the doctor said."

"Yeah, but it doesn't take a few weeks to smell sewage and waffles."

"Get in bed, honey."

"And what's with the hard-on?"

"Priapism. Another side effect."

"Oh joy."

Since he wasn't going to listen to her any other way she slipped out of her robe and slid between the cool sheets, luring him with her body. His eyes drank in her golden, oh-so-lick-able skin, her blond thatch, her little belly and compelling navel. He sucked in his breath. He might be out of his mind, but he knew that life passed in a flash and that here was his shiny girl, inviting him into bed.

Climbing in, into her warmth, he pulled her into his greedy, reaching arms. Together they clung, glued tight. After years of marriage, they still couldn't get enough of each other. It was a righteous chemistry, they'd long since agreed.

He put his nose into the warm vanilla fold of her neck.

"A Christian would let it go," she said suddenly. "And you said you admired Jesus."

"Yes," he said slowly, sensing dangerous ground, "but not to worship."

"If you'd pray, He'd help you."

"Let's not talk any more, hon."

"Better?"

On the cool sheets, under the breeze of the slowly wheeling ceiling fan, his fingertips brushed her sacral dimples, discovering her curving rump. He fit his hand to her cleft, his palm gripping her. Together they shared the fleshy taste of human mouths, moist and dark and lovely.

She kissed her way down his body . . . gave heaven's soft grip, the wet manna from her mouth, while behind his closed eyes he saw . . . what? Not that! His eyelid movie, his private horror film.

She went to work. Oh! A salivary compliment. Such a happy noise. Should he pull her up? No. She'd be hurt, insulted. Better let her proceed. He opened his eyes but the images remained.

On the desk, from under the green shade of a banker's lamp, a bright glow shone into the bloody bowl of Helmut's skull. The staved-in head dribbled blood onto the floor. A burgundy pool crept from under the desk and began congealing. Somehow, inside the well-maintained office, a fly had found it.

Barton's fingers dug into the hammer's rubber grip. Blood dripped from the hammer's claws and spattered redly on the floor. A syrupy smell hung on the air.

His knuckles went greenish-white as he squeezed the soft warmth of the hammer's handle. His ears whistled. His heart slowed. Helmut seemed so harmless – now that he'd been reduced to a bowl of crimson goo.

"You all right?" Jordan asked. She looked up from between his legs across his muscled stomach, through the curls of blond hair on his chest.

"Sure, hon – don't stop."

Compressing his lips, he thought of Graciela, who would have to get down on her knees to scrub away the stains and the unspeakable chunks of something like cottage cheese.

Tossing away his hammer, it landed in the wastebasket with a thud. The basket had a plastic liner, so there would be less mess for Graciela. Anyway, the police would confiscate it for evidence. He felt the air conditioning prickle the hairs on the back of his neck. Mystified, he inhaled, observing his chest expand. What's this? Was it possible? Yes! Dear God, he could breathe! His lungs worked. He'd got over that hump where a deep breath was satisfying, that crest of the diaphragm's expansion. He did it again. Marvelous! He could breathe freely.

Jordan sniffled and brushed back her hair, smoothing it behind her ear to give him a good view. "You sure you like this?"

"Absolutely."

Two uniformed policemen with bellies like pregnant women appeared in the door and handled his wrists in an oddly gentle, almost tender fashion. Fastening the handcuffs, one of the officers made sure the metal didn't ratchet onto bone. With his arms behind him, Barton hung his head and closed his eyes. Crime doesn't pay, he thought. Well, no – not in this case, but then he wasn't looking for money. He'd sought a more precious reward.

Jordan tried humming loudly, without success. Frustrated, she turned up her diamond-blue eyes. "You want me to stop?"

"Ummm . . . I *am* a little distracted."

"I can see that." Ever the good sport, she employed her tongue and both hands, while her husband strove to inhabit the moment. Still, his eyelid movie played.

The cops' hands were soft and warm and no one spoke as the fly settled on Barton's lip, tickling him with its tiny feet, then on some silent signal each officer grabbed an elbow and walked him down the hall, guiding him as carefully as if he'd been injured.

Barton didn't resist. Not now, and not earlier, because Helmut's shiny dome had made an irresistible target. Of course, this was hardly a legal defense. Barton understood this. But under the glare of the blue-white lights, the crown of Helmut's skull had glinted so invitingly – and with such insolence – that Barton's hand had tightened on the rubber grip and he'd swung his hammer as if he were driving a railroad spike.

The amount of blood had been a surprise. Red splotches spattered the walls and floor, as if Jackson Pollock had gone on a murderous rampage. Barton wished he could apologize to Graciela, but he couldn't risk implicating her.

Escorted down the hall with an officer at each elbow, he glanced into the display case at head shots of himself and Helmut, both a decade younger, smiling from inside gold frames. Fresh out of law school, their grins were spotless white banners for Dreams Yet to Be Lived.

Well, that was over now. The cops put him into the cruiser.

"Maybe we should try later," his wife said. She glanced up and wiped her lips. "I seemed to have lost my touch."

Outside, the rain fell from a gray sky and drops of water slid down the window in front of the prisoner's face. He would be charged with first degree murder.

"I'm sorry," he said, "but I keep imagining things. Bad things."

The prisoner smiled at the rain.

His wife's candid eyes, full of mischief, looked up and found his face. She raised her eyebrows. "Can't think of anybody?"

Can't *stop* thinking of somebody, her husband thought, but wisely kept silent.

* * *

He got behind her.

"Use the English, love."

She squeezed her buttocks, going taut and slack, wriggling just the way he liked it.

* * *

"Oh my," she said. She smacked her lips. "*Tres bien!*" He glanced up from between her thighs. His eyes shone over the honey-pale thatch. He smiled and . . . well, let us refrain from staring . . .

* * *

Done with lovemaking, they lay side by side on their backs enjoying the calm of their bodies, drowsing in bliss on the smooth sheets. Overhead, the ceiling fan spun lazily. The sun slanted through the blinds, casting the room in lines of cool green and shimmering gold.

Jordan licked her lips, making mammal sounds. "Sweet lovin' Bee," she said sleepily, yanking the sheet, "quit hogging all the covers." A swath of sunlight struck her closed eyes and she flung her arm across her face. She turned over. Kicking, she loosened the sheet at the foot of the bed, nuzzling Barton's neck with her nose.

Her husband didn't move. He attempted to appreciate the moment. Savor it like a good Buddhist. True to his vows, he *cherished* her. Indeed. There wasn't a square inch of her skin he wouldn't happily lick.

But it was no good. Helmut had infected his mind like a virus, so that he felt dirty, invaded.

He might be flossing his teeth in the bathroom or pulling a weed in his front yard, when Helmut's face would sweep into his head, plunging him into a red storm of rage. Homicidal and violent, a manic fury would shake his bones.

Worst of all, he enjoyed it. The pure furious joy of bloodlust. A gory whirl of satisfaction. Goodbye, lamb. Hello, wolf!

Observing the wild look in his eyes, his wife had insisted he see the psychiatrist, and since his appointment he'd faithfully ingested his Fokus, those tiny red diamonds designed to stop his longing to grow fangs and rip flesh, to rid the world of Helmut Knight.

So far it hadn't calmed him, and although his wife advised patience, Barton thought his psychiatrist failed to grasp that what obsessed him, to a pathological degree, was not Helmut, but rather, *the concept* of Helmut. Barton was aware of the distinction, and it gave rise to an orgy of guilt. To wit, if *the concept* of Helmut was Barton's brainchild, why couldn't that brainchild be controlled? Or if not controlled, given a strenuous whipping?

It's *my* mind, he thought, mentally stripping off his belt, so I ought to be able to loosen its hide when it misbehaves.

Turning onto his side, he found his arm and rib cage compressed. Switching sides was no better. Ah, the burden of the human carcass! He put his hand under his head, comforting himself like a child. His shoulders ached and his spine throbbed. His whole skeleton felt poorly constructed, as though afflicted with a design flaw. No matter how well-maintained, he thought, the human body was a pain in its own ass.

Lying beside his sleeping wife, he closed his eyes and saw Helmut's face, leering, then it morphed into a goat with white whiskers and yellow eyes, its lips pulled back to expose unwholesome teeth and a long red tongue. The creature bleated and Barton's eyes snapped open.

Helmut's become part of me, he thought.

Barton stared at the stucco patterns in the ceiling. Helmut the goat chewed his victim's brain and coughed it up as cud. Barton writhed.

There was only one solution.

Slaughter!

He felt himself grinning.

"What is it?" Jordan asked, her eyes popping open. Her hand

touched his hip, but her voice, disembodied in the cool green of the room, sounded strangely far off. "Your whole body jerked."

He couldn't tell her. How could he? His former law partner was a goat who needed killing? That sounded insane. Hell, it *was* insane.

On her side she snuggled into him spoon-fashion and ground her buttocks into his groin, filling his nostrils with the clean smell of her flesh. He buried his nose in her soft hair. She carried a whole climate with her, seasonal by the second, shifting from New England apples to Georgia pears to Florida lime, but now her odor faded away.

"What?" Her body stiffened.

"More side effects," he said, swallowing against a dry patch in his throat. "Scary ones."

Encircling her with his arms, the warm length of her body failed to soothe him. His jaw muscles contracted and he ground his molars, feeling his muscles go so rigid he might've been struck with rigor mortis. His heart skipped and his head ticked like a metronome – I'm old/I'm *not* old/I'm old/I'm *not* old.

"I'm not ready for people," he said, "I don't know if it's a mid-life crisis or The Kansas Incident. But I am freakin' haunted."

Jordan gasped and he felt sorry for her. Was he being forthright, he wondered, or had he sought to wound her? Candor wasn't far from cruelty, and if one was camouflage for the other, then he'd become the beast he despised: a man who was mean and petty, craven and weak.

Helmut, in a word.

Jordan struggled around and frowned at her husband. The space between them was hot. She blinked rapidly and her lower lip protruded. Her breath warmed his face. "Bee," she said, sounding injured, with tears wetting her voice, "I thought we had a pact. I thought we made vows."

"It's expired," he heard himself say. God, what was he doing? He was a fool and more: he *knew* he was a fool.

The elevator from hell rose to receive him, as it had in Kansas. His finger reached to illuminate the button, shaped like a tiny red diamond. Horrified, he realized he was going to press it. In the meantime, a goat-faced devil with yellow eyes bleated loudly and shat red diamonds onto his grave.

Neither husband nor wife said anything, looking into each other's eyes. The jagged edges of Jordan's irises began to dilate, with the black consuming the blue. The stillness roared in Barton's head.

"I'm not some kind of a contract," she said. She retreated to the far side of the bed. "I'm your wife." Her voice rose upward and the skin around her eyes tightened. "In Colorado last spring? In the aspen forest on the mountain? I thought we put Kansas behind us."

What had he said? Smacking his tongue against the roof of his mouth, he tasted gun metal.

"I'm begging you, Bee." She curled into a fetal position and grasped her slender ankles, staring at her fingernails. "Don't fuck us up, honey. You know? It's rare to see the top of the world. Hardly anyone climbs that mountain, and when they do, they do it alone . . . and so to do it *with* someone . . . "

"You're the one who fucked us up, Jordan. In college and in Kansas."

Barton shut his eyes, hearing her cry. He was appalled. Who *was* this nasty bastard? Where was Barton Squire, the man who forgot and forgave?

Dead and gone, the goat-face of Helmut bleated, his yellow eyes gleaming.

"Live in the present – isn't that what you say?" Her voice was desperate, out of tune. Her fingertips trailed across the skin of his chest. "The past is gone, right?"

His scalp crawled. They had reached the crisis, that place where certain things, if said, would tear hard and deep and long. This was the theatre of Statements You Could Never Take Back, the marital equivalent of going nuclear. Armageddon for their Civilization of Two.

A second ticked by. The Squire marriage teetered on the brink of Doomsday.

In the same instant, husband and wife drew a deep breath. This was Zen, Barton thought.

Simultaneously, they retreated. They had too good a marriage to wreck it. They were best friends. They were lovers. They traded massages. They talked baby talk. They whispered endearments. They nuzzled and cooed.

Nobody watching could've stood it. They lived in the garden they'd grown together, their own private Eden.

Not that they'd returned. Paradise was still lost.

Helmut had flicked his forked tongue and offered his apple, which Jordan devoured and whose bitter taste Barton fought so hard to forget.

Now, he thought, instead of Eden their marriage had gotten to be like a vacation at a lousy motel, where you kept finding good things to say about the rustic decor or the lovely view, even though it had rained for five days straight and the food was terrible. Still, in unavoidably bad times, frank assessment seemed self-indulgent, childish even. Grown-ups made the best of things. They constructed fictions. They pretended. They subscribed to the power of make-believe. Because what was optimism, if not a tall tale of the highest order?

Barton reached for her but she shrank from his hand. He guessed he deserved it. "Jordan, I'm sorry, honey. I seem to have gone insane."

"Yes you have," she said coldly. She wouldn't look at him.

"I'm seeing a psychiatrist."

She stared at the ceiling. "Are you being funny? Please tell me you're not being funny."

"I am *definitely* not being funny."

She snuffed through her nose and turned away and concealed herself under the covers. "Keep taking the pills," she said.

"That's right," he said for no particular reason. He was suddenly furious. His eyes ached. "Just keep Barton doped up and he'll be fine – is that your plan or Helmut's?"

"That's not fair," she whispered. She switched on the lamp as the last rays of the sun shone through the blinds. The lamp formed a yellow cone. "I'm taking a shower."

She rose from their bed and strode naked into the bathroom where she turned on the water. That was her answer. Other people smoked marijuana, gorged on food, endlessly masturbated – but when she was on the wagon Jordan took marathon showers. She'd steam her seething brain into submission. Water down her temper. Soon the faucet clinked off.

Barton sat naked on the bed. The bathroom door opened. His wife stood in a rectangle of light wrapped in a white towel, her long hair damp and stringy. Backlit, she had a shimmering gold aura.

"I'm sorry," he said for what seemed like the hundredth time that day, grimly aware he didn't *sound* sorry, then he heard himself add, "but it's all subjective. From where you're standing, *you're* in the right, and from where I'm sitting, *I'm* in the right."

She raised her eyebrows. "My word. Is that what you learned in college?" Vigorously toweling her head, she peered at him while she dried her ears. "Nobody *creates* anything, Barton." She tossed her hair over her shoulders. "Life happens and then you deal with it. That's character, hon. *How you deal.*"

Her husband kept his mouth shut, then to his utter astonishment she crossed the room and poked her finger into his solar plexus.

"Character. You dig?"

She towered over him and, finding his voice, he said, "Life may happen to *you* – but I figure – I've got what – forty years left? Max? Subtract sleep and it's twenty-five. I've got to act now. I've got to forge my destiny."

"*Forge your destiny?*" She threw her hands over her head and her pulse throbbed delicately at the hollow of her throat. She had never been more beautiful. "I mean, *really!*"

"You're right," he said. "I'm an asshole."

Standing, he opened his arms, but she stepped back. She put her cool hand on his chest. Stunned, he looked at the long tapering fingers. The pink ovals of her nails gleamed with polish.

A moment passed. Her hand hadn't moved and its palm was no longer cool. Barton swallowed. This was absolutely new and he didn't like it.

"It's the Fokus," he said, beaten. "I should go off it."

"Please don't."

His head swam and he thought he might die.

He'd never found himself so unlikable.

Though she's no prize either, a strange voice in his head informed him.

"Please don't look at me like that. Barton, please! I was drunk. He was drunk." Her voice rose and broke. "For God's sake, will you just let it go? I can't apologize for the rest of my life!"

"Well, imagine what I saw when I walked into that hotel room. You ever get behind *my* eyes?"

"Oh my – " She actually stamped her foot. "I said I was sorry. What else can I *do?* You make yourself insane. I swear you do. Now you're making me crazy too!"

"Crazy? You ain't seen the half of it!"

Shivering, he stomped naked out of the bedroom, awash in self-loathing. The last thing she'd seen was his bare ass. Brilliant. God, what a buffoon! He'd shouted at the only woman he'd ever loved, when all she wanted was to be forgiven.

Some Buddhist!

No matter. She was right about one thing. The past was gone, the present ruined, the future uncertain. And it was all Helmut's fault. The defendant had inflicted damage and he was liable.

You know what to do, Barton thought. He sat down on the couch.

Don't be a coward! He closed his eyes and pressed his face between the cushions, feeling the rough fabric against his cheek.

That snake, he thought, *Tomorrow I smash its head!*

2

NON COMPOS MENTIS

WHILE he waited for the Fokus to work, Barton required a leave of absence from Kelly, Knight and Squire. Everyone agreed on this, including me. Freshly diagnosed with Alzheimer's, even as my pancreas ticked like a time bomb, I could sympathize with maladies cognitive.

For his part, Barton pressed a bubble on a blister pack, expelling a tiny red diamond through the foil backing and the printed warnings of the drug's numerous side effects. He tossed the little diamond into his mouth and swallowed.

Outside, in the back yard, he stretched out his body in a low-slung canvas beach chair. Beyond the neighbor's house, the sun rose over the Atlantic and cast its sword-like orange rays across the grass. The sky lightened from gray to blue and a tepid breeze stirred the shimmering needles of the Australian pines and the green fronds of the palm trees. The surf boomed and crashed, and the first rumblings of traffic began along highway A1A. The clouds were flecked with gold and the cicadas whirred in the trees. Overhead, a blue jay shrieked.

Hearing car doors slam and engines rev as his neighbors began the rat race, Barton felt strangely serene, sitting there in his yard, doing nothing. No wonder retirees went insane or became slaves to strange hobbies. He looked at his watch. He'd been convalescing for fifteen minutes.

A pair of cardinals chirped merrily in a hedge of sea grape. Using his sharp beak, the male fed the female a seed. The tenderness of it widened Barton's eyes and he chuckled softly. The Fokus was lubricating his brain, washing it with serotonin.

Resisting an urge to sing at the birds, he marveled at the potency of the psychedelics doctors handed out these days. Was the DEA aware of this stuff? The legality of it astonished him.

A shadow crossed his eyes and he looked up into the smiling face of his wife. She carried his breakfast on a tray: a multi-grain croissant smeared with organic raspberry jam, a mug of strong black coffee, and a tall glass of freshly squeezed orange juice. She set the tray on the grass beside him.

"You need anything?" she asked. In a silent truce, neither spoke of his evening on the couch.

"This is perfect," he said. The coffee steamed into the morning air. Barton sipped it and switched to orange juice, ice-cold and sweet after the hot and bitter coffee. He loved alternating flavors and temperatures.

"I'll be getting on the space ship soon," she said.

Barton smiled, though he feared it was more of a grimace. Jordan looked at him oddly. Her "spaceship" was her studio, where he wouldn't disturb her unless the house caught fire or he severed a limb.

"It's okay if you need to come get me," she said gently.

"I'll be fine," he said. Disturbing her in the throes of composition caused her physical pain, so he'd take care to avoid it. They'd hurt each other enough, so that now he wanted to sue for peace, if not serenity.

Jordan knelt in the grass and put her arms around him, hugging him with great force. Feeling the warmth in her body, he knew he'd retained at least a shred of sanity, for the truly insane weren't known for gratitude.

Whatever her faults (and he had splendid collection of his own, he readily admitted) Barton adored his wife, and if there was a cure for his obsession he'd take a pass, because marriage to the right woman . . . well, call it romantic or sentimental, but it was the sweetest thing in life.

(I know, because I missed out on it.)

The magic of . . . *I thee wed!*

Watching a monarch butterfly flutter from a white jasmine blossom into the tangerine-colored flowers of a fire bush, Barton heard a crunching sound. Pricking up his ears, he heard it again.

It was coming from inside his mouth. No wonder his jaw ached. He'd been grinding his teeth strenuously enough to mill wheat into flour. He lay back. Hopefully the Fokus would arrest his mood swings. But maybe mood swings were what life was all about. When you were crazy, it was hard to tell.

"What're you doing?" Jordan asked, leaning away from him to peer into his eyes.

"Doing?"

"With your mouth? You're doing something strange."

"Sorry. It's involuntary."

She narrowed her eyes.

"I'm fine, hon. Really."

She frowned. "You want me to pray over you?"

"You're joking."

"I'm not."

She took a deep breath and slowly exhaled. She seemed older than he remembered, with fine lines spreading around her eyes, the hair at her temples sun-bleached to ash.

Their marriage had aged her. *He* had aged her.

"I'll check on you," she said.

He put his hand on the back of her neck and covered her with kisses, moving from her honey-pale hairline down her oval-shaped face to the feminine point of her chin.

Smiling, she kissed his forehead and walked toward her studio, stopping at the door to wave.

When she was gone, he tried to read but couldn't concentrate. His feelings swung between euphoria and horror, from milk and honey to fire and brimstone.

Alone, he couldn't tell what was normal. Worse, outside Jordan and Helmut, he didn't have any friends whose counsel might prove helpful. He didn't belong to a bowling league or the Elks or the Moose or a Buddhist temple or even Alcoholics Anonymous. Why bother? Most Americans had been stabilized with serotonin uptake inhibitors, so who needed clubs and a funny hat? Nobody was going to elect him Grand Poo-Bah anyway.

Washed in sun, he hugged himself. The words hadn't been spoken, but the consensus was that he'd suffered a nervous breakdown, and with the sea breeze wafting over his skin, lightly brushing the hair on his arms, he toyed with the phrase "mental illness."

If you could be mentally "ill," he wondered, couldn't you also come down with a lesser ailment, say a "mental cold," or a case of "the cognitive sniffles"? He hoped so. Yawning, he stretched his arms over his head and closed his eyes. The sun climbed behind a live oak and under the shadows of the leaves his muscles relaxed.

Abruptly his eyes snapped open, his neck jerking painfully to the right. Dazed, he wiped the drool from his cheek, realizing he must've dozed off, only to wake thinking *Helmut fucked my wife!* And more: his uncooperative mind had snapped a picture – Helmut's flabby ass between his wife's spread-eagled thighs. And it was no bad dream. That's how it happened. It was real. The lips he kissed every day had sucked his best friend's cock. Beautiful. His mind's eye betrayed him with pornography, forcing him to its squalid peephole.

But wait, didn't the body renew itself? Replace all its cells every seven years? Or was that a myth? He wished he knew more biology. Sprawled there in his beach chair like the mental patient he'd become, he found it hard to breathe.

And now, wiping his cheek – what's this? He looked at his hand. Sweat?

It was pouring off him in sheets.

"Jesus," he said aloud, flinging the sweat off his fingers into the grass, thinking, *This Fokus sure has got up on its hind legs.*

Yet maybe a fierce sweat was the only sensible reaction to his predicament. The express from cradle to grave could be a bumpy ride, even in first class, since every passenger disembarked at the same stop: Dirt Nap City, a destination not known for its flashy attractions.

Barton patted his face with his hands, admitting he might've been crying. Feeling his skin tighten, he congratulated himself on his "grief work." That's what psychiatrists called the caterwauling of the bereaved, the terminal, the cuckolded – all that blubbering was actually *work*, it turned out. He'd learned the phrase from an expert witness he'd called against a cancer surgeon who'd amputated the wrong breast. (Helmut had insisted their client bare her long pink scar for the jury, noting that a visual aid would cinch the case).

He'd complained, though, because their client hadn't accompanied the display of her scar with any hysterics. "Like showing a movie with the sound turned off," he said, disgusted. "If she'd let her eyes run and the snot flow, I could've set her up in a mansion. Being brave won her a trailer."

Remembering the courageous woman's face, Barton heaved his body from his chair and entered the oasis of cool air inside the house.

In the living room he put on a blues record and while Lightning Hopkins moaned about tears on a window pane, Barton thought about the sound of Jordan's voice.

To summon her merry laughter he'd resort to pratfalls, impressions, songs, cartwheels . . . whatever it took. Whenever she laughed, he felt his soul buffed to a celestial sheen, rubbed to glowing by a cloth of impossible softness. At the moment of his death, he meant to recall her laughter as his favorite sound on earth.

And now that music belonged to Helmut. Her pale eyes, the color of the sea after a storm, and her face, disembodied, dissolved before him.

He was losing her, he felt sure.

Hell, he *had* lost her.

Pressing his hands to his belly, he felt his intestines writhe inside him like a nest of snakes. Strange bubbling sounds, like a swamp settling, issued from his bowels.

The beast approached. Red fiery eyes, dripping fangs, meaty breath, froth of saliva.

I have what you need, its familiar voice said. Barton nodded.

The answer was simple.

He needed a drink.

Or maybe two.

God, no!

God, yes!

An unholy thirst befell him. He wanted a drink. He wanted one very badly. Marooned in the Sahara, the very marrow of his bones cried, *Slake this thirst!*

Rising from the couch, he stumbled into the kitchen. On the wall beside the fridge, framed in teak, hung the snapshot which Helmut had taken in college when they'd gone deep sea fishing. Barton stared at Jordan Kelly before she'd become Jordan Kelly Squire. The ski-jump curve of her nose, the hint of nostril. The tawny eyebrows, the blood shining through her skin, the excellent teeth.

He touched the picture.

The memory was vivid, wriggling in his mind like a live thing: that drunken nighttime road trip from Gainesville to St. Augustine after Jordan got it into her head that she wanted to see the sunrise on the ocean so she could "catch their breakfast."

And she had, on a charter fishing trip off Crescent Beach, posing long enough for the picture before releasing her fish into the blue depths of the Atlantic.

Shivering, he tore his eyes away and advanced on the cupboards, grim-faced.

Drink, he thought. Drink!

Slamming the thin wooden doors, he rifled the cabinets but found no help there, not even cooking sherry. But ah! Sugar! Better than nothing. He dug into the refrigerator where he pawed the shelves and found blackberry jelly. Fingers jammed into the jar, he stuffed his face with the sweet black goo.

Delicious. He made little moaning sounds as he licked out the lid. When it was gone, his tongue cleared his sticky teeth and he sucked his fingers, smacking his lips. Sugar was a distant cousin to alcohol, but he felt it helped. He left a purple fingerprint on the refrigerator door.

Having got some glucose into his bloodstream, he felt less maniacal, less like a fiend. But catching sight of his jelly-smeared face in the mirror over the sink, he got a nasty surprise. A strange man with wild eyes gazed back at him.

"*Non compos mentis*," he said, and quitting with the mirror he washed off his hands and face in the kitchen sink. Ever the considerate husband, even when insane, he sponged down the refrigerator, wiped the counters and shut the cabinet doors.

So much for his rest cure.

Outside, he strode past the studio and returned to his chair. He'd set a Martin Amis novel on top of his Fokus and picked up the book and popped another red diamond out of the blister pack.

Fokus, he thought, swallowing and feeling the sun warm his face, *I sure as hell hope so.*

As the sun rose higher in the sky, the world went slightly reddish, as if he were seeing it through a veil of crimson. A vision broke loose in his head. Opening his Amis novel, he scribbled inside the front cover.

Snapshot of Jordan Holding a Kingfish

Half as long and sleek as her
sea-sculpted, swimmer's body
she presents the kingfish,
aiming it skyward like a silver sword.

She's showing her teeth, jaw jutting,
mouth pulled into a hammy grin
over the astonished eye
and sharp-looking snout.

Grasped at tail and gill
she brandishes her prize
against the skin of sunset,
shouting, "Ta Daah!"
and we marvel, though it's all show,
some fun with a prop,
a trophy and pose
before the merciful release
and the deep's blue liberty.

Now she stands marooned,
caught on a hook and
mounted on the wall,
netted by a golden frame.
A fair-skinned girl
with hair gone sepia,
face white-capped with cracks,
while behind her,
the ultramarine sea
fades calmly to amber.

Yet still she dares us,
with that look, that fish

> that banner
> as if even now
> she could see, feel, hear . . .
> the deep thump of
> the fish's landing,
> the sudden cheers
> the back-slapping
> the cries of ecstasy
> the cold salt wind
> while
> so many words
> so many moments
> remain submerged
> or simply forgotten
> schools of kingfish
> awaiting the hook.

Smiling, he re-read his poem, feeling he'd got something right, because, God knew, life blew by in a hurry. And what were those flashes, those highlights he remembered? They were faded snapshots. And the people who'd burned so brightly in the past – what shadows they cast on the present!

Oh, how unbearably sweet life had been in college. The sun and the sea, best friend and girlfriend, a whole Barton-centric universe. How long could it last before some Copernicus-of-the-soul shattered his paradigm?

Not long, as it turned out. Helmut had sworn not to interfere with his pursuit of Jordan, though if he fell into the "just friends" category ("the purgatory of *agape*," Helmut called it) then he couldn't swear to restrain himself. Yet how could Barton complain? He'd won his shiny girl and he'd been spoiled and he knew it. But that was the operative word: *spoiled*. So much of life would now be rotten. He knew that too.

And startled himself. For the first time he understood her drive to paint. He felt it too, in a different way. The need to condense time.

Contrary to the cliché, he thought, time wasn't money. Time couldn't be saved. There was no way to stash a week-end in your pocket, no way to spend it later. You had to consume time when you had it or else it rotted. Human relationships had a shelf-life too, a span beyond which love soured and began its long arc toward the trash can – if you neglected it, that is, or, worse, found it poisoned.

Barton sighed. If he hadn't squandered his life on the law, he might've been a writer, or if he couldn't make art, he could've made children. Something to outlive him. In this, he wasn't so different from his nemesis.

Closing his book, the blood of his ancestors roared in his ears. *It's not too late*, they howled.

For what? he thought.

To make the blood between. That bridge between the dead and the unborn. Our heir.

"My heir," he said, flabbergasted. A light blazed in his skull. He knew what his marriage needed.

His wife was forty-three, with the same athletic body she'd had twenty years ago.

It could happen. He closed his eyes and let his book slip from his hand onto the grass.

In his feverish daydream, a baby held out its tiny hands, its mouth a crimson toothless hole.

3

Conspiracy

JORDAN hadn't planned on childlessness either, but having swallowed a birth control pill every day for nearly twenty years she'd snuffed out her eggs like a long line of candles, poor players who'd neither fret nor strut across any stage, nor hear any sound or fury. So she wondered: if she didn't give birth to children – then what? The law? She had her *pro bono* work, but that wasn't enough. Paint a masterpiece? It seemed unlikely.

She suffered bouts of "stork envy." Photos of other people's children sent her into fits of longing. So did pictures of her grandparents and earlier generations of the Kelly family. Digging out the album and staring into the eyes of long dead ancestors, she opened a hole in her heart, because as she'd explained to Barton, "They'd all love me if they knew me. They're as much my family as my contemporaries."

Her ancestors, like Barton's, simply wouldn't understand and – she felt this physically – couldn't fathom why she wasn't creating a family. Why else were you alive? So you could remain a child? So you could call yourself an artist?

Scratching her head, she steeled herself for the task at hand, because whether or not it would be a masterpiece, her job was to bring form out of chaos, to rescue the dripping stars from the blackness of her mind.

Warily, she approached her easel. She had on a tattered orange T-shirt and men's denim overalls smeared with paint. In places the paint smears were thicker than the denim. She liked them that way. With the overalls so stiff, she thought they might help hold her up.

Brush poised in the air, she surveyed yesterday's work. Smelling the sharp fumes of oil, she wiped a strand of hair from her eye, then dabbed her palette and painted a black line.

Holding her body very still, she stopped and stared at the line. It would do. Her scalp crawled and suddenly she took flight, painting with ferocious energy and speed.

Her work was oddly childlike: wide-eyed cartoonish faces disappearing into animal bodies which faded into abstraction. Whirling vortices of indigo and pink shot through a tangerine and kiwi field, maelstroms of Fauvist crimson and Warhol pea-green lay atop globs of burgundy, while through this gaseous glow a cave drawing slowly surfaced, its animal eyes and black pupils peering out from a psychedelic mist . . . watching, waiting, predatory.

A shiver zippered up her spine. She scratched and cocked her head to one side, squinting at her monster. That bit, okay. Over there, not so much. But the energy was there.

Her embryo had a heartbeat. She stepped back for a wider view, using her wrist to brush away the hair which kept tickling her eye. She blinked and smeared a streak of blue paint on her cheek.

This work might be a breakthrough, she thought, a quantum leap, and it gave her a view inside herself.

Inside her studio, with its wide skylights where the clouds sailed like passing ships, she could forget heartbreak and fear. Her painting was a hiding place, a fort, with a sign – *no boys allowed*. Her lovers lived outside. They had to. Because here she was The Creator. And who but an artist knew the thrills had by God?

But her conscience would not shut up. It opened its maw and swallowed her, hair and all.

Her painting was pretentious drivel. It showed a journeyman's talent, nothing more. Who did she think she was? A part-time attorney who fancied herself an artist? She was a dilettante. And that was pathetic.

Yet she couldn't give up. This was the definition of "artist." The worker who couldn't quit. The voluntary slave.

She heard The Big Voice when she painted, when canvas and brush and paint and body became something more than the sum of parts. "Jordan" ceased to exist. Painting herself into namelessness, she found release. The radiant void, as Barton said. The mind as clear as crystal.

The black line loomed on its angle, blocking her.

Setting down her brush and palette, she stepped outside into the humid Florida air, so sultry it felt like liquid. The live oaks in the yard hummed with insects. Atop a limb in the Australian pine, a blue jay scolded her.

Shading her eyes with her hand, she walked across the grass toward her sleeping husband. He lay dozing in the sun, his lanky body gone slack on the beach chair while a fly wandered over a dark smear of food on his chin. He hadn't slept soundly since The Kansas Incident and she didn't want to wake him.

Smiling, she noticed the Martin Amis novel in the grass. *Dead Babies*. Her husband was still the only man she knew who actually read the books she recommended. Ever since college it had been one of the things she loved about him, especially since it gave them something to talk about other than *their relationship*. They loved to read in bed together.

When he began snoring, she went back to her studio. Inside, she ran her finger over the grainy surface of the dry portion of her new work, sat down on a stool and, cutting her eyes from her workbench to her painting-in-progress, swore softly and put her face in her hands.

"It sucks," she moaned softly.

Chewing her lips, she looked up through her fingers. She couldn't find her voice. Everything she wanted to paint had been done.

Picasso, Matisse, Monet, Pollock – even that overrated Warhol. All the good ideas were taken.

And yet, somewhere inside her, she felt the flicker of originality, a guttering flame which, if only she could discover it, would lead her somewhere magical. Her work showed shards of brilliance – she was too good a critic not to see that, but she lacked vision. Her paintings succeeded on a technical level, but they weren't *about* anything. And there could be nothing worse, she thought, than a painter who couldn't see The Big Picture – *El Foto Grande*. On clear days she could see its unearthly light, but its source quivered maddeningly beyond the rim.

"You're painting Kandinsky from memory," Helmut had said on a rare studio visit, putting his face up to a canvas to inspect her brushwork. Across the room she flinched and held her stomach. Her skin crawled. She'd poured her guts and soul into *What Blood Beyond the Skin of Sunset?* And she felt she'd gained a foothold on higher ground, that lofty space where Inspiration lived, but no, in a spasm of recognition she saw what Helmut saw, and everything became clear.

Her painting was a clever Kandinsky knockoff, the product of a talented school girl. She blushed. How could she have deluded herself? She was a hack, a thief, a criminal . . .

Seeing the woebegone look on her face, Helmut relented. "The flaw is not in the execution, dear heart, but in the conception."

"Explain," she demanded.

Helmut laughed. "Nothing kills art like an explanation, Jordie."

Under the smooth brow, her eyes were clear and candid. He knew something which could help her, and by God she'd have it. She looked at him imploringly. "Come *on*," she said.

Helmut sighed wearily. "It's a matter of knowing what's required. I mean, a guy spends ten grand on a painting and takes it home and – assuming he didn't buy it just to match his couch – he wants to be entertained."

Her jaw dropped. What blasphemy was this? And in her studio, her temple! *How dare you,* she nearly said, but the rightness of his position became clear. She saw over the horizon. She'd been taking herself too seriously. Her work lacked play, that necessary leavening. Self-regard had prevented her from having any fun – precisely what was lacking in her painting – *la comedia divina!* The Dance. The Great Distraction. And her hero, Picasso? What was he if not a clown? And Dali? A chameleon. Her knees buckled.

"You haven't painted enough canvas," Helmut said, "but if you don't quit, you'll turn a corner. You understand what I'm saying? It shouldn't seem too hard. If it's too hard, you're on the wrong road."

She fetched her clipboard off her workbench and began writing. Helmut smiled slyly. His criticism was spot-on. She had to admit it. Sensing danger in this, she realized that any artist lucky enough to discover a mentor would forgive him anything.

In this way, he did for her what no other man had ever done. He allowed her to see that there might be greatness in her – if only she could get it out.

And she would do anything to unlock herself. She would bear shame and regret, but she had to have the key. She had to see the treasure inside.

For his critique, Helmut had demanded a kiss, which she had dutifully delivered – professionally, she thought, like an actress playing a scene. Her tongue stayed in her mouth, though Helmut sought it, finding only the smooth surface of her teeth.

Strutting out, he whistled as he ambled along the cobblestone path. Watching him, she plied her roller with great sweeping strokes, painting over the hack brushwork, the unconsciously stolen design.

Her husband wasn't the only one who understood *larceny,* which, for an artist, remained the unforgivable sin.

Tendons flexing, tongue tucked into the corner of her mouth, she felt cleansed with every stroke of the roller, until with the last white swath she was left with nothing – nothing which was pure and spare and above all, *hers.*

And money? At Kelly, Knight and Squire, she put in billable hours whenever she felt guilty for not selling her art. Specializing in tax shelters for the wealthy (another of Helmut's savvy suggestions), she turned on the high voltage charm and dazzled IRS auditors, explaining how her clients' offshore accounts were in fact legitimate.

"Another day of whoring," she'd tell her husband, stripping off her smart blue business suit and high heels.

Yet on the karmic balance sheet, she figured one good painting earned her an exemption in her own moral filings – themselves not the best kept records, she admitted.

Of course, she could've lived off her grandmother's legacy or her husband's paycheck, but she wouldn't freeload, even off her own inheritance. This wasn't virtue, so much as disposition. She was a born-and-bred Yankee, old school, with a New Englander's sense of thrift.

Yet this same trait had her laboring at the firm when she should've been in the studio. Offshore accounts and dubious charities – the law had aged her.

Standing before her easel while Barton slept outside in the sun, she ran her fingertips over the canvas, feeling its tiny ridges. Was it too late? she wondered. If you were still alive, could it ever be too late?

Besides, what could you paint if you were still a pup? What could you possibly *know*? At forty-three, she was no spring chicken, but neither was she an old maid.

Who knew? Maybe she hadn't squandered her best years. The law's delay might not have ruined her. Perhaps her most productive years were yet to come. Perhaps she'd had to do everything in her life up to now in order to become what she wanted to be: *an artist*, a woman worthy of that grand and seductive title.

Standing there in her studio, alone, a gray hair fell before her eye and she yanked it out with a snapping sound. Letting it fall to the floor, she rubbed her smarting scalp, feeling distinctly middle-aged, fighting for the faith to go on before she felt distinctly dead.

If other people had New York shows – why not her? Was her dream so absurd? Helmut would help. Even her advanced age might be turned to advantage. She'd already traveled to Manhattan where she'd made several cold calls, struggling down the windy streets with her portfolio.

"As long as you bring buyers!" one bearded owner had shouted after her.

The business side of art gave her a headache, but Barton was very supportive – too much so, in some ways, since he'd have praised whatever she did – bat guano on canvas, monkey dung on ceramic, whereas Helmut was more discerning. He might be brutal, but at least he was honest. An artist needed that.

And wasn't it strange how seldom candor found its way into human affairs. Honesty the best policy? Not if you wanted to keep your friends around.

Knuckling her fingers into her eyes, she crossed the studio and sat at her workbench, remembering her husband's question.

"Did you sleep with him in Kansas?"

"For the thousandth time, no!" She couldn't meet his raw-looking eyes. Why did he have to be so faithful? He couldn't cheat on her anymore than he could beat her. But Helmut, with his bold dark stare – he was a different. A predator. Sexual readiness in repose. Pure male potential. Balls, in a word.

"You know the saddest words in English?" Barton had asked.

She didn't say anything.

"It's too late," he said.

Jordan got down on her knees. "Please, Barton. Please forget Kansas." She hung her head and pressed her hands together.

"I wish I could, Jordan."

There she was. *On her knees*. Her knees! Perhaps she was being tested, to see how much humiliation she could bear.

In her heart, she was loyal to Barton, and wasn't the heart the operative organ, the deciding issue in this case? After all, sex was ridiculous. Insert post A into slot B. Rub until finished. She closed her eyes. God, one slip – even two!

For her part, infidelity didn't constitute abandonment, whereas her husband behaved as if she'd sold him to slave traders or hawked him to star in a snuff film.

What did she want from him? She hardly knew. As a young woman she'd used him to find wholeness and she'd loved him because he fixed her, but as soon as she was repaired *he'd* fallen into the emotional junkyard. And she was no mechanic. On the contrary, to her horror she'd turned out to be more of a wrecking ball.

She rose from her workbench and crossed the studio to her easel. Her eyes were lit with fire. She had it. Her subject. She wanted to practice unsafe love! Remove the condom from her heart and exchange all the loving fluids her maker had installed. She wanted to gush and paint that fountain: non-stop, free-flowing love! The elemental force, uncut by the rules of perspective or the tenets of color theory.

But before she could harness those waters, she had to put her house in order. She'd made a vow to Barton, and after cheating on him with his best man, she had to make good.

Helmut picked up on the first ring.

"So what's with all the crazy messages?" she asked.

Helmut ignored her, though he'd been calling, drunk, to tell her he was "melting down."

"How's Cuckoo's Nest?" he asked. "He better come back to work tomorrow, and tell him to bring his lunchbox. Turns out we need his sorry ass."

"Pull in your horns," she said, putting on her armor with wisecracks, "he's still off his feed."

"He's off the clock, too, you know. I don't pay goldbricks."

"Since when do you pay your own partner?"

"He didn't tell you?"

"I was testing you," she lied. "I just wanted to see what you'd say."

"Your husband works for me now – how's that?"

"Not my business. So what's your emergency?"

"Ah, well – it's a matter of some delicacy. You'd better come over. I'm at home today."

"Yeah, right."

"Don't flatter yourself, honey. This is entirely professional."

"Why would I think otherwise?"

"I have no idea," he said.

Sitting in front of one of the studio's tall windows, she gazed through a flaw in the glass at her sleeping husband. He had his book splayed face down on his chest, with a pen protruding from underneath the cover.

"Ten minutes – and I can't stay more than an hour."

"Don't forget your suit. Unless you want to swim *au natural.*"

Another of her water cures. Helmut had offered her the use of his pool, since swimming offered her some relief against painter's block.

"Earth to Jordan. Hello?"

"I'm sorry," she shook her head, "what did you say?"

"Shall I expect you or not?"

"Yes. No. I don't know."

"Damn, woman – has everyone got their pages stuck together over there? Come for a swim. And there's that financial matter..."

"I can't. Barton's been acting kind of paranoid lately."

"*Lately?* He's been paranoid since the eighties. Anyway, we're just pals, aren't we, Jordie? For twenty-five years. Can you believe it? We've achieved the Platonic ideal. Pure *agape*. Or has Cuckoo's Nest forbidden you to see me?"

"I told you not to call him that."

"It's nothing I wouldn't say to his face. Anyway, I really do need him back at work . . . so when will I see you?"

She clicked off her phone and looked out the window, chewing her lip.

That was the thing about Helmut – when he wanted something he didn't hem and haw – he acted. He knew what he was doing, or if he didn't, he had sense enough to behave as if he did.

Anyhow, she had to look after their finances.

Her husband was sleeping.

It was so hot, too, and she'd love to go for a swim. The painting could wait, couldn't it?

She'd be right back.

4

APPEALING THE VERDICT

INSIDE his beach house, Helmut sat before his computer, a far-off look on his face, his profile ablaze in the screen's blue glow. He drummed his fingers on his mouse pad. Jordan's phone call had stopped him from squaring a deal on the foreign exchange.

Impossible! Down six thousand and it wasn't even dawn in Tokyo.

He squared the deal and took the loss, then pressed his fist into his belly.

"Ouf!" he expelled a bubble of carbon dioxide and tasted acid reflux.

This particular disaster was not his fault. He knew this because his function in civil cases lay in assigning blame, that is to say, *fault*. *Ergo,* the direct and proximate cause of his financial woes was not a gambling addiction, or a research department composed entirely of chimpanzees, but rather, the editorial staff at *The Wall Street Times*.

Their writers had seduced him. They'd stuffed his head with golden dreams until his future rang out like a newly minted coin dropped into the till . . .

Ka-ching!

Who could resist that?

He'd actually believed he could join the American Aristocracy.

The paper's advertisers were also joint and severally liable, as they too had lent a hand in his financial undoing, his monetary mauling. They'd filled his eyes with private jets and luxury yachts until he could no longer respect himself. Only clowns flew commercial, and Helmut Knight was nobody's clown.

Ever the reasonable and prudent person, however, he was willing to compromise, because if he couldn't own a whole Lear jet he'd settle for a part, the time-share version, called a "fractal." Without irony, he'd tell you he deserved it. Really. If not the brilliant Helmut Knight, author of "The Charismatic Close," then who?

With his resume, he was more than qualified to be rich. He was entitled. As in the original Declaration of Independence, which read, "blah blah . . . life, liberty and *property*." Only the poor pursued happiness, just like they pursued a lot of things. Whereas the rich had already bought happiness, got it cheap from the Indians and had it in the family for years.

Besides, Helmut was forty-three. Didn't such an appalling figure entitle a man to something?

With each passing birthday he sustained permanent damage, and what with the pain and suffering of having to watch his youth evaporate, Justice demanded compensation. He was grossly disfigured. The loss of his hair alone had to be worth millions. Add to this the aggravation of the pot belly, the wrinkled skin, the creaking joints, the alienation of affection.

By God, he'd been victimized by Father Time, but Helmut wouldn't settle. Oh no. He wasn't a geezer yet.

Rubbing palms together, he set about extracting punitive damages. Using the company credit card which also bore Barton's name, he fired another twenty-five thousand into his account. It showed up instantly and he wiped his brow. One thing those administrative chimpanzees could manage was accepting money.

Then somehow it was noon in Tokyo, and things were getting gray and he had to replace that twenty-five thou – could it be? He blinked at the screen.

Twice?

No. Surely.

A mistake.

The exchange went on the move and currencies tilted across the globe. The arrow indicating a fluctuation stuck in his eye, hooking him tight. He might score millions, but money only came in one flavor, and it tasted like more.

More! More! More!

I'm on a roll, he thought, tapping the keys and baring his teeth. In a blink he made sixteen-thousand . . . seventeen . . . twenty-one!

Betting fifty large that the dollar would fall against the euro, he covered his position, crossed his fingers, tapped the wood of his desk, rolled away in his chair and waited.

Jordan was supposed to be coming over, but that seemed ages ago.

Ordinarily, she was quite punctual. He'd give her that. She was the most dependable person he knew. She was the sort of woman who'd stick by him. Even if he got bowel disease or gangrene or leprosy, he thought, wrinkling his nose. No one else would help him, of course, and honestly, could he blame them? Because . . . come *on!* Look at your face! It's like bacon. Something the dog barfed up.

But Jordan wouldn't leave. Helmut considered the rarity of this. People generally panicked and ran, but Jordan Kelly stuck around. He could count on Jordan Kelly. Bet on her, too. She was a sure thing.

He loved her. He didn't want to, but he did. That's how he knew it was love. That's why he called her Jordan Kelly instead of Jordan Squire. He had no say in the matter. It was just that simple, and horrible, too, for the same reason.

So where in hell was she?

She was a damn sight better character than her goofball husband, that was for sure. That ingrate. Did he appreciate that Helmut had saved his job? Of course not. Everything came easily to Barton

Squire except the realization that everything came easily. That was his whole problem.

With Hong Kong still asleep, the markets fell into a lull and Helmut logged off his account. He'd been beaten up enough for one day. Groaning, he stood and stretched his arms over his head, wincing at a sudden twinge in his hip. He carried his drink into the living room, a vast sunken rectangle with a white carpet, a curved white couch, a white loveseat, and a long silver coffee table. Beyond the table a picture window looked onto the thatched roof of the tiki bar and the sapphire blue of his pool.

Inside the kitchen, at his indoor bar overlooking the breakfast nook, he put fresh ice in his glass, ran a lime wedge around the rim and filled it with gin, added a thimble-full of tonic, and dropped in the crushed lime.

Looking up, he nearly choked. A fiber stuck in his throat.

Beyond the sliding glass doors, Jordan was stripping off her paint-spattered overalls. His heart skipped because for a wild moment he thought she was going skinny dipping, but underneath her overalls she had on a day-glo green bikini. Helmut licked his lips and made her a gin and tonic.

Slicing the lime, he watched as she walked along the pool's concrete apron toward the deep end where the water reflected the cumulus clouds sailing across the sky. Despite the heat, she didn't sweat. Flexing her long legs, she hopped gracefully onto the diving board. Her face was solemn as she strode to the end, her body quick and nimble. She brought her feet neatly together. Helmut admired the bold thrust of her arches, the rose-brown of her slender ankles. She stood very still. Her face had a taut look of concentration and she dove into the pool, into the inverted bowl of the sky, scattering the clouds.

Swimming underwater with bubbles streaming from her nostrils, she reached the shallow end where she surfaced with a great grasp. Seeing Helmut, she tilted back her head and spat a sparkling arc of water.

Helmut opened the sliding doors and stepped outside, hugging the cold drinks against his chest as he squinted against the sudden glare and slid shut the door with his foot. The sun hurt his eyes and his right temple throbbed. Sultry air filled his sinuses. He had on white linen shorts and a black and white shirt. He let the shirt hang open, the better to reveal the sexy tuft of hair on his chest.

Holding herself up with her elbows on the side of the pool, Jordan lazily kicked her feet and blinked at him.

"It lives," she said, and flipped over and kicked, breast-stroking across the pool, water streaming from her face. A smile twisted Helmut's lips.

Doing a racer's turn against the other side, she spun over and swam toward him underwater, keeping her eyes open, blue and wide as they broke the surface.

Helmut laughed and held out her drink. Somehow it was hard not to like the look of someone who'd just come up from underwater.

"Liquid heaven!" she called out cheerfully, turning her head and sweeping back the swath of hair which had darkened from gold to wheat. Her hand struck the surface and splashed him with sun-flecked shards. "Get in here and race me, Mutt!"

Helmut flinched when the coolness hit his legs. No one but Jordan would've dared splash him. "I haven't been swimming since I was twelve," he said. He set her drink on the edge of the pool, confounded, as he had been for the last quarter-century, by one of the great mysteries of life – how had a goofball like Barton Squire snagged first-rate talent like Jordan Kelly? "I'd rather watch," he said.

Swimming up to her drink, she closed her lips on the straw and sucked the gin into her mouth, then she paddled away on her back, wind-milling her arms over her head. Droplets flew from her hands and flashed in the sun. Turning at the far end, she swam an Australian crawl, while Helmut settled himself into a chaise lounge under the green shade of an awning.

Sipping his drink, he admired the sweeping curve of her hips, the long flanks, the narrow waist, the well-formed shoulders. Her sleek body split the water as smoothly as an otter.

The female form was more aquatic than the male, he thought, more streamlined and graceful, even as Jordan huffed loudly, doing laps. Her stroke was rhythmic and smooth and whenever she broke the surface glass-like beads pearled off her slick and nearly hairless body.

Feeling his chest tighten, out of breath from watching her, he closed his eyes and rolled the cold glass across his forehead, thinking of death. His skull throbbed from the ice. Ah, the senses. What marvelous distractions from the inevitable! Yet the mind grew a tolerance to the body's delights. Helmut sighed. He was getting old very fast. Worse, he was aware of the process, of the fact that he was beginning to decay.

Yet if Jordan stood by him he might be able to stand it. Alone, the descent would be impossible. But it didn't matter. She belonged to his new assistant, Barton somebody. He accepted this. Why shouldn't he? It was unjust, but as a lawyer he understood that Justice was a social fiction. He wanted to laugh, but found his throat constricted. God! Just when you got a grip on existence it was time to let go, wave your hand and bid the world *adieu* (assuming your brain hadn't already betrayed you with Alzheimer's disease).

Yet life's brevity didn't excuse one from soldiering on, or so he told himself. Not that he was *against* eternal life and salvation – if votes were cast he'd holler *aye*. But sorry, dead was done. An absence beyond the rim, beyond surgical anesthesia. Nowhere over the rainbow. Ta ta, self. Won't be seeing *you* again. Good riddance. Smelly old carcass. You with your gingivitis and your hemorrhoids, Helmut thought, I hope you rot!

If humans were pets you'd never have one, he recalled hearing somewhere, because the maintenance was too high. Always with the fingernails, the hair, the teeth . . . and the smell. He scratched his armpit and smelled his finger. *Pew!* What an animal. God, that joker! To cram a soul inside a bag of guts. What kind of pervert . . . well, who *would* come up with that? Unless . . . *this* was hell. He considered the possibility.

Still, death wasn't all bad. It had *some* benefits. No more paying bills or flossing teeth or answering the phone or cutting toenails or listening to the neighbor's dog bark. That had to count for something.

And yet here he was, still alive. It wasn't so easy sometimes. But the sky was blue. And his only love swam in his pool.

Twirling his glass, the rays of the sun shone through an ice cube, refracted in translucent silver. Briefly, he reflected on the antiquity of water, an ageless thing, so unlike himself, yet he was made of it. Such thoughts! Well, what did he expect, tippling liquor before sunset?

At the end of the pool, under the shade of a palm tree hung with gold coconuts, Jordan climbed out with her body streaming bubbles, her tan skin stretched tightly over her bones. Atheist that he was, Helmut was struck by the power of evolution in creating such an animal. Damn fine work, he thought. Only one hitch: her lithe body wouldn't endure much longer than his flabby one.

"Oh the humanity!" he called across the pool's blue oval, "I'm having another meltdown."

Shifting his weight in the chaise lounge to take the pressure of his sciatic nerve, he ran his hand over his head, checking for hair.

He looked at his palm. No loss or growth. His cranium was still slick.

Toweling off, Jordan came toward him, skirting the curve of the pool and walking with an athlete's grace. She caught him staring and wagged her index finger, then she picked up his empty glass and cocked her head to the side, raising her eyebrows inquiringly.

"Oh yeah, that's my kitty-cat – all tits and teeth!"

She tapped her wedding ring with her fingernail.

"So I recant," he said. "No need to burn me at the stake."

"Matrimony," she said. "It's a binding contract."

"How nice for you. Me? I've got bigger worries. Responsibilities. Keeping your husband employed, for one."

"So govern yourself accordingly, Helmut."

Barton's new boss emitted a strange barking sound which startled them both. Jordan looked at him. He shrugged and the moment passed and they pretended it hadn't happened. "I did the prenup, remember? He won't take money from you, honey."

"All the same – *honey*."

"Forget it, Jordie. That idiot would starve first."

"Please don't call my husband an idiot."

"Well, tell him not to act like one."

Inside the air-conditioned cool of the house, with its wall to wall white carpeting and its minimalist design, Jordan made another round of drinks, adding too much gin, but what the hell, she had a glow on and she felt good. Why not celebrate the near completion of *What Blood Beyond the Skin of Sunset?* Before leaving her studio she'd inserted an orange-and-white hazard marker with a flashing yellow light, signaling a dangerous boundary – a line not to be crossed, and then she said the happiest words in the English language: "*I understand.*"

For the first time in her life she realized what she loved about Helmut. He was honest with her. He was forthright about sex and death and art, and only his wizardry could transform her into a painter. He was her alchemist, changing her lead to gold.

His witty barbs and abrasive manner annoyed most people, but she got a kick out of his jokes. She knew how to take him, which was with a snowball-sized grain of salt. He entertained her. And he made her feel sophisticated, if he felt so inclined, that is. When he withheld his approval, she was perversely stimulated, desirous. He reduced her to a teacher's pet, eager to please, hungry for praise. That's how he got sex. He made *her* want it. Anyway, she wasn't staying long. One more round and she'd be on her way. No doubt about it.

Outside, she handed him a frosty glass.

"Wonderful," he said, "a polar drink and a tropical babe. *Joie de vivre!*" He put on his Ray Ban sunglasses. The pool and the sky and the palm trees sank into a deep shade of green.

Jordan stretched out on a deck chair, drink in hand, exposing herself to the sun. Hidden behind the dark lenses, Helmut's eyes traveled down her rib cage, over the concave belly and the hillock of her bikini bottom. A thin swath of day-glo green cloth disappeared between her thighs, concealing her.

Keeping her eyes closed, she said, "You know I can feel you staring."

Helmut chuckled and sipped his drink. "Is that all?"

"It's enough." Her eyes were still closed. Like him, she was forty-three, but aside from a slight loosening around the upper arms, she looked the same as she had when they'd lounged on the beach in college.

"Peeping Tom."

"Always something to be thankful for."

Eating her up with his eyes, Helmut felt drunk. His head throbbed pleasantly.

This was good greed, he thought, greed for life, which was the same as greed for a woman. She invigorated him, fueling him with a power like fusion. Basking in her glow, her Jordan-aura, he felt reborn, holy even, and less like the stinking baboon every man kept hidden under his *homo sapien* skin.

In a word, she made him feel . . . *young.*

Their twin reflections reclined in the sliding glass door. She lay with the pool shimmering behind her, while he lounged behind his shades, looking like a movie star. All was right with the world. He raised his glass and toasted himself. Salute! To Helmut Knight, Star of the Bar! Jordan laughed warmly beside him, keeping her eyes closed.

Droplets of perspiration glazed her taut belly and collected in her circular navel, running along her skin when she adjusted her chair and turned on her side. The sun caught her hipbone, casting a shadow across the cleft between her legs. Helmut ran his tongue over his teeth. The moment lingered.

Could he make it work with her? Sun himself in the blaze of her love? And if so, would he tan or burn?

The valley of death, he thought, staring at the day-glo green triangle between her legs, thinking *I would die for that*. Rattling the ice cubes in his drink, he said, "You're turning me into a pussy."

"Excuse me?" Her eyes were still closed.

"That carcass of yours. It ought to be illegal. Christ, it still tears me up – after all these years, you're still a chocolate box type."

"I'm middle-aged," she said. She opened her eyes and pulled at the skin of her thighs. "Get over it, old man." She turned her head and blinked at him in the hot pale light. She shaded her eyes with her hand. "But thanks anyway, Mutt."

He drank. "It's the whole truth," he said, "nothing but."

She propped herself on her elbow and turned over onto her stomach while his eyes climbed the twin globes of her bouncy rump and descended into the valleys of her sacral dimples, lightly dusted with the finest of blond hairs.

"Your husband is either the biggest fool alive," he said, "or else the luckiest. Anyway, I need another drink." He scraped his chair legs over the concrete and stood up. A soft breeze rippled the pool and dried the sweat from his face.

"Same again?" he asked, holding out his hand. She put her fingers over her glass.

"Can't," she said. "Husband's waiting."

"Why do you have to call him that?"

She frowned. "Cause that's what he is."

"What? So he hasn't got a name? Why do married people have this compulsion to show off? If it's not with the matching rings it's with the royal 'we.' 'We' did this. 'We' did that. It's a form of condescension."

"Call up one of your whores, Mutt. You need to get laid."

The two of them stared at each other. The moment sat still,

creating a hole. Together they perched on its edge, daring to enjoy the vertigo. One misstep and they'd fall in.

"Come on," said Helmut, raising his leg and nudging her knee with his big toe. "Just around the block, eh? I'm lonely."

She shook her head. Helmut lonely? And confessing it? It was another of his maneuvers, delivered with impeccable timing, yet even so she felt sorry for him.

"I don't really drink anymore, Bart – God! – I mean Helmut. This was a rare treat."

"What. You're an alcoholic now?"

"I will be if I keep drinking."

"Well – what are you going to do – go home and watch TV with Cuckoo's Nest? Don't be a lame-ass, woman."

"Barton doesn't like it when I drink. He says it changes me."

"That's the point, isn't it? Why drink if it doesn't change you?"

"I mean in a bad way. You've seen it. My personality. I go Jekyll and Hyde."

Helmut grinned. "I know – I love it!"

"I'm sure you do, but I'm not that person. I don't *want* to be her. Kansas was an aberration, Mutt. I hope you understand that."

"I'm not asking you to fuck me, dear. I just don't want to drink alone. Please? It's a beautiful day, we're out by the pool. Come *on*."

He raised his eyebrows, imploring her. He was terrible. She had to admit it. But he had charisma. Paunchy and bald and middle-aged, he had to have something.

And what was she? She couldn't tell. All she knew was that she had misgivings – artistic, sexual, financial and ethical. She was, she admitted, a train wreck.

Meanwhile her husband, her superego in *absentia,* flickered briefly, wagging his finger over her empty glass, but then she and booze had had such a rollicking good time together (until the party ended in Kansas anyway) and . . . what the hell, her drink was more refreshing than intoxicating so . . . just this once. What harm could it do? She knew when to quit. Or at least she used to . . . she'd have to be careful, that's all. But no, she'd refrain. Or would she?

Alcohol! Creature! Leg opener! You hustle the brain into running up a tab it can't settle, she thought. You're death on a payment plan. Fun on wild nights, but later, what a karmic finance charge. That's when the body came to collect. She never tired of borrowing, but she definitely got sick of paying. Alcoholism was the mafia of the spirit and the only way out was in a pine box. You were made and unmade. Whacked.

Lord! If you're up there, she thought, casting her pale eyes heavenward, you've damn sure got me confused. She held up her empty glass.

"Sure," she said, "why not?"

Helmut smiled and, carefully holding the glasses in one hand, slid open the door and padded barefoot over the plush carpet. Jordan watched him through the window as he poured from the Tangeray bottle. He returned with two drinks, looking pleased.

"Whoa!" she said, smacking her lips over what tasted like paint thinner. "You trying to kill me?"

Smiling with his dark eyes, he clinked his glass against hers and drank. "Only in metaphor," then, wiping his mouth with the back of his hand, "Your trouble . . . is that you don't know when to throttle back."

"Excuse me? That's my specialty."

"Sure it is."

"And you *do*?" she asked, her voice curving upward.

"Do what?" Helmut blinked. Distracted by a squirrel drinking from the pool, he'd forgotten the question. Overhead, the sun throbbed in the sky, a blazing yolk in a bowl of blue.

"Know when to quit," she said.

"Honey, I was *born* knowing." He cleared his throat, archly raising his voice. "The true hedonist maintains his body like a classic car, the vehicle of his pleasure."

He drained his glass in a single pull, creating a troubling gas bubble in his midsection. He struck himself with his fist, to no avail. Truth be known, he'd lied to her. His own alcoholism alarmed him even though his drinking consisted of the "maintenance" variety – maintenance because removing it would be like subtracting the cheese from a rat's maze.

Without a reward, why run the course?

Alcohol also fed his hunger for The Conquest. The *coupe de grace* might be diverting, but the hunt was the thing. Flooding some hapless woman's mouth was only a fringe benefit. He might've got the same satisfaction from whopping her in the face with a custard pie.

With a lawyer's sense of *fault*, he realized that, as with money, the blame didn't lie with him. He was simply human. And human nature was flawed. He'd warned his old roommate about it.

"You're going to get tired of the same old hole," he'd announced when Barton broke the news that he was marrying Jordan.

"Nice," Barton had said, "but I believe the word you're looking for is 'congratulations.' "

"You want me to fabricate a sentiment? Or do you want honesty?"

"I want a best man."

"No can do. Not if I have to stand in front of some Christian preacher."

So if in the Biblical sense he "knew" his best friend's wife, did he feel guilty? If you could ask him, he'd say, "about what?" And his question wouldn't be disingenuous. It would be sincere. He wouldn't know what you were talking about, which would, of course, infuriate you and make you want to kill him. Helmut had that effect on people.

By way of exculpatory conduct, however, hadn't he warned his victim? Barton knew that Helmut had sworn a mighty allegiance to himself. He was his own kingdom and its emperor, where all the women were serfs. And if you observed that he wasn't wearing any clothes, he'd laugh and say, *Good! Why don't you blow me?*

Fueled by alcohol, he grew more formidable. On top and in control. Oh yes. Helmut meant to wobble the world.

"Listen, Jordie. I hate to ask, but – I need more coin."

"Do you have a figure, or do I have to guess?"

"It's a loan, love. Now don't bust my *cojones*."

"How much?"

"Sixty grand."

Jordan gagged on an ice cube, spitting it back into her glass where it rattled merrily. "Jesus, Helmut!"

"Don't take the Lord's name in vain, dear."

"You're a piece of work, Helmut."

"Thanks, I – "

"Put that thing away!"

"What? No peace for the beast?"

She glanced around the pool. Tall hedges shielded it from the view of the neighbors but you never knew. Her husband had got so paranoid he might've followed her.

"Zip up your shorts. For God's sake!"

He zipped up. "Relax – I was just taking a little air. Running up the flagpole, so to speak – seeing if you'd salute." He chuckled wryly.

She tossed her drink on his crotch. The cold zapped his groin but he only grimaced and showed her his teeth, working his mouth into a lopsided grin.

He shrugged. Never shy about making passes, he'd discovered that simply exposing himself worked best. It certainly accelerated things, however they turned out. It was like handing a client a contract along with a pen you'd already clicked. Also, once the thing was out, he was always surprised at the number of women who, glancing from side to side as if they were checking for traffic, went down with all the subtlety of a truck stop hooker bent on making the rent.

"Do I still get my loan?" he asked.

Jordan clambered off the deck chair and strode to the other end of the pool where she gathered up her paint-spattered overalls and pulled them on over her bathing suit.

"Jordie, come on – don't get your knickers in a twist. I apologize, okay? It was just the gin talking. You should be flattered."

"Flattered?"

Helmut leered. "The gin's real choosy."

"How nice for the gin," she said primly. "Anyhow, you'll get your loan, but you better replenish that escrow account. I mean it. If you want to bankrupt yourself that's one thing, but do not – I repeat – *do not* ruin my husband."

"I'm not a thief, Jordie."

"I hope not. For your sake."

"Is that a threat?"

"No, it's a desire."

"You're not making sense."

"There's something else."

"I can hardly wait."

"Please be nice to Barton when he comes back to work."

"*Be nice?* What're we, children?"

"Underneath all the bullshit? Yes, I suppose we are."

Helmut held up three fingers. "I'll play along then, if it means so much to you. Scout's honor."

"Thanks for the swim."

He watched her leave and sipped from his drink, his eyes lost in the middle distance. Ice cubes knocked against his teeth. He held the glass up to the sun and sighed.

"Definitely not half full," he said.

5

CHARACTER WITNESS

HER body felt astonishingly light in his arms, or maybe it was just adrenalin. Graciela was conscious but woozy. She moaned and dribbled blood onto the sleeve of Barton's suit as he set her down in the leather chair reserved for their well-heeled clients.

"Stay there, all right?" At the sound of her employer's voice she glanced up, her moist brown eyes glistening. *"Por favor,"* he said gently. He smiled encouragingly and grabbed a wastebasket and turned it upside down and lifted her feet onto it.

"Ees okay," she said. "I getting back to work. "I – " her hand shot to her mouth and she wiped away the blood and made a sucking sound and swallowed. "Mistair Barton, thank you. I go now."

"No, you don't," he said. "I'm calling 911."

She shook her head. "Please, no. Ees only tooth." Coming to her senses, she blinked and took in her surroundings: the recessed lighting, the enormous mahogany desk, the blue river beyond the picture window. She struggled to stand. "Ees fine!"

Rifling the top desk drawer, Barton found a package of tissues and handed them to her. She dabbed her lips and held the wadded paper in her hand, spotted with blood.

He'd discovered her lying face down in the hall, passed out, bleeding from her mouth. Dropping his briefcase, he'd swept her up in his arms and carried her to the nearest office.

It was his first morning back at work.

"Let me have a look," he said. Gingerly, he touched her jaw below her right ear.

She opened her mouth and he peered inside, squinting. His guts clenched. He was no dentist but he could diagnose a mouthful of rotten teeth. Worse, she had a bloody abscess beside her lower left molar. The abscess looked raw and angry, filled with pus.

"No wonder you fainted," he said, stepping back and putting a pleasant expression on his face. A thin layer of sweat shone on her brown forehead. "*Pobrecita*. You must be in agony."

Graciela swallowed. "I go," she said. "I finish work."

"No," he said, grimacing, "that's not going to happen. I'm taking you to my dentist."

"I no afford it."

"You don't have insurance?"

She wouldn't look at him. Her long black hair, so black it was almost blue, was tied from her face into a thick ponytail which hung down her back like a rope. Her eyes were a shade somewhere between amber and chocolate, with extravagantly long black lashes. She had on a shapeless beige uniform, and Barton felt his face go hot when he took in, for the first time, that she was only in her early twenties. He knew her to be a mother and wife so it hadn't occurred to him that she could be so young.

"I don't have insurance," she said, lowering her eyes to the carpet.

Barton's stomach curdled. Was he aware that Kelly, Knight and Squire didn't pay insurance premiums for their cleaning staff? He supposed he was. It was another outrage hammered into that place inside him where he hid subjects too painful to consider.

"I'm sorry, Graciela. This is my fault, but today it changes." He held up his hand to stop her from objecting. "Don't worry, all right? I'll pay the dentist."

"Damn straight you will," said Helmut, entering with a sheaf of papers in his hand. "And since when did my office become the free clinic?"

Barton glared into Helmut's scowling face. "Graciela's got a toothache," he said. "Your door was open."

"Well, tell her to mop up that blood stain in the hall, will you?" He glanced at his watch. "I've got an appointment and I don't need fresh meat getting spooked," he winked at them, " – toughens it up." He smiled with his lips at Graciela. "Whole family got run over by a drunk in a Hummer," he explained. "Wife and son are wrongful death but Dad's a recent amputee – fresh off the chopping block."

Satisfied that he'd conveyed the gravity of pain and suffering (and more important, the law's compensation for it, for which he would receive a third) Helmut sat at his desk and stared at the two of them, who still hadn't moved. Barton was peering into Graciela's mouth again. Helmut cleared his throat and cracked the edges of his papers against the desk.

"You two about through here?"

"I think it's quit bleeding," Barton said. Tenderly, his finger traced the line of her jaw. A fat tear fell from her left eye and she stood up, blushing. Barton caught her elbow and felt a strange sensation stir in his chest. "Time to go," he said. "It won't hurt much longer."

"*Gracias*, Mistair Barton. I get my things from my locker." Keeping her head down, she pressed her hand to her cheek and walked out of Helmut's office.

"I'll meet you in front of the building," Barton called as she disappeared down the hall. "I'll tell one of the secretaries to call your husband."

Helmut clapped his hands and Barton turned to him. "Congratulations, Big Bart! It's a record! Your first day back at work and you're already off the clock. Truly, a Barton Squire move."

"We don't provide dental?"

"Not my department."

"I'm not letting somebody work for us with rotten teeth."

"So fire her ass."

Barton narrowed his eyes and Helmut shrugged, raising his eyebrows in his best "So-how-is-it-my-fault?" look. Once upon a time, Barton would've laughed, but now he only sighed and shook his head. That feeling he'd had toward Graciela, the one which had moved like a live thing in his chest – suddenly he could name it. For the first time in his life, Barton Squire, age forty-three, felt . . . *paternal.*

Helmut sorted through his papers, looking for a contract whose date needed changing. With his finances in disarray, approaching ruin, he was finding it difficult to keep track of his cases. His reading glasses and his keys, too, kept viciously losing themselves.

"For Christ's sake, she's lucky she's even legal." He glanced up, fixing Barton with his bulging brown eyes, "So why make it an issue?"

"What about her husband, Antonio? He works for us too, doesn't he?"

"Part-time."

"Without benefits?"

"Of course without benefits. This is a law office, not the welfare department."

"Unbelievable."

"Oh, it's quite believable – legal too."

"Legal, yes. Ethical, no."

"What're you, back in law school? I paid over sixty large in taxes last year. *Sixty large!* That ought to fill a few teeth. Isn't there a charity clinic?"

"You know what the wait list is at those places?"

"Again, not my department. Forget it. Gart's still fuming over the Dopolis case. You're supposed to be a trial attorney, old Squire. You better kick the EPA's ass or you're looking at malpractice. Even *I* can't help you then."

"So I'm supposed to defend a developer who dumps toxic waste in the lagoon. Do you know the dolphins all have lesions on their skins? Their immune systems have been destroyed. Apparently they've all got some form of herpes."

Helmut rolled his eyes heavenward. "Then don't fuck them, okay? If they want to be sluts, let 'em be sluts. Fucking Flippers. Anyhow, how are *you* a marine biologist? Can *you* establish a causal relationship? No! So start doing your job and defend our client."

Barton clenched his jaw and said, "Sure, Helmut. Whatever you say." Astonishingly, he felt no rancor. Rivers of sweat might be running from his armpits, staining the new suit his wife had bought him to celebrate his return to the firm, and his mouth might taste sourly of gun metal, but popping Fokus tablets as if they were breath mints seemed to be working. He hadn't hammered Helmut's skull into strawberry jam, nor had he strangled Harry Dopolis, the developer who'd been targeted by the EPA for fouling the Indian River lagoon with who knew what poisons.

Checking his temper, Barton found his rage at a manageable level, although – he ran his finger around the inside of his collar – good God it was hot! He pressed his hand to his forehead and it came away wet, and what was that hissing sound? Somewhere out of sight, a fuse was burning. And the smell! He put his nose to the air and sniffed. Homemade waffles? No. Raw sewage? No again. He distinctly caught the odor of rotting fish.

"What, *in the hell*, is the matter with you?" Helmut quit with his papers and stared across the polished expanse of his desk. "Stay home if you're still two bricks shy of a load. Goddamn. Am I the last competent man standing? You look like you're having a seizure, which as an attorney I advise you to do off the premises. I mean it, Barton. One more liability and," he drew his index finger across his throat, "*you're finished!*"

Barton wrenched his attention back to Helmut. If his sense of smell was the only part of him that was crazy, he supposed he could live with it.

"She puts in hours enough to rate benefits. So does Antonio.

Haven't you noticed how early he gets here so he doesn't disturb us with the lawn mower?"

"I hadn't noticed."

"Well, that's just it. He takes extra care so you *don't* notice. And doesn't he maintain the grounds at your house, too?"

"For greenbacks under the table he does. Huh! I wish I had a tax-free income."

"Let's not argue, Helmut. I just want them and their kids insured. Don't you think we could manage that?"

Helmut groaned and yawned and stretched his arms over his head. "*Their kids?* I don't know. It sounds like a lot to me." Feeling his back crack, he sighed and pressed his index finger against his lower lip. Here he was going bankrupt, facing disbarment and possible fraud charges, and his assistant wanted him to spend a fortune outfitting the third world with gold teeth.

What selfishness!

"If you're in need," he intoned, "you shouldn't breed. If you can't pay for the brats, you shouldn't get them."

"Yes well, they're here now, and they probably need vaccinations too."

Helmut found the missing contract and changed the date on it. His new assistant lingered. The kid wasn't showing a lot of promise, he had to admit.

"Don't give me that hangdog look, old Squire. Take a gander at the big picture. Say, for example, you want a pet zebra. I don't know. Something asinine. That's fine. It's a free country. But don't expect me to pay for it, or any other taxpayer. This ain't some hippie commune, Sunshine! It's a free market economy, or at least it's supposed to be. Truth is, half the world *already* eats out of my flour barrel. All I *do* is hand out the goddamned loaves and fishes."

Going red in the face, Helmut licked a bubble of spit from the corner of his mouth and ran his fingers through the tufts above his ears. He'd never been what you'd call good looking, but middle age had turned him into a real troll.

"So listen to me," he said a lofty, indignant voice, "if you want medical coverage for the servants, why not enlist the aid of your nurse?"

"Who?"

"Your Sugar Momma. Your main squeeze."

"We live off what we *earn*, Counselor. Same as you. Jordan donates her income to Heifer International." Helmut's stare was blank. "It's a charity for farmers – you know that. You did the prenups."

"Happily, I'd forgotten." Helmut shook his head. "Anyway, if those third-worlders ever do get your precious cows – which I doubt – they butcher the things as soon as they hobble into the village."

"One animal can start a livelihood. That's the whole point."

Helmut slapped his hand on his desk, leaving a print which quickly faded. "Christ! How can you be so gullible? I hope you don't talk this trash to our clients. Cause if you do – we'll be the ones needing a fucking half-starved cow sent to us."

Sugar Momma? It took a moment, but when the remark sank in, Barton saw red. This was not a metaphor. Crimson light bathed the office. The carpet breathed. Helmut's face sprouted a long snout and he brayed like a goat.

Grunting, Barton leapt forward and grabbed Helmut's tie and hauled him off his chair and over the desk. Helmut snatched at the edges, but his pudgy fingers couldn't find any traction on the slick surface. His limbs thrashed and Barton dragged him over the other side and, smelling Helmut's sour breath, lifted him off his feet.

Barton's eyes shot with blood and a vein bulged in his forehead. Helmut struggled and kicked, but Barton hung on.

"*Listen to me!*" he bellowed into his Helmut's face, shaking him like a doll, "the Mirandas are getting health insurance, you got that?"

Helmut clawed at Barton's chest, tearing loose a button which skittered under the desk.

Then Barton saw something in Helmut's eyes, something shiny and raw. He licked his lips. Oh yes, this was fine. He enjoyed exposing this troll who would be his boss, but then he saw the quiver in Helmut's lip and felt him trembling. Mighty Helmut was as helpless as a baby.

Swinging his head from side to side, he bawled, "Let go of me, you cocksucker!"

Barton let him go. Helmut's feet hit the floor and his desk kept him from falling. Barton opened his mouth and Helmut balled up his fist and punched him in the stomach. Barton blinked. After a quarter century of sit-ups, it was like being hit by a child. Helmut glared at him, his dark eyes boiling. The only sound was their ragged breathing.

Face to outraged face, Barton had seen the boy Helmut used to be, the one he'd roughed up during a fight back in college, the boy who was so much more innocent than the man. Barton had seen himself, too, and hung his head.

Neither of them had grown up, it seemed, and here they were in their forties.

"Helmut, I'm sorry, I – "

Red-faced and panting, Helmut tucked in his shirt and adjusted his tie and said, "Shut your mouth, Cuckoo's Nest. You *ever* try that again and I'll have you disbarred and brought up on assault. *Comprende?*"

"Helmut, I apol – "

"Ta," said Helmut, and dismissively waved his fingers. He walked around his desk and sat in his chair, fuming. Barton lingered and his former roommate looked up. He raised his eyebrows, widening his eyes. "Something I can help you with?"

Barton frowned and shuffled his feet. "I guess not," he said softly, and turned to go.

When the door clicked shut, Helmut stuck the knuckle of his index finger into his mouth and bit down on the bone to stop himself from howling. Or sobbing. He wasn't sure which.

The injustice of it all!

And he wasn't thinking of their brawl, which he'd clearly won. No, he was too big a man for that. Fistfights were for the poor. Players used money. And the courts.

Rubbing the tooth marks from his knuckle, he reviewed the fight and how he'd won it. His trophy was valuable information. To his surprise, Jordan hadn't squandered her inheritance on her ridiculous dreams of *being an artist*, because her husband had let it slip that the family fortune was still intact. And that meant she had more assets than she let on – not just the band-aids she'd applied to his minor financial scrapes – but enough to cover his losses on the foreign exchange and to restore the firm's escrow account.

Things were looking up. Jordan had resources sufficient to save his career *and* his ass, but where was the money going?

To buy every beaner in every shithole Mexican town his own flea-bitten cow, that's where! Helmut trembled with rage. Well, she'd always been a crazy bitch, hadn't she? Ever since college and especially since law school when she'd married that idiot Barton Squire, the fool with the movie-star looks, now a violent lunatic.

Growling, he banged his fist onto his desk, bruising his hand.

By God, if that maniac ever touched him again, he'd make Jordan into a widow.

A smile twisted his face.

Premeditation and deliberation had begun.

6

Mercy of the Court

OUTSIDE, the traffic roared along U.S. 1, while under the sun-dappled shade of the live oak Graciela leaned against its trunk, feeling the rough bark scratch through her uniform even as her tooth beat with a pulse of its own inside her head. She looked at the sky. A cumulus cloud, white and majestic, drifted behind the sign.

Kelly, Knight and Squire
Attorneys at Law

Stepping from shadow into sun, she shaded her eyes with her hand and peered around the building at the parking lot. Her fingers massaged her cheek, where the roots of the tooth dug into her jawbone, throbbing sharply. She tried not to cry. Swallowing, she gulped and squirmed until hot tears boiled from her eyes, shaming her. When the pain shifted its grip, she pictured a blue crab pinching her head with its claws.

Out of sight, an engine revved and tires squealed, then from around the building Mr. Squire's black pickup truck careened past the parked cars, bearing down on her. Being an important man, she wondered why he drove such an old truck. Why, it even had rust on it. Back in Cuba only farmers drove trucks like that. Through the windshield she glimpsed his face, contorted with worry. *For her.* If she hadn't been in agony, she'd have smiled.

Both Mr. and Ms. Squire did a lot of worrying, which was understandable since they hadn't been blessed with children. They were rich and they lived in a mansion, yet Graciela felt sorry for them. Watching them with her own children, when they gave them presents on their birthdays, she saw such sad hunger in their eyes that she felt like hugging them, as if they were her children too.

Screeching to a halt, Mr. Squire reached across the seat with his long arm and swung open the door. Graciela smiled wanly and climbed inside. He held out a lumpy red handkerchief, which surprised her with its coldness.

"I wrapped up some ice from the fridge in the lounge," he said.

"Thank you, Mistair Barton." Against her cheek, the compress was like manna from heaven, cool and soothing. Ah, the Squires. How could she ever repay them? They'd saved her family! First Ms. Jordan had represented them *pro bono* in court, and now Mr. Barton was delivering her to his personal *dentista*.

They weren't like other Anglos. They didn't condescend. On holidays, the Squires invited the Mirandas to their house for barbecues. They even tried to speak Spanish, but it was so broken that she'd had to kick Antonio under the table to keep him from smirking, although both the Squires seemed to think that they were fluent. Her children, Esteban and Esperanza, loved the wide grassy lawn with its view of the river, and Ms. Jordan set them up with paints and easels so they could make pictures while the grown-ups sipped strong Cuban coffee.

On the whole, Graciela preferred the United States to Cuba. She felt freer to speak about politics than she had in Havana, although the people here were colder than the ice against her face. They looked at their neighbors out of the corners of their eyes as if they might be thieves, or maybe they just didn't like each other. It was hard to tell.

Unlike her *familia* back in Cuba, Anglos weren't so good at love. Never mind the demands of *el corazón*, the romantic heart – nobody was much good at that – but these Anglos stumbled over family love too. They hardly ever kissed. No wonder they shipped off their old relatives to – what was the phrase they used? – *nursing homes.*

That was their way. They found each other disposable. Now, in her *familia*, she might not particularly *like* her cigar-chomping uncle, with his rude jokes and loud voice, but he was still blood kin. And he always would be. All her relatives could find a hot meal and a roof with her. But this wasn't Cuba. Here you spoke your mind, even if what you had to say was ugly. She'd even heard them tell each other to go to hell. In Cuba you didn't say things like that to *la familia.*

Barton glanced across the front seat. "You cold?" he asked, seeing the gooseflesh on her arms. "You want me to turn off the AC?"

"No, no – ees fine. I thank you, Mistair Barton. You are good man. You 'ave good heart."

"That's nice of you to say," he said, wishing it were true.

But it wasn't. He wanted a good heart, but all he felt in his chest was a hole.

As it was, he simply couldn't be *a have* in the presence of *a have-not.* Unfairness irked him. In fact, the whole world irked him. How could he let it go on?

He longed for a purpose. Working as an assistant to Helmut wouldn't do, because that would mean he'd wasted his life. He required a flag. A cause. He wanted to earn his existence. Because in world of starvation and sickness, where did infidelity rate? It didn't. Who cared who screwed who? Fuck fucking! He'd set too much store by his wife's loyalty . . . or lack of it.

Graciela writhed in her seat, pressing the melting compress to her jaw. "Hang in there," he said, as they idled at a red light. Glancing both ways, he hit the gas and ran it. Graciela blinked, widening her limpid black eyes.

Careening down the highway, he felt bold and purposeful. He felt – there is no other way to say it – like a man.

This was the American dilemma – down at the office you got stressed but not tested. No rivers to ford. No mountains to climb. Instead of the frontier, you got the water cooler, without risk to life and limb from wildlife, but with plenty of fear and paranoia from colleagues.

The pursuit of happiness had begun to look like a dead end.

Oh, America! Somewhere after the bicentennial his country had started showing her age, as bereft of grace as an ageing Hollywood actor who can't stop getting facelifts.

And the cure?

The panacea for all depression?

Not Fokus . . . but something even better.

Legal tender!

The currencies of the world, which even now Helmut sat trading inside his office, glancing up from his computer toward the live oak growing beside the entrance to the firm.

Braving the traffic, Barton punched the accelerator and entered the turn lane, fighting for his place amid a mass of speeding vehicles, all burning engines and spinning tires, fouling the air with their poisonous fumes.

He might not save the world, but he could act on a smaller scale, and that was something.

Graciela's dark somber eyes looked at him over the compress now stained with blood.

It wasn't much, but at least he could rescue a tooth.

7

Conjugal Rights

GRACIELA entered Barton's office and displayed her new smile. She'd needed three temporary caps and seven fillings. Grinning, she suddenly looked as young as she was, which was twenty-three.

"*Muy bonita!*" he said. He smiled and clapped his hands.

Gently, she touched his shoulder. "Mistair Barton, ees something wrong? Ees Ms. Jordan hokay?"

Her hand tightened and before he knew what he was saying, and because he had no one else to talk to, the words tumbled out.

"She's leaving me, Graciela."

Graciela's hands covered her mouth, hiding her new teeth. "No! I doan believe it. She love you, Mistair Barton! I see this in her eyes when she look at you."

"No," he said, "I mean yes. I mean, *I think* she is."

"Sometime I tell my oosban, Antonio? When he upset I say, *tranquilo, hombre. Tranquilo.* Now, I not know you so well I can say this . . . but if I did, I say it. You understand?"

He shrugged, suddenly registering the hour and the emptiness of the office. "What're you still doing here?"

"I come back, finish work."

"No, no," he said. "Go home. *Por favor.* Spend some time with your family."

She opened her mouth but Barton held up his hand.

"*Por favor,*" he repeated.

She cocked her head to the side. "Hokay," she said, "I go, but you remember and tell yourself, yes?"

"Sure," he said, "I'll remember – '*Tranquilo, hombre.*'"

When she smiled, the darkness of her eyes made her teeth look even whiter than Jordan's. "*Es la verdad!*" Graciela said. "It's the truth. You fix it sure. I know this." Her hand went to the hollow of her throat where she touched a gold crucifix, a gift from his wife. "I pray for you tonight."

"It can't hurt," he said softly, but she was gone.

Alone in the office, he reviewed a message left by a state auditor who had a question regarding unusual activity in the firm's escrow account. Sighing, he didn't have the energy to worry about it now so he filed it and locked up and left the building.

Outside, as he sat in his truck waiting to pull into traffic, the light of the sun streaked the west with red and gold, reminding him of one of Jordan's paintings. Overhead, the live oak spread its limbs, shading the driveway where it turned into the office off U.S. 1. The tree supported a vast canopy of branches and leaves, casting patches of shade onto the passing traffic, those shiny bubbles of metal and glass whose passengers hurtled along oblivious to the life-stopping power of the oak beside them, a fleet of wrongful death cases awaiting representation.

Perhaps he ought to hit the gas and drum up some business.

He shook his head. It had been long day. Awaiting a break in the traffic, he looked up at the leaves, now burnished to glassy yellow. His shoulders and back ached ferociously, but this – this was nothing, a hangnail, a blackhead – compared to the flaming knot inside his chest.

If thine eye offend thee, pluck it out. But how – how could you pluck out your own eye?

Gunning the engine, he pulled onto the highway. The wheel felt sticky in his hands. Driving home, avoiding collisions with all the other impatient commuters, his wife crashed into his mind.

The image, of all things, was of a haircut. For despite her head-turning good looks, Jordan secretly viewed herself as ugly, with all an ugly girl's insecurities. In any case, after a "shag" type haircut (which even *he* had to admit had turned out badly, a cross between a fright wig and a floor mop) she'd squared her shoulders and presented herself to him, raising her eyebrows and smiling gamely.

"So how do I look?" she asked.

Like a complete goofball, he thought, even as his blood boiled with tenderness for the little girl who peeked out from behind her eyes.

He would never love her more. Seeing that brave hopeful face, those beseeching blue eyes, he put his arms around her and hugged her roughly to his chest.

"I knew it," she wailed. "It's awful!"

He hadn't the heart to tell her it really was a terrible haircut, that her stylist must've been drunk or otherwise impaired, because what did it matter? He told her she was beautiful and she was. Her hair might be ruined, but she'd never be lovelier, nor would another day in his life, like that one so long gone, be more rich with possibility and hope.

Jordan Kelly. Barton would've sold his organs for her. Sacrificed his fortune, his honor, his life.

And now? What would he do after she left him, after she'd betrayed him?

Why, slay her, of course. She was Medusa. Pandora. Eve. What choice did he have?

Except that she was also the gamely smiling girl with the bad haircut, the one with the arched eyebrows, the sidelong glance, the mischievous eyes . . . and the goofy haircut. He had a fierce desire to protect her from all the hurts of the world. The blood. The scrapes. The disappointments.

Yet she repaid him with abandonment.

If thine eye offend thee . . . Or he could say to hell with it and blow his brains out. That was an option. Considering it as he accelerated through a yellow light, he immediately felt lighter. He pictured his corpse lying in a coffin. He shivered. In the Time Before Jordan, suicide was theoretical. Now it was practical.

He hit the gas and shot down the highway. His leg twitched and he pounded his fist on his thigh, working out a cramp.

Changing lanes, he watched the orange sun drop into the Australian pines beyond the Interstate, then he clicked his blinker and swung into the parking lot of Melbourne Guns and Ammo.

After his first meeting with the psychiatrist, he'd applied for and gotten his permit, paid his licensing fee, and today he was picking up the finest in firearms – a Smith and Wesson "Chief's Special."

Inside, the clerk checked his paperwork and ran his credit card, then in less time than it takes to buy a hamburger Barton was back in the parking lot, carrying a brand new, snub-nosed .38, along with a box of bullets. The cardboard box of ammunition felt pleasantly heavy in his hand.

At home he discovered a note taped up beside his wife's picture, the one of her holding the kingfish.

Gone for a swim at Helmut's – back soon.

The note wasn't signed. No "Love, Jordan." Nothing. He set his gun on the kitchen table and put the kettle on the stove and spooned sugar into a ceramic mug. When the kettle whistled he set a teabag in the mug and poured the hot water over it, hoping it might settle his nerves.

Sitting at the table, he stared at the snapshot. His gun lay beside his saucer, unloaded. He set down his teacup and picked it up, sighting down the barrel at her grinning face.

Tranquilo, hombre!

His wife was leaving him. Hell, she *had* left him. He was slow to believe he was a fool, but there it was. Why deny it? There were worse things. Death, for instance.

Gone for a swim at Helmut's.

Was that a new euphemism for adultery?

He shook his head. It wasn't enough that they abandon him – they had to humiliate him too. Barton Squire, odd man out. Two's company, three's a crowd. He got up and tore the note in half and let the pieces fall to the floor.

Sipping his tea, he burned his upper lip and let go of the handle. The cup clattered to the floor and broke into shards of ceramic. He eyed them impassively, feeling darkly serene. He had no intention of sweeping them up.

So this is life, he thought . . . and this is death. Oh my. No one ever warned me. It's so – so –

Tranquilo, hombre!

8

In Forma Pauperis
(In the Form of a Pauper)

BECAUSE it was Saturday and because most Anglos spent weekends at home, Graciela didn't knock when she unlocked Helmut's office. Pushing open the door and pocketing her key, she was deep in her own thoughts when she looked up and clutched her throat, tightening her fingers on her gold crucifix. Gasping, she widened her eyes and stepped backward into the hall.

Her employer knelt before his computer, his hands clasped in prayer. His eyes were closed and his lips moved silently, his bald head glinting under the unearthly light. Mumbling, keeping his eyes closed, he turned his face heavenward.

Ducking her head, Graciela pulled back the door, when the naked dome of Helmut's skull swiveled in her direction.

His dark eyes frightened her.

"Graciela," he said softly, savoring each syllable. His voice was a soothing baritone. "She whose name means 'Grace.'" He patted the carpet beside his monumental desk. "Come supplicate the Son of God with me."

Graciela swallowed. This was something new. In the past she'd seen everything in this office from steely-eyed prostitutes re-applying lipstick, to weepy clients with freshly bandaged stumps, to harassed-looking interns, to Mr. Squire's wife... yet she'd never witnessed the worship of her Lord and Savior, Jesus Christ.

"I sorry," she said, averting her eyes, "I go."

"Stay!" Helmut barked. "You're endangering my soul. Now get on your knees and pray, goddamn it!"

She caught the sickly sweet odor of alcohol. The Devil's perfume, she thought, then her eyes discovered the bottle, tipped over on the desk where it would leave a stain. Her nostrils flared. The man was a sinner and a fool. Didn't he know God turned a deaf ear to drunken prayers?

"Mistair Helmut, I happy to work for you. But you doan tell me when to pray... unnerstand?"

Helmut scowled, still on his knees. He cleared his throat and made an unpleasant sound, something between a laugh and a sob.

"Halleleujah," he said. "You're the only honest woman I know." He groaned and pushed himself to his feet. One of his knees cracked. Wincing, he said, "You're also fired. Now get the hell out of my office."

Her mouth fell open and, with trembling hands, she closed the door. She was stunned. What would she do now? Her face flushed with blood. She was insulted, but not scared. She knew he'd hire her back, with a raise, because he'd fired her before when she wouldn't join him on her knees in an altogether different capacity, but the question remained. What was she going to do with her pride? She didn't fear the fool, she pitied him. He reminded her of a bad boy who secretly wants to be whipped.

"I'm sorry, Graciela. I am! I'm sorry, honey! You know you're not fired, right?"

Contrite, his voice came through the door. She shook her head. *Echarse flores.* That's what she'd have said in Cuba. He threw flowers to himself.

She knew his type – another needy Anglo. He wanted her to mother him. Well, he could wait. He had to learn that in matters of

God she wasn't at his beck and call. Because if Helmut didn't learn humility, one day God *would* answer his prayers, with fire. *Claro.*

Twisting the smile from her face, she asked God to forgive her own terrible pride. She was a sinner and she had no right, playing with him like this . . . Helmut was also one of God's creatures.

"If you like," she said slowly, tucking a black strand of hair behind her ear and raising her voice, "I say prayer for you, because – "

The door opened and Helmut's head poked out. He looked like one of her son's toys, a thing called Mr. Potato Head. "Because why?" he demanded. Up close, his breath smelled like drain cleaner. His eyes were bloodshot.

"Because you need God, Mistair Helmut. You need Jesus." It was an effort, but she forced her mouth to make the hard "jay" sound the way Anglos said His name, although it came out more like "cheese us."

"*Muchas Grass Your Ass,*" Helmut snarled, waving his hand at her. "I don't need your Bible." *Now go spit-shine the urinals*, he thought, but her rich brown eyes, so ready with compassion, clogged his throat. She was serious. Those long black lashes, that unblinking, limpid stare . . . Jesus, she was really letting him have it!

Unnerved, he said, "So I'm going to burn in hell, right? Pitchforks and flames. Ah me. It's too late." A sob caught in his throat. He was drunk.

"I pray for you, Mistair Helmut." She darted forward and pecked him on the cheek, then turned and disappeared down the hall, pushing her cleaning cart.

Of all the goddamned blessed virgins, he thought. Envisioning Graciela beseeching the Almighty on his behalf raised his blood pressure till he heard a high-tension whining in his ears. Then, too, he wanted a good advocate, especially because he was guilty. He slapped thighs with his palms. Let her pray, he thought, because God knew he wasn't very good at it.

For Helmut's prayers were not answered. Earlier, the Fed Chairman hadn't raised interest rates and the subsequent fall in the dollar had cost Kelly, Knight and Squire seventy-two thousand dollars. Abandoning the foreign exchange, Helmut had returned to the stock market, investing what remained in the account he shared with his assistant, that idiot Barton Squire.

Which put him in mind of the idiot's wife. Where was her contribution to the firm? Her name hung on the sign outside, but did she report to the office? Put in billable hours? No. She appeared when it suited her – a crime, really, because when she strutted for a jury she was pure eye-candy. They ate her up. They loved her *pluck*. At trial in her smart blue suit, she made the jurors feel like they'd been cast in a movie . . . starring her, of course.

So what did she do with her talent? Shit-canned it, encouraged by her goofball husband. The woman and her art! Absenting her from the firm, that little painting hobby had cost him a fortune. Next she'd slice off her ear like Van Gogh! Why not? Build a mile-high gold model of Barton, studded with rubies. It wouldn't surprise him. Look at her now. Playing nursemaid to that nut-job, that lunatic . . . *that husband!* Christ. What a pair of losers.

And yet . . . with no family of his own, he realized, as the hair on the back of his neck prickled unpleasantly, those losers were all he had.

Stumbling behind his desk, he slumped into his leather chair where the cushion hissed under his weight. He clutched his chest with his hand. His heart, he admitted, ached. Jordan in her day-glo green bikini, stretched out in a chair beside his pool. She could keep her money. If only he could have *her*. But no. That timeline had forked away from him. He was alone.

He had to put Jordan out of his mind – or go out of *his* mind. She and her stupid cows, those international heifers. Grind 'em into burgers! he thought bitterly.

Jordan Kelly. Jordan Squire.

Cuckoo's Nest could burn in hell. Or better yet, he might dive into the shallow water off his dock and break his neck. That was something to hope for. Helmut smiled. Barton the paraplegic! Barton the limp-dick. In such a case, Jordan would have to be comforted.

Helmut to the rescue! Besides, who was Barton to march around as if he were the one on the crucifix around Graciela's neck? So he paid a few dental bills, did that make him God? He thought too much of himself. Anyway, Helmut knew the con games these immigrants played, because he'd have done the same thing himself, only more efficiently. In any case, he wouldn't have sought out a Squire in shining armor, that's for sure. He'd have found a Knight, someone like himself. That, or bought his citizenship and gone into politics or prostitution, something that paid. He'd have worked his way up. No depending on the kindness of strangers for him. By God, hadn't he *always* paid his way? And wasn't he paying his way now? All he needed was a little luck and he'd be back on top.

That's it, he thought, sucking air through his large nostrils. *Think positive.* Refreshed, he logged onto the foreign exchange. A multi-layered graph filled the screen, signaling deep and mysterious financial waters.

Finding nothing of promise, he bit his lip and brought up his brokerage account.

"Please, God," he intoned, closing his eyes, "let CRVQ have risen." Clasping his fingers so tightly they turned a cadaver-colored green, he opened his eyes.

Stabbed by the figures, he staggered out of his chair and retrieved another bottle from his filing cabinet, uncapped it and drank. Gagging, he wiped his mouth with the back of his hand and slammed down the bottle, shattering it. Shards of glass littered his desk, soaking the wood with vodka.

He raised his bloody fist and shook it at the ceiling, bellowing curses too vulgar to repeat.

The stock had tanked, although such a plunge ought to have been impossible. He'd piggybacked the latest insider trades and weren't those idiot CEO's supposed to know what they were doing? He burped hotly against his fist. Sour bile scalded his tongue. Tears clouded his vision and with sinking guts he realized he *still* hadn't dumped the stock.

Checking the graph on his monitor, he swallowed, feeling short of breath.

Too late! During his fit he'd lost another three-thousand, on margin no less and yes . . . here came the call. He tapped a few keys, leaving bloody fingerprints. No, sir. He couldn't cover it. Slack-jawed, he watched as his balance rang up in the red.

Consumatum est.

It was finished. *He* was finished. The null set had been accomplished.

"Fuck, fuck, fuck . . ." he moaned, "how could I?" In addition to guaranteeing his disbarment for pillaging the escrow account, he'd also destroyed the reputation of Kelly, Knight and Squire, and in a flash he saw why Colin, Lanus and Gart had let Kelly, Knight and Squire keep their names on the sign. Helmut and Barton held the bag. And the bag was empty. They were paupers. Everything became clear to him. Freeman Enterprises had set them up. Ha! He was no Knight. He wasn't even a pawn.

"Fuck *me*," he whispered, hanging his head, and his hand swept the monitor off the desk onto the floor where, perversely, the thing kept working, its cursor blinking like the eye of the Almighty, winking its silent message – *I told you so/I told you so/I told you so* . . .

Spent, he dropped to his knees for the third time that day and spread his body across the wreckage, hoping the power cord would electrocute him. When this failed to occur, he struggled to a sitting position and sat beside the monitor – a stolid thing, mocking him.

His eyes roved over the demolished office and he patted his face with his hands, sorry he'd made such a mess for Graciela. But that was his life, in the personal and the professional departments. He made messes for other people. That was his function. He was a vandal.

Aiming his face heavenward again, he prayed for all he was worth.

Outside the window, the sun turned the sky a malevolent yellow-green, illuminating the trees and the distant lawns of suburbia.

Heaven remained silent, and Helmut, being an attorney, understood that heaven had this right.

9

MALICE AFORETHOUGHT

OUTSIDE, on the green strip of lawn between the Indian River Lagoon and the Squire home, Barton planted his feet at shoulder width, took a two-handed grip, and sighted down the snub-nosed barrel of his new Smith and Wesson .38. The weapon had a heavy, balanced feel, with a reassuring heftiness to it. Closing one eye, he sighted on the target.

His finger squeezed the trigger and the humid Florida air exploded with a pistol report. A covey of fat gray doves flew from the shimmering needles of the Australian pine, flapping their wings into the pastel sky above the lagoon.

In the sudden silence, nature hung motionless, then after a beat, the insects and birds struck up their chorus, with the cicadas buzzing like tiny machines in the branches of the live oaks. Barton blinked and his mouth hung open. The loudness of the gun had stunned him. Guiltily, he looked over his shoulder, half expecting helicopters to descend and megaphones to crackle, issuing orders to surrender.

Nothing happened. Set up beside Jordan's studio, the target remained untouched. Glancing from one house to another, he ducked his head and squinted across the blue glare of the river. The way the shot echoed over the water, he wouldn't get much practice before some terrified suburbanite called the law.

Closing one eye, he took aim. He'd borrowed one of Jordan's easels, and on a discarded canvas he'd painted a crude face. Inside the egg-shaped head he'd drawn two almond-shaped, Egyptian-looking eyes, with a hawk's nose and an angry slash for a mouth. It might've been the work of a disturbed child, yet there was no mistaking its model. The face clearly belonged to his erstwhile law partner, Helmut Knight.

Barton flexed his knees and, gripping with two sweating hands and sighting along the barrel, held his breath and squeezed the trigger, obliterating the target's left eye in a thunderclap.

"Good kill," he said, the shot ringing in his ears. He puckered his lips and blew a wisp of smoke off the barrel. How could he resist? He'd seen too many movies. The acrid smell of gunpowder stung his nostrils.

Out of professional habit, he spotted the issues in the fact pattern. Textbook murder one: a killing, intent to kill, malice aforethought, and premeditation and deliberation. A capital crime, a death penalty case, for which he didn't intend to deny guilt or show remorse. Why should he? He'd resigned himself to life on the cell block, or if they wanted to fry him with chemicals, he'd hold still for the cuffs.

A lone cumulus cloud drifted in front of the sun, its wispy borders edged with gold against the sky's ceramic blue. He'd miss the odor of fresh-cut grass and blooming jasmine, and the ocean after the beach had been scrubbed by a tropical rain. Also the warm smell of his wife's hair, the citrus scent of her skin, her apple-sweet breath . . .

Yet if she was lost to him, why should he linger above ground, a ghost in his own life?

He ought to shoot himself. The gun was in his hand, its silver finish glinting in the sun.

What would it be like? The Big Lights Out. Everything dark, then everything nothing. The long dirt nap. The short road home.

And the end of that road? Was a rainbow too much to ask?

Feeling the weight of the weapon tug his fingers, he glanced at the steel barrel wondering how that bright young boy, Barton Squire, the one with the shining face, the teacher's pet, had come to waste such a promising life. Well, he'd read something about the best laid plans, hadn't he?

The grass felt spongy under his feet, and measuring off a distance of twenty paces, he turned and eyed the target while he considered other remedies. Legally, he could sue Helmut for intentional infliction of emotional distress, a tort, but suing a member of the same firm would launch their malpractice insurance into the stratosphere, and so Barton, a lawyer, found no ally in the law.

Of course, he could pay someone to beat Helmut with a tire iron or plant cocaine in his car or send him child porn, but schemes like that were sure to backfire. Barton just wasn't mean enough. That was his whole problem, as Helmut often pointed out. No killer instinct. Now that same gentleness had cost him his wife.

Well, there you had it, he thought. The bully gets all the marbles.

Staring into the face on the canvas, he raised his weapon. His fingers squeezed the trigger and he let the bastard have it right between the eyes. The air rang as if with a detonation. Birds flew from the trees. A ragged hole with singed edges gaped in the face's forehead.

Barton smiled and strode to the target where he stuck his finger through the hole.

Now that felt good.

And then he understood. Every fleeting moment was another *that could be spent with Jordan*, before they were eclipsed by the great shadow cast by Helmut's planet-like head.

With his gun in one hand and the canvas and the easel tucked under his arm, he crossed the lawn.

You'll never even hear the shot. Now, where had he heard that? And why did he remember it? Had he seen this coming and blocked it from view? Shadows surrounded him.

Inside the studio, he hid the canvas behind a sheet of plywood, realizing as he did so that he'd ceased to be any kind of Buddhist. Well, that was a shame.

It wasn't the physical act that was so disturbing. Jordan had had other lovers. He accepted this. All men had to. Your sweetheart's lips had sucked another man's hairy scrotum. Get over it, brother. Your wife's tongue had explored another man's pink palate. So what? Your lover had sucked a frightful brigade of penises, gleefully hopped on all fours for a parade of beards, stuck her fingers into squads of smelly holes, groaned and moaned for whole platoons of swinging peckers. She'd done it all, to an army! Last of all, to you, her little private, batting clean-up, bringing up the rear.

He believed that gentlemen closed the window on such peeping-Tom thoughts. This was called honor or discretion or valor. They might be old words, but he respected the privacy of his wife's past as he would a closed diary . . . but for one thing.

Helmut Knight! The man spawned like a virus in Barton's brain. He'd corrupted Jordan, tarnishing her golden spirit so that Barton swooned and pressed his palms to forehead, aghast at the thing he was contemplating.

Feeling it sag under his weight, he took a seat in a canvas director's chair beside her workbench. Light streamed through the skylights as his scalp crawled and he swallowed against a roiling, sour stomach. His teeth hurt and sweat ran from his armpits, staining his shirt.

Helmut had violated his trust, sacked his temple, raped his Eden, and for this trespass there could be no forgiveness. No mercy. The crime was capital and the sentence was death, the mandatory minimum.

He smiled. And there it came, rising like an orange sun cresting the pastel lip of the sea: *a sense of purpose. The thing itself.*

Feeling the animal grin spread across his face, he broke open his .38 and reloaded, spun the cylinder and clicked it shut.

Outside, the tires of Jordan's car crunched on the gravel and he hid his weapon inside a stack of empty frames.

Peeking from the window, he observed her striding toward the house. On her head she wore a blue beret fastened at a rakish angle with a rhinestone stick pin. She had on a smart blue suit, with a knee-length skirt, a cream-colored silk blouse and a tailor-made jacket. Unused to high heels, she wobbled as she made her way up the cobblestones. Sharp-featured, with high, angular cheekbones and a delicately upturned nose, she was still his shiny girl. Her eyes had a gem-like quality, like polished blue sea glass. Barton blinked, astonished, as ever, that he'd managed to marry a head-turner like Jordan Kelly.

His stomach clenched as he remembered that he was losing her. God, he *had* lost her. Marrying her was the action, Helmut's larceny the *re*-action. I *take* thee as my lawfully wedded wife. And what was possession?

The conscious exercise of dominion and control.

According to the law, his title was clouded and forfeiture loomed.

A screen door banged shut at the back of the house and his wife wobbled down the walk to the studio. She had a puzzled look on her face. Barton rose from the director's chair and held open the door, aware that his mouth was jerking strangely.

"Have a good swim?" he asked.

Jordan frowned as he pulled the door shut behind her.

"At Helmut's," he said.

She removed the stick pin from her beret and took it off and shook out her hair, a flood of gold. "I had to go to Orlando. File an appeal."

"I see. Nice outfit."

She hung her beret on a peg by the door, her face shiny with sweat. Her husband detected a whiff of body odor, or thought he did, but since his wife smelled good to him even with tangy armpits he couldn't be sure. That odd musky smell might be a side effect of the Fokus. Why, just that morning he could've sworn his multi-grain bagel stank of diesel.

"Deep pockets like me in costume," she said. She jammed her stick pin into the corkboard above her workbench, while her husband kept his distance, suddenly afraid he might smell of gunpowder.

"I got a message from The Mutt," she said. "The Folly's in the shop, so you're supposed to give him a ride tomorrow."

Barton sighed, remembering how Helmut had scoffed at the dependability of his truck, saying, "when mine comes out of the garage . . . *it's a Ferrari*. Yours might always start but . . . *it's a Toyota.*" He outlined the air with his index fingers. "Square, man."

Barton refrained from pointing out that the Folly spent less time on the road than in the shop, where Helmut hovered and scowled, convinced the mechanics were ripping him off.

"Bee, are you all right?"

Wiping his forehead – when had it got so hot? – her husband looked for someplace to rest his eyes, somewhere to put his body. The studio was crammed with wooden easels, rolls of canvas, tubes and cans of paint, workbenches and saw horses.

Jordan slid the director's chair toward him, but he didn't feel like looking up at her.

"You're turning green," she said. "Sit down."

Weak in the knees, he held to the edge of the chair. "I feel more yellow than green," he said. "Do I look jaundiced?"

Jordan felt his forehead with the cool back of her hand. Then she felt her own. "I can't tell," she said. He was pleased to see that she looked worried.

And she was. His psychiatrist had told her that the Fokus regimen took some getting used to, so she didn't take Barton's mood swings personally. But when she looked up Fokus in the *Physician's Desk Reference*, she learned that patients should be observed for suicidal ideation. The warning stopped her cold because she'd never connected suicide with Barton, whose disposition had always been sunny. He had a temper, certainly, so she could imagine homicide – but suicide?

Never.

"Anyway, I need the truck," she said and smiled in what she hoped was a psychologically helpful way. "The new easel, the big one? The one you got me for my birthday? It's finally come in." She held open her arms to be hugged but her husband stepped behind a saw horse, casting his eyes around the studio as if he were looking for something. The smile fell from her face.

"What's wrong, honey?"

"Nothing."

That tone. It told her *everything* was wrong. Had that fool Helmut called and told him about the loan? She stepped forward and he drew back. Startled, she blinked at him. This was new, and disturbing, but if he didn't want to be touched, she'd give him room.

"I'm sorry to mention it," she said, crossing to her workbench, "but I just played a message from the neighbors."

"Their dog get loose again?"

"They said they're afraid of you. They said they're afraid to let their kids outside. It's only because they know us that they haven't called the police."

"That's ridiculous."

"That's what *I* said, but . . . they said you were shooting at one of my paintings." She waited. "Is that true?"

Barton felt his face redden. Couldn't their nitwit neighbors distinguish between his crude target and one of his wife's paintings? He couldn't look at her. Explaining it would only make things worse.

Anyhow, did she take him for such a monster that she could accuse him of vandalizing her art, her life-blood? He examined her face for clues, raising his gaze from the feminine point of her chin, up to her full lips, driving his gaze into the twin blue stones of her eyes. The lids, he noted, were red and puffy.

"Sorry," he said, "I'm not feeling well."

"So is it true? Were you shooting at one of my paintings?"

Hearing it repeated was worse than hearing it the first time. He felt like screaming. He felt like killing.

"That's absurd," he said, appalled at how guilty he sounded. Now he understood why criminal lawyers seldom let defendants testify. Like him, they'd hang themselves.

"So they're lying?"

"I think you're a genius," he said, refusing to be cross-examined. "I love your work. I'm sorry you think I'd do anything to harm it."

"Well, I don't, Barton. That's just it. We're facing a mental health issue here, aren't we?"

He closed his eyes and slumped into the canvas director's chair. Beaten, he looked up at his wife, who'd come to stand over him, blocking a skylight and eclipsing the sun with her head. Her face hung coolly in a nimbus of blond fire. Beyond her, against the molten dome of the sky, a range of mountainous white clouds appeared to sail in one of her ears and out the other.

"I confess then – I shot *my* painting. Is that a crime?"

"Inside the city limits? As a matter of fact, Big Bart, it is."

He cocked his head to the side and shrugged. "It had a face on it. A face that needed killing."

Oh dear, his wife thought. She inhaled sharply. Her husband needed to be in a hospital, she realized, the kind with locks on the doors and bars on the windows. "You still taking the Fokus?" she asked gently.

"Are you kidding? I love that stuff."

"But you're following the directions, right? It's not candy."

"Damn. And here I thought they were M and M's!"

"Be serious, hon."

"I've never been more serious in my life."

Neither of them spoke. She was having trouble meeting his eye. And where had she really been all day? he wondered. Working her part-time practice? Or servicing his rival?

"Are you leaving me?" he asked.

"What?" Her mouth fell open. Amid its pinkness, he noted two molars with silver fillings.

"It's a simple question, Jordan. The witness will please respond."

"Honey, no – of course – "

"So you're not fucking Helmut?"

"Honey, please . . . college was a long, long time ago."

"And Kansas?"

"No. Never."

Hearing a grating sound in his ears, Barton realized he was grinding his teeth and forced his jaw to relax. She'd convicted herself with her own testimony. And her lame alibi. She hadn't filed any appeal in Orlando. She had on business clothes because of course she'd had to shower and change. She was full of Helmut. That explained her tangy smell. God! What a fool he'd been! He was no prosecutor, but it didn't take a D.A. to see how she'd incriminated herself. His eyes burned. This was not to be believed. Just look at the terror on her face. Those big round eyes.

"Sweetheart," she said, taking his hand, "I want you to lie down, okay?"

Barton allowed himself to be led inside the house, hanging his head like a condemned man. She had her hand under his arm, holding him up.

In the living room she settled him on the couch, while overhead a ceiling fan taunted him with its incessant whirling. The spinning blades cut across his body like a buzz saw. Ripping his eyes from it, he let his wife cover him with a blanket.

He'd had one hell of a day, he had to admit. Hazarding a look at himself, he got a glimpse of his reflection in the sliding glass doors and *my God* the black bags under his eyes! And the pasty skin, the three-day stubble, the mat of hair, and something new . . . a look in his eye, a darkness at the heart of the pupil, bordered by a sea of glacial blue fading into . . . what? An animal's gaze, last of a doomed species, staring from its cage at the zoo, a wounded creature, hopeless and alone, turning away to curl up and die.

"Jesus," he said.

Outside, in the trees along the river, the birds started their sunset chorus, chirping and tweeting, merrily deriding him as the sun sank into the tops of the pines and the sky deepened from blue to violet.

"You *are* still taking the Fokus, right?"

"You asked me that before and the answer's still the same."

"Well?"

"In buckets, dear."

"That isn't funny, Barton."

"I stick to the dosage."

She held out her hand. "C'mon," she said. "I know what you need. Some rubbin' and lovin'. Sound good?" She bent toward him, but her husband pulled up their blanket to his eyes and peered over it, eyeing her as he would a home-invader.

Who *was* this chattering freak? he wondered. And why was she trying to grab him? He drew breath, fearful of letting her know he was onto her. She and Helmut, those adulterers, those traitors. By God, their day was coming.

"Be right back," he said, tossing off the blanket and leaping from the couch. "I forgot something in your studio."

"Sweetie. Please stay." Her face was pinched with worry.

"I'll be right back," he said.

Inside the studio, from inside the pile of empty frames, he retrieved his pistol. Holding it away from his face, he turned it this way and that, then he inserted the snub-nosed barrel into his mouth. It tasted metallic and oily and the steel felt cold against his tongue, tasting of salt now, too, from something inside his throat.

He kept his finger off the trigger. He'd never done this before, and yet it felt so natural. Righteous even.

He rested his finger on the trigger . . . oh so gently. *Wow*. A rush like cocaine shot through his veins. His eyes dilated and he began panting. Red-faced, he removed his finger and withdrew the barrel from his mouth and hid the pistol back inside the pile of frames. He wiped his lips.

Now that, he thought, isn't something you do every day!

He shook his head, feeling giddy.

"Barton!" his wife called. "What're you doing in there?" Her voice drew closer, high with fear. "You're scaring me."

Her shoes clacked over the cobblestones and he swallowed, feeling his heart squirm inside his chest.

He was not in the best of shape, he realized.

Jordan poked her head inside the door, her eyes alight, her mouth a grim line. Barton said to himself . . . *she looks old*.

She looked, he thought, like a hag, like a witch who'd come to curse him.

"Won't you let me help you, hon?" Her voice was desperate.

"*Help* me?" He raised his eyebrows. He thumped his chest with his hands, grinning broadly. "I'm as strong as a fucking gorilla, you – "

She clapped her hand over his mouth.

10

INFORMATION AND BELIEF

INSIDE, naked on their king-sized bed with its soft, tight-fitting sheets, Jordan parted her thighs for her husband – and then she did the most healing thing imaginable. She smiled. She smiled candidly and invitingly. She smiled with her mineral blue eyes and polished teeth, and when he kissed her, she tasted delicious – healthy and female – strawberry and chocolate and cherry.

"Repair us," she said.

Letting his hand drift, his fingertips brushed her silky skin, her inner thigh, white and supple and smooth.

"Do what you want," she said.

Kneeling in the vee of her legs, he felt happy, until he looked down.

Instead of her golden *yoni*, he glimpsed a wizened face, as on a shrunken head, and in that face a gaping maw – *la vagina dentata*, the fanged orifice, a toothy hole which leered and melted, morphing into Helmut's face, dripping spittle and babbling gibberish.

Soldiering on, Barton closed his eyes and thumbed himself toward her, but his member was nothing but a tubular flap of skin. The fiend wouldn't stand up. His rubbery penis slid one way and then the other, unable to find any purchase on the slick surfaces. Yet who wouldn't stagger? His rival had cold-cocked him.

He leaned back for a better view. Facing Helmut's yammering maw, with its sharp teeth as keen as a bat's, Priapus himself would wilt. Barton groaned and sweat leaked from his temples, spattering his wife's no longer smiling face.

Ever the good sport, she whispered encouragement, cooing erotic invitations.

Slip to the left and slip to the right and . . . oh! Almost! The edge of wet bliss. But no. His hopes were raised and cruelly dashed.

Stand up, you traitor! He gritted his teeth and, employing his thumb and index finger, pinched his penis as if it were a night crawler scuttling into the earth. His eyes watered. Perhaps if he compressed the base and whipped the thing back and forth . . . but no, the thing had stage fright and nothing was going to make it stand up and sing. Barton's thumbnail caught the tender skin under the plum-shaped head and a starburst exploded behind his eyes.

"Honey, please. Stop hurting yourself!" Alarmed by her husband's twisted features, his red sweating face, she cupped his face in her cool hands and tried to kiss him.

Barton rolled off her, a failure not only as a man but also as an animal, an experience no woman can fathom. (Take it from one whose prime has passed.)

She tapped his forehead with her index finger. "Talk to me, hon. Tell me what's going on."

"How about what's going on with *you*?"

"Nothing's going on with me."

"Uh-huh. I get it. Humor the lunatic."

Jordan sniffed. Why was it, she wondered, that people reserved their most petulant, most craven behavior for the ones they really loved? It was a design flaw in human nature. Why reserve your nasty side for your spouse? It didn't make sense.

She drew the sheets over her nude body. "Is it me?" she asked. Her voice was small. She hated asking, but she couldn't help it.

Her husband squirmed. He hated that question. Of course it was her. Who else?

"No, sweetie," he said, "it's not *you*, it's *me*."

"Oh, please," she said.

"You think I'm lying?" He peeled back the sheet and let his eyes travel her naked body. "What a living sculpture," he said. She smiled gamely and let him drink his fill.

Still, her beauty was moot, for Barton was faithful. He understood the word *pledge*. As a lawyer he saw their marriage as a contract, but as a man he knew it as a sacred bond, one sealed until death did them part.

Because before dying you had to admit certain things, and one was that all you controlled in this world was your word. Either you were trust-*worthy*, or you were like Helmut, a scum-sucking dog. Of course, it might not seem that way, especially if you made excuses. Ever since college, Helmut had behaved as if he owned the world, as if he were its king, holding the game in check. Encouraged by professors and parents, Barton had also enjoyed a royal self-image, but saying goodbye to youth had hurt him more than it had Helmut, sanding the pride off his character. Who knew why? Perhaps he was made of softer stuff than his old roommate, or perhaps he was ageing differently. Time did strange things to the human heart. Some soured, some sweetened. For Barton, middle age bred a sense of urgency where every moment broke like a sunburst, one last glimpse of the sky before that long snooze in the dirt.

Looking at his wife, naked in bed beside him in the fading light, her long hair fanned out against the pillow, he was relieved to see that his rival's face had been replaced by the blond triangle curling between her thighs.

Pandora's box, he thought.

Jordan turned onto her side, covering herself with the sheet. She asked, "You're not taking diet pills, are you?"

"Why do you ask?"

"Well, it's either that, or I'm not turning you on." Her voice was thin with hurt.

What could he say? That he'd seen Helmut's face between her legs? And that it had teeth?

"It's the Fokus," he said. "Plus, I'm forty-three."

"Forty-three's young, honey."

"Is it?"

"Well, it's not *old*." She rolled onto her stomach and propped herself up on her elbows, scrunching up her buttery shoulders. "Hey," she said. She took his chin in her hand and made him look at her. Her fingers were cold.

"Remember when we read Hemingway's letters?"

"Yeah."

"You remember what he said killed Fitzgerald?"

"That he confused growing up with growing old."

"And didn't you agree?"

"Uh-huh."

"Well?"

Barton wanted to say, but Hemingway didn't see Helmut's face between your legs.

Still, she was right. She might've looked old yesterday, but today she looked young. The skin of her inner thighs was like a girl's, all silky and shiny. She'd never shaved above the tops of her knees because growing up her mother had taught her that a lady never shaved that area. There was no need. That downy skin would only be touched by her husband, the only man ever to see it.

Of course, Barton knew otherwise. Helmut too, had savored that skin, tongued its haunting softness, leaving an invisible mark, spreading his spoor. And more: the Knight had stolen the Squire's damsel and quit the field of honor, leaving the Squire alone . . . oh, quite alone.

"Goddamn it," he said, "I may have to kill somebody."

Wide-eyed, Jordan watched as he leapt from the bed and pulled on his underwear and a pair of gym shorts.

Shaking out his limbs, touching his toes and stretching, Barton considered alternatives to homicide. Perhaps he could become a

Buddhist monk. Or maybe a Jehovah's Witness. He could join the Amish if they'd have him, become an upstanding man with a horse and buggy. A man who went to church. A man who prayed. It could happen. He saw himself rising at dawn, surveying the hay field, hooking his thumbs into his suspenders, hitching up the team and setting his plow to the earth. No? Maybe a bowling league. Christ, *something!*

His wife climbed out of bed and pulled on panties, jeans and a T-shirt with *New York City* embossed on the front.

For the moment, they had nothing to say to each other. Perhaps if they ignored this wound it might disappear on its own, like a mysterious sore that blossomed and healed, never to return. At least, they could hope so. There was no other medicine but time.

Avoiding each other's eyes, they went their separate ways: she to her studio, he to the kitchen. Then a strange thing happened. As he made a cup of tea, his penis unfurled, straining against the stretchy fabric of his gym shorts. How in the hell?

Apparently the Fokus had its hand in his pants, working him against his will.

As he sipped his tea, his penis pointed skyward. What a life. He looked down. It was bigger than he'd ever seen it, a purple monstrosity. If God was in heaven, he was a prankster, planting a tree in the fork of the road like this.

His eyes dilated. *Shit!* Suddenly he remembered that his gun was hidden in the studio.

Trembling, he stepped back from the table, knocking over his chair. He stamped his feet up and down and rubbed his hair and patted his face with his hands.

"What . . . *in the fuck* . . . is the matter with you?"

That voice, that smooth melodious baritone. He whirled around as the sliding glass door opened.

Helmut winked and clapped his hands.

"Dude!" he said, smiling with delight, "I catch you at a bad moment?"

Barton froze, his feet glued to the floor. His mouth worked, but his voice was a squeak. His face was burning.

Helmut grinned and cupped a hand to his ear. "What's that, Big Bart? Hey! Looks like you're happy to see me."

Barton's jaw moved up and down. Helmut knitted his brows, suddenly suspicious. Scowling, he said, "Jesus, you're not having some kind of seizure, are you?" He recoiled.

Barton stammered, "How . . . how did you?"

Helmut advanced in a wave of garlic breath and clapped Barton on the shoulder. He swung his calfskin briefcase onto the kitchen counter. "Overtime. Some of us still work for a living, stud." He rolled his eyes toward the studio outside. "Know what I mean?"

Barton coughed, stunned by Helmut's transformation. He had on leather topsiders, pleated linen pants with a herringbone-weave and a vine green polo shirt. The sleeves of the shirt were bunched up to reveal his newly inflated biceps, and even his paunch looked smaller.

Barton felt the blood recede from his groin. "What the hell, Helmut. Don't you knock?"

"It was open." Helmut blinked and leaned against the counter, leering. Under the fluorescent light his head gleamed as if he'd polished it. Barton squirmed, but whether it was from the unexpected sight of his former partner or another hefty dose of Fokus he couldn't say.

"I'm going – " Barton said, hearing his voice rise and crack.

Helmut guffawed and slapped him on the shoulder. "Take a breath, champ. You'll pull a groin muscle."

Barton swallowed. "Someday," he said slowly, mustering his courtroom voice, "I . . . am . . . going . . . to . . . *fucking* . . . *kill* . . . *you*."

Helmut bellowed. He slapped his knee and his eyes streamed with tears. "Big Bart, stop!" He laughed and snorted through his nose. "Dude, you're killing me now!"

"Keep telling yourself that, buddy. It may ease your anxiety."

Helmut chuckled. "I'd say *you're* the one with the anxiety, or is it laryngitis?"

"Laugh all you want. I'm serious, Helmut. You're a fucking dead man."

"I am, actually. You have no idea. But I'm watching a different movie. In Barton-world, who knows? I bet I'm a blockbuster. Am I right? Ha! I am. I can see it in your eyes. Guillotine. Knife. Fists. Poison. Am I close?"

"That's what's in the crystal ball, Mutt. You ought to take up fortune-telling."

Helmut shrugged, as though another of his numerous talents had been revealed. "I don't suppose *l' artiste* can be disturbed, can she?"

L' artiste's husband frowned. God, the brass of these two. What treachery! Playing it brazenly straight, they might bluff him into thinking he was paranoid, that his suspicions were groundless. Well, he had too much Fokus roaring in his blood for that to work.

Helmut smiled enigmatically. "It's a legal matter, Barton. Entirely professional." He patted his calfskin briefcase, and they both looked at it. Flesh-colored with gold fittings, it contained Helmut's cases: the recklessly injured, the wrongfully killed, the negligently maimed – an archive of suffering within a hide of leather. "It's also confidential."

Barton knuckled his fingers into his eyes. To demonstrate his trust in his wife after The Kansas Incident, he'd agreed to let Helmut represent not only the sale of Jordan's paintings but also those of her grandmother, which were now fetching premium prices.

"She's working," Barton said, tilting his head toward the studio.

Helmut lingered.

"Spill it," Barton said.

"Um," Helmut glanced at the floor, then into Barton's eyes. "You might want to consider wearing a jock strap with those shorts, Big Bart. We're not in San Francisco anymore."

While Barton turned away to adjust himself, Helmut giggled and took his briefcase off the counter and crossed the kitchen. As he was sliding open the glass door, Barton withdrew a serrated knife from the silverware drawer. The blade glinted in the light. Testing its point with his thumb and finding it sharp, he squeezed the wooden handle and pictured himself plunging the blade into Helmut's spine.

Helmut the paraplegic. *El Castrato!* But no, he could never injure a man like that, not even the Mutt. Barton was an officer of the court. He'd taken an oath to uphold the law, and he was a man who kept his promises.

For now, anyway.

Helmut blew him a kiss through the glass, batting his eyes and waving. Barton shuddered. Turning, Helmut strolled down the cobblestones, swinging his briefcase.

Was this really happening? Was his wife's lover striding toward her studio . . . *while her husband was in the house?*

Alone, Barton's life became clear to him: he was not a serious man. He was a coward. Gripping the knife with both hands and pointing the flashing tip at his bare belly, he considered committing hari-kari. It was the only honorable thing to do.

But for one thing.

He lacked the courage.

11

INFORMED CONSENT

INSIDE her high-ceilinged studio with its wide skylights, Jordan was erasing phone calls. With each press of the button, a mournful beep ensued, a digital taps tolling for another message consigned to oblivion.

She wondered: if you could press a magic button, would you delete painful memories?

What about intangible offenses? Inchoate crimes? Simple heartache? These were difficult cases. Yet if you could appeal every verdict, alter every fact pattern, would this amount to a perfect world? It seemed unlikely. Maybe the principle quality of life was that you had to stand it. When Fate carved its initial in your forehead, maybe that was its way of saying, *Feel that sting? It means you're alive.*

The alternative?

All erase.

This was an existential truth. One false move and *beep!* You could be deleted. Permanently.

Helmut opened the door and Jordan jumped.

"I need another loan," he announced flatly.

She clutched her chest. "Hey," she said, gasping, "you ever hear of knocking?"

"Your husband just asked me the same question. Gross. You two goofballs sure read off the same script."

"You think it's okay to barge in on people?"

Helmut shrugged. He couldn't imagine anyone not being happy to see him. Anyhow, manners were a pose and he was authentic, a cut above such pettiness. He was more original than that.

"Interrupting an artist at work is a mortal sin," she said, half-seriously.

"Oh. It looked like you were on the phone."

She took a deep breath and slowly released it. She would deny him the pleasure of seeing how he exasperated her, since in Helmut's dark mind "exasperation" equaled stimulation. "How much, Mutt?"

"Buck twenty."

"Thousand?"

"I had a tough week."

"My God, Helmut." She picked up a pencil and tapped the eraser against her lips. "Even *you* must see that you've got a problem. You need therapy. I mean it. Between you and my husband – "

"Would you rather I tell Barton he's about to go bankrupt?"

Jordan shot him . . . *that look*. "You leave Barton alone, mister."

Helmut peeked under the paint-spattered cloth covering an easel. Jordan smartly smacked his knuckle with the pencil and he let the cloth fall over the painting – a man with a fox's head baying at the moon. Other paintings, both oil and acrylic, lined the walls in various states of composition. Watching him survey her work, Jordan squirmed.

None spoke to Helmut's personal taste, though he had eye enough to realize she'd progressed from gifted amateur to low-grade professional. Hitching his thumbs into the waistband of his pants, he was surprised to find himself slightly impressed.

"Maybe we can make some coin off this mess, after all, eh? My Tokyo guy is itching."

Feeling her neck muscles tighten, Jordan cast her eye from one painting to another. No doubt about it. Her work was hideous. It ought to be burned.

"I should just quit," she said. "I'm delusional."

"Self-loathing is a form of vanity," Helmut said. "Get over yourself and just keep painting."

She chewed the wood of her pencil and examined her tooth marks. Art-making was so damn *hard*. One second you were a fraud, the next you were a genius – an anus, she thought, dreaming it was a mouth.

And then there was *the work*, where she filtered the material *through* herself, a giant liver straining the blood of the universe. Or some such picture: her mind was full of disturbing scenery.

She'd earned good reviews for her shows in New York, although her best work wasn't commercial. Her paintings were too unsettling. Surreal, expressionistic, like Dali, but with a sensibility more inebriated than psychedelic. Chagall came to mind. Certainly no one accused her of being decorative – apart from her one "pretty" painting, *What Blood Beyond the Skin of Sunset?* – the one she later sent to yours truly after I was incarcerated here at Green Glade.

Her work also had a strange ethnicity. Mexican low-riders engulfed in sparks – wide-eyed, raven-haired virgins – Christ figures dripping with stigmata. Goya showed his influence – honor in the face of cruelty: terrorists in black hoods lopping off the heads of TV reporters, with pages torn from the Q'uran glued onto the canvas. Fearless, she'd die for art. Let a martyr come get her. She'd install a knee in his groin before he went to his virgins.

"Helmut. I want you to feel this – you're going to Gambler's Anonymous – understand?"

"It's not gambling, love. It's day trading."

She smacked his knuckles with the pencil. "Don't call me 'love.' And what do you mean 'day trading'?" She frowned. "I thought you were in currency speculation."

Helmut put his face up to a painting of a convict staring out from his cell. The convict had rabbit ears painted on his head and a stylized American flag draped over his shoulders. "Currency spec is for losers. I'm in the market now, cooking with gas." Rubbing his knuckles, he inspected her workbench for wet paint, then swung his briefcase onto it and opened the lid. He handed her a folder. "Check it out, *love*. I got you in the Nalle gallery."

"No!" Jordan blinked and stared at the contract. Helmut allowed himself to be hugged. She'd been angling for a show at the Nalle Gallery for as long as she'd been painting, because the owner didn't just show the work – he supported the painter, *as an artist*.

Helmut preened, strutting around the studio, inspecting her offspring.

The artist frowned. Leave it to him to coat the pill with candy. This victory would be followed by a request for more "backing," as he called it. She should have known.

"Call your investments what you want, Mutt. I call them losing money. *My* money."

Helmut stiffened. "Then I rescind this offer and resign as your agent."

Ignoring the stricken look on her face, he hastily stowed the contract and snapped shut his briefcase. What an ingrate! He didn't need this. She was as bad as her lunatic husband. He'd been carrying them both for years and what thanks did he get?

Nothing but ridicule, as if he weren't as sensitive as the arty Squires. Well, he had feelings, too, thank you very much.

Anyway, Barton and Jordan's friendship was the last thing he needed. They were bad luck. Always had been. Hadn't they been present each time he perched on the rim of success? They had. And they'd been there to gloat when he failed, too, though in their demented minds they'd helped him recover.

He couldn't afford them. Wading into the stock market, he needed to think positively. Sure, poetry and art and beauty and even love had once figured in his accounts, but now his world was mathematical – graphs and digits and decimals – these were the bottom line of his existence, and in some secret place inside, the poverty of *that* was more than he cared to contemplate.

"I need something else," he said abruptly, feeling his mood change, sweeping him back to her, "to tide me over."

Jordan peered over his shoulder at the door. It was unlocked. Would this fool ever change? Or, more to the point, would *she*?

"What about my husband? What about him?"

She had her hands on her hips and Helmut deftly slid his arms under her elbows, crushing her to his body, feeling her muscular back with his hands, her hard breasts against his chest.

When Barton held her, she had to crane her neck to look into his eyes, but with Helmut she returned his level stare, which was bold and dark and penetrative, undressing her, making love to her. Their eye contact was different in tone than what she shared with her husband. Together, she and Helmut vibrated along a darker frequency. The sound was not a harmony, or a dissonance, but something else, other-worldly, something ancient.

She cut her eyes to the floor and twisted her body out of Helmut's arms.

"I need my hands on you," he said.

With her athletic build, she was relatively sure she could beat him up. One good tag on the jaw with her hard little fist, she figured, and he'd collapse like one of the personally injured.

"*I can't*," she said. She balled up her fist and smacked it into her palm, "I should just beat the shit out of you."

Helmut swallowed. Physically, he was a lot more afraid of the wife than of the husband. Jordan could hurt him. "You know you *won't*," he said, bluffing, trying to keep his cool.

Jordan narrowed her eyes. Was that a flicker of doubt she saw, a twitch in the corner of his mouth?

He rubbed his jaw, somehow reading her thoughts.

"Come *on* – the room's paid for. You don't want to waste a room. You know what it cost?"

"I'm sure you'll put it to good use, Counselor. I have every confidence in your ability to fuck things up." She waited, risking eye contact. "Goodbye, Helmut."

"Jor – "

She poked her index finger into his solar plexus.

Helmut winced.

"*I said goodbye.* Barton's in bad shape and I don't need you stirring him up."

"Seems to me you've already done that."

Jordan swung the flat of her hand at his face but Helmut caught her wrist and squeezed it. He was much stronger than she'd anticipated. Her face reddened and each felt the other's hot breath.

"Let go," she said calmly, "or I'll knee you in the balls."

Helmut released her and they stood glaring at each other. The moment simmered. Helmut pressed his mouth to hers. His tongue was a wet creature, striated with tendons.

"Get out," she said, spitting him from her mouth and pushing him away with her hands on his chest. "My God – you're insane."

"I'm in love with you, Jordie."

"Now listen, Helmut. I need you to *stop being a freak!* I *mean* it."

Helmut sneered. "I thought you liked freaks," he said bitterly. "I thought that's why you married one."

Jordan closed her eyes. Helmut excited her, there was no denying it. They'd done things in bed she'd never do with Barton. Things she wouldn't even suggest because Barton was a New England prude and if she so much as . . . he'd leap from the bed as though she'd zapped him with a cattle prod.

She opened her eyes. Somehow this short bald man always set her to gasping, and if in her heart she knew why she didn't want to admit it. "I'll transfer the money," she said. "But you better know what you're doing." She cleared her throat. "I have limits, Counselor."

His dark eyes flickered. "Not that I've seen, *Counselor.*" He scuffed the floor with the toe of his shoe.

Nobody said anything.

"The wonderful Jordan Kelly," he said at last, caressing her with his smooth baritone. His brown eyes went deep and she had to look away. He sighed meaningfully. "You know, Jordie, out of the three of us you've aged the best. A few laugh lines maybe, but you look the same as you did in college."

Knowing she was being hustled, she fought his dark charisma, yet she couldn't resist the drug-like high of a Helmut Knight compliment. *Had he really said he was in love with her?* It seemed impossible, yet she felt herself blooming inside. The Big Man on Campus had noticed her.

She was pathetic and she knew it, but that didn't mean she understood it. Why did she want to please this tyrant? Barton was ever-eager to please *her*, to idolize her even, and sometimes that got on a woman's nerves. Sometimes she wanted to be dominated.

"You're like a fine wine," Helmut said, not touching her. You've grown into yourself." He held up his hands defensively. "No irony, Jordie. You wear the years well."

She met his gaze, then looked away and picked up a brush, tipped with blue paint. She had the urge to poke him in the eye with it.

"Don't even think about it," he said.

She'd always be transparent to him, so that now she blushed, as if she could hide behind her own blood. She hurt him sometimes – she knew that, but a woman had to choose. She slid his calfskin briefcase across the workbench.

"Goodbye, Helmut."

His appeal was denied. Still, he'd got his money, and if he couldn't content himself with that she was sorry. He had his settlement, and their case was closed.

"I said *goodbye,* Mutt." She looked away.

Helmut didn't say anything and walked out the door.

So there was an end to it. She'd chosen the Squire over the Knight and there went the game.

Selecting a clean brush and holding it at arm's length, she felt something like serenity. Like her art, her love for Barton might not be perfect, but it worked, and it would go on working – until death did them part.

12

Pari Delicto
(In Equal Fault)

FROM an upstairs window, Barton watched his rival cross the lawn toward his burnt-orange Ferrari, which waited by the curb like a machine from the future, low-slung and sleek. A 612 Scaglietti from Prancing Horse Motors, Barton's eye roved over the streamlined body, the curve of the wheel arches, the scalloped sides, the projector headlights.

Striding down the sidewalk, Helmut swung his calfskin briefcase, shaking up the cases inside, all his divorcees and amputees, whose duty it was to offer up their percentages to pay for his mighty ride.

His tuneless whistling invaded Barton's ears. *First let's kill all the lawyers*, he'd read in his Shakespeare class in college. Not a bad idea. Ever fair-minded, he included himself.

Squinting at the round globe of Helmut's head, he imagined it framed by the cross hairs of a telescopic rifle sight.

He licked his lips, feeling the weight of the rifle in his hands, the stock pressed against his shoulder, the sense of glorious, impending release.

First let's kill all the lawyers!

Except one, he thought, when his wife ran onto the lawn, her long legs pumping, her hair flying out behind her like a yellow flag. Pursuing Helmut's gleaming head, she stormed across the grass wearing her paint-smeared overalls, waving a folder and hollering. She was barefoot.

Barton swooned – in love with her at first and every sight.

Helmut was sliding into the Folly when she handed him the folder. He opened it and pointed and said something and handed it back to her. They seemed to be having an argument, but no . . . now she was patting him on the shoulder . . . and what's this? She leaned against his precious car and wrote a check on the roof and stuck it through the window.

Helmut saluted her with it and pulled away, the great Ferrari roaring, bearing him off like somebody famous.

Remembering his gun, Barton thundered down the stairs and made his way along the back of the house. Inside the studio, he rifled the drawers of her workbench until he found the card she'd inscribed with her computer passwords, then he retrieved his weapon from inside the pile of old frames, broke open the cylinder, emptied the bullets into his pocket and stuffed the gun down the front of his shorts.

These might be dire times, but a reasonable and prudent person wouldn't shoot himself in the groin.

Hearing his wife's footsteps, he pushed the weapon further down, wincing at the cold metal against his flesh. He tucked the card beside it and, looking down over his stomach, shook his head in wonder. He sported another bulge in his shorts.

"Hi, Bee!" Jordan called out cheerfully. Her lilting voice came from behind him. The hairs on the back of his neck prickled. He hadn't put on a shirt and he felt exposed.

Turning, he reigned in his face, attempting to compose an expression which might resemble that of a sane person. The gun had slipped and the barrel rubbed against his scrotum, holding it hostage.

Knitting her brows, his wife said, "Honey, what's wrong?"

There's a pistol aimed at my balls, he thought, but wisely kept silent. Then too, at least the weapon was unloaded.

"Always something to be thankful for," he said.

"Yes, that's true," she said hesitantly. She pressed her palm to the stubble on his cheek, "Something on your mind?"

Barton smiled, certain his grin must look demonic. He'd never make it as a criminal – not with a face like his, which telegraphed every secret in the brain behind it.

"Honey? Love of my life – why're you searching my studio?"

"I was looking for a stapler."

"Can I help you find it?" The look of her clear, candid eyes filled him with shame. She still trusted him, even as he lied and spied on her. Traveling down that road, he wondered, what would come next?

Intent to kill, a voice answered inside his head. *Malice aforethought. Premeditation and deliberation.*

His wife kissed him, her breath warm on his lips, her tongue a mischievous wet wonder. "Oh my," she said, feeling the bulge in his shorts. He stopped her hand when she reached for him. Finding her password was easy – *concealing* the fact that he'd found it was another matter. Concealment was Helmut's department.

"I can't," he said. "I'm working on a heavy case."

"I want you to rest."

"Graciela cleaned my office last week and now I can't find anything."

"You know, hon, that girl worships you. I think she has a little crush."

"You're the Mirandas' hero, rescuing them from the beach like that. Most people would've kept on jogging. Can you imagine Helmut stopping?"

"I can't imagine him jogging."

"And you send their kids to private school."

Barton swallowed a yawn which returned alarmingly as a fragrant belch, tasting of fish. He brought his fist to his mouth and excused himself. His medication was tying knots in his digestive tract.

"Um . . . so, Barton . . . what were you hiding just then?"

"What did you say?" He frowned unconvincingly. He was no actor.

His wife assumed the sorrowful expression of a woman who knows she's being deceived. Her long face wounded him but he felt committed to what he'd begun. He was, by nature, an honest man, or so he thought, and she was the last person he wanted to mislead.

Yet how could he confess? She'd be horrified. He'd purchased *a firearm* and hidden it from her, in her own home. He met her eyes. Big mistake! Her glacial-blue irises cut into him like diamond drill bits. He dropped his gaze before all his secrets gushed out. He had a permit for a *concealed* weapon and he saw that he'd better keep it that way.

"Barton Squire," she said, as though the emphatic pronunciation of his name communicated something, which it did.

"Have mercy," he said. "Don't ask."

Turning her body sideways to squeeze past a painting of a violent blue whirlpool, she gripped his upper arms, squeezing his biceps with her fingers. She shook him lightly. "Honey, I'm nothing but mercy. Just work with me, all right?" Using a finger to raise his chin, she forced him to look her in the eye as if he were a larcenous child. She let him have her stare – point-blank. "You can fudge the truth with juries, hon, but not with me. I'm all yours. *Confide in me.*"

She was offering him an escape, he realized, for the trespass of searching her studio, because what had so far been comic might turn tragic. There was a reason laughter sounded like sobbing. And for that, he was distinctly not in the mood.

"I was looking for pot," he said suddenly. He grinned sheepishly. It sounded absurd enough to be true.

Jordan arched her honey-pale brows, wrinkling her wide forehead, giving him *that look,* the one she saved for clients who weren't good liars, the look that said, *don't even try.* "You want to get high," she said. She made it a statement.

"It's for my article."

"Philosopher's eye?"

"Nature's bullshit detector."

"Ah! The old Helmut trick – write sober and revise stoned."

"Or write stoned and revise sober." Barton felt the handhold of an alibi. From now on if anyone caught him acting strangely he'd blame it on marijuana. Still, he had to go easy and not slip into caricature – reefer madness he didn't need.

Jordan frowned. She seemed to be buying his story. She *wanted* to buy it. "I never paint stoned," she said. "I don't trust the work. Not like the old days."

"No doubt," he said, nodding, "but legal writing's about as far from art as the moon."

"I might be able to find an old pipe you could scrape."

He shook his head, feeling the gun slip further down so that now he looked like he was carrying a load in his shorts. The edge of the business card positioned itself for castration. Shifting his weight from one foot to the other, he wanted desperately to adjust his testicles, but he was afraid if he moved his legs the gun would fall at his feet.

"I was thinking of my friend Bill," he said, remembering the joint they'd shared at the conference in Kansas, "I thought it might break loose a few ideas." He laughed in a way that sounded utterly false, earning him another odd look from his wife. "No worries," he said.

Overhead, the studio skylights admitted a sudden stream of sun as a mass of clouds sailed over the house toward the Atlantic. The doves in the pine tree whistled and cooed.

She touched his shoulder. "Honey, is there something you want to tell me?"

Shrugging off her fingers, feeling the gun shift again, he clapped his hands with mannered enthusiasm. "Never mind. I best get back to it."

His wife detected the false note in his voice. He was hiding something, but she didn't want to become his interrogator. Well, so be it. Like so much in her life, whatever it was – perhaps it was better left out of sight.

"The ostrich philosophy," she said.

"What?"

"Nothing. I've done my procrastination dance. Now *I've* got to get to it."

Barton didn't take the hint. He suddenly wanted to take her in his arms, even with the steely bulge in his shorts.

"Why is every artist in such a rush?" he asked.

She showed him the pink tip of her tongue.

"So spill it," he said. "Educate me."

She cast her eyes toward the skylight and said, "Well, I've got . . . what, maybe four-hundred months left in this carcass? That's not many paintings, or not a lot of good ones."

Unnerved, he wished he hadn't asked. Four-hundred months before The Long Dirt Nap? What an appalling figure.

"Sorry I asked," he said. Shivering, he threaded his way through the maze of easels toward the door. The paintings draped with sheets brought to mind corpses in a morgue. "Break a leg," he called, turning the knob with one hand and grabbing his crotch with the other, feeling something slip.

Jordan widened her eyes, leaving her husband to his odd ways.

Outside, the sultry air hit him like a wave and beads of sweat broke on his forehead. Walking toward the house, he dug the business card from his groin before it unmanned him. He'd have to return it before she discovered its absence, but his wife lost small objects so frequently – car keys, reading glasses, cell phones – that she wouldn't find its disappearance unusual. Like him, she had the ability to dispatch tiny but important items to an alternate universe, never to be seen again.

Also, he was eager to remove the pistol from his balls.

Shading his face with his hand, he studied the card. All the user names were the same: *Cubistlover@1Bee*, and so were the passwords: *Liketothelark@1Bee*.

He stopped on the walk and stood blinking in the dazzling light. Overhead in the west, the sun sank beside a thunderhead, dropping toward the horizon like a peephole on the inferno.

Extracting the gun from his shorts, he concealed the weapon in front of his body and slid open the sliding glass door, thinking *forgive us our trespasses . . .*

Some Buddhist! His stomach bubbled into his throat.

Inside, sitting at his computer in his office upstairs, he stared at her password. Sighing, he looked out the window at her studio. She would be painting and sketching, aglow with inspiration. The pistol lay beside his mouse pad.

I don't have to do this, he thought.

He could trust his wife.

Then he flipped over the card.

Helmut Knight, Esq.
Attorney at Law

As we forgive those who trespass against us . . .

13

Hot Pursuit

THAT night a gentle rain fell from oyster-colored clouds whose ragged edges were lit by the full moon. Raindrops dotted Helmut's pool, illuminated by underwater lights which were warm to the touch.

On a lounge chair next to the diving board, lit by the pool's blue glow, Jordan's rear end sagged on rubber slats. She sat straddling the chair with her feet on the concrete, buttoning up her blouse. Distracted, she misaligned the buttons, discovered her error and tore her shirt open. A tiny pearl button rolled into the pool and sank spinning to the bottom.

"Self-pity," Helmut said, "is emotional hypochondria." He stood under an awning sipping vodka from a martini glass. Barefoot, he had on a black silk bathrobe embroidered with orange dragons, and as the alcohol hummed through his veins he shivered against the smooth fabric. Under the black sky, the pool shimmered bluely as Jordan hid her face in her hands.

Stepping from under the awning, feeling a cold droplet strike his neck, Helmut quickly ducked back. His robe had been handmade in China and it wasn't the sort of thing you wore in the rain. As with his Ferrari, he had a deep respect for objects of value.

Jordan's eyes fluttered up to him, brimming with liquid. They were extraordinary things, those eyes, more blue than his pool, even if they *were* washed up. Maybe now that they were fading he could escape her spell.

"So are those teardrops or raindrops?"

"What?"

"On your face."

She sniffled and wiped her face and stood up. Her khaki blouse, woven from hemp and now missing a button, hung open over a sports bra. Her shirttails flapped against her tan stomach, which was muscular and flat apart from the small roll of feminine fat resting atop the waistband of her shorts. On her feet she wore leather sandals with espadrille laces. The laces wound upward around her slender ankles and crisscrossed her muscular calves. The sandals looked vaguely Roman. Helmut approved of them. During their romp, he'd asked her to keep them on, which she had, without comment.

Crossing the concrete, she removed the drink from his hand, contemplated throwing it in his face, then tossed it to the back of her throat. She handed him the empty glass, enjoying the solvent taste of the alcohol.

"You're welcome," he said approvingly.

"I shouldn't have come."

"But you did, love."

"That's right," she said brightly. "My husband's going insane, and instead of helping him – instead of standing by his side – I fuck his business partner." She laughed hollowly, making a high, shrill sound, so that Helmut frowned. She was slightly hysterical and he disapproved of hysteria.

"Well," he said slowly, not wanting to alarm her, "technically he's no longer a partner."

Her eyes widened and her hands shook. Helmut raised his arm protectively, thankful he'd gotten the glass away from her. The last thing he needed was to cut his foot around the pool. Under the influence, Jordan liked to break things, especially *his* things.

"Let me get you a Valium," he said. "Cuckoo's Nest isn't worth it." He held up his hand as though he were being sworn in. "So help me God."

"Huh! You ain't my daddy, Helmut." She leered and the wobble in her eyes alarmed him even more than her demented laughter. No more hard liquor for this one, he thought, fixing himself a drink at his outdoor tiki bar.

Stumbling toward him, she groaned and took a seat on a wicker bar stool. Helmut narrowed his eyes. "Turn off the waterworks, will you? Come *on*." He set his drink on the bar and stroked the downy hair on her forearm. It was as close as he got to tenderness. Beyond her blond head, the rain increased with a rushing sound and dotted the mirror-smooth pool with tiny expanding circles.

Jordan's eyelashes flickered, beaded with moisture. "Touch me again and I'll break your jaw, you – " Helmut withdrew his fingers. "Wait," she said. She grabbed his hand and squeezed it. Helmut wondered what he'd done to deserve her. Suffering her moods and her drinking, it occurred to him that he was better off without her. She was a bad influence. That was the long and short of it.

"Listen to me," she said, seeing his eyes drift and squeezing his hand so forcefully he pulled it away and glared at her. "I keep thinking of his face! He's so lost." Helmut held her eyes but she couldn't look into his. They were too dark. He had no shame, but she was bathed in the stuff. She pictured her husband at home, staring out the window at the rain, wondering where she was. His face would be long with worry.

Christ, I am a shit, she thought. She shuddered, unable to abide herself. She was a disgrace. She couldn't look at the past. And she couldn't look at the future, leaving only the intolerable present.

"It's funny," she said. "I got a room of my own, and it had a view. Yet of my own accord I've blacked out the windows."

Helmut drained his glass and fixed another drink. Coping with a weeping female, he figured he'd earned it. He checked his watch.

"Virginia Woolf," he said. "Filled her pockets with stones and jumped in the river. Is that your role model?"

"I don't know. Right now I can see the appeal."

"*You don't know?* Jesus. Make sense, will you?" He looked at the half empty vodka bottle on the bar, remembering not to offer it to her, although in her present state she was really depressing him. "You want a coke?" he offered.

"Coke? That's the last thing I need. I'm already wired. What the fuck, Helmut? I'd probably have a heart attack."

"A Coca Cola, dear. A soft drink."

"Oh. No, thank you." Then, "What I want is my husband."

"So call him! What the hell. We're adults."

She let him have *that look,* though it was blunted by drunkenness. She smiled bitterly. "What's being adult got to do with it?"

Helmut pretended to inspect the fine Italian tile bordering his pool. Nobody but Jordan could stare him down, but perhaps that explained why she was the only woman who'd ever been more to him than a pair of breasts and a receptacle for his precious spunk. Like the liquid glinting in her eyelashes, a blend of rain and tears, she was a mixture. Half her soul belonged to the church, the rest of it to the circus, where it belonged, Helmut thought, under the whip.

"Quit acting," he said coldly, fortifying himself with more vodka. "You seem fake."

She held up her index finger. "Ah. The master speaks." She pointed at the cocktail napkins on the bar. He pushed them toward her.

"Keep up the auditions," he said, burping against his fist, "you need the practice."

"He's going kill himself, you ass. Don't you understand that?" She dabbed at the corners of her eyes. She wasn't wearing make-up – she'd given it up, although out of habit she made as if not to smear mascara. "He bought a gun he thinks I don't know about. So I have to stay. Otherwise, I'm a murderer. You *do* realize that, don't you?"

"*Murderer?*" Helmut scowled. "Where did you say you went to law school?"

She didn't say anything.

"Where ever it was, you must've flunked Criminal Law."

Jordan set her mouth in a hard line. Always the teacher's pet, the world expected her to bear teasing and even ridicule with a good-natured smile. To her disappointment, Helmut was no different. Well, she'd had enough of returning insults with smiles. She let her face look how she felt.

"Oh, that's right! You got the only 'A' in the class. Problem is . . . *you didn't learn anything*. That's the difference. You want to stay with that worm? That pathetic puppy?"

She hid her eyes with her hand while Helmut glared at her. Suddenly he growled and stepped around the bar.

"I said quit acting!"

He seized her shoulders and shook her. "Hollywood's that way, Jordie." He pointed west.

Jordan gasped and gulped air, breathing shallowly from the tops of her lungs. "I'm nuh-nuh-nuh-not acting . . . you asshole!" She coughed and swallowed and blew her nose into a napkin. Helmut's mouth fell open. Feeling his grip loosen, she twisted out from under his hands.

Smacking himself in the head with the heel of his hand, he began applauding. The sound of his clapping echoed loudly over the pool.

"*Brava!* Ladies and gentlemen! What a performance!" The palms of his hands were stinging and he swept his arm over an imaginary audience, "I ask you – have you ever?"

She swung her arm and caught him across the face with her fist. A terrific *crack* split the air as his head swung sideways and he had to grab the bar to keep from toppling over. She stood over him, panting, nostrils flaring, her fists balled tight.

Helmut massaged his jaw and slid his rear end back onto his bar stool, checking for loose teeth. A red welt emerged on his cheek.

Raising his arm, he made as if to slap her, but she caught his wrist and slammed it onto the bar, cracking his knuckles.

"Stay still," she said calmly. "Or I'll beat the living shit out of you."

It was an ugly moment. Helmut was no athlete and Jordan was. She could put him in the hospital. Of course, he could beat her up in court afterwards, but such a settlement would be moot. No man wants to get thrashed by a woman. That damage couldn't be compensated.

"If you've finished your assault and battery," he said, as the rain drummed on the leaves of the trees, "I'd like to fix myself a drink."

She released his wrist.

"Helmut, I – "

He didn't look at her. "Hit the road, Jordan." He fixed his drink. "Or I'm calling the cops."

"He doesn't know anything, Mutt. Not about the money. Or about us."

Staring down his long nose, Helmut's eyes were flat and merciless. Dropping to her knees, she caught his hand and kissed it, knocking over her bar stool. "Please," she said. "If you ever loved me please don't tell him. Please, Helmut? Please don't tell him."

Helmut yanked his hand away. "Quit your blubbering, you infant." He glared at the top of her tawny head. She was a wreck. Just like her husband. He wrinkled his nose. How had he ever got mixed up with these two losers? "Your problem," he said, "is that you don't know what you want."

"I want my husband to be well."

"Then quit cheating on him, you whore!"

She cried into her hands and he thought, *Jesus! Look where love has got me.* An ageing beauty, on her knees, bawling on his patio, his pool, his life, everything he'd worked for. She expected too much.

"As your attorney," he said, "I advise you to find a priest."

She hugged his legs. Her body shook. Feeling her tremble,

a tingle slithered up his spine, though whether from pleasure or revulsion he couldn't say.

She unclasped her hands and slid backward on her knees, scraping over the concrete, sniffling and wiping her nose. What had come over her? Barton's mental illness must be contagious, she thought wildly, because . . . *I seem to have picked up a dose.* She looked around the pool, tilted her head back and peered upward into Helmut's hairy nostrils.

"What do *you* want?" she asked. She felt like spitting, but there was only the pool so she swallowed it, tasting her body's sourness. She grimaced.

"Right now I want you to stand up and get that fucking look off your face. I'm not a shrink, Jordan."

She picked up her bar stool and looked at him. She held his eye and shrugged. Her crisis seemed to be passing like the rain.

What *did* he want? he wondered. His best friend's wife? Well, yes. He admitted it, after all. He wanted her to be his lover, but also his possession, and more: his fan, his audience. He could do without other people. They bored him. *She* was the one he wanted to entertain, whose merry laugh he loved above all sounds on earth. He couldn't hide it anymore. Ashamed, he *longed* for her. He couldn't help it. His fame required a witness, and she was it. She was his cheerleader.

"You're higher maintenance than my goddamn Ferrari, Jordie. But Cuckoo's Nest can keep you." Hearing his voice, he winced, but it was the right move, the disciplined approach.

"That's the booze talking," she said. "I've seen the real you, Mutt."

Silently, he agreed. Deep down, where it mattered, he was a good man. Anyone could see this. He sighed.

"I'll keep your precious secret, Jordie – as long as you don't crap out on me. What a waste though – with me you could've been . . . well, who knows. As it is you're a housewife." He snuffed through his nose. "A dilettante."

Jordan cleared her throat, turned her head and spat into his pool. Helmut didn't flinch. She hadn't expected him to. Helmut set great store by his powers of foresight.

I'm not a shrink, he claimed, and yet he shrunk her, although she couldn't say why or how, or even if she found it unpleasant. He made himself into a hero at her expense, she realized vaguely, but the thrill was worth its price. Sometimes. Perhaps she wanted his approval because he bestowed it so grudgingly. When it came, then, it was a blood rush as nerve rattling as cocaine.

"We still picking you up tomorrow?"

"Unless you know how to change the plugs on a Ferrari."

"And you won't say anything?"

"Are you deaf? No! Now go. Hit the bricks!"

He didn't look at her as she pulled on her paint-spattered overalls and stomped off his property. Scowling, he noted the wad of snotty napkins she'd left on the bar. Using a swizzle stick, he nudged it into the trash.

A car door slammed and he thought, *You're letting her get away!* His entire past became clear, and for one crystal moment, he understood himself.

The glass fell from his hand and broke with a musical-sounding crash, its shards glinting on the concrete.

His brain swam.

He'd spent his life in duplicity. Lying to get women on their knees, lying to win cases, lying to Barton, lying to the IRS . . . the inventory of his falsehoods was the story of his life. And now that he was getting older, he wanted a story with a moral.

Yet how he could he find it with a liar, an adulteress? What a joke. Only God could've concocted it. Well, what had he expected?

He spat into the pool himself, smiling at her nerve.

In the moonlight, the crickets chirped. Life had forked. And it was strange. Sometimes he saw it coming, but other times, it was like a blind turn on a mountain road.

It didn't matter. He knew what he wanted.

Racing through the house with his vodka bottle, he crossed the living room and glanced out the front window.

She was getting away, ditching the Knight for the Squire.

A capital offense.

And the penalty?

Death!

For only now, in this second, standing drunk in his living room, did he find the courage to admit what he'd known for the last twenty years.

He loved Jordan. He'd *always* loved her. His precious career was a joke. He wasn't young anymore and his dreams had packed up, a fact which struck him every time he touched his bald head. Jordan was all that mattered, the damsel he couldn't buy, but had to win.

Outside, her headlights swung out of the driveway and shot halogen beams down the dark street.

Clutching his bottle, he chased after her, dashing onto the lawn where a cool wind blew across his skin and a cold rain struck him like a shower of icy needles.

"Jordie!" he screamed, hollering into the rain, into the grayness, stamping barefoot over the wet pavement. His voice caught in his throat and he shouted himself hoarse. The gutters ran with dirty water and the rain pelted him, soaking his robe and ruining the embroidered dragons. The black silk clung to his skin.

He charged on, jogging down the street, bellowing her name. He brandished his bottle at the sky, which answered him with a thunderclap and a jagged flash.

He began to run. The naked soles of his feet slapped the pavement while the black street glimmered under the lights with petroleum rainbows. A sudden gust blew open his robe and he dangled in the breeze, bathed in cold air.

Jordan's red tail lights receded.

"Jordie," he said. His eyes filled. "Sweetheart! Honey. Come back!" His throat was burning and he tasted blood. Doubling over, he stopped and pressed his hands to his knees, gasping. He hawked and spat in the gutter.

Across the street, a yellow light blossomed in an upstairs window. Helmut thrust out his pelvis. "I expect you've seen human genitals!" he bellowed. The window darkened and he threw his bottle against the house, hitting it squarely in the front door. The bottle exploded with a crash and the upstairs light winked on again.

Helmut fled. The police were probably en route and he had no wish to represent himself.

Safe at home, he walked through his living room, where a trail of bloody red footprints followed him across the white carpet. At the tiki bar by the pool he found a fresh glass and poured himself a pick-me-up. God knew, he thought, his lungs popping, he'd earned it.

Rotating the glass in his hand, he caught his breath and studied the alcohol. At least booze didn't lie. It didn't tease. It fucked you good and hard, without any lube, and buddy . . . it knew that was how you liked it.

Overhead, the rain ceased and the stars shone through a break in the clouds. A sensation like bee stings shot from the soles of his feet and, lifting each one in turn, he found them bleeding from numerous tiny cuts, sliced up by all the glittering shards of glass surrounding the pool.

My personal stigmata, he thought, suddenly smiling. A great weight lifted off his heart. He had a plan. A mission! With the stars shining down on him, alone by his pool, he felt touched by God.

Or perhaps it was the Devil, or the hormones in his blood, or the alcohol in his brain. He didn't know or care, because from the lightness in his heart he knew he'd been redeemed. Blessed even.

Murder would be his salvation.

Holding up his drink, he toasted the holiness of homicide.

"Here's to crime," he said.

14

MITIGATING CIRCUMSTANCES

JORDAN switched on her wipers and pulled away from Helmut's house. In the rearview she caught sight of his pale body running down the street, his robe flying open like a pair of black wings, his vodka bottle held high. His mouth opened and closed – a toothy hole baying into the night.

Shuddering, she hit the gas and sped over the reflections of the streetlights glinting on the pavement.

She didn't see any point in stopping. Drunks loved to talk but seldom had anything to say. In this she was an expert witness.

Stopped at a red light, she checked herself in the rearview. Awful! Who knew the human eye contained so many veins? Crimson rivers wriggled across her whites, the blue buttons of her irises straining through a net of bloody threads.

"Not what you'd call a pretty sight," she said, shaking her head.

The light turned green and she hit the gas and lurched forward. So what if a cop arrested her? At least she'd be relieved of the burden of holding her life together.

A night in jail, she thought – hell, a lifetime. No more decisions. What freedom! Getting locked up was what she deserved. *Quantum Meruit*. As much as you merit.

Overhead, the clouds congealed and a fresh squall of rain pummeled the windshield. She advanced her wipers to a setting she thought of as "frantic." The glass fogged up and she hit the defroster. Its heat blew the hair from her face, tickling her ears.

Tonight, she decided, she'd paint a picture of love. A slobbering, fanged wolf, snarling at the gates of hell. Or maybe a black-eyed angel?

"Gross," as Helmut would say, "too obvious."

Lifting her phone from the center console, she called her husband. He answered immediately.

"Where *are* you?"

"Driving. On my way home. Listen, if you don't need me, I'm going to paint."

"Say again. You faded out."

"I'm going straight to the studio, if that's all right. You want me to come in and check on you?"

"No, no . . . go ahead. I'm slaving on my article."

Jordan exhaled. No matter how bad things might get between them, they seldom interfered with each other's work, a habit which had smoothed over more than a few rough patches on the long road since college.

It was weird. So much of love consisted of gratitude, but sometimes it was gratitude for not having to see the loved one, for not having to pretend to *be* in love, even if you were.

Well, what *was* love, anyway? The freedom to remove your mask and show your homely face. And who did the loving in return? Someone who embraced your unabashedly goofy, childhood self. Someone who'd talk to you in silly voices and make inside jokes which ended in side-splitting fits of hilarity. Only One True Love could tickle her, free her inner brat and make her merry.

Who needed grown-ups, with their mortgages and retirement? Love was Eden, a paradise. Why leave? She and Barton grew their own garden, spawning sprites in every brook and glade – green and secret places where magic lived, where lovers whispered and kissed and giggled.

Ah, those were the days!

Pulling all-nighters in college at the corner coffee shop, their friends had joked, "Don't even try to talk to them – Romeo and Juliet can't be disturbed." Writing, painting, screwing, reading, sleeping, eating, swimming: their young bodies bred a universe, with a physics all its own. Later – *oh, so much later* – she wondered if even Einstein could've discovered its laws.

What had she done? She clicked her signal and turned onto their street, passing the large ocean-front houses as the rain tapered to a slow drizzle. She switched her wipers down from the frantic setting. Her husband was coming apart, and by hooking him on medication, she'd unfastened his grip on sanity as surely as if she'd had him lobotomized.

Barton was a delicate man. His soul beat close to his skin, and since those glory days in college she'd vowed to protect him, to preserve the radiance he harbored and around which she and Helmut had so long orbited. Without admitting it, they'd fed their dark souls on Barton's stellar glow. He was their holy joy, their innocent center, their luminous fusion.

Pulling into the driveway, sweeping the beams of her headlights across the lawn, she wasn't surprised to find that she still loved her husband. In college, her Classics professor had shouted: *Cupid was a god the ancients feared!* He wasn't the cherubic baby on Valentine cards, holding his cute little bow and arrow. Cupid was demonic. Lanced by his poison tip, you fell into bondage, a slave not even the gods could liberate.

Jordan accepted this.

And yet . . . in her core, she wasn't a bonder. Not like Barton, who craved total intimacy. Objectively, she judged her level of attachment to other human beings to be within clinically "normal" bounds, but as an artist she was more of a single-celled organism than part of a colony. Only the existence of Barton sentenced her to live in love. If she'd never met him, she'd have been happy alone or else as part of a marriage of convenience. In this she was like

Helmut, who, if Barton were subtracted from the world, she would certainly have married.

Clutching the wheel with both hands and breathing hard, her chest inflating and deflating as though powered by a respirator, she crunched over the gravel in the driveway and parked in front of her studio. Killing the engine, she rested her head against the steering wheel, listening to the drizzle patter against the roof while the engine ticked in the cool air.

The windows of her house glowed with light. Her husband would be inside, paranoid and sick, working on his article and waiting for her. Beside the house the windows of her studio were dark, waiting for her to illuminate them, presumably with inspiration. Her lungs hurt, and for the first time in many years, she wished she had a cigarette.

Clearly, there were two ways she could go. Love Barton, or love Helmut. On this gray evening, the road less traveled bore no sign.

Staring through the windshield at the low clouds scudding across the moon, she prayed.

Hearing no answer, she banged her forehead on the steering wheel. She was tired of crying.

Parked in the Florida drizzle, thinking of her husband with his need and despair, she watched herself blossom like a poisonous flower. Her stare glued itself to a spot of fog on the windshield. Her fingers tightened on the steering wheel, turning her knuckles a corpse-like shade of gray. She grunted. She felt like howling.

What if she abandoned Barton?

Her eyes widened and she gulped the moist air. What if he killed himself? She had in that horrible moment, when every nerve in her body sang, done what every living thing was born to do.

She grew.

Then Helmut and Barton stomped into her mind, dragging her back to earth. God, she wanted to forget them. She had to. Between Helmut's lust and Barton's love, they were ripping her in half, tearing off her wings when they were still wet.

Enough! Her lovers were as dark as black holes in their wants, their terrible *gravitas*. Only painting yielded light. Let painting be her lover then. It asked everything and promised nothing and it brooked no refusal. Painting met her on the field of honor, daring her to show cowardice, her yellow belly.

"Time to step up," she said. Climbing out and slamming the door, she walked into her studio and turned on the lights. She hid her torn blouse in the closet and changed into her paint-spattered overalls. Propped on easels around the room, her blank canvases spoke accusingly of neglect. Well, that was going to change. Now she was painting for her life.

Squeezing a tube of cobalt blue onto her pallet, she blinked and stared at the tiny blob. A single fat tear fell beside it and sucked up the pigment till it quivered like a drop from the sky.

Barton wouldn't survive without her.

But could she sacrifice herself? She couldn't redeem him. She'd fail him. She knew that. But where did duty to husband and duty to art come together? That was the front, the no woman's land where she sprawled in her trench.

"Good heavens," she said softly.

From the studio refrigerator, she retrieved a frosty bottle of gin and fixed herself a drink. She drained her glass and let the ice knock against her teeth. She wouldn't have another. That would be too easy. And shameful. She'd drunk more than enough at Helmut's.

Taking up a painting knife and dabbing it into a blob of orange, she committed to her canvas.

And there. Two fiery dots on a white field. Her mood brightened and she went light on her feet, feeling the aesthetic fight the anesthetic, a war between states. Blood versus blood-alcohol. The thing in front of her might not be art, but it protected her. It locked out her demon, that grinning fiend with eyes like embers, the beast himself.

That thing which wanted another drink.

Ignoring it, she painted rapidly, switching to a fan brush because it was turning into one of those nights, where regret had fangs, where misgivings had to be painted over.

Overhead, the rain drumming on the skylights reminded her of a saying she'd always despised – the pitter-patter of little feet.

Another tear hit the palate and turned itself tangerine. She wasn't a crier but . . . She hadn't used protection with Helmut.

Could I possibly have gotten pregnant? At forty-three?

It seemed unlikely, and it struck her as oddly painful that she didn't have to sweat out the calendar as she had in her younger days, when she'd been even more irresponsible. No more anxious waiting for the blessed blood, because when it came it was moot.

I never had children. I never even got pregnant.

Of course, she'd never *tried* to have a baby, but that didn't make childlessness less baffling. Somehow life had gone on without her. No use fighting it. She shook her head. Apparently, her unused maternal instincts meant to torture her all night. Well, so be it. There was nothing she could do to appease them. Biology had conjugated her, shifting her reproductive tense from present to past. Egg-wise, she'd gone bad – from fertile to barren, a field gone fallow. Somehow she found the change unexpected, though nothing was more natural. Blinking rapidly, she sniffled and wiped her eyes, smearing a streak of blue along her cheekbone.

Focusing on hue and brushstroke and perspective, the lens of her mind refused to come clear. Groaning, watching it prepare to unload, she thought, oh lovely, another truckload of guilt . . .

What would her ancestors have thought her? Shoving every manner of device into her womb, ingesting God-knows-what hormones, calling on lovers to withdraw – Lord, her reproductive life, or the lack of it, was *la comedia divina* incarnate – except she wasn't laughing.

On the canvas she painted a mask of agony and beside it one of joy. Ah, those Greeks – what a bunch of wise-asses. The inventors of *hubris* thought they knew it all.

There was a gentle tapping on the door. That would be Graciela, who knew how to knock without surprising the artist while she was composing, lest a startled hand abort a future masterpiece.

Jordan had forgotten that this was Saturday, when Graciela earned extra money scrubbing the studio.

"*Buenas noches, Graciela,*" she sang out cheerfully, wiping the tears from her eyes and crossing the room, paintbrush in hand.

Graciela stepped inside, averting her eyes and hunching her shoulders, cowed by this tall American woman, so confident and successful. Ms. Jordan wasn't like the women in Cuba. As far as Graciela could tell, she had no fear of men. Why, she even sued them.

"Come in, come in," Jordan said, gently taking Graciela's elbow. "I want you to see my latest."

Graciela admired her employer's work with her intelligent brown gaze. "I like," she said, eyeing a tangerine wolf's face with a nimbus of indigo spattered with gold glitter.

Frowning, Jordan watched her study the painting. Graciela had on a beige maid's uniform, with her hair tied onto her head in huge blue-black knot, fastened with a plastic clip. Crossing the room to another easel, she smiled with her dazzling new teeth. "My favorite," she said, nodding at the picture and tracing its lines with her finger without touching the canvas.

Seen from the back, a naked man and woman waded hand in hand into the ocean, awash in a riot of gold and rose.

"It's called *What Blood Beyond the Skin of Sunset?*" Jordan said, "the first of a series with these orange-and-white hazard markers."

Graciela cocked her head to the side, looking puzzled. Jordan stared into her brown eyes, finding kindness there, a feminine warmth which was new to her.

"This one's too sentimental," Jordan explained, looking away, "like the cover of a bad novel." Blowing a wisp of hair from her face, she used the end of her brush to flip a paint-spattered canvas over the easel. "It's sort of embarrassing in its subject matter, but I can't bring myself to ditch it. I'm going to send it to an old friend. He's got Alzheimer's so maybe he won't think it's so terrible." She laughed, but the laugh was hollow.

Graciela thought her employer might start weeping and wanted to hug her, but Anglos weren't comfortable with affection. Thinking how strange this was, she caught the sickly sweet odor of alcohol on Jordan's breath. Graciela formed her lips into a smile but felt very sad for Ms. Jordan. She was a beautiful woman, but her eyes were bloodshot and she had worry lines around her mouth. She smelled sweaty. A streak of blue paint ran down one of her cheeks like a clown's tear. Graciela couldn't stop herself. She hugged her.

Startled, feeling Graciela's small breathing body tight within her arms, Jordan was careful not to smudge her hair with the brush in her hand.

Holding each other an extra second, neither woman said anything. When they separated, both looked away. They cleared their throats in the same instant, made eye contact and laughed, releasing the tension.

"You're a sweetie," Jordan said.

Graciela smiled shyly and let her employer show off the rest of her new work, which didn't look all that different, she thought, than the paintings her children, Esteban and Esperanza, did in art class at school. *What Blood Beyond the Skin of Sunset?* remained her favorite, by far.

Graciela scuffed the toe of her work shoe on the floor. "It's getting late, *Señora* Squire. I should start, no?"

Jordan apologized. Here she was inflicting her painting on this woman whose feet were probably hurting and who wanted to get home to her family. For an agonizing instant, she wondered what that would be like – to have children waiting for her – would it be as good as a studio of one's own? The question wasn't fair, she decided, eyeing the glass on her workbench. Somehow the beast had emptied it. She was momentarily confused. If Graciela was here, why was it dark outside? Daylight had somehow escaped from her.

"Why're you here so late, *Compañera?*"

"I come after I clean office. Mistair Barton help me set up a college fund, so I stay late."

"And how are Esteban and Esperanza?"

"So good! They always fixing my English."

"Here. Let me do that." Jordan retrieved the cleaning supplies from under the workbench and got down on her knees beside Graciela. Together they scrubbed a splash of green watercolor from the baseboard.

"*Señora*. Ms. Jordan. I do this. You go see your oosban. He not so happy today. He waiting for you."

"No. I want to help."

Graciela shrugged and the two women worked side by side on their knees, scrubbing the baseboard. These Anglos didn't do enough physical work, in Graciela's opinion, and sitting at their desks all day drove them *loco*. Jordan scrubbed at another stain, a splash of crimson in the shape of Texas.

Feeling the other woman's eyes on her, Jordan glanced up. Graciela's gaze was full of tenderness, which Jordan hadn't known she'd been craving until it was offered. The two women stared at each other. Jordan's eyes were lost and cold and blue. The moment was intimate and they both recognized it, but a vast distance lay between them. Both saw the chasm, of culture and of class, and regretted its existence, each feeling sorry for the other.

Jordan shivered. Perhaps there was hope. Her heart thumped against the wall of her chest. She wanted there to be hope.

So did Graciela. Despite the *pro bono* legal aid, she and her husband Antonio were struggling, members of the invisible class whose job it was to scrub toilets and haul trash. Guiltily, the Squires skirted a careful course around the Miranda family pride.

Hence the citizenship, the dental insurance, the private school tuition and now the college fund. Over Graciela's strenuous objections, Jordan had made her a present of her old Mercedes after Barton had bought her a Land Rover to transport her easels and paintings.

Yet when the Squires spoke of the bright futures of the Miranda children, Graciela would narrow her eyes and nod without conviction. Jordan got a better response from Antonio, who would stop trimming a palm tree and grin, showing off his new gold teeth, saying, "*Sí*, they smart, maybe lawyer like you some day!"

Graciela would cringe. Hopefully, Esteban and Esperanza would become something more than lawyers.

"You want a drink, sweetie?"

"No, no – I never."

She covered her employer's slender white hand with her tiny brown one. "Ms. Jordan – why you crying?"

"Oh, well. You know. Nothing. Everything." Jordan tipped up her empty glass and swallowed an ice cube. "Let me help some more," she said, feeling the ice cube squeeze down her throat. Her eyes watered. "Please let me help. All right? I'll pay you the same."

Graciela's face tightened.

"Please, honey. *Por favor.* I need to." She looked into Graciela's coffee-colored eyes. *"I need to."*

Graciela nodded. She felt sorry for Jordan painting out here all by herself while her husband worked alone inside the house. These married Anglos! They spent so much time getting away from each other. She didn't understand them, but then so much of this country was strange. Her people were poor in Cuba and they had to fit too many people into one house, but that was the difference – they *liked* being together. It was special. *La familia.* The bonds of blood relations. And more, through your flesh you knew God. The cold ways of the Anglos gave her a headache.

"Graciela, do you know the saddest words in English?"

"Saddest words in English?" This sounded like a trick. A frown creased her smooth forehead.

She's so young, Jordan thought, smiling sadly, taking in the taut skin, the unlined face, and yet she's already a wife and mother. She's *connected.* Jordan shuddered. Graciela made her feel like an old maid, but then she thought – *feel* like an old maid. Hell, I'm forty-three. I *am* an old maid!

"*It's too late,*" she said.

"For what?"

"No, I mean those are the words. The saddest ones, *en ingles.*"

Graciela considered this. She pursed her lips and nodded. "*Sí,*" she said. "In Spanish too, I think."

Jordan quit with the sponge and the water and stood up. Already, her lower back ached. "I'm going to pay you for the whole night," she said. Graciela opened her mouth but Jordan held up her hand, putting on her lawyer's voice. "But only if you go home. *Por favor?* Go home to your family, hon." The artist's voice went thick and caught in her throat. Her eyes wobbled. She'd stood up too fast and she was lightheaded. Drunk, too.

Graciela didn't argue. She gathered her cleaning supplies and stored them under the workbench and left the studio, feeling rude but rushing anyway – because that was another funny thing about these Anglos – they couldn't stand for anyone to see them cry.

Outside, in the cool air, she turned her face to the sky and let the rain sprinkle her skin. The mist against her cheeks was heavenly. At church on Sunday she'd say a prayer for the Squires. It hurt her heart to think about them. She was sorry they were so unhappy, although she couldn't see why. They were healthy and rich and they had each other.

What could be wrong?

Crossing herself and walking toward her Mercedes, she even felt sorry for God, who'd have to figure out why this husband and wife had lost faith in their marriage, their sacred vows, because from what she could see, glancing up at the windows above the wide grassy lawn – the one her loving husband Antonio so carefully manicured – the Squires owned everything money could buy.

And wasn't that the American Dream? The pursuit of happiness?

Felicidad?

Her fingers gripped her car's door handle. She was supposed to clean the house, but Ms. Jordan had dismissed her. Thinking of her children and how much she wanted to snuggle up to their compact bodies, Graciela felt love like an ache in her bones.

But no, she wouldn't leave. Her feet tingled and her spine throbbed, but these were mere inconveniences. She felt loyalty more than pain. God and the Squires had been good to her and gratitude made her strong.

For the divine as well as the mortal, Graciela would put in the hours.

15

FRUIT OF THE POISONOUS TREE

WHILE his wife was helping Graciela clean the splashes off the baseboards in the studio, Barton sat at Jordan's computer inside their study. Propped against the monitor, he'd set up Helmut's business card with the password written on the back. Jordan would be painting all night, leaving Barton his motive, method and opportunity.

Now he began the crime.

Downstairs a door slammed. He froze, wide-eyed and red-handed. His eyes darted to and fro and his fingertips hovered over the keyboard. Sitting rigidly, he pricked up his ears and listened intently to the sound of a woman's footfall. It didn't belong to his wife. It was Graciela's. Squaring his shoulders, he closed his eyes, steeling himself against a hot wave of guilt.

Muttering an obscenity, he opened his eyes, exhaled, and logged onto his wife's email account. The cursor blinked accusingly. He typed her password.

Liketothelark@1Bee

Its origin was familiar. In college they'd taken the same Shakespeare class, one where the professor, so old and frail you half expected him to have *known* Shakespeare, had required them to memorize a sonnet.

Barton could still remember it:

Like to the lark at break of day arising
From sullen earth, sings hymns at heaven's gate;
For thy sweet love remembered such wealth brings
That then I scorn to change my state with kings.

He stopped, fingertips poised above the keys. Would Shakespeare have stooped to this? It seemed impossible.

But Barton had probable cause, a warrant. With his wife about to abandon him, he'd weighed the evidence. Figuring a lifespan of eighty, he had a balance of thirty-seven years and change. About eleven thousand days, or a few million heartbeats.

Given that bottom line, what choice did he have? How else to cure his loathing for Helmut? He could feel the man polluting him, stinking him up, fouling his soul.

Killing his old roommate was the *right* thing to do. He felt this now as a holy cause. Not only for his sake, but also for the sake of the world. How many marriages had Helmut ruined? How many lives had he poisoned? If any fault obtained, it lay with Barton, who ought to have put down his rival years ago. Hell Mutt. Bad dogs had to be destroyed. The act was both just and right, reasonable and prudent.

Why, just a few days ago, Jordan had said, "Helmut paid me a nice compliment when he brought over the new contracts." His wife shifted her weight from one foot to the other. Her husband remained silent. "He also got me in the Nalle gallery."

She pursed her lips, waiting. Okay, then. He'd play along. "So what was your compliment?"

She smiled. "Well, as we were talking, suddenly he pulls his head back and says, 'You know, I like you better now that you're older. You've grown into your age.' Wasn't that nice?"

"And did you reward him?"

Her smile evaporated. "Are you making fun of me?"

"You didn't blow him, did you?"

His wife's mouth fell open.

"I just ask because that's the line he uses on all our secretaries." Jordan shook out her hair as if to shake out fear.

"Barton. I want to ask you something. Are you jealous of me because I paint and you still practice? Is that what's behind all this skullduggery?"

He raised his eyebrows. "*Skullduggery?*"

"You know what I mean"

"And live off you? I wasn't raised that way."

"Well, if you're unhappy you can't blame *everything* on me, honey. We write our own scripts. Don't you believe that anymore?"

"I'm just saying that's how he's got all our secretaries to blow him. It's a fact! Why do you think we have such a turnover?"

"He meant it, though. He was sincere."

"Jordan," he took his wife's hand. "That's his job. *Seeming sincere.* It's method acting. I do it, too, but there's a difference. I *know* I'm doing it. Whereas Helmut's never offstage, never out of character. It's been years since he played himself."

"So you don't think I've aged well?"

Oh boy, Barton thought, recognizing the trap with the eye of an experienced trial lawyer.

"Of course you've aged well. Don't we eat sawdust and tree bark and other health foods?"

"He was being honest, hon."

Clenching his jaw to stop himself from talking, he let it go. Clearly, the compliment had meant something to her, so why spoil it?

Irked, he knew that Helmut knew that she'd relay his compliment and that it would bother him, which it did.

Sitting at the computer, Barton wished his old roommate would get drunk and plow his Ferrari into a tree.

But that wouldn't happen. When Helmut saw double, he produced the souvenir pirate eye-patch he'd bought on vacation with Jordan and Barton in Key West and put it on. According to him, it eliminated double vision, enabling him to drive with a blood-alcohol content which would've put down an elephant.

And that damned Ferrari! "I'm on your way," its owner often pointed out, without imagining Barton might prefer solitude.

In any case, the act wouldn't even be a crime, really, since if Helmut wasn't the Devil neither was he was fully human. He was a demonic little troll deserving of his ticket to the underworld. Startled, Barton made a discovery: *it felt good to hate*.

And Jordan? The Devil's concubine? She'd betrayed her One True Love and so he accepted the unthinkable, knowing in a secret corner of his heart that she, too, would have to be punished. For this creature she'd become, created by Helmut, had murdered the Jordan he loved, the girl who'd taught him the meaning of *cherish*.

The Jordan *he* knew had expired. The one whose citrus-smelling skin filled his nostrils even now. And the frankness of her gaze, the blond lashes, the sapphire irises flecked with gold – what nakedness. Jordan's stare was obscene, candid, sexual . . . if only she hadn't become the corpse of herself, her own killer, whose sentence must be death.

Barton coughed but the air stuck in his lungs. *Gone forever.* Oh my. This was new. This finality. A gray tombstone jutting from the cold ground, his wife's name covered with moss.

Jordan, my love, he thought. My wife! *Where are you?*

His spine stiffened.

He was done being Squire. He would anoint himself with the blood of his rival, drained from the fiend's own skull.

Liketothelark@1Bee

Enter. And he was there, at her inbox, for all his sense of purpose feeling as guilty as if he were rifling her diary. Vaguely, he was aware that no matter the provocation she'd never do this to him. She had more integrity, or she had, once upon a time.

Then he read Helmut's message.

Jordie, please forgive my disgraceful conduct. I assure you that it wasn't me running down the street but my evil doppelganger, Helmut Hyde. I must speak with you.

Lawyer/client privilege will obtain. Bring the necessaries and have the one notarized.

Your K.

Barton blinked. *Jordie?* What the hell. Where had *that* come from? He'd never in his life heard anyone call her by that name. His face burned. Reading her reply, he noted the location of the wastebasket in case he had to vomit.

Why are you doing this? I've done all I can. You're asking too much!
SO LEAVE ME ALONE!

Barton wiped the sweat from his forehead and spat into the wastebasket. His wife wasn't the sort who typed in upper case, and her font alarmed him as much as her words.

Jordie, I swear this is the last time. Just meet me. Please. And bring the stuff. I won't ask again. Please, Jordie. I'm not crazy, just desperate.

And her reply – *All right then. I'll be there.*

Barton picked up Helmut's business card, crumpled it into a ball, tossed it to the back of his mouth and swallowed it.

So *Jordie* was leaving him. *Had* left him. Well, he'd expected it. Ever since he and Helmut had watched her stroll past their dorm room window so long ago, way back in the twentieth century, he'd seen this coming.

There would be legal hurdles, of course. The dissolution of the firm. The dissolution of their marriage.

Surprisingly, he found himself calm, serene even, with an even, steady pulse, or maybe that was the Fokus working. It was difficult to identify the author of his moods, whether composed by himself or the drug. Either way, his life was over, which was something of a relief.

Taking fate by its clammy hand, then, he would escort them, an unholy trio, down the road to the place where college never ended and they were still young, before Helmut stole his life . . .

Larceny: the trespassory taking and carrying away of the personal property of another with the intent permanently to deprive the owner thereof.

Downstairs in the kitchen, Graciela heard him moaning and froze beside the snapshot of Jordan holding the kingfish. She sucked in her breath and closed her eyes and prayed, holding a bottle of Windex in her hand. Sensing the tension in the house, she'd continued cleaning, feeling the Squires shouldn't be left alone.

It frightened her to imagine the desolation of their lives. Still, you made your own happily-ever-after, she thought, or God didn't mean you to have one. It was just that simple.

Hearing Mr. Barton make the sounds of grief, she asked God for courage and climbed the stairs and opened the door of the study, pushing her vacuum ahead of her. Reaching around to pull the cord she pretended to jump when he turned away from Jordan's computer. And his face! She knew that look. It was the same one her little boy Esteban, *el gordito de la allegria*, got when she caught him eating the baking chocolate.

"Graciela," he said, blinking rapidly and covertly wiping his eyes.

"I'm finishing now, Mistair Barton. Ms. Jordan want me to go, but I still clean."

"She's home?"

"In studio outside. You want – "

"No," he said, and spun around and switched off the computer.

These Anglos and their electronics, she thought. Always with the email, the cell phones, the pagers, the text messaging, they had a thousand ways to keep in touch yet they were the loneliest people on earth.

Barton fumbled in his pocket and handed her a crinkled ball of money.

"Mistair Barton, this is too much."

"No," he said. "Esteban told me he wanted a clarinet."

Reluctantly, she pocketed the cash. If it helped her children, whose futures she cradled in her mind like delicate eggs, she'd eat her pride.

"Um . . . I find this on the floor outside." She handed him a pill shaped like a red diamond.

He popped it in his mouth and swallowed it.

"*Muchas gracias.*"

She looked away from his bloodshot eyes, his blotched and mottled skin. Mumbling good night, she hurried from the study and down the stairs, certain that God was testing her faith. If Mr. Barton was such a good man, why was his life disintegrating?

Outside, she breathed in the green odor of the lawn her husband had mowed. It was good to be alive, she thought, no matter what happened.

She'd learned this at sea, on a homemade boat, waiting to drown.

Shivering, she observed the Squire's brightly lit house standing against the blackness, holding its own against the night.

Part IV

Green Glade

It is I, Alexander Colin. I wish to disclose that I've translated the following dialogue from Spanish, which the Mirandas still speak at home. Also, just as I was approaching the climax of our story – toward which I hasten before Alzheimer's disease tangles my brain and pancreatic cancer devours my innards – I discovered that a nurse threw away seventeen pages of my manuscript. Luckily, I was able to rescue them from a trashcan marked "biohazard," albeit stained unspeakably.

I don't blame her. What could a man with a dissolving brain have to say? Yet as we all tend toward liquid, I persist, a still cohesive solid, one determined to finish his story before his own conclusion. (In the future, I shall conceal these pages in a strongbox below my inadequate mattress.)

On another front, I received a parcel today, wrapped in scuffed brown paper. From what I gather, it fell behind a cabinet in the mailroom where it remained until a new employee had the wit to deliver it to me.

Its contents now hang on the wall at the foot of my bed, a gift from Jordan, the oil painting she called *What Blood Beyond the Skin of Sunset?* It's a gorgeous, colorful work, a splash of exuberance in my otherwise gray world. I am, of course, deeply touched by its creator's generosity, although its tardy delivery gave me quite a start, I must confess.

Bedridden now (stage IV pancreatic cancer is always mortal) I enjoy staring into the painting until I become one of the figures wading into the sea, awash in rose and gold, my hand held by the woman whose face is forever turned toward the sinking sun.

So Jordan has come to my rescue after all, if not in body, then in design.

In any event, the work lies beyond my powers of description, so I won't mar it with words, except to say that if light has a melody, this painting sings.

– Alexander Colin, Attorney at Law (ret.)
Green Glade Assisted Living Community
Sebring, Florida
September 15, 2008

1

THE PURSUIT OF HAPPINESS

UNDER ragged silver clouds lit by the full moon, Graciela strode along the cobblestone walk toward the Squire's driveway where her teal Mercedes coupe stood waiting. "I don't want to go to my grave as some floozy," Ms. Jordan had told her. "You'd be doing me a big favor to accept it."

Behind the wheel, Graciela felt like an important person. In Cuba she hadn't even owned a bicycle. Mr. Barton had taught her to drive and now her husband, Antonio, was taking lessons from *her*, although he was secretly frightened of the fancy car and preferred that his wife play chauffeur.

In Cuba such an arrangement would've been considered unmanly, yet in this they were well-suited to the States, since Graciela "wore the pants," while Antonio was mild and shy and more than willing to let her drive, both in the car and toward the bright shining place they called their future.

With the studied care of the apprentice driver, she cranked the key in the ignition, checked over her shoulder and pulled away from the Squire's house.

Piloting the Mercedes, whose luxury still amazed her, she ascended the ramp of the causeway, pressing the gas and hurtling under the amber streetlights whose reflections shot below her, a long line of gold spots shimmering against the black of the water. It was a thrilling view, and as she drove, gaining altitude, she felt as if she were flying off a runway.

From the top of the causeway, the lights of Melbourne and Palm Bay twinkled like constellations.

All those houses. All those beating hearts.

Life cut her to the quick. What right did she have to happiness when the Squires were so miserable? Especially Mr. Barton.

She drove from the barrier island to the mainland. She and her family lived in a tiny concrete block house in Palm Bay, a working class suburb across the Indian River from Melbourne Beach. Mr. Barton had helped her find it, insisting that the structure be made of concrete rather than wood in case of a hurricane. Coming from Cuba, she would've made the same decision, but Mr. Barton enjoyed explaining the dangers of hurricanes, so she let him talk.

That was another funny thing about Anglos – since she spoke English with an accent, they assumed she was uneducated, when in fact she'd graduated near the top of her class from one of the best high schools in Havana. She also intended to continue her education. As soon as both her children were in school, she planned to enroll at the community college.

She smiled. Soon she'd be home. There she'd read to her children and put them to bed and make love to her husband, if his back wasn't hurting him. When he complained, she allowed him a single aspirin. "Pain is natural," she'd tell him, rubbing his sore muscles with her strong hands. "Pain is weakness leaving the body." Why else were Anglos so sick and depressed? Too many pills!

And they were all so fat, too. The Squires were tan and fit, but most Anglos were so pasty and round they reminded her of jelly donuts. Picturing all the fat people in America and all the skinny people in Cuba made her sad, though, so she thought of her children, of Esperanza with her chestnut-colored eyes, and of Esteban with his curly hair and high piping laugh. *La familia.*

Descending the causeway, she tightened her hands on the wheel, gripping at ten and two as Mr. Barton had taught her, when a sport utility vehicle roared past her belching clouds of exhaust.

On the mainland in Melbourne, she stopped at a red light, and when the light turned green, she entered a neighborhood of squat, functional houses, home to the people who cleaned the houses of the people on the other side of the causeway. She shook her head, laughing to herself. Without the brown and black-skinned people, the white-skinned people would be helpless. They were like children. They couldn't patch their own roofs or do their own plumbing or even mow their own lawns. In fairness, the Squires had asked her to call them by their first names, but she insisted on keeping it professional, compromising with "Mr. Barton" and "Ms. Jordan." She was a professional too, after all, even if she did scrub toilets.

Pulling into her driveway, she was grateful that the Squires had volunteered to help her with her education, because what if Antonio got hurt and couldn't work? Always a quick study, she was sure she could have a real career, whereas her husband, who she loved as much as her life, wasn't the smartest man in the world, which he was the first to admit.

What mattered was that he was faithful. He had a twenty-four karat soul, she liked to say, and he was a provider. Hadn't he risked his life when he'd jumped off that cruise ship into the oily waters of Port Canaveral, hoping he could find work so his family could follow him to the United States? She was so proud of him. Then too, she was secretly grateful to her savior Jesus Christ for letting her children inherit their mother's brains instead of their father's.

Shutting down the car, she sat motionless, listening to the sound of her breathing. The engine ticked and the stars shone through the windshield, silver sequins glittering on the black cape of the tropical night. Climbing out of the Mercedes, feeling a twinge in her spine, she slammed the door and started up the walk, feeling a cool breeze off the river tickle the wisps of hair at the nape of her neck.

Inside, the house smelled of candle wax and roasting beef and burnt pepper. Her stomach growled. Sniffing the air, she found herself suddenly ravenous.

A gleeful howl arose as she sank to her knees and her children thundered down the hall, squealing. Sailing into her arms, their hot compact bodies hit her in the chest and she nearly toppled over. Hugging them in their soft cotton pajamas, she pressed her nose to their cheeks and inhaled the scent of their skins, freshly washed and baby powdered, faces scrubbed to glowing. Blinking their dark eyes and black lashes, were Esperanza, age two, and Esteban, age four. Their pajamas were the kind with the feet sewn on and were decorated with jungle animals. Bouncing in her arms, unable to contain themselves, they pressed their faces to her neck. She grunted under the weight of their arms.

She covered their faces with kisses while Antonio looked on, smiling. Children were at their most adorable, he thought, right after a bath, when they seemed not so much young as *new*.

"Be careful of your mother," he said, kissing his wife, "she's worked all day and you don't want to hurt her."

"Mama loves you," she said, standing and letting her children slip through her arms so that they stood clutching her legs, "but she's very tired."

"Daddy said we could say goodnight," chirped Esteban, her little fat boy of happiness. His eyes shone out of his plump face. In Cuba, plumpness was a sign of good health, but she was learning about carbohydrates from Ms. Jordan and so she'd begun to wean him off custard and cakes, substituting fresh fruit. He was having none of it. Esperanza, though, who already had pierced ears with gold hoop earrings, had developed a passion for pears, a rarity in Cuba.

Antonio set up a tray for his wife in front of the fireplace, and the family gathered in the living room. The children climbed onto the couch, nuzzling their mother, while Antonio set down plates of goat cheese dip and bread pudding, roasted pork in a citrus marinade, garbanzo beans in a mojo sauce, and fried plantains and yucca, with coconut flan for desert.

Antonio loved to cook, which was another thing he liked about America. In Cuba, his talent in the kitchen would've made him a laughingstock.

Graciela closed her eyes and let the aromas fill her nostrils, a heady mix of Cuban spices they could never have afforded back in Havana. Her little fat boy of happiness licked his lips and opened his mouth. Graciela fed him a bite of pork.

"My sweet Antonio," she said, smiling and making a show of appreciating all the trouble he'd taken, "The yucca smells like home."

Her husband's eyes glowed. Back in Cuba, when the ribs of his wife and children pressed like brittle sticks through their thin skins, he'd fantasized about being able to put food on the table. And now here it was. A miracle. Happiness pursued and captured.

"Please," his wife said, chewing a spicy bean and feeling it burn her tongue, "switch on the fireplace."

"We'll do it!" the children screamed. After a brief struggle, Esperanza beat Esteban to the switch on the wall and the fireplace roared to life, if you could call it roaring. A dim orange bulb flickered behind tin foil flames made to flutter from an unseen fan. The children cheered.

Together, they made as if to warm themselves from the heatless flames. Lit by the specially flickering bulb, they joined the magic circle of *la familia*.

Graciela hiccupped and sucked in her breath, pressing her small fist to her mouth, grateful to God.

They had braved the dark waters and they had found the sun.

Felicidad.

On a plank nailed over the fireplace, which served as a mantle, *Felicidad* had been painted in crude white letters on a burgundy field.

Antonio had hammered the plank off the stern of the ramshackle boat which had borne them to freedom. Each morning Graciela crossed herself in front of it to remind herself to be thankful to Jesus for answering her prayers and for bringing her family to safety.

Truly, she thought, tasting the salty pork on her tongue and smelling her children's bodies as they snuggled close, God had seen fit to reward her.

She kissed them on the shiny black hair on the tops of their heads. When she closed her eyes, she could remember the delicate fleshy odor they'd had as babies. If the soul possessed a scent, she believed, that must be it

"How are the crazy ones?" her husband asked. He sat across from her in a perfectly good Lazy Boy Recliner he'd rescued from the trash in Melbourne Beach.

"Don't call them that," she said, covering her mouth with her hand and swallowing. "Your father forgets to be grateful," she told the children. "When you say your prayers, ask God to help him remember who he is."

"I know who I am" said Antonio, standing and stretching and holding the small of his back, "I dug out a stump today and I'm the man whose spine is killing him."

"Yours isn't the only back hurting, my husband."

"Shall I rub you with oil?"

"You're not too tired?"

He thumped his chest with his hands. "Antonio is never too tired for his wife."

Esteban said, "Tell us a story, Mommy!"

"You go," she said. "Help your sister, my child." Esteban opened his mouth but Graciela raised her eyebrows and he quickly closed it. He took Esperanza's hand and, trailing her blanket, they went to their room.

Finished with dinner, Graciela fingered the smooth gold of her wedding band. "I think the Squires are getting a divorce."

Antonio cuddled up next to her on the couch. He smelled of strong cologne and she stroked the black curls on his head. He loved the feel of her nails scratching lightly across his scalp.

"What makes you think so?"

"They've stopped sleeping together. And he takes those nasty pills. I found one today and he took it right in front of me. They're supposed to cure sadness but – "

"Is Ms. Jordan sleeping with that Helmut?"

She shivered. "I don't know."

Her husband shook his head. "That man. He's not as smart as he thinks he is."

"Oh?"

Antonio chuckled. "In front of other people, he likes to show off with me. He pats me on the shoulder and pretends we're friends, but as soon as I walk away he makes jokes about 'that *loco* beaner, that greaser I rescued'."

Antonio gazed up at his wife, showing her the whites of his eyes. The fan whirred inside the fireplace and the tinfoil flames danced in the light of the flickering bulb. "If he were any richer, I'd say that Helmut sold his soul to the Devil."

Graciela yanked out a gray hair from her husband's head. "Antonio, hush."

"I'm serious."

"Stop it." She plucked another hair and Antonio winced and rubbed the sore spot with his hand.

"You'll make me as bald as he is," he said, massaging his scalp, "anyhow, they're all crazy if you ask me."

"Well, they don't have any children. No family. No blood. It's not natural. No wonder they're crazy."

"They'd be terrible parents."

"And how does the wise Antonio know this?"

"They're cold fish. There's something wrong with them."

"They thought they'd stay young forever."

"But then they ran out of time."

"I don't think they believe in God."

Antonio's tongue caressed his gold incisor, another gift from the Squires. Good people, he thought, but very strange.

Come to think of it, nearly all Anglos were strange. He didn't understand them. They didn't sing songs or touch each other, and they had such closed faces and they hardly ever kissed. He wondered how they could live like that.

"You really think they don't believe in God?"

Graciela sighed. "Even if they do, they don't bring God into their lives. They keep Him away. Even the ones who go to church. They pray for football games."

Her husband grinned. "Then I guess we better say some prayers, my wife."

"Yes, my husband."

Pressing his hand against the threadbare couch, Antonio groaned and clambered up, pressing his other hand to his back. He held out his callused palm to his wife. She clutched it and, leaning away from her, he helped her to her feet, then together they padded down the hall to their children's bedroom.

2

CRUEL AND UNUSUAL

"WHAT in God's name are you doing?" This was Jordan's voice, high-pitched, coming from behind him. He didn't look. His hand gripped the neck of a vodka bottle, which he turned up and bubbled. Lovely! Like drinking gasoline. Setting it down on the table and feeling the burn descend from his throat to his belly, he smacked his lips and wished he had a cigarette. The kitchen spun lazily so that he grabbed the edge of the table until the fridge landed in its place by the door. The floor grew steady. God, alcohol was good. A mighty healer, a stauncher of wounds. How could he have forgotten his old friend?

From a bowl on the table he snatched up a lime wedge and sucked out its juice. A shred of pulp stuck between his teeth. His tongue worked at the sour-tasting fiber and for an instant it comprised his whole universe. When it broke loose he returned to the larger world, one less palatable than a piece of lime – his marriage, his life, his future.

"Bee, what's wrong?" His wife's voice had dropped into its normal range, but there was another note. It was the sound of fear.

She touched his cheek and turned his face toward her.

Her husband squinted, trying to focus, but her face blurred, floating like a blond balloon. He opened his mouth to laugh but belched into his fist, feeling his esophagus burn with acid.

"What's that?" she asked, her voice quavering. She aimed a trembling finger at the pistol he'd set beside his bottle, its stainless steel barrel glinting in the sun slanting through the window.

"Allow me to introduce you," he said grandly, sweeping his arm toward the weapon, "Jezebel, this is *El Jefe*."

"Excuse me?"

He inhaled her fragrance through her clothes: jasmine and sandalwood.

"The Smith and Wesson 'Chief's Special.' " he said. "A thirty-eight caliber revolver – prophet of the old school."

Her face tightened. "I see."

"I don't think you do." Employing the nail of his little finger, he worked loose another shred of pulp from his teeth. "*El Jefe* is the resurrection and the life. But first he punishes the sinner. Ever hear about sin, *Jordie?* "

She didn't say anything.

Her husband raised his eyebrows. "Something wrong, Jordie?"

She put her hands on his shoulders and looked him in the eye. "Firearms and vodka?" she demanded, shaking him. "*Prima facie* – something's wrong." She released him and crossed her arms, tapping her foot and frowning. Her husband chuckled. He thought she looked like some kid's pissed off mother. "You think bullets and booze are good combination?" she asked, using her cross-examination voice.

Her husband picked up the evidence. *El Jefe!* He spun the cylinder and his wife jumped back, surprising him. He'd never thought of himself as a man who could be intimidating. Yet there she stood – wide-eyed, and clearly frightened of him. A chamber clicked into place with metallic precision. Closing one eye, he held the pistol at arm's length and sighted along the barrel at the palm trees outside the window.

"I think it's a fucking great combination," he said.

"Is that thing loaded?"

"*I'm* loaded, but *El Jefe's* sober as a judge."

"I'll ask again. Is it loaded?"

"Wouldn't work if it wasn't," he said cheerfully.

His wife sat down at the table. Her face was pale. She picked up the vodka bottle and drank, bubbling it, working her throat and reminding him of how much fun they'd had in their drinking days. Well, that was over now. If they spoke of that time at all, they referred to it as "the bad old days."

Slamming the bottle onto the table, she made a gagging noise. Quickly, she grabbed a lime wedge and sucked it vigorously. Her face turned red.

"You off the wagon?" he asked.

"I am now." She coughed into her fist.

"So have another. Let's party." His voice was full of false good cheer, which made it menacing.

Subdued, she asked, "Why're you drinking, Bee? You've been doing so well. You haven't been drunk since – "

"Kansas?"

"Why?" she asked. "Why now?"

Her eyes followed his hand as he set the gun on the table. Its barrel was aimed away from them, pointed at a picture on the wall – the one of her holding the kingfish.

"Take a wild guess," he said. "Go ahead. Free associate."

"Well," she said, keeping her voice level, "alcoholics are like mountain climbers. We drink because it's there. The gun? I don't know. It's very scary. I wouldn't know. It's not like you."

"It's not like me," he repeated mechanically, staring at the bottle and burping hotly into his fist. His throat burned as though he'd swallowed a red-hot coal.

She flinched.

"I'm drinking," he said.

"We've established that."

"No, really. I want to get fucked up. *Really* fucked up, then I want to *fuck* someone up."

"And that squares with being a Buddhist?"

"Fuck that. I'm drinking with The Big Dude."

The Big Dude. College slang for the quart-sized Smirnoff bottle. Barton lifted it, catching sight of Death, the Reaper who held his heart, whose long gray talons pierced the pulsing red muscle . . .

Mea culpa! Barton thought.

Outside, beyond the sliding glass doors, the setting sun seared a yellow dot onto his retinas, and he realized he was drunk. Drunk enough to stare down the sun.

His wife's hand closed over his and he felt the strength in her fingers. She rested her eyes on his face.

"Please stop, honey."

Wrenching away from her, he upended the bottle and drank, his Adam's apple pumping as the bubbles rose through the vodka.

"Can't," he gasped, slamming it onto the table, "don't want to." He studied the label. " 'Because I could not stop for Death, he kindly stopped for me.' "

His wife closed her eyes. The drink she'd taken had turned her stomach and she swallowed against a wave of nausea, fighting it down, then when she opened her eyes she found herself staring down the black hole of a barrel. Her husband's bloodshot eyes hovered above it.

"Give it to me, Barton. Give it to me and I'll do it myself."

For a woman facing death, she looked strangely at ease. Her face was unlined, her eyes clear. He thought of how different they'd look with a hole between them, spouting blood.

"Hand it over," she said.

A moment passed. So she thought she was tough, did she? He pressed the cold barrel to her forehead.

Two fat tears rolled down her cheeks. With her big eyes, she reminded him of a young deer standing alone in the forest, nursing a broken leg, facing a future of fangs and death.

"No point in you going to jail," she said, her voice breaking as she stared into the blue eye behind the gun sight, "now put that fucking thing in my hand."

Her husband lowered his weapon and stuffed it into his waistband, then he picked up the bottle and drank.

"Tell your lover his day is coming," he said, swallowing. "Tell him it's the end of the goddamned world. Tell him it's the fucking apocalypse."

"He's not my lover, Bee."

Barton snorted, flaring his nostrils. "You want to explain your emails?"

She drew back. "I told you. He's not anything. Oh God, Barton. *He's not.* I shouldn't have hidden it, but Helmut's bankrupt. And so are you, honey. Helmut's sunk whole the firm. He's gambling. He calls it day trading or currency speculation, but it's gambling. He's completely out of control."

Reaching down to his crotch, Barton ran his fingers along the cold barrel of *El Jefe*.

"There has been crime," he said, "and there will be a punishment."

"I tried to fix things before you found out . . . and that was wrong." She waited. She forced her lips into a smile. "You forgive me?" Her voice curved upward.

Her husband drew a long, slow breath, sighing like a judge about to pronounce a penalty.

"Of course I forgive you."

Jordan's face lit up and her eyes brimmed, sparkling like wet sapphires.

"However, the sentence is still death."

"*I'm sorry, honey. I am.*" Her voice was so high she might've been singing.

"Sorry?" he asked. "Why don't you be sorry when you're mopping up my fucking brains." He pulled out his gun and stuck the barrel into his mouth. Jordan screamed and he pulled the trigger.

Nothing happened. The hammer clicked with a metallic *snap*.

It was no accident. Knowing he couldn't trust himself with hard liquor, he'd unloaded *El Jefe* before he got out the vodka. He'd double checked it, too, breaking open the cylinder and blowing air through every chamber, making sure they were empty.

Slamming it onto the table, he said, "*Damn* – was that a rush or what?"

His wife couldn't speak. Her lower lip pushed out and she started crying. He felt like slapping her. He felt like taking her into his arms. He felt like killing her. He looked at his hands and saw them shaking.

His wife ran to the sink and retched, spitting and fouling her hair. He stood behind her, watching her tremble.

"I don't believe you," he said. "And you can tell Helmut I'm coming heavy." He laughed and waved his gun. "And this time, *El Jefe's* going to be loaded." He spun the cylinder. "No more games, *Jordie*. Helmut's a fucking dead man."

3

Alibi

JORDAN rinsed her mouth at the tap and dashed upstairs, pumping her legs and taking the steps two at a time. In their room she glanced at the bed where they no longer made love, found her husband's truck keys in the nightstand drawer and stuffed them into her pocket. She pressed her fingers to her throbbing eyes, hearing him step up behind her.

"Barton Squire. If there's a gun in your hand, you best use it. Otherwise, I'm calling the cops."

"I'm unarmed," he said. His voice was thick with alcohol.

Jordan faced him. His eyes were like twin patches ripped from the sky. His sandy hair, she noticed suddenly, had gone gray at the temples, though on top it remained thick and wavy – enough for the handfuls she'd pulled with such happy abandon in their now sexless bed.

With his long limbs and flat stomach and thoughtful ways, it occurred to her that she was a lucky woman, or that she might've been, if only she wasn't a . . . what? She didn't know what to call herself.

Adulteress? Cheater? Whore? Whatever she was, it wasn't good.

Barton braced his hand against the door frame.

He had dark bags under his eyes and his cheeks had sunk into his face. He looked like an out-of-work actor. With a start, she saw that the stubble on his chin had gone gray.

How had she failed to notice this earlier? She blinked. For the first time in her life, or his, Barton Squire was showing his age. She guessed she was, too.

There was no use talking to him. If he remembered anything, his memory would be shrouded in fog, as if he were trying to recall a movie he'd seen years ago. She knew this, having shot a few of those films herself. She called them Blackout Reels.

"How about fixing me a gin and tonic?" she asked.

Her husband frowned and nodded, agreeing in a besotted voice quite unlike his own. Distracted, he stumbled downstairs to the kitchen. She didn't want a drink, but like most people under the influence, Barton was easy to control as long as his instructions involved obtaining more alcohol.

Hearing his footsteps recede, she made a phone call.

"Yeah? What do *you* want?"

She clenched her free hand and stifled a scream. Helmut's voice was thick and throaty, also drunk.

"Jesus Christ," she said.

"I'll see if he's here," he said, "Yo, Jesus! What? Okay." His voice returned. "He's says to please quit calling him. What's that? Oh. Yeah, I'll tell her. He said to tell you you're a goddamned harlot."

"At least now I know what to call myself," she said.

"What?"

"Never mind."

"Pull the other one," he said, "it's got bells on it."

"Barton knows," she said.

"Barton knows," he repeated.

"That's right," she said. "He *knows!*"

"You've lost me. What does he know?"

"That his best friend fucked his wife and stole his money."

"Oh *that*," said Helmut, and she heard liquid pouring over ice.

"Yeah," she echoed, "*that*."

Helmut hawked the phlegm from his throat and she held the phone away from her ear. In the meantime she got an idea for a painting. A female lifeguard, in a red one-piece bathing suit, dragged underwater by two drowning men. She imagined six white arms jutting from the azure sea.

"Hey," Helmut said, "how 'bout some phone sex?" He held the phone to his fly so she could hear the zipper slide. "Just let me free the monster, babe."

"I'm hanging up, you idiot."

"Whoa there. You called *me*, sweetheart."

"Oh, Jesus."

Helmut clucked his tongue. "I told you, babe. Jesus shit-canned you. Gave you walking papers. But not me. I understand my Jordie. Who'd have thought? Old Helmut's all you've got!" She heard ice cubes rattle in a glass. "You still bringing the coin?" he asked.

A shooting pain stabbed her in some vital organ she couldn't identify. "Helmut, please tell me you didn't plan this."

"Plan to bankrupt myself? Plan to ruin my law firm? Plan to be disbarred?" His voice grew suddenly sober. "Screw *you*, Jordan fucking Squire." He held the phone to his crotch and she heard the zipper go up. "You think this was a conspiracy to win you away from your husband? You give yourself too much credit. You and Cuckoo's Nest deserve each other."

Jordan suppressed a scream. "Just cover the escrow, will you? You're the agent, Helmut. *It's your job.*"

"So you trust me now?"

She laughed humorlessly. "Consider it my last act of faith. In you, I mean."

"Okay, okay . . . Jordie. Leave it to me and my genius. All will be well."

"Mutt, I'm telling you. If you ever put this in Barton's face, I'll go straight to the D.A. Depend on that. You're looking at embezzlement and fraud. Got that, *amigo*?"

"*Sí, Señora.* You'll ruin me. I got it."

"No, I don't think you do. Not ruin, *imprison.*"

Helmut hung up. Startled, Jordan stared at her phone. A long blond hair was caught on it and she pulled it off and let it flutter to the floor. Maybe Barton was right. Maybe somebody should kill Helmut. *Quantum meruit.* As much as he deserved. Perhaps it was time she got a pistol of her own.

But no, this wasn't the movies. Life didn't work like that. It was much more boring and painful and sad.

In college, the trio had shared youth and health, and despite Helmut's weird ways. . . Barton and Jordan had accepted him . . . loved him, even.

Crying, she thought, he's right, I *am* a stinking harlot, and whatever happens, *I will deserve it.*

4

Closing Argument

ACROSS the river, inside his corner office at Kelly, Knight and Squire, Jordan's phone call cast Helmut into the past, into that secret place where he was still a young man, one with hair. In college, cavorting on his roommate's bed, his locks had been so long that they'd tangled with Jordan's.

Oh, the smoothness of her honey-butter skin, the smell of her girlish curls! He screamed *I love you* when he came, thunderstruck at having spent an hour sporting in the nude with the fetching Jordan Kelly.

But there was more to it. She'd seen him naked, stripped of his many skins, and he'd felt beautiful. Hell, he'd *been* beautiful.

What of it? Now he was ugly. Forget self-pity. Life was horrible, and there it was. You saddled up and soldiered on.

But it was hard. On the foreign exchange he'd been losing money like blood from an arterial wound, because it was a far more dangerous arena than the stock market, what with its 100 to 1 leverage. What's more, the labor department had announced the latest non-farm payroll numbers, resulting in a financial hemorrhage of over two-hundred thousand dollars.

Christ, he thought, personal best and rock bottom were two sides of a coin.

His fingers furiously tapped the keys as he bet all the credit on the business card he shared with Barton. Numbers and graphs flew across his screen and a red polluted dawn broke in Taiwan, a Chinese government official bit his fingernail and . . . *ka-ching!*

Hello, Big Zero!

Using his code as escrow agent, he dipped into the sacred, untouchable account, and as the sun's yellow rays fell across Hong Kong harbor, Helmut put his head in his hands and bent over his keyboard.

Damn the dollar! Damn the euro! Damn the yen!

With astonishing speed he wiped out his clients' insurance settlements, his partners' business account, and Barton's credit rating, all in less time than it took a minimum wage earner to grill a hamburger.

Outside, beyond his picture window, the Florida landscape steamed in the subtropical heat. Well, it hadn't been a good week. Nobody could deny that. Yet it wasn't *all* his fault. No, your honor. The birth of the new millennium had delivered an exculpatory circumstance.

High speed internet connections made losing money too easy. Why, back in the pencil-and-paper twentieth century, he could never have lost so much money so quickly. It simply wasn't possible. Whereas now . . . with powerful computers, you could really screw yourself in a hurry.

Username and password and . . . wham bam, thank you, Sam.

His eyes rested on the brown bark of the century-old live oak beside the driveway. It was even older than he was.

He pictured himself dangling by a rope from one of its limbs.

Now that would be a slogan for a law firm: "Don't hang yourself when you can sue somebody." Then again, maybe he'd get a chainsaw and cut the thing down. Show the old bastard who was boss. Count the rings. Discover the one where he was born. Trace the steps of little Helmut, toddling into nursery school.

For by now his own rings were contracting, each year a tightening loop, until one would become the noose which crushed his windpipe and he floated free and clear.

But he wasn't beaten. Not yet. Step up, Big Mutt. What the computer taketh away, it also giveth. Bank transfer. Wire transfer. Rifling his files, he discovered two valid credit card numbers and during one thrilling ride he made eighty-three thousand dollars.

That's the way we do it! Oh yeah. His blood sang as if he were doing cocaine. Only this was better. Sweet Jesus! It was good. His numbers soared. At last! He clapped his hands and ran his palm over the hot skin of his head. Now, *this* was more like it.

Grinning and typing, he was bathed in pleasure. He felt he was being caressed by the Lord.

Gleefully, he watched the figures rise. Then his luck went south and he tried three other credit card numbers, none of them his. Gleaned from client records, he sank another ten thousand into his account. With his 100 to 1 leverage, salvation was still an option. But no. Another ripple in the financial world two oceans away, another bank transfer, another wire transfer and that was it.

Helmut Knight was broke.

The computer's cursor blinked like a winking eye, merciless and robotic. Barton had gone broke too, though he didn't know it. Helmut sighed. What had Jordan told him? *Just cover the escrow.* Well, that was going to be a problem, unless . . .

He called her up.

"About that escrow," he said.

"Barton's going to shoot himself," she said.

Helmut blinked and the magical phrase *life insurance* rang in his head. "I've missed a transition," he said. "Fill in the blanks."

"Are you insane?"

Helmut didn't say anything. A loud beeping sound came from beyond his window, followed by a metallic clink and the roar of a truck engine. Jumping from his chair and crossing the office, he cupped his hands to the glass and peered outside.

What's this?

A tow truck with a flashing yellow light on top. And on the back? His sleek orange Ferrari, its nose raised in an obscene wheelie.

"They're repossessing my car!" Glancing at the calendar on his desk, he tried to recall the last time he'd made a payment.

"Helmut, I'm talking about my husband's life."

"What?"

"Barton's going to kill himself."

"Oh. Yeah. But *hey!*" He banged his fist on the window, shaking the glass, "Stop, thief! That's my Ferrari!"

An obese truck driver with a red bandanna tied around his head and tattoos on his arms glanced up from the parking lot. Helmut bellowed. His face was red and he jumped up and down. The driver shrugged and secured the front of the Ferrari with chains.

"Jordie, give me a credit card number."

"Dream on, Mutt."

"Just trust me."

"Ha! You *are* insane."

"But it's my *Ferrari!*" Helmut set the phone on his desk.

"Helmut?" She could hear him typing. "Are you listening?"

Helmut stared at the fluctuating graph on the screen, willing it to move, then he hit a few keys, betting the yen would rise and . . . damn, there it went! Down. No, up! Up! Up! Yes! Oh, no . . . down.

"Pick up, or I'm hanging up."

"Just a sec!" he hollered, tapping his keys, "I need to concentrate." *Because I'm stealing money*, he thought wildly.

Even at a distance he could hear her sigh. "Helmut, are you familiar with the phrase, 'a matter of life and death?' "

"If only, babe."

"Barton's threatening to kill you, and then himself."

Helmut laughed. "Great. Saves me the time."

"He's serious, you idiot."

Helmut set down the phone. Outside, his Ferrari was being towed, its streamlined body disappearing around the building.

As fortunes went, this was a low point, no question.

Grunting, he patted his pants pockets, where he discovered a quarter, a dime and two pennies.

Well, you had to start somewhere.

Nestled in his sweaty palm, he stared at the coins and picked up the phone.

"You can stop worrying," he said. He jingled his change so that she could hear it. "I've started saving my money."

5

PER ASPERA AD ASTRA
(THROUGH ROUGH WAYS
TO THE STARS)

UPSTAIRS in the bedroom, the wooden floor creaked under his feet as Barton tiptoed to his dresser, slid open a drawer and removed a sock filled with .38 caliber bullets. With their stainless steel casings, they were mean-looking, surprisingly heavy little things. He arranged them like toy soldiers awaiting inspection, then scowled as they morphed into a squad of stubby silver penises.

Pugnis et calcibus, he thought. With fists and heels, with all one's might . . .

Six caps busted in Helmut's head. Thick burgundy blood pulsing from the holes in his dome.

Barton shivered down his spine, thinking *thrill kill*. No wonder human history was a chronicle of homicide. Malice aforethought was entertaining.

Set atop his dresser, his ammunition brought to mind a miniature army, armless tin soldiers standing at attention, awaiting his command.

Hearing his knees pop, he opened his bottom drawer and retrieved *El Jefe*. The barrel was cool and its handle fit snugly into his hand. Savoring its heft, he stood up and aimed *El Jefe* out the window, feeling like a god.

Turning his head, he stole a sidelong glance at the mirror. He was armed! And dangerous. His chest throbbed and the veins in his arms stood out, faintly green under his tan skin.

He felt younger than he had in years.

Still, he couldn't make eye contact with himself. He didn't dare, afraid he might look insane, afraid his reflection might sap his will.

Turning from the mirror, he raised *El Jefe* and sighted down the barrel toward the lawn, picturing Helmut's astonished face. He'd put a bullet straight into the adulterer's gaping mouth. He'd spatter the wall with his hair and blood and brains.

The back of Barton's neck prickled and he understood *bloodlust*.

Shivering, he lowered his weapon. *El Jefe* would replace his pen. He'd use it to represent himself. The corners of his mouth turned up and he faced the mirror, making eye contact.

His pupils were limpid black pools, swollen with Fokus. He felt like a demon and he looked like one, too. He smacked his lips, tasting metal.

Hey, Helmut! Won't you come out to play? I've got a treat for you!

A spasm gripped his belly and he pressed his hand to it. Did Helmut have any kin, any family to mourn him? Barton swallowed at the prospect of inflicting grief on any innocent bystander, although if blood bound you to Helmut, perhaps you could never be wholly innocent.

Yet the killer was rattled. Would anyone miss Helmut? Barton had difficulty imagining him as a child, but he must've had parents, been cuddled and read to, nursed through chicken pox, presented with birthday cakes . . . or perhaps he'd burst from hell fully grown, licking his chops over the mincemeat he meant to make of the world and all the women in it.

All Barton knew of his former partner's youth (apart from the soft-core abuse he'd endured at the hands of his older sister and her friends) was that in a high school he'd ruptured an opposing player's testicle during a football game. Chuckling, Helmut had recounted how his mother had forced him to go to the hospital to apologize, which he'd accomplished through the side of his mouth.

Helmut! Barton had become his mental slave. He understood this. He also knew that to free himself he'd have to forgive the man, but for what? It was more than screwing his wife and ruining his career. Somehow he'd have to forgive Helmut for *being* Helmut, for even existing. Barton sagged at the knees. This was the very thing, the heart of Buddha-nature. For what was required of him was that he forgive Helmut the sin of his birth, the transgression of coming into the world.

Barton set *El Jefe* on the bed. Atop the dresser, his six-little-silver-penis army stood waiting. But they'd never fly. They'd remain unfired, forever virgin.

He sat on his bed and pressed his hands to his eyes, feeling the cool skin of his face against his hot palms.

The end had come, his personal Armageddon. He picked up *El Jefe* and placed the barrel in his mouth and tasted steel. An acquired flavor, but he was getting there. He removed the weapon and set it down.

He wasn't ready. He held up his right hand and watched it shake.

El Jefe glinted dully. If he put it to use, it would be outside. Polite to the end, he couldn't abide leaving a heap of gore for someone else to mop up.

Anyhow, what *was* life – that ending his own should be a crime? It was a series of moments. Some formative. Others illuminating.

He recalled an Arizona camping trip in the painted desert, where he and Jordan had stood beside the trunk of a petrified tree. Three hundred million years earlier it had fallen beside their feet, when the parched orange landscape had been a lush green swamp.

"The rings are still visible," he said.

"Like a giant fern." She shook her head, amazed. "And where were we, I wonder?"

"Hmmm?"

"When this was growing."

Jordan! Her oval face, her fair hair, her ultramarine eyes.

"Un-evolved. DNA in some of kind of weasel," he said.

"Our Great Grandpa."

"Old Grandpa Weasel."

"I love that guy!"

"But we must've existed *somewhere*."

She grabbed his shoulders and squeezed him, shaking him with mock ferocity. "Aye, laddie – you'll drive yourself mad with such questions. Mad, I say! Caress ye woman and love ye life – that is all ye know on earth and all ye need to know!"

"Paraphrast!"

She bowed deeply from the waist. "Guilty as charged."

"But even if we were eons in the future, we came from *something*."

"Happy accidents. All our ancestors hooking up. Weasels unto hominids.

"It's a wonder we're even here." She whooped and bounded off among the rocks, jumping from one boulder to another. Her musical laughter echoed off the canyon walls. Her future husband smiled. She knew how to enjoy herself and he knew how to enjoy her. There was no other word for it, that something more than love.

Jordan patted her hand against her lips, hooting so that her cries bounced off the rocks.

Barton shivered in the Arizona sun. His body hummed with a steady droning happiness. She hid behind a boulder and he looked up, startled, as if he'd heard the crackling of the universe suddenly fade and quit. The Big Bang gone still, dead as their fallen tree, toppled.

He hollered her name and his voice echoed off the canyon,

surviving to echo inside his head in his bedroom, so many years later, so many miles away.

No wonder people got religion. *She* was his religion. And more – in the theology of Jordan, before marriage, Barton was stuck in the Old Testament, then Jordan saved him. Now Helmut had brought the apocalypse, or rather, he'd summoned it with his trumpet, spewing bile over Creation.

So be it. Judgment day had come. With bowed head, Barton accepted his anointment. He was a prophet now, bringing justice swift and terrible.

Sitting on the bed, his body quivered with that lovely nameless sensation that something wonderful was going to happen.

Another . . . *big bang!*

6

Clemency

STANDING beside his garage with its stucco walls and Spanish-tile roof, Helmut stood sweating in the sun when Jordan pulled up in Barton's black pickup.

"What a piece of junk," he said, opening the door and climbing inside, the crown of his head bright pink. He thumped the dash with his middle finger. "What's it made of – recycled plastic?"

Jordan stuck out her tongue. "Morning to you too, Mr. Mutt."

Helmut blinked. She still didn't get him. Nobody did. Never had, never would. He wasn't nasty by nature. He just told the truth. Why couldn't people accept that? Honesty the best policy? Not in this world. People wanted lies.

"Well excuse me for using up your air," he said, furrowing his enormous forehead.

Jordan made the shame-shame sign with her fingers. "Bad, Mutt!"

Helmut snatched her slender hand and kissed it. "Let me start again." He cleared his throat. "Good morning, dear Jordan. Pray tell – dost the Lord bless and keep thee?"

"See? You can be nice when you want to."

He ran his slippery tongue down the groove between her pinkie and ring finger. It was like being invaded by a worm. She yanked her hand away and wiped it on the front of his shirt. "Why do you have to be like that?"

Helmut smacked his lips, tasting her. One honest gesture and this was her response. Who did she think she was? Christ! He lied professionally – did he have to work as an amateur too? Personally, he was a man of honor.

"Do we do this here?" she asked, annoyed. "Or do you follow me?"

Helmut's eyes welled up.

"Oh," she said, "sorry."

"I really loved that Ferrari," he said. His voice broke and he turned away, looking into a hedge of Hawaiian berry and grunting as the sun streamed through the windshield, slowly roasting him. His shirt tag rubbed the back of his neck and his scrotum itched ferociously. "Can't you hit the AC?" he begged. He tugged at his collar and rolled down his window, feeling the sweat trickle from his armpits. A faint sea breeze caressed his face. Beyond the dune line, a white ridge of sand covered with sea oats, the waves crashed and a seagull shrieked.

"Broken," she said.

"So let's go," he slapped the dash with his palm. His breath smelled like something slain in a swamp. Truly, she wondered how he managed it. With all his malpractice lawsuits, perhaps no dentist would treat him, fearful of the pain he could inflict.

They didn't move. Overhead, cicadas hummed in the palm trees.

"We need to talk, Mutt."

"I can't wait. Can we do it somewhere air-conditioned?"

"I'm not coming inside."

"Where's the Land Rover?"

"What?"

"The one with the AC! I'm dying here." He struggled out of his suit coat and bunched it up on the floor.

Jordan glanced out her window, wrinkling her nose. The man

must've had stewed garbage for breakfast. "I lent it to Graciela," she said. A blue jay chased a cardinal from the Hawaiian berry. "The Mercedes needed brakes."

Helmut laughed and scratched his ear. "Man, those beaners are really working you."

Peering out from under her yellow hair, her eyes flashed and she gave him . . . *that look*.

He held up his hands defensively. "I just hate to see you get hustled, that's all."

"With all your degrees," she said, "it's a wonder you have no sense of irony."

"Oh, please," he said, although he had no idea what she was talking about.

"I put my money and time where they do the most good," she said. "Anyhow, you should talk. You're another of my *pro bono* clients." She raised her eyebrows. "Like that? You're in the same league as *those beaners*." She patted his shoulder. "Ha! You could end up mowing *their* lawn."

"They have a lawn?" Outside the truck, the birds and insects chirped and buzzed. Helmut clapped his hands. "Brava! You really ought to get back in the courtroom and – " *quit playing with fingerpaints,* he thought.

Jordan felt a frown creasing her forehead. Leave it to Helmut to nettle her before the sun had climbed off the ocean.

Unbuttoning his collar, he loosened his tie and fanned his face. "Is refusing AC some kind of hippie ethic? I mean, Kee-Rist! Why can't your husband live like a real person?"

He scratched what remained of his hair, a semi-circle of fuzz traveling from over one ear round the back to the top of the other, so that with his protruding brown eyes he had the look of a dog which has been propped upright and shaved for surgery. Jordan was startled. Somehow he'd had aged without her noticing – in canine years, it seemed.

Looking away from him into the hedge, she considered her

own age. Having thought herself ugly despite a lifetime of hungry stares, she was still on speaking terms with mirrors, although that would change, and soon. One second she was squeezing pimples, hoping she could pass for legal, and the next she was yanking out gray hairs.

"Whatever," he said. "Let's get it over with."

He looked at the fabric of the seat between their thighs. His life had become disgustingly clear. He was the object of her pity. And his voice. He'd heard himself whining. A desperate man. God, he thought, I sound like Barton!

How'd things come to this? His Ferrari repossessed, his credit cards cancelled, malpractice charges looming. Jordan was right. Soon he'd be kicked to the other side of the bridge where he'd end up mowing Graciela's lawn.

"So where's your not-so-better half?"

"Home freaking out. That medicine was a mistake."

"Hmmmm," Helmut said, smelling a lawsuit, "I heard some guy in Oregon blew out his brains on the stuff."

"That was Bliss. Barton's on Fokus."

"Fucking pharmaceuticals. Whatever happened to being miserable? The whole country's on antidepressants. No wonder we're fucked. Character never came in a bottle."

The blue jay shrieked, defending its spot in the Hawaiian berry against the cardinal. "This country's changed since we were kids," Jordan said, "these days being sad's the same as being sick."

"Huh? Oh, yeah. So. You got my money or what?"

His money? She rolled her eyes. One thing about Helmut, the man was consistent. If the sun went supernova, he'd be scowling over his declining property values. Careful not to touch him, she reached across his lap to the glove compartment, accidentally brushing his thigh. He looked up, smiling lewdly.

"Put a cork in it," she said, removing a thick brown envelope. She dropped it in his lap. Greedily, Helmut tore it open.

"What's this?" he demanded. He slapped a thick green stack of cash against his palm, frowning.

"It's a hundred-thousand dollars."

"I can't use this!" He glowered. He'd been expecting a check, something negotiable. Nobody accepted cash. It was *so* twentieth century. Worse, it reeked of criminality.

"Not my problem. Now settle with your creditors, and if Barton ever finds out, I swear to God, Helmut, I'll – "

"You'll what?"

"I don't know, but . . . *I'll do something!*"

Helmut laughed in her face. He had a bit of egg stuck between his teeth. The reek of his breath was so pungent she felt she'd been slapped.

"You think I'm kidding?" she asked. She grabbed his face in her strong fingers and wrenched his chin toward her, surprising them both. She put her nose up to his. "I'm fucking serious, Mutt. Barton's losing his shit and I can't take it anymore!"

"Jordie – "

"This is your last chance. Understand?"

"Let go of my face, Jordan."

She released him and he massaged his jaw. She and her husband deserved each other, he thought – the sentimental losers. Really, what a pair of assholes! Why was he even friends with them? Why had he *ever* been friends with them?

"I said I'd pay you back," he said, hurt, "but you think I'm some kind of monster – "

"No, I don't. You've always kept your word, Mutt."

He cupped his hand to his ear and turned his head to the side. "What's that?"

"I said you've always kept your word! God! Happy now?"

"Quite." He grinned.

Nobody said anything and they looked away from each other. They'd been too close to bicker like this, and they weren't young anymore and life was too short. So as old friends will, they forgave each other, letting their hard stares soften.

Jordan spoke first, her voice mellow. "Just don't tease him, all right? He's in a very dicey state right now."

"Ain't we all," said Helmut.

"Yes, but he's doped up on Fokus."

"I told you it was a mistake. That stuff hasn't been around long enough."

Jordan didn't say anything. Helmut's face alarmed her. "Helmut?"

He drew breath. His whole body seemed to shrink. "I'm ... I'm, uh," he gagged and swallowed.

"You're what?"

"I'm not doing so good myself."

She closed her eyes and rested her forehead against the wheel. "Just pay your creditors and fix the firm," she said, "I can only take care of one lunatic at a time."

"Let me look at you for a minute."

"Are you serious?"

"Please."

She opened her eyes and looked at him. "I thought you wanted to get moving."

"Please, Jordie. It's the last time."

"What do you mean?"

"I don't – " Helmut choked and swallowed. He looked out his window toward his house. Perspiration beaded the crown of his head.

"Hey," she said, touching his shoulder, "you all right?"

"Don't talk," he said. "Just let me look at you, okay? Then I'll go."

"What's gotten into you? Helmut? You're freaking me out."

"Just shut up, will you?"

Jordan opened her mouth and Helmut buried his face between her breasts, framing his head with her hair. He laughed sadly and she thought he might be crying. She patted his back, finding it soft and damp. In the quarter-century they'd known each other, nothing like this had ever happened.

Helmut allowed himself to be comforted. His old friend rubbed his shoulders and told him it would be all right.

She was lying, of course, but so what? She was the only woman who'd ever "known" him, in a Biblical sense anyway, when he still had hair and innocence, youth and a future. Now, it seemed, he was spent, and who'd want to know a man like him? Only the guilty, his partner in crime.

Yet she'd been innocent once, too, with her unlined face so unafraid of the sun, and while she and Helmut had grown brittle and sad with age, somehow Barton had retained his youth, at least until he got hooked on Fokus.

Growing older, Jordan and Helmut had left him behind like the boy on a playground who still wants to play kickball while his friends sneak off to smoke cigarettes in the woods.

Yet Helmut wasn't all bad. When he still had a shining future, he'd been a nice guy. Affable. Charming. Quick to slap your back.

Jordan pitied him because she understood that only someone very delicate could be so twisted by the world, wrenched to the point where he'd never be straight again.

Seeing the same defect in herself, she embraced him. Barton could never understand this. His universe was comprised of himself, his girlfriend and his best friend. Sun, moon and earth. Barton, Jordan and Helmut.

But that system wasn't energetic enough for Helmut, even if he *had* been the one to marry her, even if the Knight had defeated the Squire. He needed more, and Jordan was the only woman who understood this. Helmut didn't need a solar system. He required a galaxy. The more attention shone on him, the brighter he burned. He was a maker of shadows, and Jordan was his fuel, his fusion, his atomic cheerleader.

He needed her now because he wasn't young, with a calendar of glory days spread before him. He was ageing at the speed of light. The skin on the backs of his hands! Could that wrinkled hide be his? Everybody was getting old. It seemed to be going around. You saw a face from your past and stopped short, thinking *what the hell happened to you?* And worse, what the hell happened to *me?*

Life was so much losing, so many goodbyes. Hair, teeth, friends, mother, father. One day you looked up and the house you'd struggled so hard to build was a charred spot on the earth. Chaos trumped form, always. But wasn't that the point of life? To be the eyes and ears of the Universe, the Big Bang's antenna?

Smelling the soapy odor of Jordan's hair, he decided to leave such hippy nonsense to her husband, *Señor Cuckoo's Nest*. Let *him* be God's fingertip.

For all Helmut knew of redemption, and of grace, he found in this woman's warm lap. Let the rest of universe burn itself to hell.

Of course he hated Barton. Who wouldn't? All I really wanted, Helmut thought, was his way of seeing things, even for an instant. *Because I don't see the wonder. I don't see God. I see Guts.* And I wanted him to help me, to accept me . . . and Barton, who thinks he is good and kind and sensitive . . . he said no and spat in my face.

He killed me.

Barton fucking Squire. He could've forgiven me, Helmut thought. And Jordan, too. We three had no need of society – its silly rituals, its hypocritical approvals. We were above it, Barton Squire!

You could've had us both, you ass.

"Helmut, I – "

He pressed his finger to her lips and they held each other and then Jordan showed a terrible mercy. She and Helmut broke another taboo. Right there on the front seat of Barton's truck.

She couldn't say no. She didn't *want* to say no. Brushing her forehead against his belt buckle, working down his zipper, she suddenly understood herself.

She wanted this because some secret part of her adored submission. Surrender gave her an awful sense of freedom, of release, of flight. And yet, as she accepted him into her mouth, she felt, paradoxically, as if she were the one in control. And wasn't she? With her steady rhythm, her savvy grip and her flickering caress, wasn't she the mistress of his house?

She wouldn't let him touch the back of her head. She wouldn't let him touch any part of her, other than the orifice he occupied. Her skin belonged to her husband. This was her show, by God, and she'd run it. Their relationship might be a circus, but she was the ringmaster.

Groaning, he arched his back and pounded the seat with his fist. Jordan nicked him with her teeth.

Hearing him yelp, another thought assailed her. She was no circus ringmaster.

She was the sideshow geek.

7

Corpus Delecti
(Body of the Crime)

LIFTING it by the handle bars, Barton concealed his beach cruiser inside a gnarled growth of sea grape, emerging from the tangle of broad, fan-shaped leaves to hide behind a Banyan tree. Overhead, the sun shone from a cloudless sky. Resting his hand against the trunk, he stuck out his head and peered down the street.

Partially obscured by a hedge of Hawaiian berry, he could see his truck. Through its back window he discerned two heads, one blond, one bald. The heads touched and parted. Barton swore and ducked behind the tree and caught his breath. He'd made himself a witness, and like most witnesses, he regretted having seen anything.

Crouching, he rested his cheek against the tree's cool bark. High in the sun-dappled leaves, a blue jay shrieked, scolding him. He leaned forward and peeked out again.

Next to his wife sat . . . who? Rival? Nemesis? Colleague? Roommate? Boss?

The truck's door swung open. Were they arguing? Barton could see their hands moving but he couldn't make out a word. Overhead, in the tree's green canopy, the blue jay shrieked and the cicadas buzzed, invisible in the leaves but as loud as tiny motors.

Barton squinted, trying to get a better view through the layer of dust obscuring the back window of his pickup.

Inside, Jordan's hand touched Helmut's shoulder and Barton felt the contact like a boot driven into his belly. Resting his hand against a branch, he bent at the waist and held himself, spitting into the grass.

The two of them were talking excitedly – lots of head movements and hand gestures – and cautiously Barton's spirits lifted.

Were they breaking it off? Was she confessing her sins? Swearing undying love to her husband?

And what about Helmut? Was he renouncing his betrayal? Renewing his loyalty to his friend? Acting as his best man? Perhaps there was hope. Barton felt it fill his lungs like the fragrant, tropical air.

He hugged himself, overcome. Covering his mouth, he slowly exhaled. The adultery was over. Helmut was getting his walking papers.

Closing his eyes, Barton rested against the tree, which, like him, was now planted solidly in the earth. Sweet Buddha-nature! He'd kept the faith. He'd resisted revenge and he'd been rewarded. His heart leapt.

Strengthened by gratitude, he vowed not to make Jordan feel shame. He'd eat his pride. He'd forgive Helmut. Why not? He was human. They were all human, and humans made mistakes, God knew.

Peeking out again, he saw the door close. Framed in the back window, the bushy blond head moved beside the shiny bald head, turning to and fro before it abruptly it sank from view.

Alone, the bald head made a circular flesh-colored spot where it pressed against the glass.

Barton's mouth opened and his knees buckled and he sank to the ground, scraping his back through the underbrush. A glaze settled over his eyes and he stared unblinking into the middle distance.

A branch snapped off in his hand as he struggled to his feet.

Jordan's head hadn't reappeared, and the flesh-colored circle of Helmut's head hadn't moved. Barton looked at the branch in his hand. The end was jagged and white and he considered plunging it into his eye.

The bald head's face might not be visible, but he could imagine its expression of slack-jawed bliss.

He'd seen it before.

In Kansas.

The man was a repeat offender. And his crime? Not disloyalty. Not adultery. Not betrayal. Not lust. Not even coveting his neighbor's wife. But vandalism. Senseless emotional violence. This was Helmut's felony.

For while Helmut scorned love as sentimental and even pathological, classifying it alongside obsessive compulsive disorder, he didn't know what *it* was, not really, except to know that . . . *he didn't have it.*

Love for him would always be contingent – on good health and economic self-sufficiency, so that if you suggested love was a burden which had to be borne, that love for an imperfect other had to be *accepted*, he'd stare down his hawk-like nose as if to say – *what species of mental-defective are you, anyway?* And in Barton's view, Helmut hadn't *become* jaded. He'd been created that way, with bitter ingredients, by a bitter God.

Whereas Barton had searched for One True Love since childhood. And he'd found her too, only to find himself duped, exposed as a fool and a bumpkin, so that by the time he discovered that God or Buddha-nature really *was* love, his love had fled, seeking whatever it was her husband didn't possess.

Helmut had swiped his birthright.

And now . . . *it was too late.*

It was larceny.

The trespassory taking and carrying away of the personal property of another with the intent permanently to deprive the owner thereof.

Crashing through the sea grape, Barton heaved his bicycle out of the mass of shiny green leaves and thorny branches. Mounting up, he began pedaling, fighting for balance as he cycled over the asphalt.

At the end of the block he passed two little girls riding around in the driveway in front of their house, silver streamers blowing from their handlebars. The smaller one in pigtails waved a grubby hand but Barton only smiled in return, living as he did, in a country where grown men didn't wave to little girls.

A sea breeze cooled his face. Riding above the swaying shadows of the palm trees growing along the sidewalk, he was unaware that the two little girls had stopped and stood over their bikes, staring after him.

Wide-eyed, their tongues stained pink with Kool-Aid, their mouths hung open.

Who was that man? And what was wrong with him? His face reminded them of the bully next door on the day his dog got crippled by a car, that day when his father carried the whimpering dog into the back yard and put a bullet through its head.

The shot echoed through the neighborhood, shaking the leaves on the trees, but the bully next door hadn't made a sound, only a face like that man's on the bicycle.

8

PRO CONFESSO
(AS IF CONCEDED)

"BARTON doesn't need to know about this." The sweet, sea-salt taste of Helmut was fresh in her mouth. She swallowed, grimacing.

Her lover laughed and adjusted his balls and zipped up his pants.

"Silence makes no mistakes," he said.

She narrowed her eyes.

"You think I'd forgotten your college motto?"

Jordan sighed. At the water cooler at Kelly, Knight and Squire, Helmut was a well-known storyteller, of the locker-room variety, the type of man whose sex life wasn't fully realized until he'd drawn you a picture. She could imagine him chuckling with glee as his fans were struck dumb by his outrageous charisma, his irresistible joint.

Gripping the steering wheel, she banged her forehead against it and turned and pressed her nose to her window. Her breath caught in her throat and she closed her eyes, thinking *I am such a fucking whore. I am such a goddamned foolish bitch!*

Outside, two little girls rode their bicycles along the street, silver tassels dangling from their handlebars. They waved as they pedaled by and Jordan waved back, wondering if they'd grow up to be faithful wives or cheating cocksuckers such as herself.

Ah, childhood. What big eyes you have! All round and terrified – don't judge our Jordan too harshly. She still remembers you. Hello, little girl! See her in the car with her mother, with her hair tied in pink ribbons. What innocence. Where did it go? Did she abandon it that day in the car?

Her parents had divorced and she'd ridden out of town wearing her Girl Scout uniform, twisting around under her seat belt to stare out the back window. In the distance, her house was shrinking.

"Your father is dead to us."

"I don't get it."

"He has a new woman. He doesn't want us around."

"He said *you* had a boyfriend!"

Mother and daughter rode in silence. At the time, Jordan weighed seventy-two pounds. Crying silently, she caught a final glimpse of her house, where her Daddy lived. She wanted to go home, to feel his strong arms around her, the rough stubble on his chin scraping her cheek, the minty smell of his aftershave . . . but there wasn't much you could do if you only weighed seventy-two pounds.

Beside her, Helmut inspected his fingernails, preening. If the bastard started to whistle, she'd push him from the truck. The hanging judge in her head wasn't disposed to mercy.

Helmut began humming tunelessly. He was so *cocksure*. He was Helmut Knight. He was everything Barton Squire wasn't.

And yet, she'd never divorce her husband. Not now. Or ever. Their sex life lacked the white-hot energy she shared with Helmut, but orgasm wasn't everything, was it? She shuddered, feeling her age, when her life suddenly became clear.

There's no fool like an old fool.

Yet as the wrinkles bloomed around her eyes, she still felt seventeen. How else to explain this lust, this jealousy, this madness?

God, a little air! That's all she asked. But no, Barton had to own her. He had to *know* her. Yes, she loved him. And during lovemaking she wanted to give him – what? Everything? But she wouldn't surrender. Never. She reserved a secret space for herself, a private part Helmut respected, but which her husband felt compelled to excavate, no matter that she felt violated. This was the difference between them. At their most intimate, Helmut kept his hands to himself.

"Catch you later, Jordie." He opened his door. There would be no kiss. There never was. Helmut lingered. His eyes felt heavy on her.

"Goodbye, Mutt." Helmut closed the door, careful not to slam it. He didn't look back as he entered his house, nor did she expect him to. A wave or, God forbid, a blown kiss, would've humiliated them both.

Driving off, turning the corner on the narrow, palm-lined street, she glimpsed a tall man on a bicycle and the hair stood up on the nape of her neck and her fingers tightened on the wheel. It looked like . . . but no . . . she shook it off . . . it was her imagination. She moaned low in her throat. Her imagination was driving her wild. Wasn't that its job? Home to the poet, the lover, and the madwoman? What a trio.

Clicking her signal, she assured herself that her imagination would soon be confined within the canvas she meant to attack when she got to her studio. That was the thing about emotional scars and high art – the one gave rise to the other, on the anvil where pain got hammered into beauty . . . or at least into something flat.

"Always something to be thankful for," she said.

Blinking rapidly, she squinted into the sun.

9

THE REASONABLE AND PRUDENT PERSON

BARTON stood on the dock staring across the blue stretch of the Indian River. Five pelicans, flying in a vee, creased the cloudless sky. A mullet jumped and landed with a splash. The sun sparkled on the water, creating a world of comforting pastels and gentle brush work.

El Jefe felt heavy in his hand. He broke open the cylinder and, one by one, emptied the bullets into the water. Tensing his chest, he drew back and with a forceful sidearm hurled *El Jefe* into the river, half expecting a hand to burst from the depths to catch it.

With a soft *plonk,* it splashed and sank, sending out ripples from a final bull's eye.

"Adiós, El Jefe!"

Rubbing his palms together, he immediately felt lighter, glad to be rid of the thing. The naming of firearms by persons under psychiatric care could never be described as healthy, he realized.

The morning air hung motionless on the river, balmy and sweet. He sucked in a great draught through his nose, filling his lungs and smelling jasmine. A seagull landed on the dock and studied him with its round black eye.

The seagull blinked, angling its head, hoping for a handout. Barton shrugged.

"Sorry, Jonathan, I'm all tapped out."

The seagull squawked and flew off the dock, wheeling in a white arc against the sky. Turning from the river, the wooden boards flexed under Barton's feet as he walked toward his house, while on the shore, beyond the expanse of his lawn, the royal palms towered over Jordan's studio. The tips of the fronds swayed in the breeze wafting off the Atlantic, blown west from other side of the island.

Inside the kitchen, he banged open the cupboard doors and removed all the hard liquor and poured it down the drain, turning his face away from the smell, then he took the bottles – four of vodka, one of whiskey and two of gin – and tossed them into a recycling bin.

He was making progress. He was cleaning house. From his pocket he withdrew an amber pill bottle and removed two Fokus pills. Nestling the twin red diamonds in his palm, a ferocious tremor assailed his hands, a side effect he dared not mention to his psychiatrist lest his prescription be revoked.

Because the stuff was well-named. *Fokus.* Indeed. Without it, his life went by in a blur. Medicated, he was invincible. Ignoring his shaking hands, he tapped out another red diamond and popped it into his mouth.

I can do anything when I'm Fokused, he thought. He smacked his lips, doing his best to ignore the fishy taste in his mouth.

It was going to be all right. His doctor said so. Why, the doctor had even assembled an intervention, an emotional pow-wow starring all the principals. They'd put each other through enough, Jordan said, and it was time to put the past to rest, to forgive and forget, to take it one day at a time. *Easy does it* and so on. The clichés of recovery were exchanged and agreed upon, although a group hug remained out of the question.

Jordan then directed "their reckoning," as Helmut dubbed it, toward money, striving to keep a civil tongue as she delivered a stern lecture on financial responsibility. At her insistence, Helmut confessed his financial – if not carnal – sins. Barton took the news of this new larceny quite well. He wasn't a greedy man, and the more he thought about poverty, the more he liked it. It was the end of the road, at long last.

* * *

Jordan had taken your narrator, Alexander Colin, into her confidence, and with Jordan's assets, and mine, we set things right at Kelly, Knight and Squire. The senior partners insisted that both Helmut and Barton begin "a program," with Helmut attending Gamblers Anonymous while Barton returned to AA.

His wife hadn't given Barton a choice, because no one likes to have a gun pressed to her forehead. She remembered the cold barrel, its muzzle pressed against her skin, and the rank smell of fear coming from her armpits.

"We'll get through this together," she'd said at the end of the intervention, and clapped her hands. "You'll see!" Bright-eyed, smiling, she glanced from one to the other of the men in her life, first pleading and then demanding that they be of good cheer. They could be dead, after all.

The doctor and yours truly agreed.

"Always something . . . " said Helmut.

Jordan shot him *that look*. He was getting off easy and he better know it and be grateful. Barton remained in the merciful dark regarding her own conduct, which she'd privately begun to see as a sex addiction, and she didn't need Helmut upsetting him – not now that their lives had been returned to what might pass for normalcy.

And so, with the crisis tucked safely into the immediate past, where it throbbed unseen, a new day began.

It was a fresh, bright Florida morning.

"We have to pick up Helmut," Jordan said, staring into the steam radiating from her coffee cup. She didn't raise her eyes.

Her husband didn't say anything.

"The Folly's taking another vacation."

"Already?"

"As of yesterday."

A lie, thought Barton. Already! His wife looked up, her eyes puffy with sleep. Was lying another habit, another vice requiring a program? So much for reform, he thought, and suddenly his mood shifted, swinging toward fury. The force of it clenched his fists, startling him. Quickly, he hid his hands behind his back, not knowing what he might do.

"Of course it is," he said, pulling up the driveway at Helmut's Spanish-style house. "Why wouldn't it be?"

His wife held her coffee cup with both hands, hiding her face behind it, eyes peeking above the rim.

Sauntering down the walk with his calfskin briefcase, Helmut piled inside, grunting in the heat.

Headed off the island, the three of them sat jammed onto the bench seat of Barton's truck. With the sun slanting through the windshield, they sat waiting at a stop sign, on their way to another meeting with the senior partners, minus your narrator (since committed to Green Glade) to continue repairing their careers. Jordan had brought along her mighty checkbook, and her willingness to make restitution was their only hope, their final plea.

Turning his head and checking the quiet intersection, Barton eased onto the gas.

"So we're agreed?" his wife asked. With her husband on one side and Helmut on the other, she clasped each man's hand in her own, squeezing them tightly. Barton's palm was warm and moist, Helmut's cool and smooth. "Soldier on," she said, mustering cheerfulness and driving it into her voice. "Time to kick ass and take names."

The two men, her best friends, grumbled and looked away from each other, appeased if not settled. Barton sped up and headed for the highway.

Why not make the best of things? she wondered. They'd been

trained to think like lawyers, after all, so they were conversant with *the reasonable and prudent person,* that mythically even-tempered individual toward whom all hotheads and depressives might aspire. And for the luxury of this second chance, she thought, they should be thankful.

Holding their hands, she enjoyed the pressure of their legs on either side of her. Barton's thigh was long and muscled, Helmut's short and surprisingly firm, a contact which, though it was intimate, felt in no way sexual. That was finished. The three of them shared too much history to throw it all away in bitterness and hurt.

(Meanwhile your narrator, Alexander Colin, who'd recently gone public with his Alzheimer's diagnosis, came to rue that decision, as he was promptly Baker-Acted for a perfectly innocent mishap concerning a toaster and a bathtub. The fact pattern is that I was forcibly dragged from my home by ruffians and cast unceremoniously into the back of a van, thence kidnapped and incarcerated here at Green Glade, although I confess, now that I've been granted my freedom, I've nowhere else to go.)

But I digress. As I said, before my imprisonment, I lobbied Gart and Lanus on the trio's behalf. Doing it legally was a risk, but Barton insisted on total honesty. With Jordan replenishing the escrow account, the hope was that Freeman Enterprises might forego disbarment or prosecution, although some form of censure seemed inevitable.

All things considered, she felt optimistic.

However, the fact pattern, as she knew it, remained incomplete. For her husband was tossing back his red, diamond-shaped tablets until he glowed with them. He'd come to the conclusion that he had to alter his brain chemistry in order to forestall his drinking, for the alcoholic path led to disaster, sure and certain. In this way, he convinced himself that he was doing the right thing.

Intense self-medication was required, yet the more he considered its necessity, the more he blamed it on the people sitting next to him.

They had driven him crazy, and now he was driving them toward their bright shining future, the one without him in it.

Clenching the wheel, his mood darkened until his face was almost purple.

"Anything wrong?" Jordan asked, an edge creeping into her voice.

"Not a thing," her husband hissed through clenched teeth.

"Your face is all red."

He flipped a switch on the dash, feeling his wife's hip press snugly against his own. "Damn AC only works when it's cold outside."

In the rearview he intercepted a secret glance between his betrayers. Helmut had something of a poker face, but Jordan – she looked as guilty as a smuggler facing a customs officer. A solitary bead of sweat trickled down her face, wetting a strand of hair.

For a moment, her husband wavered.

Imagining a life without her, all those blank years, he felt, physically, as if the organ tree inside his body had been ripped from its roots. His future loomed, a featureless void. He might survive, but the day would come when he'd be doing something simple . . . making a cup of tea perhaps, when in the midst of taking off the kettle the sudden absence of her bright merry eyes and musical piping laugh would smite him like a fist from the Old Testament.

And he'd howl – like a dog with its spine crushed, left to die on the street without its master.

I don't know where you are. And I don't know where to look for you!

The wet taste of her mouth – cherries and chocolate and honey – the lively muscle of her tongue.

Let me remember her kiss when I die, he thought.

For he hadn't planned it.

Yet as they approached the oak tree beside the sign for Kelly,

Knight and Squire, he understood that he'd been imagining this for a long time, perhaps since birth.

When his hands swung the wheel and he aimed the truck at the tree, his wife turned to him and said, "Barton, please."

Helmut screamed and covered his face with his hands.

If thine eye offend thee, pluck it out.

Why not? You spent your life burying former loves, until your own bell tolled and you waved goodbye to the ultimate lover, the one who'd been with you through all the lonely hours – *all* of them – your one and only – *you*. Goodbye, old friend. Farewell, lover. Farewell . . . self. We sure took a trip, didn't we? I love you. Goodbye, goodbye, goodbye . . .

Screeching to a halt and parking in the shade of the oak tree, Barton cut the ignition. Helmut and Jordan stared at him with round eyes. They had the blank, dumbfounded looks of survivors after a natural disaster.

Helmut's mouth worked in his pale face. "Jesus. How long's he been doing that?"

"It's new today," Jordan said. Her voice was high and strained.

"Fuck *me*," Helmut said, opening his door and climbing out of the truck. "Tomorrow I'll get a ride from Graciela."

10

THE TOTALITY OF THE CIRCUMSTANCES

JORDAN'S phone rang. It was Helmut. She cast her eyes heavenward and drew a long breath, as if the air itself might contain the courage to face another day.

"Hey. Graciela's already left . . ."

"Right," she said, smacking her dry, pasty-feeling mouth, "her day starts at seven."

"Good God. She *gets* there at seven?"

"Yes, Helmut. You work in an upscale office. How do you think it stays that way?"

"Tidy trolls? The cleaning fairy? How do *I* know?"

"Call a cab, Counselor."

Helmut didn't say anything. He was too ashamed to tell her he didn't have cab fare. Dead air hung on the line.

"I'll be late if you don't pick me up. I don't have time to wait for a cab."

"Aren't you *always* late?"

"Yes, but today I'll be *extra* late . . . and I can't be – not with Gart putting me on probation."

"It was Alexander Colin who saved your ass, you know."

"Good old Alzheimer Colin. Diminished capacity to the rescue, eh?"

Jordan scratched her scalp with her fingernails and discovered a pimple forming in the hair at the back of her neck. Picking it, she broke off a tiny crust and winced, flicking it away with her nail.

"You're making me break out," she said.

"Of what?" For a wild moment, he thought she referred to her marriage.

"Helmut, I need the truck today. I'm dropping Barton off."

A pained sigh came into her ear. "But I'm on your way," he said.

Jordan adjusted the volume on her phone. "It's not a good idea," she whispered.

"Three nuts make a fruitcake," he said. "Come *on*. I'm not worried about it. Let the past alone. It's so much *easier* to be friends, isn't it?"

Jordan shook out her hair, groaning. "I honestly don't know," she said. "I think what we are is . . . *all fucked up*."

"Jordie?"

"Please tell me you didn't start the day with a drink."

"Jordie . . . I . . . there's something – "

"Shit. Barton's coming downstairs."

"You're all I've got, honey."

"What! You *are* drunk!"

"I'm not. I love you. *I do!*"

"Then please don't wreck my marriage."

"You've already done that." Helmut didn't say this in a mean way. He was being himself, as sincere as ever.

"Tell him we'll pick him up," he heard Barton say from a distance. "I knew he'd never wake up early enough to catch Graciela."

When she spoke again, Jordan's voice was different. "Wait outside," she said brightly. "We're on our way."

"I have to tell Barton," Helmut said.

She ended the call. Apparently her sins didn't mean to stay buried. *Quantum Meruit*. You got what you deserved, she thought. In the end, life's rough justice was all you could count on.

Outside, the sun was low in the sky, casting sword-like rays across the lawn onto the east wall of her studio. The grass looked orange in the Florida morning and the birds chirped merrily. In the west, over the river, clouds massed against the blue of the sky like a range of snowy mountains.

Ambling down the cobblestones, Jordan said, "So, Big Bart – you think I should come back to work?"

Her husband looked at her. *So you can see Helmut?* "Do you want to practice?" he asked, "or do you just want to keep your name on the sign?"

Shading her face with her hand and looking at him across the truck's black hood, her shoes crunched on the gravel as she walked around to the driver's side. "Let me drive," she said. "You look a tad green."

"Jordan, if I'm not competent to drive, I'm not competent to represent a client."

She let it go. It was too early to get on to the subject of mental health, especially as her own wasn't in the best of shape. "I just thought that since I'm taking the truck – "

"Get in," he said. He opened his door and swung in under the steering wheel, watching her through the windshield. The tag at the back of his shirt irritated his neck and he reached around and tore it off, letting it flutter to the floor. Leaning across the seat, he opened her door and she climbed in, smelling of honeysuckle.

Heading east toward Helmut's house, they pulled down their visors to shade their eyes from the sun, whose rays had shifted from orange to gold, shining through the windshield onto their laps.

"Music?" Barton asked, reaching for the radio.

She shook her head. "Too much static," she said. She tapped her temple. "In here."

Along the beach, the seagulls shrieked and the breakers crashed against the sand. Through the open windows, a cool wind blew over their faces.

Such a beautiful day, she thought, gazing over the turquoise water, and such sour moods.

The pursuit of happiness, she thought. You might as well chase the horizon.

Barton drove slowly along the ocean road, stopping at a crosswalk to let a thin young man carrying a surfboard dart across to the beach. The two men, one in the beginning of his prime and the other at the end of it, exchanged nods through the glass.

Barton supposed Jordan and Helmut would soon be leaving him. Well, he didn't blame them. Who would? He was deranged. He could hardly stand his own company, so what could he expect of others? He was *non compos mentis*. Why should his wife stay with a lunatic?

And there was something else. He'd known it for years, ever since college. Helmut had won her after all, because he was a country club man, because he was royalty, and when did a Squire ever defeat a Knight?

He didn't know her anymore.

His wife. His friend.

Lover. Lawyer. Liar . . .

He pounded the horn and Jordan jumped.

"So help me God." He held up his hand and pressed the other one to the wheel, giving it a long blast.

"Sweetheart," she said, flinching. Her cool fingers brushed the skin of his forearm, stroking the fine blond hairs. "He's not deaf, honey."

Barton revved the engine. The front door of the house opened and Helmut's shiny dome popped out. He waved and closed the door.

"I'm leaving," Barton said.

Jordan's hand gripped his thigh and they waited.

"Top of the morning!" thundered Helmut. He opened the door and the salty odor of the ocean blew into the truck as he climbed onto the seat. Jordan slid over and wedged herself into her husband's side. "And how is the happy couple this morning?" A dollop of shaving cream rode inside a fold of Helmut's ear.

"Scooch over," Barton said to his wife, nudging her with his rear end. "You're crowding me."

Jordan pulled her elbows into her lap, making herself small. On her left, her husband was flying on Fokus and sweating through his suit, while on her right, Helmut's drunken hand explored her knee.

Barton hit the gas and the truck lurched away from the curb, squealing the tires.

"Way to go, Speed Racer!" Helmut grinned. Jordan and Barton looked at him, astonished. Helmut beamed. His teeth were twin rows of flashing pearls.

"You got your teeth whitened," Jordan said. She socked him in the arm.

Helmut's fresh breath filled the truck. It was like riding in a cloud of mint. Barton leaned toward his window and let the wind blow across his face. He didn't want to smell Helmut's breath, fresh or otherwise.

Soaring over the causeway and the blue swath of the river, he turned onto U.S. 1 and headed toward the firm, accelerating into the morning traffic as they careened past strip malls and fast-food restaurants.

"They look fantastic," Jordan said. "I mean it."

Helmut shrugged.

Highway lines shot along below them, while the truck's tires hummed along the asphalt, vibrating the cab.

" 'Parting is all we know of heaven,' " Barton said, " 'and all we need of hell.' "

"Spare us," Helmut said, closing his lips over his gleaming teeth. The shaving cream had melted in his ear and trickled down his cheek. Thinking it was an insect, he slapped himself and wiped it off, frowning at the smear on his palm.

"It's Emily Dickinson," Jordan said.

"I know who it is," Helmut said irritably.

Jordan clucked her tongue. "Once an English major – "

"Jesus," said Helmut. He shook his head. "It's a little early."

"Actually, it's too late," Barton said.

Helmut raised his eyebrows. His prominent nostrils sprouted fresh black hairs. "Brilliant," he said. "You're a real man of mystery."

"That's right," Barton said.

Helmut narrowed his eyes. "What're you up to, young Squire?"

Barton shook his head as if to say it was nothing.

Helmut elbowed Jordan in the ribs. "Mr. Cryptic. Secret agent man."

Up ahead, alongside the oak tree, their names rose high in the air.

Kelly, Knight and Squire
Attorneys at Law

Approaching the sign, Barton's body jerked and his hands yanked the wheel and he swerved toward the tree.

Helmut screamed.

Cramped in the seat between them, Jordan hauled her legs up to her chest and braced her feet against the dash.

Barton didn't turn. His eyes were wide, pinned on the oak's brown trunk.

Saliva flooded his mouth and white froth dribbled down his chin and his muscles convulsed, shaking the seat.

"He's faking!" Helmut yelled. "Get the wheel!"

The oak tree roared into view, filling the windshield with its massive trunk.

But Barton couldn't see it. His teeth severed the tip of his tongue but he didn't taste his salty blood because he was far away, amid a green field of clover atop a hill, somewhere in childhood where grape vineyards slid down mossy ravines into distant valleys.

Blinking, the boy looked at the world. *How had he created it?* In the hilltop clover, white butterflies flew around pink blossoms stained with purple, dancing on air so sweet it stung his nose. Honeybees buzzed his ears and clouds of gnats flew into his eyes, and yet, wiping his face, there was that blue horizon, that never-ending sunshine . . .

I am God, he said softly. The child smiled.

The boy gazed over the cloud shadows wheeling over distant pastures. Overhead, a solitary black bird spun lazily against the white boundaries of a cloud, pulling the boy's eyes into the sky. All that light and space! The boy swelled gloriously, expanding beyond his skin till he was free of his small body and the earth which cradled it.

And then everything was black and then everything was nothing.

11

EYEWITNESS

IN the picture window of Helmut's corner office, Graciela stood with a paper towel in her hand, polishing the glass. Leaning up to it, she fogged the window with her breath.

Wasn't that Mr. Barton's truck? *And why wasn't it turning?*

She shut her eyes and opened them and grabbed the gold crucifix at her throat. Dropping to her knees, she crossed herself and prayed. And then came the sound of metal striking wood, of tires squealing and glass shattering, of metal scraping along the asphalt.

Graciela covered her ears with her hands.

Moments earlier, inside the truck, Jordan grabbed the two men beside her and crushed their hands until she felt their bones below the skin.

In her last moment she turned her face toward her husband.

The tachometer redlined and the engine kicked into a higher gear, whining with sudden power. Helmut pressed his feet against the dash, bracing his legs with his hands.

"Barton," he said. "Barton, no . . . "

Reaching behind Jordan's back, Helmut shook his friend's shoulder. Barton foamed at the mouth and his eyes rolled back in his head, the whites quivering. Jordan put her lips to her husband's ear.

"Mother lode," she whispered.

Her husband's mind cleared.

Coming to, he cranked the wheel toward the sun-dappled shade beside the tree and into the lane leading into the parking lot.

What he hadn't reckoned on, oddly, being an attorney, was what in the law is known as "the totality of the circumstances."

To wit, on that particular day on that specific stretch of asphalt, a shallow skein of water a millimeter deep had spread along the highway, glazing it with iridescent petroleum rainbows so that when he swung the wheel away from the oak, he over corrected and the rear wheels broke loose and the truck spun sideways, striking the tree broadside.

12

Lawsuit

AT the inquest, when Graciela testified, she admitted that from her perspective the collision with the tree appeared intentional, although she wouldn't swear to it. For insurance purposes, and for the benefit of her family, your narrator interceded, arguing his last case, which he won. The official report found that the death of the truck's driver and that of his two passengers was accidental, the result of hazardous road conditions.

In an unrelated settlement, Glib and Stone, the makers of Fokus, withdrew their product from the market after a series of suicides was linked to prolonged exposure to the drug. Expert witnesses testified that grand mal seizures had earlier been reported as an adverse effect, but this finding was not addressed by the court.

13

INNOCENT BYSTANDERS

GRACIELA'S husband, Antonio, kept watch from the Land Rover, guarding his wife while she planted three small wooden crosses, each adorned with a plastic lily. He wiped his eyes as she hammered down the second cross.

So Mr. Squire went *loco* at the end, he thought. Well, life was hard and Antonio was the first to admit it. He narrowed his eyes at other groundskeepers when they made jokes about Mr. Squire, telling them that they were too *tonto* to recognize a good man when they saw one.

"*Vamos!*" he hollered, "the kids will be late." He stuck his head out the window and smiled, showing his gold teeth, the ones Mr. Squire had paid for. Esperanza and her Esteban, *el gordito de la allegria*, their little fat boy of happiness, bounced on the back seat, pummeling each other. "Be gentle," Antonio said, looking at his children with his kind eyes. "She getting to be a lady." He touched her face. "Eh, *la consentida?* True, my princess?"

"*Momentito,*" Graciela called. On the grassy side of the highway under the shade of the oak, whose trunk was still scarred from the wreck, she surveyed her work: a trio of white crosses. Esteban and Esperanza had helped with the lettering, and Antonio had applied a coat of marine varnish.

Using a rubber mallet, she pounded the final cross into the ground.

Each was carefully inscribed:

> Barton Squire
> 1965 – 2008
>
> Jordan Squire
> 1965 – 2008
>
> Helmut Knight
> 1965 – 2008

Antonio sounded the horn. When Graciela looked up, he pointed to his watch. He was worried. His wife was kneeling in a dangerous place, on deadly ground.

"*Momentito!*" she called again.

Bowing her head, she made the sign of her savior over the crosses. In the west, a storm cloud hung like a violet bruise on the pastel sky. From around her neck she removed her gold crucifix, kissed it, and carefully wound it around Jordan's cross, which stood between the ones for Barton and Helmut.

It was an offering. *Pro bono.* For the good.

Esteban stuck his face out the back window. "Mama, Esperanza's pinching me!"

Traffic roared along the highway, stirring her hair with hot blasts of wind.

Antonio held open her door and she climbed inside and buckled her seat belt.

The Squires had left the Miranda family their entire estate.

Helmut died without a will.

Esperanza leaned forward and pressed her face between her parents.

"Papa, why is Mama crying?"

"Because, *mi querida.*" With his muscular arm he squeezed his wife's shoulder, "She loves us so much."

Double checking his mirror and glancing over his shoulder, Antonio pulled off the grassy right-of-way and entered the traffic racing along U.S. 1.

14

Pro Memoria

SO that's the end of our story, my beloved reader. And if you've come this far, I expect you've outlived me. Still, having set down this history, perhaps in some small way I persist. It may be so.

You hold in your hands a valentine from a dead man.

Endings are painful, sudden things, and they hurt a great deal, which is their nature. It's also how you know you're alive. Life is sorrow, I don't mind telling you. And I should know, expiring here alone. But we are creatures of an instant, and our friends – and they were our friends – weren't they? Our friends Barton and Jordan and Helmut, they have passed away.

We must let them go.

They had their faults, just like the rest of us – real characters in the stories of each other's lives. Please don't judge them too harshly. It's unkind to speak ill of the dead, who cannot defend themselves.

They were real people, you see, but they were also figments of my imagination. This is how human beings appear to one another. We're all fictions, in the end.

Farewell, my beloved trio.

Adieu!

Let your shadows fall beyond these pages, silhouettes against the earth, arrows aimed toward all our happily-ever-afters.

Barton and Jordan and Helmut – they had their moments. They had their exultations. And as Barton would say, there's always something to be thankful for.

They enjoyed the day's yellow fire, its saffron dawns and crimson sunsets, they scrunched their toes against the hot sand, let the waves break against their skins, gave their bodies to the Atlantic's cooling hiss and the white froth of the waves, while overhead the sky shone as blue and serene as Jordan's eyes.

Oh, my reader – gentle spirit of the future. You should be so fortunate.

I hope that you are!

It's not too late.

For we are no less imaginary, no less substantial, than the ocean's blue mist at sunrise, which shimmers and burns away, sweeping us onto a new calendar page, that grid of future yesterdays . . .

Oh, my characters . . .

My friends!

The lamentations of your creator shall be omitted.

Post Scriptum

Leaving no survivors, Mr. Alexander Colin passed away without a funeral.

Per his instructions, his ashes were scattered in the Atlantic ocean.

Given the absence of a headstone, I offer these pages as his epitaph, his testimony.

– Graciela Miranda
University of Florida School of Law
Class of 2015